I0652823

A Diabolical Bargain

Mary Catelli

Published by Wizard's Wood Press, 2015.

A DIABOLICAL BARGAIN

First edition. January 30, 2015.

Written by Mary Catelli.

Chapter 1 —Studies

With the sky flaming red and orange, the dirty streets lay in shadows that hid details. Such as where the snowmelt was freezing again, making the footing treacherous.

Nick eyed the roughly clad men before them. Stephen stood next to him. His hand edged toward his sword, and Nick wished he wouldn't. They—sailors, carpenters, or some such—carried no swords, but they could overpower three men who had them, especially when—

"Who you calling a drunken fool?" said Edgar.

You, thought Nick—drunk at this hour and picking fights to boot. Spells might protect them, but magic could enliven matters more than Nick quite cared to.

Edgar raised his voice. "I said. . . ."

Nick dropped an arm about his shoulders. "You said we would visit the Golden Fish."

Puffs of white rose from their breaths. Time inched on, and the men facing them glared. Muscle bunched under Nick's hand; Edgar could shrug him off.

"Why are we waiting?" Nick said.

"Yeah," said Edgar, slurring the word. He eyed the men but walked off with them, down the dark street. The sunset darkened as they walked. Snow haunted the corners, but no footsteps followed them.

Stephen came up beside Nick. "Did you have to tell them where we're going?"

"Well, then," said Nick, "let's not go there. We've got a city."

"Why don't we go to your home, Nick?" Edgar said.

Edgar *was* drunk, Nick thought. "My father's home."

Edgar scowled, and Nick grimaced. Edgar knew what Mortimer Briarwood was like. Though at the moment, he saw what his father enjoyed in solitary misanthropy—no. Nick forced his breath out. Edgar could turn into a drunken fool; *he* would not turn into his father.

"Let's go to the Golden Fish," Edgar said.

A breeze picked up. Puddles were growing white feathers of frost. Any minute, the enchanted lights would shine.

"We were going to the Golden Fish."

Where Edgar would proceed to get even more drunk. Nick wondered why he had not stayed home and studied. He would have enjoyed that.

Just like your father would, said a cold thought. Your mother dragged you to all those parties so that you would not turn into another Mortimer Briarwood.

Even that thought did not make the notion of having stayed unpleasant, and if he could get home—

"There's a sleighing party, tomorrow," Nick said. "If we roam the streets through the night, we'll sleep through it."

Edgar said, as if he had not heard, "There's the Bird. Old Watkin. . . ."

As if Edgar were sober enough to play cards! "I don't—"

Edgar rounded on him. "You're a prig, Nick."

I don't get drunk nightly, thought Nick, I don't gamble money I don't have, I don't visit the whorehouse weekly, —and in our circle, that is impressive virtue. In face of such temptation, it would be more astounding if I weren't a prig.

Edgar already ignored him to look about. After a minute, he said, "What the devil's that?" The shock in his voice made both Nick and Stephan look up.

A man swooped, pitch black against the sunset. A wizard's robes billowed about him. Nick stared. What wizard would be fool enough to cast that? If the spell failed—

A mischief-making university student, of course, who cast it without thinking ahead. Perhaps Edgar's age.

Nick mouthed, "University," at Stephen, and turned to Edgar. "What's what, Edgar?" He looked over the sky again. "Maybe you ought to go home."

Stephen grinned for a moment, behind Edgar's back, before he wiped it off his face. Edgar stared at Nick for a minute; then his gaze went to Stephan.

Stephan said, "Maybe we should go home. The Golden Fish, the Bird—they'll be there tomorrow."

Edgar nodded and staggered down the street. A cart trundled, far ahead of them, but most people had sagely gone to their homes during the sunset.

Several strides behind Edgar, Stephen said, in a low voice, "Unscrupulous."

Nick shrugged. Edgar had a nasty edge to him, even sober, but one could hardly cut him, not in their circle. He was a rich man's only son. More, his father was indulgent and would make a good marriage settlement.

The buildings blocked off the sight of the flying man. Ahead of them, an enchanted light sprang to pale life; as if it were a signal, all down the street, the wrought iron pillars were crowned with light.

"You make me wonder," Stephen said. His voice was low, and his glance sidelong. "Why do you come to parties at all? When you are so fascinated with your books."

Because, thought Nick, my mother dragged me. When I was old enough to resist, the old gardener, surly old grumbler that he was, still greeted my protests with a grunt and said I would turn into my father if I didn't watch out.

And you, as much as Edgar, can make me wonder why.

"If you were that fascinated," said Stephan, "you would go to the university."

A young wizard walked across a university square. Despite her youth, she wore a master's colorful robe—a yellow robe more brilliant than most masters would wear.

"Mistress Janet!" A student hurried under an arched gate, his black robes streaming.

Janet Whitehall sighed. It had been a long day. Already.

"Mistress Janet, diabolerie!"

Her gaze fixed on him. "*What*?"

"A man flying through the air. . . ."

Dozens of spells could make a man fly, but—Janet strode to the gate. A moment later, someone swooped against the sky.

She scowled. With the robes dark against the sky, she could not see whether they were a student's black, but he swirled and circled, like a leaf in a maelstrom. The spell caster had no control.

Her mouth felt dry. "Once his will-power is exhausted," she whispered, "we will have a murder on our hands." What need did the university have for diabolists as long as it had fools? She strode on, ransacking her memory for a spell to avert falls. The student scurried behind her, but if he could help, he already would have.

A scream rang. The man plummeted, his robes sweeping out behind him. Futile shouts rose toward him. Forcing the noise from her thoughts, Janet rattled off her spell. His weight bore down on her. His fall slowed, and slowed, as sweat beaded on her forehead, and he sank into the next square. He vanished behind a building, without unburdening her, but then, so abruptly that she nearly staggered, the weight lifted.

She ran.

In the square, a student sat on the stones. His friends crowded around and congratulated him—the same voices that had cried out with such distress. "That was really something!"

In other words, thought Janet, I did not avert a murder, but a suicide.

"It doesn't have the control—" said the student.

"You mean you don't have the control," Janet said. She drew some gazes, not many.

He shrugged. "Turned out all right."

Her hands itched to slap him. She was not more than a decade older than the youngest of them, possibly less, but she had been that age without being such a fool. "What are your names? And from what colleges do you come?"

That drew their eyes. From the gawking, many had not realized who she was before that. Some tried to sidle away.

Her brilliant yellow gave warning enough. She cast a light spell in the air. It shone on them all and removed any shadows where they might hide.

Nick whistled under his breath. He walked alone toward the bridge—and home, and his studies. The last of the sunset only colored the west crimson and violet. The quarter moon gleamed overhead, not brightly next to the spell lights.

The university appeared ahead of him.

Spells whitely lit the buildings. His hands hitched on his belt, and he cursed Stephan for being right. Even if he were never halfhearted about them, his studies at home were frivolous. He studied as he pleased. He doubtlessly had great gaps in his knowledge from distaste for some subjects.

But his father would never pay his tuition.

He walked again. The still air was cold.

Even for his allowance, the arrangements had been made by his dead mother, not his father. The university gave scholarships—meant for the poor, not for the children of the rich. He would never need to support himself with his magic.

He skirted the buildings. Between the university and the town, the Cathedral of the Magi loomed. Melted snow had flooded the cobblestones in front; ice crystals glittered on the water.

Nick jumped up on the low wall in front of the cathedral. Frost feathers made the stones a little slick, but it would not soak his boots.

The spell lights shone. Nick paused. Well, he was no older than Edgar and likely younger than the flying student. He gestured, with an incantation. The first light glowed red as he pointed—the second orange, the third yellow—green, blue, indigo, purple. He smiled. He could learn in his father's library, if only he applied himself.

Snow had muffled the garden, and the melting had not freed it. Nick eyed the dips and rises and thought he should do something in the spring. The gardener had taught him enough. Though old Warin was years dead, he would have snorted in displeasure to see what his merely competent successor had wrought. And surly as he had been, he had admitted, once or twice, that Nick might manage as a gardener.

In his father's study, the lamp was lit. Nick slowed and glanced at the windows. Nothing moved within. He slipped to the door, opened and closed it as quietly as he could, and stole over to the study. The door was shut, but the maid lit the lamp whether his father was there or not.

He slid the door open and found the study empty. Inside, he studied the shelves. He recognized one tome instantly, a ponderous work on disenchanting, but its dullness had defeated him before. He glanced over more bindings. Some, he had learned the hard way, were beyond him, and some he had already surpassed, but one, he had sampled before, without mastering.

He pulled it out. A miscellany of spells. He could find something he did not know in it.

Mortimer approached his house, lit only by a few windows. The parchment crinkled in his pocket.

He would regret it, some, when the bookseller betrayed himself. Easily frightened rabbit though he was, the man found some useful manuscripts. He served more uses than the other merchants in this city, the haughty, self-righteous lot.

He pushed open the door. Something moved in his study. His eyes narrowing, Mortimer walked over.

By a shelf, Nicholas paged through a book. He stood next to the entrance to the secret chamber.

"What—are—you—doing—here?"

Nicholas blinked. He raised the book. "Getting this."

Their gazes met. Man and woman had told him that his own eyes, dark, indeterminate in color, neither blue nor purple nor green, made his expression hard to read. On occasion, that had its uses.

For the brat to have inherited the same unreadable eyes annoyed him beyond measure.

"You've got it. Get out."

Nicholas raised his eyebrows and walked toward the door.

Mortimer eased his breath out. He had permitted the boy run of the library, to all appearances, but that had been folly. The boy might have realized that spells had kept him from some books. He was enough of a mischief-maker to try them.

He watched Nicholas go up the stairs. Marrying Phillipa Greenleaf had been prudent. So had been fathering Nicholas on her. The actions had convinced the master wizards that he was settling down and forgetting diabolerie as youthful folly.

That use was long exhausted, and he should have foreseen that it would saddle him with other troubles. Phillipa had not cared about the library, but it had been too much to prudently hope for, that their son would resemble his butterfly mother.

Upstairs, the door closed behind Nicholas.

Mortimer shut the study door and pulled the parchment out to reread. Immortality. Since such magic exceeded any human enchantment, the parchment described how to deal with those with power to work it. It described the summoning, meticulously, and mentioned two ways to pay—which was well. One way, he had used up long ago.

But the other—no wonder the bookseller looked queasy. Unless he could claim not to have read the work (and the sanctimonious master wizards would hardly believe that), he would be party to murder. Mortimer did not doubt that, money or no money, the only reason the bookseller had not burned it was from fear of him.

Wise of the bookseller to fear a man who dealt with demons.

Mortimer had examined it thrice at the bookstore, but now he looked again, there being no such thing as too much care when dealing with demons. But he could see no flaws, and he could not hunt forever. Letting time fly without such a magic held dangers of its own.

Let it work, and he would never have to worry about lack of time; concealing his work would not drain the precious hours from his studies, for time would be plentiful. Selling his soul had granted him the power to make demons bring him lore, but this spell would let him gather lore throughout ages.

He lit the lamp, fetched himself wine, and read with an eye to casting the spell.

First of all, payment. He could have sold his soul, had he not sold it already, but he could also offer a blood sacrifice.

"It must be human and unflawed. A blood relation is best."

Mortimer looked at the darkened window. It reflected back his study and himself. When young, he had never wasted time with frivolous company, and gone wenching with them. Nicholas was too much of a prig to have gone with his shallow friends. That meant no bastards of his blood were convenient. Nicholas was the only choice there.

Mortimer sat back. It would eliminate the risk of his prying, but Nicholas had friends of good family. He might be Mortimer's son in his studies, but he was enough Phillipa's son to gad about.

Mortimer's mouth pursed. Those friends know how little love there is between us, he thought; they might believe I turned him out of the house.

He eyed his desk. This parchment was the fruit of years of labor. He would not stint a few moments to consider his choices.

Most of the servants had served him for years, and they were all akin to each other. His fingers drummed on the desk. A servant would draw even more note than Nicholas.

A beggar, now, or vagabond. Half the children who cluttered the streets would never be missed by anyone. Their parents, if they paid them any heed, would be glad to be unburdened of a mouth.

Mortimer leaned forward to take the wine glass. A master wizard who had wasted his time on charity might not be noticed, but he would. Even giving a beggar child a coin to lure it would attract eyes. His studious reputation had its disadvantages.

But he had a city to select from. When the demons had capriciously declared that this spell did not fall under his original pact, he had searched the world for it—without slacking, but without undue haste to betray him.

And here, he did not need to search so far. He should look before he dismissed the possibility. He drained the cup, lowered it to the desk, and refilled it, this time to the brim, where the least jostle would spill it. With care, he poured in the last drops. The wine rippled, absorbing them, and went still. The ruddy surface showed the walls and his face. His incantation was swift, and then the wine reflected the road outside, tinted red.

Swiftly, he sent the vision down the road, over the river, toward the poorer quarters. Nightfall had put them where they might most easily vanish.

The vision flitted over the buildings, redly revealing scenes plunged into darkness: beggars gathered under bridges; apprentices slept in shops; vendors crowded into tiny rooms. No one alone. One room caught his eye. A mother and father hung over a bed made of two chairs, where a child lay swaddled in blankets. His lip curled. Half a dozen others clung to their mother's skirts or peered at their sister, but the parents were as anxious as if she were their only chick.

"She may prove as awkward to you as Nicholas to me," he told them, and brought the vision closer to study the girl. Thin, ragged, and filthy, of course, but beneath that—even with the red cast the wine lent her—he could see her pale face and the sweat.

White sickness. Nothing else brought both fever and pallor. The plague was not far advanced, or he would have heard—The vision broke. In his meditations, Mortimer studied his own reflection. During a plague, if he took an urchin from the streets, or a beggar, people would lay it to the door of the white sickness, but the spells to cure white sickness were wearing, and an ailing victim was unquestionably flawed.

On the other hand, the white sickness began in the poorer quarters, but it would not remain there. It never did. If he quarreled with Nicholas and turned him out of door when the white sickness raged, the disease would likely strike him down before he reached anywhere else. No one would be too startled if no body could be found. His friends might make a show of distress, but they would have no grounds to suspect.

His mouth twitched. He would have a blood relative to offer and be free of Nicholas's spying.

Still, he had to take care. The white sickness had sprung of an ill-mastered demon. He would profit by that fool's example and do all that was necessary.

He read on. In the next section, it repeated that the offering must be flawless. He would have to ensure that Nicholas had not injured himself in a prank.

But, what would Nicholas's life buy? He flattened the paper to ensure no shadows. A fiend would ignore everything except the exact wording, and the most perverse interpretation it could make of that. Mortimer read with care. The demon would take the heart from his chest to bespell it. Unless his heart was harmed, he would never be killed. The text assured him that no diabolist had ever had this pact fail, and the circle forced the demon to grant immortality.

That was, he noted, the only thing it mentioned. He sat back and considered. Another diabolist had learned a like spell—Master Oliver, at the university—but Master Oliver had not found this spell. His preserved health as well as gave immortality. Then, that was how he—and every other soul in the city—knew that Master Oliver had cast it. To give the spell the power to restore his health, the demon had put Master Oliver's heart where it could be destroyed. And a rascal of a student, Janet Whitehall, had found the heart and murdered the master. For all that, the university had made her master.

The surface of the wine trembled. Despite the chill, Mortimer opened the window to fling the wine into the gloom. He put down the cup, fetched another and poured his wine into that. He would profit from Master Oliver's folly and seek only immortality.

And with his friends expecting Nicholas on the morrow, he would await his return from those festivities. He could check the pentacle in Nicholas's absence, and years of patience should not be wasted for a day.

Nick contemplated the book on his desk. At the university, no one would order him out of the library, but then, the master wizards would direct his studies as they wished.

He flipped through the pages. He would not master any fundamental principles from this miscellany, but he could learn some clever pieces of enchantment.

Nick grinned. He flipped more slowly, considering. One page held a spell for warming one's self, which might prove useful on a wintry day. He turned on. Another page described moving small objects.

He considered the warming spell. Why expend the effort magically when the same effort, mundanely, would get you inside, instead? He studied the other spell.

Half an hour later, he looked at the candlestick. A short, sharp invocation, and the candlestick wiggled on its broad base, rattling against the table. His eyes narrowed. It slid toward him.

He put his hand out to keep it from sliding off the table and setting the house ablaze; it hit with a smack, and the candle flame quavered.

For a moment, Nick contemplated the flame. He had not considered how similar this spell was to the smoke-shaping spell. He cast that, to twist the candle's smoke into an impish little dragon. It grinned at him.

He put the candle down and let the dragon dissolve. He could study the warmth one now, or master refinements on this one—stopping the candlestick by spell, rather than hand.

He pushed the candlestick back along the desk. At times, he realized how his father had come to live as a hermit on the outskirts of the city. The thought made him shudder. He could not study too much later. He had to be awake for the party. His father would scorn it, but he was not his father.

Besides, he had had all the time in the world to study these spells.

Sunlight gleamed off the snow. It was colder than the day before; nothing was melting.

Nick wished he had mastered a spell to keep watch for the sleigh. Then, even with such a spell, what would he do instead? Study anything, and he would have to cut it off in the middle.

Dark against the snow, a sleigh came briskly down the road. A soberly clad servant sat with the reins. Behind him, young people, bright in wool and furs, filled the benches. Nick pulled on his own winter mantle and hoped that he was the last one intended for that sleigh as he descended the stairs and out in the crystalline afternoon. The sleigh was still drawing to a stop, the harness bells jingling.

"Why, Nick!" called Lucia, laughing, "one would almost think you eager to see us!" Other women smirked at her. Nick climbed into the sleigh.

"You're the last," said Fliss. Some of her long black hair escaped like a banner; she caught it to push it back under her mantle. "Now we will go—"

Stephan leaned toward Nick. "The old women agreed that out in the open, we could meet without chaperons, but they still had three women together in the sleigh before one man—as if we were not to be trusted." He was smiling.

Nick answered as lightly. "Are we to be trusted?"

Stephan looked sharply away, coloring. Nick blinked and glanced at the women, wondering which one—

Fliss looked at Stephan and said, tranquilly, "If you hated the notion of this party, you should not have attended. But to foil any future one by making tongues wag—" She spread her hands.

After a moment of ringing bells, Lucia said, sweetly, "Dear Nick, you got me in trouble with my mother this afternoon."

Nick gave her a sideways glance.

Lucia giggled. "We talked of whether you would come—" She glanced at Agnes, who nodded. "And I said that I would bet that you didn't."

Her uncle had left the country because of his gaming debts. "I did not know that your mother was still so distraught over the scandal."

Lucia pouted. "If you did not neglect us for those—studies of yours, we would have no occasion to."

Nick smiled wryly.

The horses reached the open fields, and the sleigh driver set them to move faster. Ahead of them, beside a frozen lake, soberly clad servants set out braziers and tables.

Nick grinned. No, Stephan should not foil such ventures.

Sleigh bells went jangling off. From his study, Mortimer watched. With the sunlit day and gleaming snow, neither Nicholas nor his friends could see clearly inside the study. Still,

Mortimer waited for them to vanish down the road before he went down the secret stairs.

At the bottom, he opened the door. The walls' gray stone arched into the roof, over the golden pentacle and the slab, like an altar, in one of its points. A smaller table stood to one side, and books cluttered it. He stacked the books higher to clear the space for his lamp.

The door opposite, with its tunnel to the countryside, he ignored as a piece of youthful folly. He walked to the pentacle. The gold and the haggling with imps had served him well—the pentacle had held the demon for his first pact—but even demonic work did not last forever. He bent over to inspect the pentacle inch by inch, moving with care to ensure that his shadow never fell on the gold, to hide any flaws.

Having traced over it, he let out his breath. He had waited until Nicholas left; he could wait until he returned. He did not need to conjure up needless tasks.

He picked the lamp up and took to the stairs. The chamber being so far underground, the stairs were long, but he climbed steadily and emerged into his study. There, he looked out the window. The sky was orange in the west, but Nicholas had said he would not be back before sundown. Mortimer's mouth twitched. His son and his gad-about friends could easily be much later.

At least, waiting for Nicholas gave him time to prepare, when no detail should be neglected. He put the lamp on the oaken desk. Its light glinted off the decanter there. He poured himself a glass—no more, though he knew the wait would be long—before he wrapped the wine with soporific enchantment.

He sat back to wait and to ponder what to say, to lure Nicholas to his study for the wine. He considered the youngsters he had seen in the sleigh.

Chapter 2—Festivities

A breeze ran from the dark forest, over the ice-bound lake, the snowy shore, and the party, brightly clad in red and green and blue wool. Nick turned his back on it and warmed his hands at the brazier. The breeze tugged at his hair, damp snow squished underfoot, and a burst of laughter resounded.

Lucia looked over at him. "Stephan told how you abandoned him and Edgar."

"Stephan and I delivered Edgar to his doorstep," said Nick.

"But then, you could not wait to be off." Lucia glanced at him through her eyelashes.

Nick spread his hands. "You would have been distraught if we had grown too weary to come here."

Lucia smiled and spoke to another woman. The young women nearest to Nick chattered about one guest: Luke, a young man new to the city, and his prospects, and whether his father would make a good settlement.

George's hands hovered over a candy. Nick's gaze went up to his face. George grinned at him and sidled through the party to Robina. With a deep bow, he offered her the candy.

Robina beamed and popped the candy into her plump face. A second later, her mouth popped open again, and she spat out the flaming candy. It flamed orange against the white.

"Why you...."

Many suppressed smiles. Some laughed outright.

George's grin deepened. "Ah, it wasn't dangerous."

Fliss Seaborn cocked her head, glancing at the candy. The flames went out in the snow they had melted. The breeze blew her long black hair back from her pale face—like a banner. "Oh." Her voice was colder than the breeze.

"It wasn't!" George said, his grin vanishing. Nick suppressed a smile.

Robina sputtered. "You impudent...."

George's grin returned to insolent. "Ah, don't be such a baby, Robina." His hand on his sword, he swaggered toward the brazier.

Nick held his hand over the fire. He ran through some spells, chose one, and muttered under his breath.

He pulled his hand back as George held out his.

From the coals, blue-black flames surged—taller than either of the men—and singed George's fingers. George jumped back, and gawked. Nick smiled.

George stiffened. "YOU!"

Nick spread his hands. "Don't be such a baby."

Laughter erupted. George seemed likely to choke.

After some minutes, the laughter sank. The breeze whipped through the snow, which cascaded and hissed.

Fliss turned to Edgar. "I heard you intend to go to the university."

"My father insists," Edgar said, looking none the worse for last night's drunkenness.

Fliss laughed, sounding almost natural.

Edgar looked about the party. His gaze settled on Nick. "Are you going?"

Briefly, Nick wondered what Edgar remembered of last night. "You know my father."

"I'm going on scholarship," Marie said. Her sweet face set in mutinous lines. Even beneath her massed blonde curls, she almost looked severe. "My father says I would waste the money, but *I* have not let that stop me."

We knew you when you were small, Nick thought with amusement, when you had a governess. We all saw her running after you in the garden. You will waste the money.

Marie looked about. "Are any of the rest of you going on scholarship?" Her eyes settled on Fliss.

Quietly, Fliss said, "Lady Alicia will pay."

"Oh, yes, you have to go," Robina said. She garnered baneful looks all around. It was tactless to remind Fliss that she was Lady Alicia's ward, and a baseborn foundling, accepted here only because of the great rank of her guardian, or that she would have to support herself after her guardian's death.

Nick reached for the mulled cider. However true either statement was.

The conversations broke up into little circles. Nick poured himself a cup. Fliss would go to the university unless compelled not to, but Robina would think that Fliss's folly. And his saying that the scholarship were meant for the poor would only inspire quarrels.

"Of course Nick doesn't want to go—he'd rather be a *gardener*."

Nick could not pick out the whisperer. He lifted his cup rather than try. That rumor, he had heard before. He walked among the partygoers.

"There is white sickness in the slums," said Robina to Marie. "Or so they say." She shuddered. "Now there is a dreadful magic."

That was a dreadful magic, thought Nick. Now it is a dreadful illness, but not a spell, nothing that could be broken. He wandered past them, the snow crunching underfoot, and asked Fliss about the university.

"Oh, yes," Edgar said, "you would want to master the studies. You helped with that dead hermit's cottage, the one he wanted as a traveler's refuge." Nick looked at his flushed face and wondered if Edgar was drunk again. He had heard of that cottage: a hermit had lived in the Wizards' Wood, and had left his cottage for whatever unfortunates happened on it.

"Of course," Fliss said. "They wanted someone who could do the spells."

Nick raised his cup. The spells might be fascinating, but questioning Fliss before Edgar would not prove instructive.

Edgar said, "Not a *poor* hermit, with an enchanted cabinet and all."

When Fliss said nothing, he added, "didn't he have a magical cabinet that fed him?"

"A benefactor—" said Fliss.

Edgar cut her off. "Anyone who owned *that* was rich." He eyed Nick as if expecting him to have his back.

"Oh, Nick," called Lucia. Nick turned. Her wet snowball hit him in the face. A chilly bit broke off and slid wetly into his collar.

"This means war!" someone shouted. Snowballs flew. Nick ducked, wiping the snow from his face, as the snowball fight became general. He tried to pull the snow from his collar without getting under his shirt; it melted under his fingers, icy water trickled down his shoulder, and the last bit of snow spurted from his grip, down his back. He shook his head and reached for snow. What did it matter that he could not pick out Lucia in the confusion?

"Look at that!" Robina shouted.

Across the snow, Edgar stood. He must have walked away as soon as the fight began. Snow clumped before him and rose into a wall. It reached his knees. Edgar grinned. His hands raised in spell-craft as he pushed snow before him. It grew higher, like a wave gathering at the beach.

"No fair!" Lucia shouted. Edgar's grin broadened. He strode forward, as if chasing the snow. The wall rose until it hid him from view. Nick scowled. Mischief was one thing, but

Edgar was not *thinking*. Fliss, looking pale, grabbed the brazier. Galvanized, the rest of the party scattered.

Let him win that easily? thought Nick. He threw up his hands for a spell of his own. It made not a visible trace; his companions looked at him, baffled whether they had heard the incantation or not, but he did not budge.

The snow loomed. Nick braced himself. Fliss called, "Nick, he can't see you! Don't be a fool—"

The snow hit his invisible shield—the wall of will—like a wave against a cliff. Nick staggered. He strained, concentrating, reminding himself that Edgar must find fighting his spell as difficult as he found fighting Edgar's.

The snow bore down on him. Sweat beaded on his face. His arms trembled. He could not last much longer. Perhaps Fliss had been right about folly—

Snow cascaded backward, toward Edgar.

The moment's distraction that caused broke his spell. Snow avalanched through where his wall had stood, filling the air like a dust cloud. Snow poured over his knees until it knocked him over, and something stabbed his arm.

Nick hissed with pain. Struggling through the whiteness, he pulled his arm free. His jacket and shirt sleeves were torn, and blood welled from a dirty scrape. Edgar had picked up things besides snow in that wall.

The air slowly cleared. The collapsed snow, sprawling, had knocked half a dozen others over. Pieces of ice had slithered into his clothing and now melted there. Nick tried to stand and realized he was exhausted. He had misjudged the strength of Edgar's spell.

He wrenched himself from the snowdrift. His sword caught, and he pulled it after. He shook himself, trying to knock off the clinging snow, but his clothing was already damp. Removing some snow would help little there. His fingers and feet already felt numb.

"Nick, Edgar!" Fliss shouted, sounding more exasperated than anxious. "Are you all right?"

"Pretty much," he called, looking for her.

Fliss was bent over beside Catherine. Giles stood beside her, as if ready to help—but she, her expression furious, glanced over her shoulder; her blue-violet eyes met Nick's gaze. "What about Edgar?"

A mumbled affirmative answer came from Edgar. He thrashed out of the snow. He had to be even more tired, with pushing the snow to where it fell. Nick's mouth twisted. Served him right.

"A pretty pair you make." Fliss stalked over the snow, her black hair streaming like an army's banner. "If you *could not* get out of the way, Nick, why didn't you push his wall into the lake?"

He blinked. That would even have been easier for him. Still—"If Edgar had to be stopped *properly*," said Nick, "perhaps you should have done it yourself."

Fliss sniffed and looked at the blood on his arm. "One day, your foolish spells will get you into deeper trouble than this—and no one will help you up again." She took his wrist and muttered a spell. The scrape knitted back together, the blood pulled back into his hand, the grime vanished, and the cloth joined together over it.

Nick looked it over. He knew a spell of mending, and another of cleansing (the first spells a mischievous boy learned to cover his tracks), but he could not have cast both together. He straightened his sleeve. Fortunate for Fliss that the healing spell did not exhaust quite like others; there were bruises and cuts all about.

"You will need to rest," said Fliss. "Healing spells can only repair damage, they can not restore vitality."

"I know that."

"Really?" said Fliss. The wind blew over the ruins of Edgar's snow wall. She added, "I could not be certain, with the knowledge of spellcraft you displayed this evening."

Nick looked at her. "Have you ever known me to lie to you? Or to anyone else?"

She stalked off, toward Edgar.

"What a prig," muttered a voice behind Nick.

Without turning, Nick flexed his fingers against the chill. Perhaps, but she had some grounds for complaints.

The revelers were bruised and shaken, and most of them wet. Lucia said, "I hope the cold doesn't make me ill."

In the west, the sun colored the sky with flames. Robina said, "Weren't we going to go home now?"

Nick walked up the stairs. The sleigh bells rang and then faded, behind him. He opened the door. The lamp glowed in his father's study. Nick walked by it. He was too tired to study tonight.

"Nicholas."

Mortimer's deep, cavernous voice stopped him. When he turned back, Mortimer looked up from his books, at him. His pale, lined face, and those dark eyes of indeterminate color, were unreadable. Nick walked into the study. The walls of books surrounded them, fading back into the shadows where the lamplight did not reach.

"I saw you return," said Mortimer. "Felicity Seaborn was among your company."

Too startled to speak, Nick nodded.

Mortimer rose. Lean build, sharp, pale features, black hair, and dark eyes of indistinct color—it was looking into a mirror that showed how he would age.

I do not, thought Nick, want to resemble him.

Mortimer poured out a glass of mulled wine and offered it to his son. Nick took it.

"I wondered about that," Mortimer said. "The scum of the docks, gaining acceptance on strength of her bastardry."

She's the only one who studies magic—or anything—seriously, thought Nick; not even I am serious. He sipped the wine. But then, his mother had been no scholar, not when Mortimer married her, not after. Mortimer would not fathom his interest.

"She is Lady Alicia's ward," said Nick. "A foundling. No one knows her antecedents."

Mortimer snorted. "They knew to name her Seaborn."

So, thought Nick, with a pang, I can draw his attention, with the threat of a misalliance. "Shall gentry tell a nobly born woman that her ward is unwelcome?" He raised his head. "And, Fliss is no more to me than any of the others among our circle." She would never let herself be more—

"What?" Mortimer lifted an eyebrow. "You were not taken with her today?"

"I was showing off," Nick said. And Fliss knew it.

He yawned and blinked. The exertions of the day had left him tired, but this sleepiness was sudden. He yawned again, and Mortimer smiled. Nick looked at the glass in shock. His father had bespelled it, he realized.

Mortimer slid the glass from his hand. Nick watched it go; he barely felt the smoothness of the glass on his fingers. Black blotches appeared in his vision, blocking out ever-larger bits of the study.

The sleigh plodded through the empty city street. Fliss sat back. The others were as tired and silent as she; the only sound was the clop of the horses' hooves.

A cat skittered across the way. The sleigh drew to a halt. Giles leapt from the sleigh and held out his hand. Fliss, not too tired to wonder, still took it, and he handed her down.

"You had reason to be displeased with magical studies, today," said Giles, his voice low. "Prudence is more difficult to show than folly." His hand moved through the air and snatched a bouquet of white and pale blue flowers, from nothing. Fliss gasped. "But Edgar and Nick are not the only students among our number."

Fliss cast down her eyes and took the flowers. She could smell the sweetness. She thanked him—and wondered what inspired this attention. She hurried toward the door. The sleigh driver told Giles to climb back or be left behind.

Within the doorway, the flowers almost glowed. She knew this spell, knew how they would dissolve by morning, but no one else would have given them to her. Certainly not Nick, showing his true face with that wall of his.

With a snort, she climbed the stairs.

Chapter 3—Plans Awry

Waking, Nick shivered.

He lay on his back, on cold stone. Icy metal weighed on his wrist and ankles, and a draft ran over his naked body. He shifted one arm, and a chain clanked. Slowly, in disbelief, he opened his eyes.

A windowless room, built of dark gray stone, stood around him. Two heavy doors, their wood almost black, stood opposite each other. The slab he was chained to stood in one point of an enormous pentacle—gold inlaid in the stone. Against the wall, a table stood with alembics, books, and bottles, like a wizard's laboratory. His clothing lay in a neat pile beside it.

Too dazed to feel anything, Nick rose to half-sitting, but a rush of dizziness knocked him back down. A bitter taste hung in his mouth.

The dizziness faded, but as his mind cleared, Nick wished the haze back. He shivered again, not from the cold. This was no dream. He wrapped his arms about his legs, huddling against the chill. Once, long ago, he had heard that, when a student, his father had dabbled in diabolerie.

His breathing was light and shallow. Every year some foolish student at the university summoned up a succubus and lost his place. The gossip about his father had been so blatantly spiked with malice that he had dismissed it as no more than that, if it had happened at all.

Nick let his head drop against his arms. He had been a fool, he had been three kinds of fool; as distant as Mortimer was, he knew that Mortimer was a fanatic for his studies.

He shivered for long minutes. He means to kill me, Nick realized; he can not show me this and let me live. The chains chattered about him.

Think, he told himself, fiercely. Terror would not rescue him. He looked at the chains, but they were nothing out of a chivalric tale: not rusted near the breaking point, but new. He studied them and felt even colder. In this, they came from a tale: these chains bore no locks, and no hinges on the manacles. Bespelled about his wrists. Even if he had known a lock-picking spell, it would not have availed him.

Despite the icy air, he dragged in a deep breath. He had nothing lose. He braced himself and pulled his right arm as far as he could, straining every muscle. His heart hammered in his chest. Even in the chill, sweat beaded on his body.

The chain did not budge.

After a long minute, Nick admitted that. He slumped. His arm ached from the effort. He wrapped his arms about his legs and dropping his head to his knees. The sweat felt chilly on his body. Deliver me, o Lord, from my enemies and the hands of those who hate me.

A door slid open. Damp and smelling of stone, an icy breeze swept from the doorway. Mortimer looked at him.

Nick stared. Mortimer had been a cold and morose father, had left him to the servants after his mother's death, but now he inspected his own son like a housekeeper inspecting meat at the butcher's. His flesh crawling, Nick tightened his arms about his legs.

Mortimer's mouth twitched. "You look as horror-struck as the chancellor was."

Horror choked Nick into silence.

Mortimer walked over to the table. "What petty minds the master wizards have."

Thinking aloud, Nick thought; not speaking to me. Mortimer picked up a parchment. . . . "They will stop you." Nick's voice echoed hoarsely. "The master wizards."

Mortimer lifted an eyebrow as if surprised that his son could speak. He unfolded the parchment and chanted.

Nick dropped his head to his arms. As if he could, in moments, throw awry a long-laid plan. His burst of anger faded into dread. Lord, have mercy on me. His thoughts roved over his life. It seemed a flimsy thing to face eternity with.

His father's face was not implacable, but serene. Nick looked away, his mouth as dry as bone. Lord, have mercy on my soul.

Mortimer's voice rose to a shout and fell silent. The silence seemed to resound. Nick could not help looking up. Then he could not look away. A tendril like red smoke rose in the pentacle, from no fire. The air grew warmer. Nick inched as far away as the chains would let him. His chains rattled. O God, he prayed, unable to make a more coherent plea.

The smoke rose, thickened, and coalesced, taking form until a red and sexless figure stood in the pentacle. Its muscular body bowed over beneath the ceiling, and it glared at Mortimer with tiny but burning gold eyes. It grumbled, the noise deep and bone-shaking.

The air stank of iron and fire and grew heated, but Nick, gagging on the smell, still wrapped his arms about his legs, though neither Mortimer nor the demon looked at him. Between Mortimer's cool mask and the demon's irate expression, he felt like a mouse between two cats.

Mortimer laid the parchment back on the table. "I summoned you." Next to the demon's grumble, his voice was small, but steady and clear. "I summoned you for an exchange. I will give you this one's life, and you will give me immortality." He looked up. "My own flesh and blood, the child of my body."

Nick choked. His heart felt as if it stopped.

The demon grumbled again, looking Nick up and down; its gaze passed Nick's, but could not be said to meet it.

Nick forced himself to pray, Lord have mercy on my soul; he was dead now. His tongue felt dead in his mouth, but he would not implore anything of either of them. He swallowed. That was a brag—as if he could speak.

The demon turned to Mortimer. "So you found your first bargain insufficient? You were so proud of it."

"It sufficed for its purposes. For new purposes, a new bargain."

"Such cunning," said the demon. "Did you not mark the disease in the city? Did you not know where it comes from?"

Mortimer spoke placidly. "I will not ask for a disease. Nor for a weapon to strike down my foes, or anything else where a disease might fulfill the bargain. You need not trouble yourself. Especially as I have already made my request."

"So, despite such a warning against over cunning, on your very doorstep, you find the gumption to offer this, this time?"

A mad attempt to discomfit his father, Nick thought. He wished they would strike the bargain and be done with it—and him.

The demon smiled. "Have you been afraid for so long? You sold us your soul, long ago. What made you find your courage for this?"

"What matters it to you? I have made the offer, with flesh of my flesh and bone of my bone—if you can fulfill your portion."

The demon's smile deepened. "Did they frighten you, those master wizards? They caught you, and they punished you, and they frightened you."

"They heard me confess to a tenth of my doings, and were appeased. How could such fools frighten me? When I wed and sired a son, they thought I had put away youthful follies."

Mortimer smiled. "Nor can you discomfit me. I offer you that son. My flesh and blood."

Nick drew a deep breath, though the air stank. He would neither grovel nor plead before these twain—but he thought it wise to remind himself of that.

"And yet—you ask for so little. You know that more can be done."

"One of you did it for another. I have heard of Master Oliver. I would be less than pleased with such a bargain. Putting my heart in the Wizards' Wood? Who but a fool would entrust anything to so treacherous and wild a place?"

The demon pondered a moment. Then its deep voice made the slab tremble. "And if I find your own flesh and blood not enough for your new bargain?"

Mortimer smiled more deeply. "Do you think you have a choice?"

The demon ceased to smile. It did not frown, but Nick looked uneasily between them, wondering whether they could fight. He thought the magic circle trapped the demon, but its face took on an ugly look, and he could feel the heat. Oh God, let the demon just reject the offer; Mortimer would have to devise some way to kill me, and I might escape. His heart hammered.

"Have you never heard of the magic circle that will hold until the demon grants what is asked?"

The demon glared at him. Nick's heart seemed to stop, and settled to a normal pace in defeat.

"You may have never seen one before." Mortimer put his fingertips together. "But this one is for immortality."

The demon's lips pulled back from its fangs. Its broad shoulders stretched until they strained against the pentacle—but even at that, it seemed more bent on testing than escaping. After a minute, it subsided. "Clever mortal."

Nick felt cold, weak, and queasy.

"I require that you give me immortality, in return for my giving you my son."

The demon's expression turned calculating. Nick shivered, remembering tales his nurse had told him, of the folly of devil's bargains. If the demon had its way, Mortimer would not find the immortality a blessing.

"Let us make all clear," said the demon.

"Everything must be clear," Mortimer said.

"You give me your son, to do with as I please."

Nick gagged. Not even a clean death, then. Scraps of possibilities raced through his imagination, all the more horrifying because he could not detail them.

"Even so," Mortimer said.

"In return," the demon said, "I must give immortality." Its expression reeked of secrets.

"Not only that. Will not this means of immortality entail taking the heart from the body?" Mortimer asked.

The demon nodded. Mortimer's face held no trace of revulsion. Nick felt ill. He had heard the fairy tales, and the tales of Master Oliver.

"You must keep my heart safe from harm."

"I will give immortality through taking the heart from the body," said the demon, like a child reciting a lesson, "and protect that heart from its enemies and all who wish it harm."

For all its sniping, the demon had yielded easily, thought Nick.

Mortimer said, "Even so."

The demon nodded. I was wrong about its expression, Nick thought; it has no secret, and Mortimer has outwitted it.

One enormous hand, with clawed fingers, reached out. Nick pulled back, but the hand flattened him against the stone. It lay against his stomach, pinning down his arms, and burned against his skin. Nick's heart hammered in terror. Lord, have mercy on my soul.

The demon's other hand swooped in on Nick's chest. Midnight black claws delicately touched his skin, burning like coals, and then tore into him. Nick opened his mouth, but the pain was too agonizing for him to scream. Half-blinded, he saw the demon pull something red—his heart!—from his chest, leaving no wound behind. For a second, Nick closed his eyes, but the demon did not pull away. He felt its touch once more and opened his eyes. The demon pushed a black lump into his chest with its burning touch.

A minute later, in the silence, Nick realized that the blinding pain was gone. His chest ached. Therefore, he was alive. Past terror, past horror, past comprehension, he stared at the demon. It straightened, his heart still red in its hand. No blood, Nick thought weakly; why is it not bleeding?

The demon rumbled, deep in its throat. A horror-struck expression dawned on Mortimer's face.

Nick looked between them. The demon had, after all, found a loophole.

Golden light coalesced around the heart and entombed it. The demon pulled its hand back. Gleaming like amber, the light hung in the air; Nick could just see his heart inside.

Mortimer gaped. Nick's hand went to his throat. The chains clattered, but he barely noticed. He was alive, he breathed, but though his fingers dug into his throat, he could not feel his pulse.

The demon smiled, displaying its fangs. "I have given immortality." It hunched down, bringing its face almost to Mortimer's level. "I have given immortality—to him!"

"You." Mortimer's lips formed the word.

The demon's smile widened.

"You!" Mortimer screamed, his voice distorted. "HOW DARE YOU!"

The demon grinned.

Mortimer looked at Nick, his face contorting. "Not for long. I know these spells. . . ."

"What manner of protection did you bargain for?" The demon chuckled. "The spell protects the heart against anyone who wishes your son harm."

Still grinning, the demon rose until its head brushed the ceiling. It stretched its arms as if it did not fear the pentacle.

Mortimer's face contorted. "You cheat."

The demon, laughing deep in its throat, vanished.

Silence reigned. The stones' chill seeped back into the room as Mortimer stared at the pentacle and looked blank. Nick, growing cold, shifted his weight. The chains clattered.

Mortimer turned toward him. His lips pulled back from his teeth. "You. . . little. . . wretch."

Nick met his gaze, but felt too dreary to keep it. His chest still ached.

"You. . . . How could you get what I have bargained for, I have studied for. . . ."

He meant it, Nick realized, temper rising through his shock. *As if I wanted such unnatural, damnable immortality.*

"All *my* work, destroyed by *your*. . . ." Words choked. "What *I* slaved for."

Nick sat up as far as the chains would let him. "And I was to be sacrificed for. The law will burn you at the stake for this. "

Mortimer drew a deep breath.

Serves you right, Nick thought.

Mortimer's voice gentled. "No, Nicholas, they will burn *you*." He raised his hands. "What evidence have you that I had any part of this—wickedness? That is *your* heart." He shook his head sadly. "For once, you have gotten yourself into a mischief that I can not get you out of. I am deeply distressed that you fell so deeply into folly."

Words choked in Nick's mouth.

"What was the evidence against Master Oliver? That his heart had been changed. After the way you ruined my spell, you wretched thief, it serves you right."

Mortimer's hand flashed. Chains fell from Nick's arms and legs. The manacles, still closed, rattled on the floor. Mortimer swept the air with his hand, toward the door he had not used. "Go. To the master wizards if you wish. Or to hide in some corner until you give yourself away. But go!"

Nick swung his legs off the slab, stiff in every limb. His chest ached. He could still feel the touch of each claw. He drew a deep breath, rubbing one wrist. The master wizards would believe him. Wouldn't they?

"Leave, Nicholas." Blue sparks danced between Mortimer's fingers. Nick's face set, and he stalked over to his clothing. He would not let Mortimer turn him out into the cold naked.

Even if it would not kill him. Nick swallowed.

"GET OUT!" Blue fire blazed around Mortimer like a halo. Sparks leapt out to lick and scorch Nick's arms. His hands full of cloth, he leapt back. There were evils besides death that Mortimer could inflict. Nick glanced at the bolted door. His father would not give him time to unbolt it, let alone to dress.

Mortimer's face contorted. One hand stabbed at the door. The bolt rattled and slid loose; the door opened a crack. Icy air gusted inside the chamber, blowing the door open—knocking it against the wall. "Now. . . ." Mortimer said.

Nick fled. The lamplight gave him a glimpse of the narrow stone tunnel, but the moment he stepped out, the door slammed shut behind him. The heat the demon had brought did not reach this far. Nick stood, shivering; the stone underfoot burned with cold, and the air licked at him with icy tongues, but still, he could not move as the bolt slammed into place, and the echoes of its fall died away.

Chapter 4—Flight

In the silence, Nick groaned. His own father. The boots slid from his hands. Clothing, he remembered, in a panic. He had to dress before he froze.

Half the clothing fell to the ground as he tried to identify the pieces by touch, with fingers that grew chilled until aching. Nick dropped to his knees to pick them up and scrambled back at the stone's burning touch. Crouching, he sorted through the pieces with shaking hands. More than once, he dropped the cloth before he could identify it. He bit his lip and drew the clothing on, piece by piece, though it was icy from the chamber's floor.

Minutes later, he still shivered in the black tunnel, but the cloth held out the draft. An owl hooted. The noise carried down the tunnel, distorted almost behind recognition by the echoes. Nick closed his eyes, glad beyond belief for the sound. It came from outside; this tunnel did not trap him underground.

He felt not terrified but grief-stricken and lethargic.

He took a step and grunted in surprise. His foot struck stone; the ground rose almost at once. He had not seen even that in the moment's glance. He walked on with more care. Though the slope was uneven, he kept to his feet. His breathing grew harsh, and his clothing warm, but his heart did not race.

Faint light crept down the tunnel, or else his eyes adjusted. Walls extended before him. Nick walked on, trying to see in the dimness. Mortimer had to have protected this passage. He had not kept his work from the master wizards by leaving an open door. Not when he conjured up demons.

Nick's chest ached.

Minutes later, the tunnel widened. Stairs stood there, with alcoves to either side. Moonlight shone on the snow that had drifted inside to cover more than half of each step.

"What I would not give for Edgar's spell now." The words echoed in the stillness. His eyes narrowed. If he fell and broke his leg, he could be trapped here until Doomsday. He picked his way to the first slippery steps.

Something moved in the shadows, making no more noise than a faint scrap on the stone. Nick turned, but the moonlight left the corners invisible with shadows. He pulled back, trying to probe the gloom. With a hiss, a creature leapt from the darkness. Nick glimpsed a bewilderment of batwings and a long tail, claws and goggle eyes—all gray by moonlight— and then it was upon him. Cold claws dug into his side, and icy teeth bit his arm. Nick struck with his free arm, trying to break its grip; he slid on the snow and went down, jarring the creature loose. He kicked it. A solid blow made his foot ache but knocked the creature back. He rattled off his spell.

The creature leapt forward, striking the wall of will. It hit with more force than Edgar's snow, and Nick cried out in pain, but it fell back.

He gasped for breath, watching it.

The creature hissed again and clawed at the wall. Its serpentine tail lashed the air behind it. Nick moved, gasped, and looked at the blood staining his side.

The creature strained up on its hind legs, pushing against the wall, reminding Nick that he was already tired. He climbed, ignoring the track of blood he left.

He staggered into the moonlight, into a grove of birches. Barren of leaves, their branches were lattices against the starry sky. A stream ran nearby, gurgling faintly beneath the ice, and in breaks, the water showed dark against the snow. By the stream, a small dark form moved. Nick froze. A rabbit stared at him, its eyes glowing by moonlight, and scurried off.

With a hiss of pain, Nick leaned against the nearest tree. He let drop the wall of will. If the stone creature could follow him out here, he was too weary to hold it back.

The stream gurgled, on and on. His breath steadied. The creature did not climb the stairs. He could go on.

The quarter moon hung low in the west. Trees and hills cast shadows over the snow. Nick braced himself and worked the spell of mending, knitting his flesh together. An easy spell, urging nature as it would go of its own. The skin sealed up, and he closed his eyes. If the spell were any harder, he would have bled forever.

His arms shook with weariness. He had been tired when he returned from the sleighing party, and he doubted that the hours under Mortimer's spell had given him any true rest. God help me, he prayed. He wished for Fliss's help. Then, the memory of her scorn struck. If she tried to heal him, he could not hide what had happened to his heart.

He thought of his friends: Edgar's drunken attempts to start a fight, Lucia's heartless prattle and George's heartless pranks, Stephen's contempt for his studies, Fliss's cold glances, all the young men who had drawn him into pranks, and all the young women who considered him a poor match. Perhaps they had never meant him any real harm. Then, he would have said that his father meant him no real harm.

Nick looked miserably about. From feeling merely exhausted, he felt nearly dead. It was not merely casting the healing spell; the spell only repaired injuries, it did not restore vitality. He had a long recovery ahead of him.

His fingers bit at the tree. He could not recover here, where he would freeze. If he had mastered the warmth spell, last night. . . . he would be too tired after it to move, and the warmth would not last long enough. He let his breath out. He was too tired to think straight.

His feet grew numb from the snow. Nick looked down the hillside, over the drifts, to the farmland below. His father's mansion stood near the city; he had come out in the country, by the woods. Nick looked over his shoulder. The city glowed in the night. The university—Master Oliver's heart had been found in the Wizards' Wood, but the student had come from the university. Nick looked at the woods, a vague mass in the moonlight.

He plodded down the hill. In one boyish adventure, he had reached the hermitage in a day and returned—late enough to be punished, but this night, he only needed to reach the sanctuary, and there would be no one there to punish him.

He slid on a piece of ice and caught himself on the nearest birch. His side stabbed with pain. A summer day, when he had been in good health—but where else could he go? He shook his head. When he had rested at the hermitage, he could think.

Slamming the door on his impudent thief of a son relieved nothing of his rage.

Mortimer turned, his hands still filled with blue fire. The table held all his preparations, with the papers ready to spill in disorder. He glared at it. With such a conclusion, he did not dare try again.

The demon's spell, warding Nicholas's heart, glowed in midair. He hurled the blue fire on it. It shot up, for a moment obscuring the heart—but not completely—and the fires died as if water had been thrown on them.

He stormed up the stairs. In his study, where the lamp still gleamed, he threw himself into his chair and glared at the mulled wine. He had to disenchant it. Half the servants were thieves. If the wine enchanted them, someone might guess what had happened to Nicholas.

"The little wretch." His hands tightened into fists. He had never heard of such impudence. A demon not even claiming its sacrifice!

He reached for the wine but, seeing that his hand was unsteady, he forced himself to stop and draw a deep breath. His hands had difficulty moving smoothly through the gestures, but he disenchanted it. The wine sat innocuously on the desk. Mortimer poured himself a glass.

He took a sip but brooded over the glass without drinking further. This—it could not be coincidence, that Nicholas had the immorality that he had studied for, strove for, and bargained for. His eyes narrowed. Phillipa's one virtue had been her disinterest for the art—she had been no rival—but Nicholas was his son as well as hers. The boy had to have guessed about his studies and *stolen* from him to warp the spell. He had stolen his own father's immorality.

"The little thief," he whispered. "The infernal little thief. I will show him, and that demon—" His eyes narrowed. Despite the demon's brag, no spell was unbreakable.

"And then Nick's theft will not benefit him." Mortimer's mouth twisted. "He should have done his own studies."

He let out his breath. He would need another spell, without even a sacrifice as good as Nicholas had been for this one. He had no doubt the demon would prove impish if summoned again. He drained his cup. He could search for both at once—he glanced about the room. The books were barely visible in the lamplight. He should search here for some way to get at Nicholas's heart. It would be folly to hunt all over the world for something that might be within his grasp.

Empty of every living thing, the fallow fields spread around Nick. Snowdrifts and stubble cast shadows. Nick plodded toward the woods. The moon sank.

Just before the wood, a village stood, a cluster of cottages around a church. Nick hesitated. Something moved, by one house, but when he looked, a cat flitted between two buildings, its head low. Feeling more lonely, he walked into the village. The church loomed, higher and higher, its cross a sharp black shadow against the stars.

Nick swallowed. He thought he could feel the demon's black thing against his chest. I wonder, thought Nick, if the demon's spell can endure holy ground.

He plodded over to the church, and its shadow engulfed him. A statue of St. Lucy, with an insipid expression, stood there, looking over the square, as if staring over his head. He stood under it, in the churchyard, and he felt no weaker than he had been. He could feel no relief.

He closed his eyes and prayed for a second, without words, trying to shape his imploring. The demon had spared his life, but he felt worse than he had when he first woke, chained to the altar. Alone and with such things about him that he dared not find company. He shivered. His walking had warmed his feet, but now they grew numb again.

Nothing stirred, not even the cat of before.

He walked from the village and into the trees. The moon set, and he walked by the glimmer of starlight. It was well that he needed to make out nothing more than the road.

Skeletal trees surrounded him, interrupted here and there with pines. The road was only a place where the snow had been beaten down. It was as hard as stone, underfoot, and his feet ached; the one that had kicked the stone creature hurt the worse.

Long hours later, dark gray touched the eastern sky. It spread and paled as the hours trudged on. Haze spread over the sky and took on a pale eggshell color. Dawn touched it with a fragile pink.

Nick climbed over a hill to see the small building. The hermitage stood in a small field. A garden held only snow with a few dead stalks, and leafless oaks towered on all sides. A stream ran by it and gurgled faintly, through the muffling ice.

The road went on. He did not.

Snow covered the stoop, but not enough to block the door. Nick staggered up and pulled on the latch. For a fearful moment, he thought the door would hold; then, with a groan, it slid open. Nick walked in, letting snow spill in from the step. He pulled the door shut. The windows let in too little light for him to see, so he leaned against the doorframe. At least, he had reached the hermitage.

He shivered. The air was still, but the cottage held the damp chill of a place unopened for months. The fireplace was empty, and no firewood stood stacked beside it, but blankets covered the bed.

Nick crossed the room. The blankets carried a faint lavender spell of enchantment. He smiled a little. At least they would not be musty and mouse-nibbled. Not, he added as he fumbled with his boots, that I would scorn such a bed. His boots clumped on the floor. He collapsed into the bed and pulled the blankets up.

They felt like sheets of ice, not only cold but rigid. Bone-weary though he was, he could not sleep. His breathing was harsh in his own ears. Then it steadied, leaving him hearing the silence where his heartbeat had been. He swallowed, feeling a mounting panic. He had to do something. Every fairy tale about such sorcery ended unhappily for the sorcerer—but the blankets grew warmer as he thought, and exhaustion overwhelmed him.

Chapter 5—Troubled Times

In the gray sky, a few stars still shone, though dawn had washed most away. Her hood up and her mantle drawn against the chill, Janet hurried through the square.

Something flitted by, about buildings, in shadows. When it dashed between two buildings, it caught the dawn and glinted metallically. Janet watched with narrowed eyes. Tiny, no bigger than her hand, it flew on a path as uneven as that of that idiot student. Though, she had to concede, it would not die. More swiftly than she could work out a spell to stop it, it rose to the garret of a college and flew in. Janet glanced down at the doorway, to be sure of the name: St. Agnes's.

The new term would open soon, and she always had things to do. Still, she pulled her hood forward to shadow her face and walked the other way.

She found a handful of students—men—talking of their feat. She stepped forward, pushing back the hood.

At the sight of her, one said, "*I* didn't fly."

Janet's mouth twisted. "I suppose it is just a coincidence that your automaton flew into a women's college."

The men colored, guiltily. At least, they were still young enough to feel abashed.

"I shall speak with the headmistress there. I suggest that you produce proof that this automaton was destroyed. Then we may talk further." She smiled mirthlessly. "Your names, and your colleges."

After a minute collecting them, she left for her office. She stalked up the stairs. She had too many papers to ready for the king, before she even could prepare for the term. Mischief, she thought. She spread her papers out in the gray dawn light and picked up her pen.

She moved steadily through them when footsteps sounded in the hall. She kept on writing, but the steps stopped in the doorway.

"You've heard of the white sickness," said Mistress Elise.

Janet's hand tightened on the pen.

A plump middle-aged woman, with gray peppering her brown hair, hovered in the doorway of Janet's office. Her robes were colored, of course, but the violet was not vivid—even if no other master but Janet favored a color as brilliant as Janet's yellow. She looked ready to fade into the woodwork, but Janet knew she would not.

"We have wondered whether diabolerie might be involved."

As if every wizardling did not learn that with his first spells. Janet cut out the words as if with a knife. "It was, once. That is legend. But now that it runs loose, there is nothing magical in its striking a city."

"Are you sure? These things are easily hidden."

This woman, thought Janet, is old enough to be my mother. She ought to have *some* sense by now. She laid down her pen. "The white sickness originated in diabolerie—a century ago—but it spreads on its own." Her lips curled. "It took off the diabolist, which he could not have wanted."

Mistress Elise's tongue touched her lips.

Oh yes, I listened in lecture, Janet thought, however much the thought shocks you.

"They say," said Mistress Elise, "that it spreads where evil magic is practiced."

Janet gestured at her papers. "Then it is a wonder that it ever leaves this city." She sat back. "I dare say your spells could help ward off the epidemic. I helped, last night."

Mistress Elise looked aghast.

"It's a simple spell—involves only similarity. I could teach you myself."

Mistress Elise muttered and hurried off.

Janet let out a long breath. If the master wizards minded the finding of diabolists so much, they should not have inflicted the job on someone who would do it. It might have been the easy way, with the fire lilies, but it returned on them. Her mouth twitched.

Those students had assured her that they could deal with the automaton within an hour. If so, she would give *them* a new spell to master.

Fliss combed out her hair. Nick's impish expression appeared before her again. She scowled and combed on. He studied more industriously than even those who intended to go to the university, he neither drank nor gamed like most of the young men, but he would not be serious. Even if he were more handsome than most—she hacked at her hair with the comb, refusing to be distracted. Except that Edgar's snow could have ended badly, however stopped.

She threw down her comb. She could never tell Nick that. She should stop mulling on those walls and consider Giles. She had never marked him out among their company before, but he had not shown any interest in her before, and the spell—she remembered her hands laden with sweet flowers—the spell had not been slight. She studied the comb. Giles had never shown interest in magic before.

A clatter sounded at the window, like a pebble being thrown—as she used to be roused when a child, and the others wished not to let Lady Alicia know.

Opening the window let in a blast of chilly air.

Lucia stood in the street, her maid behind her. "Have you heard about Marie?"

"Not since last night," Fliss said. It was only noon. What news could be less shocking than that Marie had not stirred? A chill breeze touched her. She pulled the window closer to shut.

"They talked about the white sickness, last night. Down by the docks. Didn't you hear?"

Fliss's voice was flat. "Rumors." At the orphanage, during her last visit, the sisters had seemed worried, but they had not spoken of illness.

"It was there, and now. . . ." Lucia spread a dainty hand. "I would have shopped this morning, but after Marie. . . she fell ill, and I couldn't risk it—would you?"

She hadn't even been hectic last night at the party, thought Fliss—showed not even a trace of fever.

"Oh—and Stephan and Agnes." Lucia put a finger to her mouth. "They *kissed* when she was dropped off at her home. The servants saw them, can you believe it?"

One way to get around Agnes's father, thought Fliss, as long as they did not mind a meager dowry. If they did not sicken— "We will all hear soon enough. Her father will not delay having the banns read."

Lucia nodded, beaming, and left. Fliss shut the window and leaned against the frame. White sickness.

She let out a long breath, trying to calm herself. When last white sickness had struck, she had been seven. Lady Alicia, having just taken her from the orphanage, had tried to shield her from the sickness, but no one could have. Any vagabond the watch caught was put to work digging graves.

She wondered if the orphanage could use her help.

She wondered if any of the others would help. Enough of them had mastered - *some* magic. Then she remembered the party, and her mouth twisted.

She stepped from the window. It would be wise to cut loose of that group when she went to the university. She would need to concentrate on her studies. Nick had probably exhausted himself with his little trick and lay abed, where he would do no one any good.

Nick smelled lavender as he woke. His stomach growled. Trying to ignore it, he rolled over, where a jab of pain woke him with a gasp.

With more care, he rolled over again. Afternoon sunlight shone over the strange room: whitewashed walls, a wooden stand with a breviary under the window, and a cabinet next to the gray stone fireplace. His chest ached, making it impossible to forget why he was here.

His stomach growled again.

He pushed back the blankets. The air was chilly, though the sun must have warmed it some. The hearth was empty of wood. Some dry twigs and leaves lay by it, but a fire would consume that in moments. Fire, Nick thought, he would have to get some firewood—after eating.

He swung out of bed. His legs ached; he had walked far last night. He closed his eyes. He had to eat.

He forced himself to stand, and his legs carried him. His foot was tender where he had kicked the stone creature, but he could walk on it.

He crossed to the cabinet. Praying that the rumors had told the truth, Nick opened the cabinet. Dried fruit and meat lay there, bread, uncooked porridge, and a small jar of honey. He snatched a piece of fruit and bolted it.

More fruit appeared on the wood. He did not see it emerge, but a glance away sufficed. Edgar was right, the hermit had not been poor. Still—

"God bless that wizard, whoever he was." He ate another piece, taking the edge off his hunger, and eyed the porridge. He had made a nuisance of himself in the kitchen, driving the cook to teach him how to make porridge one morning. He did not see any pot and turned toward the fireplace. Pain shot through his side, killing any thought of hunger.

With care, Nick pulled his shirt from his belt and bared his skin. He had staunched the mauling that Mortimer's stone creature had given him, but the wounds were still pale against his skin. He had been too weary to do more, last night. His mouth tightened. Wounds that set awry were harder to heal.

He dropped the shirt. Breakfast, and then enchanting the wounds again—as if last night had not sapped his strength enough.

If it had been last night. He did not know how long he had slept.

He looked about. Then he shook himself. The cottage would not tell him what day it was. He could judge from the moon at night, but he had to wait for that, and he could not wait for a fire, and food, and to tend his injuries.

From the sunlight's slant, it was mid-afternoon. He went to the door, hoping there was wood in the woodpile.

A few logs lay under the shed—and they could be rotten. Nick bent over to pick them up. His side stabbed again. His mouth set. Thumping on them showed they were still sound, but this much wood would not last through the night, and he was too weak for the cold. He had to gather more before nightfall.

His hand touched the bark. Of course, he would not freeze to death if he did not.

He shuddered. But he took the logs into both arms and turned.

A bird flitted over the snow. Its wings gleamed blue and gold. Its ruby-red head turned to look at him with a flaming orange eye. Nick did not twitch. The bird flew on, under the trees, where the shadows showed that it glowed with its own light. With a chirp, it flew deeper into the woods.

Nick stared where it had vanished. He wished he had read more deeply. He could not remember any works on the woods in his father's library, but there had to have been some. Mortimer would not ignore such power on his doorstop.

His arms started to tremble from their burden. He shifted the wood to ease them. This was the Wizards' Wood, and it had not received that name because of the nearby wizards. The university had started because the students had followed the master wizards, and the wizards had come here for the woods.

The wizards still came here for the woods.

A breeze made him shiver. You have to risk a wizard happening on the hermitage, and you, Nick told himself. The city, where the wizards *stayed*, was hardly safer.

Besides, what would be wise did not matter; he was too weak to travel.

He walked over the snow and into the hermitage, dropped the logs in the fireplace, and collapsed on the hearth, breathing hard.

He had been bone weary before he had walked here. If he had gone to his friends in the city—why had he fled like that? Fliss's scorn had been for the foolish way he had hindered Edgar's spell, and no proof that she would name him a liar about this. Even—the master wizards might have believed him if he had gone to them at once. Now, on top of the other evidence, he had hidden something from them.

The floor was cold beneath him. He wondered what the rumors said of him. Rumors would fly; nothing else would fascinate them quite so much.

A minute later, his stomach grumbled. With a groan, he pushed off the stone. He arranged the logs and stoked the fire until orange flames licked the wood.

Water, Nick told himself. He ventured out to fill the pot from the stream. Water ran in the gaps in the ice, looking black against the snow. Some gaps came close enough to the bank that he could fill the pot.

Cold water lapped at his fingers. Do not fall in, he reminded himself; wetness would chill him more quickly than anything. But the bucket filled, and he could leave.

He rose, holding the bucket with care to avoid spilling it. A golden eye appeared in the waters and looked at him. Nick could not make out any form behind it. It blinked, and he pulled back. The water sloshed, and he walked slowly. The water weighed like lead. He imagined the eye watching his every step until he got inside again, into the welcome warmth.

Tired as he was, he enchanted the water to cleanse it. Somehow, he set it to boil and collapsed on the hearth again. His arms still trembled.

Nick stared into the fire, unable to see anything but flames. He should not have fetched so much water.

The logs shifted, and the water started to steam. Nick turned his attention to making porridge. He wondered if he could stay awake long enough to see how full the moon was.

Janet walked through the university. The sick she had treated would live until tomorrow—and so need the spell again. The white sickness would spread. She was mildly tired, which was well; she would need more strength ahead.

Something flew through the air. Her eyes narrowed. Slowly, she turned her head to see three metallic things flitting through the air, dancing about each other as if drunk. It took her a minute longer to pick out the excited whispers, but the students were so bent on their little tricks that she walked up to them, unnoticed. One jumped, and she smiled. He made some frantic gestures at a flying thing—which did not make it to descend. Her smile twisted.

"You will bring them down," she said. "And, on the morrow, since you have so little to fill your hours, and you are so eager to learn, you will learn another spell, and gain ample practice: to help the victims of the white sickness."

A couple of faces contorted.

"We don't—"

"If you are so eager to learn new arts," said Janet, "this is a new spell, and not a common variation."

"We don't want to learn *that* one," said one young man.

"How do you know you will not find it *fascinating*?" said Janet, sweetly.

A minute later, she walked on. She had their names. She did not have time to write the report of their misdeeds, but she would find it, after the white sickness.

A dry cough, across the square, stopped her. It took her a minute to find the source. She had not dreamed that a purple robe could be *drabber* than Mistress Elise's.

"Isn't that severe, Mistress Janet?" His hands twisted together.

She had to have seen him, the masters were not that many, but she could not remember that face. "I would not have imposed the sentence if I thought it too severe, Master—"

"Simon," he said, with restraint. "But—it's dangerous. They could contract the sickness, don't you know that?"

"So could anyone in the city," said Janet.

"Some are safer than others. Those who keep themselves safe." He spread his hands. "Is it fair to expose them for so trivial a matter?"

Janet cut out her words. "They—could—not—control—them. Their—spell—ran—wild."

He looked ready to protest.

She stepped toward him. "How dare you! With the white sickness raging, you yet act as if *control* were unimportant!"

Master Simon sniffed.

Janet wished she could slap him like an impudent child. "The knave would have been a murderer if he had only conjured up the illness. But that would have required him to *control* it. Now he murders again and again and again, long after his death."

"Comparing the white sickness to stray automata is folly. You have no sense of proportion. You treat the most frivolous of pranks as if they were foul—"

"Do you deny that diabolerie is foul?" said Janet.

"You treat everything as if they have signed a pact to sell their souls! I know students you have rebuked—"

Janet glared at him. They were nice young men and women, no doubt, which was proof enough they could not be guilty of any serious evil.

"I have no doubt that you badger the priest into his sermon on diabolerie, every term!"

"If you went to cure the poor," said Janet, "you would not be here to have your propriety offended."

He glared at her. "Two young gentry dueled with spells. They engulfed each other with snow. You should go after them."

"Students?" said Janet.

"No," said Simon.

"Perhaps I should appeal to the king. The masters can not grant me authority over those outside the university, and the king, thus far, has only let me deal with criminals."

Simon scrambled off, and Janet walked. Perhaps she would hunt down those gentry wizards—after the white sickness.

Evening sunlight spilled over the room. Its gold turned to orange. Nick lay on the bed, unable to do more than stare at the sunbeams and the motes in them. The dust moved lazily, but more than he could. Since he pulled his clothing off and slid under the blankets, he had barely moved; he had drowsed now and again, but now he felt wakeful and unable to rise.

Disgusting laziness. This time, he had undressed, but he had not washed, and his beard was sprouting.

Gilded dust drifted about. He had been injured, Nick reminded himself. He needed to recuperate. He needed patience.

And then what? a thought retorted. He would not need forever. What would he do once he was healed? He stared at the ceiling. Live here forever?

As a child, he had dreamed of quests in the wilderness, of fighting colorful dragons and black-hearted magicians.

Firewood. He needed firewood—and he had no fire-breathing dragon to fight. He pushed thoughts of later aside. The gardener had told him that the lower boughs of a tree were often deadwood, and dry for burning—and he remembered a contemptuous twist of mouth, when a small boy had wandered, pleading exhaustion, from the weeding he had begged to help with.

He rose to dress again. At that, what choice did he have?

Even as he walked to the nearest trees, the sky darkened, and the air chilled. The snow underfoot grew harder, turning to ice, and the wind picked up. Shivering, Nick bent his attention to the nearest boughs. They broke off in his hand, and he slowly accumulated an armload. The sky and its clouds turned to scarlet and purple.

He walked back to the cottage. The moon shone through the trees. It was little larger than the night before, he had not slept through a day, but he could not care. One day would be much like the next here.

The wind grew more chilly. Shivering, Nick dropped off his armload and headed back out. If it were that cold, he would need more wood.

Something flitted through the trees. He could not make out the shape, even whether it was a bird. He collected the second armload faster than the first, despite moments of nearly sprawling on the snow.

With the wood, he headed back to the cottage. Something flew between him and the moon. Nick moved more quickly. Something flew behind him as he opened the door. He lunged inside and slammed the door behind him. A sound echoed—a sound half way between a bird cry and laughter.

His shoulders hunched, he laid the wood beside the hearth. From the corner of his eye, he saw something flying by the window. He should stay there, cook himself more food, and eat. He was ill.

He walked to the window. The moonlight shone on half a dozen birds flitting by, as black as a starless sky.

They flew closer. His fingers bit at the windowpane. One flew at the glass, making Nick jump back. It stared at him with an inhuman eye, as black as its feathers. Nick tore himself away and returned to the fire. He fed it another branch.

Laughter echoed.

Nick looked away from the orange flames. Two birds flew by the windows.

Ignore them, he told himself. You would not have left tonight, whatever happened.

A bird brushed the window. Though he flinched, he did not look back. The birds flew on and on, their mockery resounding. Nick rested by the fireplace. Every now and again, he fed the fire. The moonlight shining in the window shifted, and shadows raced through it.

The wall of will could hold them off, Nick thought, though it would exhaust him even further.

A bird let out a wild cry. Not that they tried to get in. Nick's mouth tightened. The clamor would keep him awake. He faced the window and tossed the wall in their path.

One cry stopped abruptly, with a thud; the pressure was short, and none too strong. Silence reigned a moment, before the air erupted into offended calls.

He thought he heard one bird-like scream, "Not fair!"

Nick smiled and, as the cries faded, yawned. He was glad he had not been standing while he did that. He banked down the fire and yawned again. The coals glowed a dully red. He leaned against the fireplace. He had been gravely wounded. He had to rest. Throwing about spells at will—he would sleep fully clad tonight, as well. He was too tired to undress.

He could get his boots off, he thought fuzzily.

The charity hospital's ward was dark and dingy. Two small windows, neither one clean enough to see through, let in light on row upon row of beds. Every one held its pallid victim. Half a dozen more lay on the floor, on pallets roughly built from blankets. Some patients were fretful; others, too weak to fret. All were sweating, though winter and the want of charity had left the room chilly.

"I haven't time for this if you aren't serious," said the doctor.

"I learn quickly," said Fliss. Her voice was faint, but she kept it steady. A young man thrashed against the blankets. She looked away, wondering if she had the stomach.

"God knows we could use more wizards," muttered the doctor.

Fliss let out a breath. It had taken her all the day before and part of this one to find someone who could teach her. "I will not stay long. At the Orphanage of Holy Innocents, the orphans are sickening."

After a moment, the doctor snorted. "Better than they should send them here." His voice grew clearer. "All these patients are running a fever, yet see how pale their faces are. This is because the white sickness attacks the blood. Ordinary spells do no good."

Fliss nodded. "The demon didn't mean them to."

The doctor looked annoyed at the interruption. "You must cast a similarity spell, which will multiply the redness in the blood. Like this."

Fliss cocked her ears. The woman beneath the doctor's hands grew rosier. The doctor gestured at the next patient.

With one example? Fliss felt cold, but walked over. A miscast spell could doubtlessly kill. Still, the plague spread throughout the city, and she had no time to study. The old man on the bed stared at the ceiling. Fliss wondered if the doctor had chosen him because she could not shorten his life by many years. She drew a deep breath and began the spell.

When she finished, the man was not dead, but he looked only slightly more pink. She felt more tired than she had expected.

"You'll improve," said the doctor. "For now, repeat it on each patient. When they grow pale again, you must do it again."

Fliss whispered, "I feel tired." She swallowed the "already."

"It's not a healing spell," said the doctor. "It's a similarity spell."

Her mouth tightened. Then, she should not have been such a fool before him. She repeated the spell on the old man. Before she finished, the doctor went to another patient. Fliss could only inspect his color and conclude that twice was enough. She went to the next bed. She ought to be sure of doing it right before she wielded it with no other wizard near. And no orphan was as ill as the patients in this ward—but the sickroom weighed on her.

She wondered what gossip spread. She would not mind if only some pranksters heard enough to join her. But she had known enough to not ask.

The doctor stood over her at the last bed. Flustered as she was, Fliss cast the spell once. Color bloomed in the old woman's face.

"Well done," said the doctor. His voice held more exhaustion than approval.

She hesitated. "The orphanage?"

He waved a hand.

She thanked him, promised to return if she could, and fled. She hurried down the stairs as well as she could when three ill patients came up the same flight.

Outside, in the wan sunlight, she pulled her mantle and hood more closely about her. The street was icy.

The church bells clamored. A small church stood ahead of her, and she saw no one entering for the service. Then, they all had grave cause not to come.

Two days. After only two days of this.

Janet looked at the wiry sailor in the cot, now less pale. The sick all ought to come to the hospital; it was too much for the wizards and doctors to go house to house, even the houses of the wealthy.

She went on. She had heard of a wizard in love who had walked through a garden, turning all the roses from white to red in tribute to his love. She could disprove it, now. He could not have endured it.

She cast the spell on a weather-beaten old man. The ruddy color was paler than it had been. She would have to rest soon.

With the wizards up at the university thinking the white sickness no concern of theirs. . . no, she had seen Master Bernard and Mistress Meghan, and she thought Master Francis—and the city was large. She might not see them all.

She went to the next bed. Still, none of them would see that the worst diabolist did not begin by creating the white sickness, and would continue to demur on the grounds that a student who summoned up a succubus was not dangerous.

"At least they won't track me down," she muttered, "to complain while the white sickness reigns."

In the three days, the break in the stream had been frozen over. Nick clambered out on the rock, with the pot in one hand and a brand from the fire in the other. The steadiness of his pace pleased him.

Despite the breeze, flames licked the air. He dropped the wood on the ice. It fizzled. He cast the spell he had used on George at the party.

The brand erupted, searing the air about. In moments, it slid through the new hole in the ice. He wondered how the hermit had managed during the winter, but dropped to one knee to fill the pot. Nothing looked back at him.

"Maybe it was curious the first day," Nick said. The words echoed oddly. If he had studied harder—he shook his head and walked back into the cottage. The water slopped, freezing on the snow, and his arm shook before he reached the inside.

He put the pot down and rested by the hearth. Wood lay by the fireplace, and more outside in the shed, and even with both wood and water, he was less weary than his first day here.

Still, he should rest, and not outdo his strength. He could hardly study here.

He looked at the breviary, neatly lying on a kneeler. He smiled. The hermit had wished it to be ready for any traveler. He rose and opened the book. It fell open to a Psalm.

"Keep me safe, O God, I take refuge in you. I say to the Lord, 'You are my God. My happiness lies in you alone.'...."

Nick drew a deep breath and collected his thoughts.

"....who even at night directs my heart."

His fingers felt numb on the book. He stared, blankly, at the wall. He had forgotten. Since he had risen that morning, he had not thought on it, but now the silence seemed loud.

A long minute later, he collapsed on the kneeler and buried his face in his hands.

About the university, the streets held not even a stray cat. Janet walked as swiftly as she could, though the frost on the stones made them slick. She wished she could believe that the masters and students diligently assisted against the sickness. She knew better.

She came about a corner. The Cathedral of the Magi stood before her. In the graveyard beside it, men dug four graves, next to three covered with earth, but bearing no snow.

Janet shuddered. She had found the lights before the Cathedral colored, once, just before the illness; she almost wished it back again, not to catch the culprits, but to know that the student could do mischief. She had known the white sickness would reach the university, she had warned Master Simon of it, it came as no surprise to her—

"There you are, Mistress Janet!"

Janet stopped. Students hurried toward her. One grinned and held out the remnants of an automaton.

She raised an eyebrow and took it. They did seem to have found all the parts. "I heard that the Orphanage of the Holy Innocents has need of wizards who can bespell the orphans sick with the white sickness."

They shifted uneasily. "We could catch it," one said.

"Then you should go to confession, first," said Janet. "And be glad of the effort." Her voice turned poisonously sweet. "If you know the spell, you will be able to use it on your fellows— and on yourself. And, at the orphanage, someone would notice if you fell. Many a man died, last time, because he fell ill with no one to aid." She glanced at the Cathedral graveyard, causing more uneasy stirrings. "When death spreads like this, only a fool would not remember futurity. Better to die, having done good in your last hours, that go to your grave with nothing but cowardice to mark you out." She smiled. "And if you live, which is more likely than you seem to think, you will have mastered a new spell."

"Fliss," said Sister Helewise, sounding constrained, "you must come to the Mother Superior. At once."

Fliss looked at the orphan beneath her hands. This one was healed. For now. Five days at this, and no end in sight. Some orphans had recovered. Two had died. Whenever she ventured home to rest, she saw new graves in every graveyard. Wizards, down to the hedge wizards, scuttled along the streets, and priests, to attend to the ill the wizards could not aid.

"Fliss?" said the sister, sharply.

Fliss followed Sister Helewise down the stairs—not to her chamber, then—and to the receiving room where, Mother Humiliata waited with half a dozen young men. Their robes were not merely dark but black, of students not masters.

Her heart sank. She was not even a student, herself, but that reflection did not raise her spirits again.

"These young men," said Mother Humiliata, "say that they were told that the orphanage could use wizards."

"We could," said Fliss, wearily. "Did you learn the spell?"

One nodded. Another said, "Yes." All of them looked sulky, but she did not care. They could sulk while they cast spells, and she would bless their names forever.

Mother Humiliata said, "Three of you will go with Felicity to the girls' wing. The rest, follow Sister Helewise to the boys'." She picked off the three and gestured toward Fliss.

She led them down the dimly lit corridors. From their accents, she guessed them to be scholarship students, and one muttered about the place looking like a college. Any university student was more serious about magic than one dabbling on his own. Even Nick, evading parties to study, had not applied his magic to this horror, and a scholar needed to study for his scholarship.

"Have you practiced with the spell? It's unusual—"

"I heard," said one, sourly, "that it's the same spell that an undertaker uses to keep a corpse from making a stench."

Fliss's laughter was so shrill, even in her own ears, that she slapped a hand to her mouth to silence herself. The students gave her wary glances and made no more such comments.

The travelers' footsteps were not loud, and their voices came only occasionally.

Nick stood still in the forest, though his arms were laden with wood. When he came here, the road had been beaten down, but he had not thought ahead, to realize that people traveled through here. He could only hope that since the road

did go on, they would, too. To huddle here like a fugitive
would convince anyone of his guilt.

"Huh," said a voice. "Someone's at the hut."

Nick closed his eyes. Smoke. He had not fed the fire, but
he had not banked it, either—as if he had to fear its going out.
His arms ached, and his side reminded him of the stone
guardian's claws.

"Warn him?"

"Probably hiding—or carrying. You want it?"

Nick shifted his weight. His feet felt cold.

"What's that?"

"Huh?"

"*That*?"

The voice grew sharp. "That's smoke and nothing m—"

Silence fell. For a moment, Nick thought they would hear
his breathing. Then their flight down the road drowned out all
other noises. He let out his breath. Any man who chose to
walk through Wizards' Wood could not be easily frightened.

When the sound of footsteps faded, Nick walked back.
Smoke came from the chimney but not in dissipating curls. It
gathered, took shape—a wyvern's shape.

He went to the wood shed. The wyvern's head had formed;
even in the even gray of the smoke, it had eyes. The nape of his
neck prickled, as if it stared at him.

He laid down the wood and walked outside. The wyvern
eyed him and stretched its gray wings, flexing its gray tail.

Shaping smoke was none so marvelous, thought Nick in
irritation. He rattled off the incantation. It snagged curls of
smoke before the wyvern drank them up and formed a smoky
knight. The wyvern pulled back in surprise. The knight waved
his sword, and the wyvern flew off, past the column of smoke.
Without that, it fell apart.

Nick smiled. Then, with a sigh, he released the knight. It
dissolved into wisps, which the air ate up.

Inside, the fire looked innocuous, but he gave it a few stirs. Whatever had inspired the wyvern was no longer visible.

He stared into the depths of the fire, where the flames burned blue against the wood. From their talk, something was happening in the city.

He let his breath out, exasperated. If he had to wonder, perhaps he could do something besides gather wood and eat: he could wonder how to free himself from the demon's spell.

The fire crackled.

He should have studied harder at his father's library. He might have learned his father's secrets, enough that he could plan a spell at least. His hand formed a fist. He fought down the impulse to hit it against the hearth.

In the ashen shadows by the bed, Fliss held the little girl's hand. Occasionally the child stirred, as if to ask something, but Fliss ignored her and repeated the similarity spell the four times needed to turn her rosy again. The girl's parchment-colored face slowly gained color. Either she was far sicker than the earlier patients—or Fliss was too drained to cast the spells well. Even with the scholars, the orphanage held patients enough to exhaust them all.

The girl shifted. Her cheeks turned up from the pillow, her brown, sweat-laden hair shifting. Fliss grimaced; with the tangles the girl's thrashing gave it, it was just as well the fever would mean she lost it. She laid down the girl's hand and rose, though her arms and legs protested.

Through the window, Fliss saw the rising moon—past full and waning again. She blinked. No noise came in the window from the street, but the white sickness accounted for that. Fliss shook her head. That morning Lucia had told her that Nick had not been about since the party—over a week before. Even he could not study for so long, and the folly of stopping the snow at least showed him no coward. She leaned on the doorway to steady herself. He must have taken the white sickness, and early. She had slandered him in her thoughts.

She could not bring herself to care.

Fliss pushed herself from the door. After a moment, she walked into the hall. Lord, help us, she prayed silently, Lord, help us. A cart rattled by. Fliss swallowed. Lord, have mercy on the souls of the dead.

Lamplight pooled at the corridor's end. Mother Humiliata talked with Sister Johnette in a low voice. She looked at Fliss with sharp black eyes.

"Fliss, are you well?"

Fliss blinked. Three children had died. What did they expect her to feel?

Like a small bird, Sister Johnette tilted her head to one side. "We promised Lady Alicia to send you home if you sickened."

"I think," said Mother Humiliata, "it is time for it."

I'm not sick, thought Fliss. I don't feel sick. She opened her mouth to say so.

"And hope," said Mother Humiliata, "that you have not waited too long for the spells to work quickly."

"But," said Fliss.

Mother Humiliata took her arm. "Lady Alicia sent a sleigh for you."

Mortimer glared at the books. The master wizards had told the truth in one thing. The fruit of laborious years, the carefully drawn-up pact—all proved useless. Nothing held a way to break the protection, to end Nicholas's insolence. His hands clenched into fists. He had been foolish to be so pleased with the pact, when he had not tried to find something they would hide from him. *Now* he knew that too much of it came from the hands of the imps; the demon must have known his powers too well. Or the imps had taken care not to bring those spells. Or both of them being untrustworthy, both.

He forced his breath out. There was nothing for it but to look for new spells in the hands of mortals. It was not as if the Wizards' Wood held a charm to help him.

The bookseller would be simple and straightforward, and cost only the coins and no other effort—the bookseller was too frightened to be troublesome. He glanced at the window. But the white sickness had come.

He remembered the bookseller's fearful glances at the door. A man so cowardly—Mortimer drew out a cup to fill with wine. With no need to search, the muttered spell summoned up the tiny red image of the bookstore: unlit windows, locked door, and stillness within.

Mortimer dismissed the image. The street outside had been as empty as if the middle of the night, but the fool frequently had few customers. How did he plan to eat without selling? And he could sicken at home as well as at his store.

He opened the window to toss the wine into the chill; it splattered on the snow. He closed the window and thought. The imps of his last bargain were still bound by it. He had not asked them for these specific spells before. It would be folly to assume that they could not aid him. How Nick would laugh if he learned his father had overlooked so obvious a possibility. He put down the cup. He had hid all his arts when the masters had watched him. He would not cower in defeat now.

Nick walked through the hemlock grove, in shade as dark as the evening. The needles overhead had kept most of the snow off; dead needles crunched underfoot, faintly scenting the air.

"Now, this red berry is the winterheart."

The chirpy voice carried over the snow, and Nick froze. He had been a fool to forget, because he had only been lucky. The university's wizards were charged with preventing the misuse of the Wizards' Wood and its magic. So far from the road, the most innocuous stranger would be questioned, and the master wizards would learn that he had no heart.

My heart ought to be hammering, he thought.

Among the leaf-bare trees outside the hemlocks, two young men and a young woman, in black robes, trailed after a plump man in green robes. It felt strange, hearing a human voice.

"Winterheart flowers and fruits in the winter. This liveliness in the face of difficulty is a valuable trait for similarity spells, particularly ones of healing."

"Then it would be valuable in the city, now," said the woman.

"Even so, Eva. Look for it."

The students dispersed across the snow. Nick, careless of being seen, pulled deeper into the shade.

Snow crunched under his feet.

"What was that?" said a student. "In the grove...."

Nick could not move. He was too drained to even think of trying to escape, if they came after him.

The master wizard tutted. "If you try to track down everything in the Wizards' Wood, Drew, you will never master your studies, even if you live long enough. If you do not heed my advice, I will not chase after you to ensure that you happen on no perils beyond your skill."

In turmoil, Nick hurried away. His hand went to his face and the half-grown beard. A student might take him for a wild man of the woods. He was shaggy and filthy enough for one.

He burst from the hemlocks into the sunlight, where leafless branches had not kept the snow from underfoot. He stopped to drag a deep breath of the chilly air.

"What a coward you are becoming." His voice echoed strangely. He knew spells to clean his clothing as well as a laundress, and that spell Randall dug up when his father thought him too young to shave. He had hidden any number of pranks that way, and how much he did in the garden—and that when he could have washed like anyone else.

If he only were not so tired.

Fliss's voice chided him again, as if from the party, and his injuries had been trivial, then. Still—

The master wizards, he assured himself dully, were mastering whatever evil the city found.

A blood-red squirrel ran over the snow before him, leapt to the nearest tree, and chittered, as if scolding him for his flight. He stared at it, remembering the master's words to his students. So many strange things, and they were as impenetrable as the heraldry of a distant land.

His eyes closed. Even if he had stayed in the city and won the masters' trust, he would have been healing, not studying. To feel pangs of envy for those students was mad.

Lamplight surrounded Fliss's bed and left the rest of the room dark in brown and gray.

"She should not have stayed so long," Lady Alicia said. The words seemed awkward in her mouth.

"Many a young woman has sickened without going near the orphanage," the doctor said. "Your ward is likely to recover. Though she will lose her hair; the fever has come on too hard."

Lady Alicia blinked. Fliss's hair was not so lovely now: tangled, matted, and soaked with sweat.

The doctor bowed and left. Lady Alicia sighed.

Fliss looked brightly at her. "I'm going to the university at the Annunciation," she said, with startling clarity.

Lady Alicia winced. Perhaps, if Fliss made a remarkable recovery, it might be possible. She had thought, when she went to the orphanage, that she would be charitable and generous and give the girl, whose cleverness the sisters spoke, of a chance to master her gifts.

"Nick," said Fliss scornfully, "says he wants to go but I don't believe him. He's lazy."

Lady Alicia's eyes closed. It was far, far, too late for her to be up, her old bones would ache in the morning, but she sat by the bed. She had mastered the spell.

By the window, Nick looked at the evening. The sky was flat and gray. Plump white snowflakes drifted down. The warmth he and his friends had sleighed and chattered in—only two weeks ago; it felt like years—had been a thaw. The scars from the mauling were fading, but his arm still ached, and the weariness lingered.

The fire crackled. The nearest groves had surrendered their wood, and the new snow would be harder to find wood in.

He turned from the window and felt the thing in his chest, like a weight. Unlike his arm, his chest showed no scars, and the pain had long faded. But from time to time, he felt the absence of his heartbeat.

He wondered how his father had accounted for his absence, or if his friends had noticed: Edgar, Lucia, Fliss. . . . The pang he felt surprised him with its strength, but he was not sure that they would notice before he missed several parties. They would gossip about his absence, he doubt there would be enough else to preoccupy him, but they always gossiped when he studied.

Which, he had to concede, he had done often enough.

What had he told Stephan? That a retired life would be delightful? He had mistaken how fond he was of solitude.

He looked at the breviary. The healing spells had not utterly exhausted him; he had managed the spells to clean his clothing and himself, and to shave, and it was not as if wizards or monsters breathed on his back. He opened the book.

"O God, come to my assistance,

"O Lord, make haste to help me.

"Glory to the Father, and to the Son, and to Holy Spirit, as it was in the beginning, is now, and shall be forever more."

He read on, until he came to the Psalm. He looked at the line for a long minute before he read, keeping his voice carefully steady, "Who even at night directs my heart. I keep the Lord ever in my sight: since He is at my right hand, I shall stand firm. And so my body rejoices and my soul is glad." He swallowed at the next line but read on. "Even my body shall rest in safety."

The window showed the falling snow.

Robina pouted. "Another reason." She turned to the room, where her sister Ursula and her aunt Dora sat with Lucia. "You're the only one I've seen since the sickness broke out. Once it snows, everyone will appeal to it as insurmountable."

"Some have excuse," said Lucia. "Agnes took the white sickness—and Stephan is too distraught to think of anything."

"Well," said Robina reluctantly, "that would be an excuse."

Lucia lowered her voice. "I saw Fliss creeping out of the orphanage with half a dozen students from the university. *Scholarship* students, no less."

Ursula's eyes grew large. Robina took care not to look at her. If she realized that Robina let her overhear, Ursula would think she was no longer a little girl—but if she stopped her, Ursula would not realize what she knew.

"I'm sure Nick was about—casting spells like Fliss."

Lucia raised an eyebrow.

"It's a new spell, he never let anything get in his way, with spells—"

Lucia's mouth pursed.

"Edgar and others study magic, but they have limits—did you know? When Nick was a boy, he used to help the *gardener.* Digging, weeding, everything. Mistress Phillipa had to take care to summon him in time to get him *clean* for a party." Robina sniffed. "He scorned our parties so young. Can you imagine anything so common?"

"I swear," said Lucia, "Nick Briarwood would have abandoned us entirely if Phillipa Briarwood had not watched him like a hawk. After that fever took her—" Lucia shook her head. "He's doubtlessly glad of both the white sickness and the snow. Anything to avoid us."

Said Robina, sadly, "After all her efforts to see to it that he didn't turn into an image of Mortimer Briarwood."

"He still," said Aunt Dora, "is not on such good terms with his father that he could get a marriage settlement."

As if anyone would want to marry such a killjoy! thought Robina. "Let him turn hermit, then."

The white sickness had ended. The bishop proclaimed services of thanksgiving—well attended by people ready to drop from exhaustion. Janet heard the bells as she walked. Thanks were fitting for a plague that had only lasted two weeks, but she would not join the streams of haggard people to the church doors. She would give thanks after she slept for a week.

Or two.

"Mistress Janet?"

She looked at Master Otto, as angular as ever. He did not look at all weary. Pompous fellow, she thought.

"You were not at the funeral," he said.

What had the chancellor to do with attendance at funerals? And after these weeks, "the funeral"? How many new graves were there in the Cathedral of the Magi's graveyard alone?

Master Otto folded his hands together. "Whatever we think of our fellow masters, respect is important, lest our students learn disrespect from us."

"Which master?" said Janet.

Master Otto's mouth pursed. "Really, Mistress Janet. Bad enough that you could not break your labors to attend when others could, but to not even remember his name—"

"Who claims to have told me his name?" said Janet.

Master Otto hesitated. "The others, the message reached them."

"The wizards," said Janet, "who attended the funeral—any *one* of them could have preserved the body long enough to have the funeral after the white sickness. And ensured that everyone *could* attend."

Master Otto sniffed. "We still have to replace Master Simon before the term."

She blinked. Master Simon. In muddy purple.

"A servant found him, dead in his chamber."

"May God have mercy on his soul," said Janet. She hoped he made his confession before he hid himself away.

"And, I heard tales that some young wizards, among the gentry, committed some folly about spells before the white sickness. And you have not investigated."

Even I, thought Janet, can not do twenty things at once. "Not *yet*," she said.

Mortimer flipped through the pages. The sailors' shouts, outside, reached through the bookstore walls. For all his follies, the bookseller usually was right when he said a book was worth looking at.

Mortimer snapped the book shut. But not always.

"Sir? Is everything all right?"

Mortimer handed the book back without a word, not listening to the bookseller's apologies that the white sickness had barely ended and had stifled his trade. Without a glance at another book, Mortimer left.

Outside, the sun shone on the bustling street and dazzled on the snow lurking in every corner—new snow, not yet grimy. He stalked down the street. Other spells had to exist; Master Oliver had found one, and not the same one that he had found. That meddlesome student had killed him, and all his papers had been burnt, but the spell had existed.

If it required dealing with the Wizards' Wood—but it could not. Wizards cast the spell all over the world.

Mortimer bumped into a plump woman. She turned, scolding like a bird. He scowled. She cut off her protest in mid-word and scurried off.

Mortimer's hands clenched. He needed that spell. Or else the boy would live forever and laugh him to scorn.

In the slanting sunlight, Nick staggered into the woodshed and leaned over the pile of firewood to release the wood. They clattered as they fell. His arm aching, he stayed leaned over, his hands on his knees, and fought for breath. A prudent notion, to fetch enough wood to last out a storm. Last weeks' snow fall had been warning enough that the weather could trap him, and laziness here would make him suffer far more than it had in his studies.

His breath finally slowed.

He straightened. Before him, the road parted the trees to reveal charcoal clouds in the west. They were far thicker than they had been the week before.

He looked at the wood stacked at his feet. His arms ached, he wished he was not so sensible, but tripping over it in the cottage would be better than fighting a snowstorm to fetch it. He braced himself and picked up an armload of wood. He paused for a second, then bent to add another branch.

His grip slid before he took three steps. Nick gritted his teeth and walked on. Water pooled in hollows on the ice. He picked his way more slowly, but his arms trembled. He took one quick step, trying to reach the doorway, and a slick patch caught his foot, making it slid out from under him, dropping him on the rock-hard ice. The wood jumped from his arms to fall on the ice and on his legs.

Nick sat without moving for a minute. The sun set behind the storm clouds. The ice was slick with water. His clothing was getting wet, which the gardener had warned him against; it was a good way to freeze in the winter.

The gardener never lied to me, Nick thought. He pushed off the ground and looked at the wood, sitting on top of the ice, before gathering an armload—a smaller armload. He limped into the cottage, to drop the wood by the hearth, and back out for the rest. Water dripped from it. He had not given it time enough to soak in, but he would have to let the wood dry before he fed it to the fire.

Patience, he told himself, as he propped it up to drip freely. If he had had patience, he would have carried two loads, and dropped none.

Inside the cottage was dim, even beside the storm-threatened evening. Nick fed the fire a log. As the flames leapt, the wind picked up. He shivered.

What was he going to do?

He let his breath out. His folly with the firewood might slow his recovery, but it would not stop it. He stared into the blaze. He was no hermit; abiding here, even if it were safe, would drive him mad. And if the solitude did not, his curiosity about the creatures would. He could flee aboard to study wizardry—he hardly had the learning to study anything else, or to make his living otherwise—but he would not find a university the match of the one on his doorstep. Foreigners came to study here.

Nick turned his head to stare into shadows. They trembled as the fire danced, and the orange light played with them.

Perhaps, if he became a master wizard, he could find some way to undo the spell.

His hands clenched into fists. If he had gone to the master wizards at once—but now he was too weak to make the return journey. Even if they would believe so wild a tale, hidden for so long. And so he lingered, useless, futile.

Among the skeletal trees, brown leaves blew in the wind; caught, they piled up in every corner of the garden. Nick walked down the path, turned a corner, and saw a flowerbed, filled with flowers: yellow and red tulips nodding over daffodils, and pink and purple hyacinths.

No, no, Nick thought, confused; it's autumn, they will freeze, they will die, they will be too weak to survive the winter, and unable to bloom in the spring.

Then he woke.

His face against the pillow, Nick drew a deep breath. The dream dissipated into fragments. He rolled over to face the window. Outside was charcoal gray, but the wind was calm, and nothing fell. He pulled the blankets closer. A strange dream, he thought; he had known it was the garden at his father's house, but the dream garden had not much looked like the real one. And no autumn ever had that many leaves.

A dream, he thought, and burned his face in his pillow.

Sleep did not return. Minutes inched by, until finally, he rose. A glance out the window showed snow lying everywhere. His footprints had been muffled into hollows, such as the wind made, and he could not pick out the road.

Nick walked to the fireplace and stoked up the fire to make breakfast. He stared into the yellow-orange blaze as the porridge bubbled. He had no skills to earn himself a living, and hardly enough to learn anything but wizardry at the university. He stirred the porridge. And he had a diabolic thing inside his chest. It would keep him alive, but health was another matter. He had heard of an immortal man who had withered into a grasshopper. Not to mention that anyone who trusted a demon's gift was a fool.

He lifted the pot from the fire and spooned the porridge out, to stare at the steam rising from the bowl. His old reason for not attending the university was that with a father who would not pay, he would need a scholarship meant for a poor man, when he was not poor.

He was poor now—if that had been anything but an excuse for sloth.

He ate.

Chapter 6—Preparations

Wrapped in blankets against drafts, Fliss wondered whether she was slothful or merely bone-weary from the white sickness. She had risen from her bed, but Lady Alicia had forbidden her to rise from this chair.

Low voices came from below. She sighed. Life returned, even if subdued by Lent, and Lady Alicia received visitors.

Footsteps sounded on the stairs. Indolently, Fliss thought that they did not sound like a servant's. Then Lady Alicia showed Giles into the room.

Fliss managed to stop gaping like a fish.

Giles conjured up the bouquet again, white and blue, and scented. "Christopher is giving a party. I thought to bear news of how you fared." He smiled. "After the fearful warnings your guardian has given, not to weary you, I think I shall have to limit how good I make the news."

Fliss smiled. After a minute, he left.

As he descended the stairs, Lady Alicia said, "Those were the flowers you brought back form the sleighing party."

"So they are," said Fliss.

"He seems taken with you."

Fliss's finger brushed one petal. She knew little of him, and only from attending so many of the same parties. But, if he wanted to overlook her birth—she looked out the window to nowhere.

"Is there something about his character—"

Fliss shook her head. It would be folly to reject a good match rather than consider whether they would suit.

Especially—she smelled the flowers—if he attended to studies.

The door closed and cut off the chill.

Laughter echoed from the room. Smiling, Catherine handed off her cloak. The first party since the white sickness struck was bound to be merry, when they had not lost any of their circle. Even most of the ill had recovered enough to come.

Ahead of her, a guest muttered that they were frolicsome for Lent. Catherine shook her head. As if Lent had not arrived early, with the white sickness! And they would not dance. She walked in. For those who wanted more gloom, the city held processions, filled with moaning, ill-clad penitents; they should not attend parties.

Half a dozen revelers stood about the buffet; a handful played cards at one table; one woman at the harpsichord sat with a company about her. The chaperoning aunts and mothers, in sober dress, sat in the back of the room. Their low voices did not carry, but she knew their grave talk with the husbands and widowers—and that their eyes were sharp for scandal.

"Catherine!" Christopher appeared at her elbow. He looked pleased with himself; then, he had reason.

"A charming party."

Christopher sketched a bow, offered her his arm, and ushered her toward the buffet's fruit. He had to be proud of it. Pyramids of fruit awaited her, as ripe as any that grew in the summer. She took a peach and complimented him, and then looked about.

By the buffet, Giles assured them that Fliss still ailed. She had guessed that—was anyone else missing?

Her gaze was caught by the cards. Randall dropped them on the table. They leapt up and shuffled themselves, to the card players' exclamations, and Randall's grin.

Catherine shook her head and took a bite of her peach. Juice trickled onto her fingers, and she stopped her survey to lick it up. For a moment, the plague seemed like a bad dream.

Nearby, Marie tossed her head. Her face was still pale. "You might be well enough attend the university, Edgar, despite the white sickness. You've always been hardy. I found it more—enervating than you did." Her eyelashes sank to veil her eyes.

Ah, poor, delicate Marie, Catherine thought. "Fliss plans to attend after the Annunciation. I hope you were not more sick than she." She took another bite.

Marie's mouth pursed. "Oh, Fliss. Her parentage is not in much doubt now: hardy peasant stock."

How vulgar to say so, Catherine thought, and continued her catalogue of the party-goers. She frowned. She had not even heard that Nick had taken ill. She swallowed and said, "Nick must have suffered badly. I haven't seen him since the party by the lake, have you?"

Marie shook her head. Shrugs and head-shakings came all around.

"Perhaps," said George, "he decided that he would rather study." He rubbed his hand. "Or he doesn't have a good prank to play on us."

That childish retort did not change anyone's expression. Catherine wondered that even George managed to say it.

"Perhaps," said Edgar, "the Briarwood servants could tell something."

"They couldn't," said Christopher.

Marie gasped. "Why, Christopher, whatever do you mean?"

Catherine thought her melodramatic but felt cold herself. The music at the harpsichord stopped, and even the chaperones looked at Christopher.

"I sent an invitation. The housekeeper told my footman that she hasn't seen Nick since the party by the lake—since before the party. Neither have the rest of the servants"

Marie gasped again. Catherine shivered and thought that gasp less theatrical. Nick had been delivered to the very door.

"According to the housekeeper," said Christopher, "Mortimer said he quarreled with Nick and turned him out of the house."

Catherine felt the blood seep out of her face. All about the room, people murmured their horror. "Shocking!" exclaimed Robina's Aunt Dora. For once, Catherine did not find her vulgar.

"I wonder that he didn't come to any of us," said John. "He knew he could be a guest at my father's house at any time."

"Unless he sickened," Catherine said, not loudly, but the room went silent. She had not even intended to speak aloud. Still, with everyone looking, she went on, "Hadn't the white sickness had started by then? You were sick that morning, weren't you, Marie?"

Marie bobbed her head.

"So Nick might have been." She stopped again. Alone, in that bitter cold, and ill.

"That would be *dreadful*," said Marie.

A minute later, the conversation broke up again. Catherine returned to the buffet. Someone said, "Perhaps Nick ran away to study elsewhere, to avoid *us*." Catherine grimaced and took another peach. Without leaving the city, Nick Briarwood had avoided them whenever he wished.

"Dear me," said Edgar beside her, "you were as anxious about Nick as if you and he had been kissing in the corners."

Catherine gave him a baneful glance. "If I had been that fond of him, I would have learned of this before this party—he would have come to me, after his father threw him out."

She bit the peach. She could do nothing for Nick now, and it would be morbid to dwell on it.

Marie came up to the buffer. "Have you seen Randall's cousin?" She glanced at Catherine through her pale eyelashes.

"I think so. He was at the party by the lake."

"A charming young man—and a nobleman's grandson."

Robina said, "I guess the advice about Nick was good. If Mortimer would turn him out for a quarrel, he would not make a settlement for Nick's marriage, would he?"

We knew that, thought Catherine, without the quarrel.

Something glittered to one side, catching her attention. A young man—John—on one knee, offered a bouquet of flowers to Beatrice. The petals were too evenly colored to be real, Catherine thought, and they glittered. The scent reached her. Yes, he had conjured them up on the spot. Catherine smiled indulgently. No wonder Beatrice looked bedazzled.

Papers, thought Janet, and more papers.

She had done the right thing, setting those students to fighting the white sickness, even if she had not formally written the sentence. A time of plague was not time to palaver about details.

But she had to write them all for her next information to the king, and her hand already ached. She rubbed it, glaring about her chambers. She was the only master in these chambers, but if she left, she would be the only one *awake* in the lodgings.

A rap on the door made her snort. She did not need distractions, but she called, "Come in!" After all, a visitor who bothered to find her at this hour—

Symond looked in. Janet blinked. Like the rest of her kin, her cousin was not one to visit her at the university. Certainly, none of them ever hunted her down to her chambers.

But she could guess why. And it was not to report diabolerie.

"Good evening!" she said. "A delightful surprise. I did not expect you, but I am glad of your presence." She gestured at the papers. "You may find yourself a messenger—but a *royal* messenger."

Symond's mouth twitched. "You could deliver them yourself."

Janet blinked. "Term's too close."

"You don't *have* to teach here," said Symond, "and scandalize all the nobility."

Ah, that had been a new opening in an old argument. Symond, sent to make it, *would* come at the hour he came to the city, as if swallowing a bitter medicine.

"I *am* teaching here," she said. "I can not drop my duties."

"They could find another."

Janet let her breath out. "They're still looking—"

"They would have managed if you had taken the white sickness and died, Janet. They don't *need* you."

Janet sat back. "I'm not landed. What better way to earn my bread than to engage in the noble occupation of tracking down miscreants?" At Symond's flinch, she pressed, "That was what nobles *did* for the king. That was *how* our family became landed."

"You could be landed. With our blood, you could find—"

"An upstart willing to overlook a bride who loves wizardry?" She resolved to *load* him with messages for the king. Either her blood was worth something, and she was entitled to as much in her bridegroom, or it wasn't.

Nick looked down the hillside. The slope was slick with glittering ice, and the trees far apart.

"I hate this rain that freezes." His voice echoed oddly, but after this long, he did not let that squelch him. "I wonder how the hermit ever survived."

As the echoes died, a bright thought came to him: the hermit had never recovered from injuries like his.

Nick ran a hand through his hair. He was recovering, he had even cleaned himself—no one would take him for a wild man of the woods—but he had exhausted the wood near the cottage. The hermit must have laid in wood over the summer.

He walked toward the oak grove below. By stepping firmly, he broke through the ice to the snow and inched down the hillside with foot holes of his own making.

Something brown skittered over the ice. For a second, Nick took it for a windblown leaf, but the wind did not blow that way; then, it was too small to be a squirrel. His eyes narrowed. It turned a human-like face, no bigger than his thumb, at him. Nick stared. The creature darted behind a tree and, he thought, climbed it.

He walked on. A wordless scold came from a tree, but he could make out no words, the Wizards' Wood contained many marvels, and he still needed wood.

"Nuisance," he muttered. He reached the bottom of the hill and walked under the boughs. Something hissed, and he jerked back. A green and blue snake wound about a branch. A snake? In this weather?

It slithered forward, so that its head—a woman's head—and a woman's body to the waist, both blue-skinned, came into view. She hissed again, showing tiny fangs and a forked tongue.

Nick stepped back.

Something flew through the air by him. Then a second thing, and it lodged in his jacket. Shrill scolding echoed, and two human-faced but squirrel-like creatures danced among the trees. Anger contorted their faces. One lifted something to hurl at him, and Nick fled to the nearest tree. The ice broke, underfoot, making him lurch through the snow, but he put a great trunk between him and his assailants. He glanced about. Three creatures lurked beneath a snow-laden tree, ready with—he could not see.

His hand went to his collar. It came away with a stone arrowhead. His breath hissed between his teeth. He would fare farther to gather his wood, once he escaped.

He looked at the tree. He did not have Edgar's spell, but— he cast the wall of will and knocked it against the boughs. Snow cascaded. Screaming in rage, the creatures darted for shelter. Nick ran for the hilltop.

Half way up, he slipped on the ice and did not catch himself on anything. He landed hard enough to knock the wind out of him, but before he slid, he caught the nearest tree. The rough bark bit at his hands. He looked down. He could see nothing moving in the grove, but the creatures had been small. He moved with care, but with the tree's support, he climbed to his feet.

He looked for his tracks down, and inched over to where he had already broken the ice. Farther to gather wood, but not as far as he would need to go anywhere else.

Mortimer emerged from the bookstore into the frozen day. Bad enough that the bookseller had sold him that foolish parchment that Nicholas had so easily subverted, but now the fool acted as if a book about breaking spells held danger.

"The foreign wizard!" Two boys pelted down the road as if see a marvel. Despite himself, Mortimer looked. On the docks, a man, wearing a master's robes in flame red, stood. A big man, tall and solidly built, he loomed over all the boys and even the sailors. His dark brown skin and black hair showed he was indeed a foreigner.

"Come for the marvels of the Wizards' Wood!" called a boy.

Mortimer walked up the street. The useless marvels. He had been born here, and the nuisance of moving was all that kept him here. He would not have come for deer that bled flowers, or golden eyes that appeared in the midst of springs, or anything else of Wizards' Wood. Their only use was to make fools wonder.

In a reasonable world, the people would wonder at a master wizard's skills. They would tell a master from a merely skilled man, they would know the folly of not distinguishing, and they would be impressed by mastery. Mortimer snorted. The masters stood between him and undoing a demon's work, now. . . in such a world, Nicholas could have found his own lore, rather than steal it—he snorted again, this time at his own folly. In no world would everyone be willing to work for their honors.

"Master Mortimer!"

He thought he recognized Master Francis's voice, but did not turn to see. That would betray that he had heard the hail, and his search meant that he had no time to chatter.

He remembered tales of diabolists chattering with imps. His mouth twisted. If a man could not bear to keep his own counsel, he would be wise to avoid every form of diabolerie.

The servant ushered Umberto into a paneled room. The two tall windows lit the vast oaken desk, and the chairs with their embroidered cushions. Master Otto, an angular man of middle years, with thinning brown hair, looked up from behind the desk. "Master Umberto."

Umberto nodded and took the chair the chancellor offered. The day I arrived, he thought; it offers a good hope.

"I heard that you came from Metharia and want to join the university."

"Even so," said Umberto. He remembered the fresh graves he had seen walking here. To profit from such misfortune— but it had been no fault of his. "I only regret I came no sooner, when I could have aided during the plague."

"Well, that ended over a month ago," said Master Otto. "And there is much here to draw any wizard."

"The fame of your Wizards' Wood has spread over the world." Umberto spread a hand. "And the university that is beside it."

Master Otto hemmed, and Umberto suppressed a smile. The university was founded because of the woods; the woods did not grow because of the university. Master Otto knew that.

"The university," said Master Otto, "is always glad of a wizard who can teach lore of far countries."

A woman swept into the room. Her yellow master's robes rustled, and her coppery hair swept back. Her gaze fell on Umberto, but she turned to the chancellor. "The papers you requested, Master Otto."

The chancellor glanced at her. The intruder's mouth set in a thin line. She looked young for a master wizard, and while all master wizards, who could teach as well as learn, wore colored robes, hers were notably brilliant.

"Ah, later, Mistress Janet."

Mistress Janet, Umberto thought—Mistress Janet Whitehall, perhaps?

Her voice was clipped. "Had I known you entertained a foreign guest, I would have waited, but you called it urgent." She held the papers out.

"Mistress Janet Whitehall?" Umberto rose.

She looked startled and then wary, as if readying a retort.

He inclined his head. She had claim to such vividness in her robes. "The fame of your dealings with diabolists has spread far."

Mistress Janet flushed—a brick red that did not become her—and looked down. Master Otto looked sour. Ah, thought Umberto, bad blood.

Master Otto took the papers, and Mistress Janet left, her robe swirling, her footsteps hastening down the hall and growing quiet with distance.

Master Otto cleared his throat. "I do not know what tales have reached you, but I assure you that they are overstated. Mistress Janet lacks—proportion." His fingers came together in a steeple. "She treats every case of diabolerie, down to the foolish youths who summon up succubae, as if it were another white sickness."

At Umberto's glance, Master Otto flushed. "She treats wrongheaded students, or even careless ones, as if they were criminals of deepest hue."

The Wizards' Wood, thought Umberto, does not exhaust the intriguing aspects of this land. He weighed his words . "Until you look into their work, you can not tell how grave the case is. I had the sad duty once, when a student had not properly dismissed a succubus." He paused. The demon had, of course, changed its form, the succubus and incubus being merely appearances, and as an incubus, had assault a maiden. From Master Otto's contorted face, he knew that much of diabolerie. "The poor young woman conceived, of course. It took the labor of several wizards to restore the infant to a human form. I would have been glad if that student had been frightened by relentless scrutiny of diabolerie."

The moon was waning but still almost full. It shone on the tiny room, and the table and the oddments on it were colorless in light. Luke reached for the lamp. Randall's heart hammered.

After a muttered spell, yellow lamplight brightened the room and cast distorting shadows on Luke's face. "Here's something you've not seen before. Better than those cards."

Randall's heart hammered harder.

Luke slid the lid off a box, revealing a stack of thin papers.

Randall pulled the top one out. It looked yellow with age, though by lamplight, he could not be sure. He read. His breathing grew shallow and rapid, and after a minute, he lowered the papers.

"It would stir up the university." Luke grinned.

"It's diabolerie."

Luke's grin turned smug.

"We can't do that! What if we're caught?"

"Caught?" Luke's lip curled. "Half a dozen students have been caught at automata. By Mistress Janet Whitehall herself. You know what *she's* like, but she only made them stop the automata and help with the plague."

"I heard. . ." said Randall, weakly.

"And those were scholars. Paupers. Nobodies. For all her noble blood, she would dare less with men of gentle blood."

"She didn't know if they were diabolerie."

"Then what have we to fear? I won't tell her."

Randall drew a deep breath. "I won't do it."

Luke's lip curled. "Well, if you're a coward. . . ."

Randall managed to keep his tongue for a moment.

"I thought help wise, but if you're so inadequate, I would be better off without you."

"Of course I'm no coward," said Randall.

In his underground chamber, Mortimer glared at the stone and the chains. He ought to remove them. Not that he found them galling reminders, but that they might interfere with the pentacle, and be dangerous.

The demon's spell, protecting Nicholas's heart, gleamed in midair. He turned his back on it to prepare. It made a few movements awkward, but the spell could not taunt him.

At least these demons were bound to obey him or forfeit their bargain. They could demand no further concessions, and they could hardly be more difficult than the bookseller. His voice crisp, Mortimer recited the spell.

Three tendrils of smoke rose up, one red, one blue, one green. Smoke or not, the air remained chill; these were not great demons. He watched with narrowed eyes. They always came in company—perhaps to encourage each another in mischief. His hand tightened on the list. That, he could not allow tonight.

The smoke coalesced into three imps. None of them stood as high as his waist, their figures sexless and with long, barbed tails. Their smooth skin kept the color of the smoke they sprang from, but they slowly took on detail, until sharp black eyes peered at him.

Mortimer remembered Master Jasper's declamations on how demons were liars, and the devil the father of liars, and how not one of them could be trusted. Sanctimonious old fool, thought Mortimer. His hand tightened still further on the page. Jasper was fit only for the monastery he ended up in, afraid of bold quests for knowledge. Demons were liars—as if men were ever honest.

The imps giggled and poked each other. Their little hissing voices rose just high enough to grate on his nerves, without making their words plain.

"Imps." His voice was thunderous. "Look on this spell." He gestured at the golden case. They chattered, but the green one poked a finger toward Nicholas's heart, and all three glanced at it more than once.

"Fetch me a spell that may break this spell, or the lore to devise it."

They chattered on. The blue one giggled, setting off the other two. Mortimer's eyebrows drew together, for they lingered longer than usual. Usually, they vanished more swiftly, to fetch the spell and be done.

The green imp looked at him. Its hands went to its midriff as it hooted with laughter. The other two echoed it. The red one fell on its front and kicked its legs and tail in the air.

His mounting rage made it hard to think straight. He had to, he had to—but was there such a spell in existence? Had the demon concocted something new, that there was not even lore on how to break it?

The blue imp doubled up. Mortimer felt a cold weight of certainty in his stomach. The demons were famed for the variety and depth of their lore. That was why dealing with them was the best way to find new lore. The demon could have devised something that no human wizard had ever seen.

Or were the imps being facetious? The paper crinkled in his hand. They could dream up some explanation about the lore: that no human wizard had ever broken it or, perhaps, written down the lore to break it did not mean that lore on the spell was nonexistent.

"Fetch me lore on the spell that protects the heart there."

For a moment, the imps stopped their laughter and looked attentive. Then, they laughed again. The green imp fell on its back to rock like an infant in its cradle.

Nick looked out the window. The crescent moon was vanishing before the rising sun. It had waned to nothing, grown full, and waned again—a month and a half, more or less.

He wished he had counted the days. Some time before, the cabinet had ceased to yield cheese and meat, giving him dried fish instead. Too late, he had realized that it must be Lent; he had not marked which day had been Ash Wednesday.

The day before, the snow had started to melt. It might freeze again, as it had frozen twice while he was here, but only a fool would count on it. The night had turned the snowmelt into a slick layer of ice, over the road and clearing, but the day was melting the ice again. Now, the glistening pools still formed on the ice, but before noon, it would transform the road into mud. Either condition was less passable than the snow.

Nick collected his thoughts before self-pity mired him more than the mud ever would. He could not return before he was strong enough to face the road—however sorry he was to be trapped here, however much he need to break the demon's spell.

Snow slid off the nearest branch with a plop. He sighed. Not while the roads were icy. He walked back, by the hearth.

The fire snapped, and the noise echoed oddly. Nick frowned and looked for the log that had produced it. A pair of red eyes glared back.

He stared. The smoke creature, he thought, but that had left no traces in the blaze.

A thing like a flame crawled from the log, toward him. Nick threw a wall of will up and was glad the spell was invisible; he would not like to let that thing out of sight.

With the air cut off, the flames shifted. The creature, as orange as the flames, but distinct, crawled forward, hissing, and hit the wall. Nick flinched, but the wall held.

The creature's eyes turned crimson, and it flattened itself against the wall. Its eyes darkened further, to pure black, and burned in the midst of that mutable body. The creature pressed harder, with tiny yellow hands like candle flames. Nick held the wall and wondered how so small a thing could press so hard. Their eyes met. The creature glowed brighter, turning from orange to pure yellow. The logs burned faster, crumpling into ash. The creature, spitting out a crackling noise, glanced down and shoved against the wall. Nick braced himself, and the creature, with a final hiss, dissolved.

For a minute, Nick watched where it had vanished. It must have slept in the firewood. He let the wall collapse and was surprised at how tired he was. Not recovered yet, Nick thought. He banked down the fire, still pondering it. No wonder the university had come after the wizards. For any student, the forest was frustration: all marvels, inexplicable.

He gave the fire an unnecessarily severe jab; the poker rang against the stone. For a moment, he leaned against the stones of the fireplace, sick with longing. He had no choice. He could not have studied even at the university when he had yet to recover. To recover, he needed to sleep.

He crawled into bed, and fell into a dreamless sleep.

He did not wake as the snow turned to rain, and drummed on the roof before it washed away snow.

In the morning, Nick woke to a new smell in the air, and a steady dripping noise. Outside, blotches of brown spread through the snow. Nick pushed the door open, and warm air brushed against him. A robin—an ordinary robin—flitted into the field and looked at him with bright eyes.

Edgar drew a deep breath. He read the paper again. This would show Nick. Humiliating him with that wall—well, Nick would learn that humiliation was not merely something he dished out. *He* would find Nick, and Nick, who could not keep himself from getting lost, would *have* to thank him.

He carefully memorized the spell and went outside. Servants worked about the garden; a housemaid, with a basket slung over her arm, walked down the path, for the market. He muttered the spell and found each one: a pale glow burst from his fingers to brush the head. One gardener looked up with a grunt, but his gaze went over Edgar, and he bent back to work.

Knows his place, thought Edgar. Whistling under his breath, he went back inside. He could find now, but at a suitable party, the revelers could watch, and if Nick tried to deny it, they would jeer at him.

Silverware clattered about Janet.

She should have taken notes. White sickness or none, the notes would not have taken long, and then she would not be in ignorance.

"Before the white sickness," Janet said, "I heard reports of young wizards who misused spells of snow."

"I never heard that," said Master Francis. He spread butter on bread.

Janet wondered if only Master Simon had heard. She winced. She should have taken notes.

"I did," said Mistress Elise. "I can not fathom why anyone would pounce on them so long after—for so minor a matter."

"If you are willing to write to the king," said Janet, "to assure him that it was minor—"

"It was among the gentry," said Mistress Elise. "I do not follow their gossip."

Janet ate some soup. The masters knew no more, but some students came from the gentry. Indeed, she had one this term. She would fish among them.

Afternoon sunlight washed over the table. The teapot sprang up, scrambled across the table, and poured tea into a cup. Fliss smiled at the enchantment and took the cup. Across the room, Luke pointed out the teapot to Randall. Perhaps, being new to the city, he had never seen such a thing before.

The graves were still new, just sprouting grass, but they were back to normal. She sipped. Normal, if she avoided looking a mirror. Her short hair might shock the rest, as it still shocked her. Marie had glanced at her and put a hand to her own blond curls.

Still, she was well. She could learn what had happened in her illness. She looked about at the clumps of people—the flirting couples, the older generation gossiping about prospects and matches—and walked toward the harpsichord when she noticed something. She remembered Nick's impish smile, the night of the sleighing party.

From the card table, Edgar called, "What inspired that scowl, Fliss?"

Fliss said, "I wondered where Nick is." No one had mentioned his taking ill—or anything else that would have kept him away.

"Vanished," Edgar said. "He quarreled with his father, and Mortimer turned him out."

Vanished? Fliss stared at Edgar. He did not blink. She looked about. All the others nodded in agreement.

Catherine said, "The night of the sleighing party—we did not learn it until Christopher's party." She shook her head. "A bad time for the quarrel, with the white sickness about."

Fliss forced her breath in and out. If he had sickened in his father's house, the *servants* would have helped him, but outside—

If Lady Alicia kept this from me because I was ill, I will never forgive her, she thought. Before her shaking hand could spill it, she put down the tea. "Where did he go?"

"No one's seen him since," said Edgar.

"He can't have *vanished*!" Fliss said.

"He's not that good a wizard," said Marie, waggishly, and Fliss hated the woman.

"Nick is gone," Lucia said, as if trying to interpose herself, "and it's very like Mortimer to turn him out."

"Once out," said Fliss, "Nick would not be ruled by what Mortimer wanted."

"If we had realized at once. . . ." Stephan spread his hands. "But he had vanished weeks earlier, so we could hardly search. Between snow and the wind, any tracks had long vanished."

"Well," drawled Edgar, pushing back his chair, "I might be able to find something of him—without footprints, even."

"Really?" said Marie.

"A new spell—follow me!" Edgar rose.

Fliss remembered Edgar's last spell, but. . . if he could find Nick. . . . She trailed along with the rest.

Outside back door, in the muddy garden, green sprouts stood among dead leaves and patches of snow. Fliss stopped in the doorway, several strides from Edgar. The others clumped between the door and Edgar.

Marie pulled back her skirt to look at her shoes. "It's filthy out here. Why are you insisting on this?"

"Inside," said Edgar, "the walls are between us and Nick. It'll work better outside." He intoned the spell. Despite the mud, the others clustered around.

If the walls were a barrier, Fliss thought, what if Nick were inside? She frowned.

A pale glow formed between Edgar's fingers. Small exclamations arose from the crowd. It hovered without moving. Fliss thought she saw Edgar frown. Then, in a silent but blinding flash, the glow burst. Fliss turned her head away, but still blinked at the effect. The partygoers were vocal in their objections.

Edgar grimaced, rubbing his fingers together, and his face contorted. Trying to come up with an explanation, Fliss guessed scornfully.

"Enough," Marie said. With her head lifted high, she led the way back inside.

Fliss let out a long breath—as if she could do better than Edgar, when she had not studied the spell at all—and followed Marie and the rest in. It prickled her pride a little.

Giles appeared by her. "I dare say that *you* would not have done anything that foolish."

Snow still lay in splotches on the brown of earth and dead leaves. Umberto walked with care. Rain enough to make a forest this sodden came but seldom in Metharia—and even in those rains, the air was warmer.

But pale snowdrops blossomed, though he was but strides from the forest edge.

Though—he had students to consider, and he knew little of the woods. Prudence should measure the length of his walk.

He walked over a hillock, and then to the height of another. Before him, a vale spread, filled with violets. Some flowered purple and white. Others—red. Orange. Yellow. Some were as parti-colored as a harlequin.

He let his breath out. He had heard of yellow violets, but this—dyer's shop was a marvel of the Wizards' Wood. He glanced at one blossom, an unfortunate mix of purple and orange. He would fetch back flowers to the university, to remind himself that he had not dreamed, and to learn more from them.

She heard the whispers first, but it was the hissed "It's *Mistress Janet*," that drew her. The dank alley was narrow and dark, and the sunset already colorful, but she could make out the students: half a dozen women. One gave a guilty start, which drew the others' attention. One glanced upward, at the automaton flitting overhead. Janet's mouth twisted. She might not have seen it in the shadows, without that glance.

"I trust you will destroy it," she said.

One, very young, drew herself up to her full height. "*They* sent an automaton into *our* college. . . ."

"I have never known a youth to be reluctant to let a maid spy on him," said Janet, dryly.

The women giggled, and the young one looked annoyed.

"Summon it," said Janet.

The women looked startled. One gestured. The automaton flittered about. She scowled. Then she gave Janet a nervous glance.

"You let loose an automaton that you have no mastery of," said Janet. "If the white sickness were still here, you could atone swiftly and master a new spell in the process—but I will not let this go unpunished."

His mother's hands fluttered about the tea set. "Some of your friends came by. They said they would play cards—"

Edgar said, "I know, Mother."

"Oh," she said.

"I have to prepare—the term is coming up." He remembered the parchment, still lying on his desk. Count on Nick Briarwood to make him look a fool without even being there. He wondered what spell Nick had cast to make it fail.

"Fool me once—" he whispered, but Nick had fooled him *thrice*. First with the flying student; he'd bet Nick thought he had gotten away with that one. Then with the wall of snow, and now with location spells.

His mother put the tea cup before him. Edgar leaned forward and brooded, without drinking.

Bernard's hand hesitated over a chess piece. Umberto watched.

Elise walked in, her robes swirling about her, and collapsed in a chair. "The students are arriving in force," she said. "You can hardly pass from one building to the next."

"And the new students," said Bernard, in his quavering voice. "For all the deaths, I do not think that either places or scholarships will go lacking." He moved a piece. "You were wise to arrive when you did, Master Umberto."

Elise cocked an eyebrow. "You knew they would arrive a week early, Master Umberto?"

He had reached the university over a month ago, himself, Umberto thought in amusement. "Mistress Janet mentioned it."

Bernard snorted. "Mistress Janet."

"Master Umberto," said Elise, "you may want to consider prudently any friendship with Mistress Janet."

Umberto's eyebrows went up. "Her skill in wizardry is great, if she uncovered the crimes of master wizards while still a student."

Bernard and Elise said nothing. Neither master looked at him.

Umberto kept his tone mild. "Are the tales false? Did she not catch the master wizards in their crimes?"

Bernard looked at his gnarled hands.

"Janet Whitehall is a woman of noble blood," said Elise. "When she was examined for her mastery, she threatened to gain authority from the king to examine us all for diabolerie if we found her incompetent." Color rose in her cheeks.

Umberto considered Mistress Janet. She was bold enough to do such a thing. Was she petty enough? "What was her weakness, that she should not be a master?"

They both looked away.

Alas, Umberto thought, lightly, I may have alienated them both. He gestured at the chessboard. "It is still your move, Master Bernard."

Elise's mouth tightened. Bernard leaned forward, but the silence was broken by shouts arose outside. Umberto rose.

The students had scattered before he reached the window. A small gray creature scrambled toward the building opposite. Umberto scowled. "Something enchanted is running loose." The creature vanished through a doorway.

"Another flying automaton?" said Elise.

"Walking," said Umberto. "Skittering, actually."

Elise looked startled and came over herself. "If *flying* fascinates them so, I don't see why—"

A woman in green master's robes, her brown hair flying, ran to the door. Her hands moved to cast spells that Umberto could not recognize at once.

"*What* is Mistress Martha doing?" said Elise. "I can't see it. . . ."

"It reached the basement of All Angels'." He had helped Master Timothy find something there, just the other day. Remembering the clutter, Umberto shook his head. "A fit place for an unwanted enchanted thing, if it is harmless, but not one still running about."

"An out-of-control spell," said Elise. Her smile was sly. "Your Mistress Janet will have more to do."

A rap sounded on the door to the street, down below, but loud enough for her to hear. Fliss stopped in the midst of straightening her shift. After a minute, the door opened. The maid, and then Lady Alicia herself, spoke with the visitor. She pulled on her gown quickly and left the room, to look down the stairs. A soberly clad man was already leaving; the door shut behind him.

Lady Alicia stood in the corridor. "Come to breakfast, Fliss."

She could already smell the sausages; she hurried down, but Lady Alicia did not move, and Fliss stopped, looking at her.

"That man came about Nicholas Briarwood."

Fliss looked accusingly at Lady Alicia. After all her worries. . . she had slept horribly these last nights. . . .

"No, I had not heard." Her mouth set in severe lines. "But when you came with the news, I sought news of all those found dead. None of them were clad as gentlemen."

Fliss nodded. She might find hope in that news, if it did not leave her more bewildered.

"Or naked."

Her stomach lurched. To imagine Nick dying in the cold, and his body being robbed, perhaps even while he lived —she drew a deep breath, trying to steady herself, though the image of his impish grin flitted before her face.

Lady Alicia's face grew grimmer. "Which means that Nicholas Briarwood has vanished without a trace."

"She shouldn't have trapped it," said Bernard.

Umberto sat back. The master wizards filling the room looked grave. For the last week, the stone guardian had been trapped in the basement of All Angels'.

"When I got my degree," Bernard said, his voice quivering as much from indignation as age, "we would have destroyed it, not trapped it. It would never have come this far."

Ah, the glories of ancient days, Umberto thought. "How could we tell what spells would destroy it without proper study?"

Master Bernard scowled.

At the end of the table, Mistress Janet dropped one hand on the papers before her. "The spells are containing Mistress Martha's stone guardian. For now. Master Lawrence and Mistress Elise have inspected Mistress Martha's papers and found that it appears to be only a ramification of the spell she was not aware of." She looked sour. "Therefore, there remains only the service she must perform for the university for letting it run wild, and the destruction of the creature itself."

She garnered several glares.

"Several irresponsible students are being sent to maintain the roads. Mistress Martha will take charge of them."

The spells to restore the magically laid stone were grueling, but to Umberto, being in charge seemed light. About him, the master wizards looked discontented.

"Her guarding spells will last months. It will give plentiful time to study her work."

"Master Umberto," said Bernard. "He feels it important."

For all the spite in his tone, such duties were part of being a master here. Umberto inclined his head.

A few minutes later, the meeting dissolving, Janet caught him by the door.

"You do realize they expect you to hand this to a student," she said in a low voice. "To learn how to dissolve spells."

Umberto considered that. "Do all the master wizards palm off their work on their charges?"

Her mouth twisted. "It *would* be a good way to learn to dissolve spells. I myself have given such things to my students. And for all the contrasts drawn between students' works and the masters', automata do not vary much." She glanced aside, through a window, at All Angels'. "I should rebuke the students. They have set a poor example and led astray an innocent master of the university."

"On the other hand, if none of my students need to learn it, or are suited to?"

Her smile was bitter. "At that point we learn whether you resemble the other masters."

A good thing that Master Umberto had taken on Mistress Martha's creature, thought Janet. She had not had to fight off the duty herself. She made a note on one paper. Before the term open, and already the students dug up the books to summon the succubae. She scowled. The demons always made sure that they were close to anyone who might be tempted— she had lain hand on such texts once or twice herself—but it seemed that this year's new students were fools beyond common.

"At least they haven't set one loose in the city."

"What are you talking about, Mistress Janet?"

Janet wished she had gone to her rooms before working. "Some fools enrolled in the university."

Master Otto's eyebrows went up. "When temptation is so ready? At every hand, to students who have just left their fathers' houses and guidance? You judge them so harshly."

"For diabolerie?" said Janet.

"You might as well expect every student to be sober, with all the alehouses about."

"And Mistress Anna did nothing drastic? Nor Master Oliver?"

Otto drew himself to his full height. "Come, Mistress Janet. Solid, reputable wizards—they did wrong, I concede you that, but even you attend the Good Friday service."

They both of them nearly killed someone, thought Janet.

"Holy Week begins tomorrow," said Master Otto. "Blessed are the merciful. Mercy shall be theirs. I commend these poor students to your mercy."

"On Good Friday, at the Cathedral," she said. "They have a ceremony called Creeping to the Cross. I suggest you attend it, and consider the cost of the mercy you consider so cheap."

Nick leaned against the door's frame. One squirrel chased another through the sodden dead leaves—proper squirrels, not the creatures that had harried him out of their oak grove, nor even the colorful one he had seen earlier. The first squirrel leapt up an oak, and the other ran after, vanishing into the veil of new leaves. Only the sound of their scolding emerged.

Nick tucked in his shirt. He had cleaned it, and it was not worn to rags, but he would melt in this clothing. He would need to replace it in the city.

There, everyone would have questions, and he had no answers. "Lord willing," he muttered, "nothing will happen."

A child's voice echoed from the trees. "Over here!" A girl, wearing a green peasant's dress, stopped on the road to look over her shoulder. "The hermitage! I told you. . . ." She spotted Nick. Her mouth turned into an O. A boy and another girl came up beside her.

"I thought the hermit was dead," said the boy, wide-eyed.

"He is," said Nick.

"Are you the new hermit?" said the first girl.

The second girl scowled. "He doesn't look like a hermit."

The peasants would expect things of a hermit: a man at least holy, if not wise. "I'm not. Nothing but a poor traveler, taking refuge."

"Oh," said the first girl.

Perhaps she doubted *poor*, she was looking at his clothing, but that was no matter. The peasants would expect a hermit to pray for them and offer them guidance. The bolder among them would expect an occasional miracle.

He wished the hermit had lived longer. He was desperate enough to be among the bold.

Chapter 7—Inquiries

At the edge of the woods, Nick stood in the shade.

In the village graveyard, bright green blades had pushed through last year's dead yellow, but on several new graves, only scatterings of grass grew. Nick looked past, to where the road ran through meadows. Peasants walked toward the city. Many drove geese or cows or sheep; others carried bundles or baskets. Market day, he guessed. Behind him, birds sang, content in their nests and the Wizards' Woods.

He let his breath out. O God Our Father, who led Israel through the Red Sea, and guided the Wise Men by a star, bless my journey, that I may reach my destination, and in due course, the gate of eternal salvation.

He walked on. The weather had left only a puddle here and there from the snow. Sheep bleated in the flower-filled meadows, and lambs frolicked. In the procession of peasants, geese, sheep, and cows, some glanced at his clothing—clothing of the prosperous, but shabby and out of season—but looked away again. Perhaps they thought it secondhand. Servants sold cast-off clothing, he had bought such clothing once or twice, for a prank, but it surprised him, how much it smarted.

He fixed his attention on the road. Many peasants carried eggs, some had donkey-pulled carts filled with them, and he had to stop for a herd of lambs that filled the road.

Easter was late this year, wasn't it? Nick pondered as the lambs bleated. No more than half way through April—and the moon had been full last night. He edged about lambs, as the days settled into place. Market day, the week before Easter—Tuesday of Holy Week. The term had started two weeks ago, with the Annunciation. The sleighing party had been on Candlemas. He must have spent two months in the woods. No—over a week more than that.

In the sunlight, his heavy clothing made him sweat. Every new path that joined the road swelled the crowd, and he drew curious glances. But birds cheeped and swirled in great flocks overhead. Flowers bloomed across the meadows and filled the ditches with color. Little children, their faces rosy and grubby, ran across the road, squealing with delight, and Nick smiled. Spring had come, and it was good to be on his way.

Near noon, the road flowed over the river that marked the city bounds, now that the city had outgrown its walls. Sunlight glanced from the waters, and peasants crossed the bridge.

Nick slowed. Leaving the hermitage had been easy, but— on the rivers' bank, the ivy-grown buildings of the university stood. They were built of stone, and the ivy concealed the strange colors that stray spells had touched it with. Trees were so laden with bloom, rosy or white, that he could not see the leaves between the petals. Robed students stood, or walked, or hurried, about them.

This would have been easier if he had left earlier. He was late for the term.

From the rushes on the river's edge, a red-winged blackbird took flight, startling him from his thoughts. He crossed the bridge. Not the university first, but Benedict. Nick's tongue touched his lip as he picked out the right street. Mortimer had been angry enough to cut off his allowance, but whenever he did not need the money, he had left it on deposit. Less than he could use now, but Benedict would give him it.

He hoped. He prayed. And if he was not the spendthrift of his circle, he had never stinted himself.

The stone about the university gave way to the practical brick—here and there an odd color. He knew that one purple one stemmed from a miscast protective spell; it had not changed for his time in the woods. Indeed, everything on the street looked the same, down to the vendors' crying their wares. Then, what had he expected, in three months?

The churches were subdued for Lent, but the children were bright-eyed with excitement. People glanced over him, but not to mark him.

Randall came out of a building. His gaze met Nick's. The other man froze, except for his eyes, which moved up and down, taking Nick in.

Nick wondered if he really looked that odd. He had not thought that shaggy hair and shabby winter clothing would disguise him.

Randall looked away, as if embarrassed, or thinking he had mistaken Nick for someone else. Nick let his breath out in a rush. He had never been close to Randall, or fond of him. He had known that poverty was fatal to their society. Yet Randall hurried away, and he had trouble breathing for the pain.

But people walked by. One hurrying maidservant brushed by with her basket and gave him a foul look. He walked on, until he picked Benedict's sign, with its quill pen and lion. He needed money for more than what it made others think of him.

The clerk looked idly up. His gaze flickered over the clothes. Disdain settled on his face, and he looked at Nick's. For one frozen moment, his face held nothing. Then he flinched. Before Nick could speak, the clerk babbled about Master Benedict and sidled off.

Nick hooked his hands on his belt. At least the clerk had known him. Randall, he did not actually need.

Master Benedict filled the doorway with his drab brownness. The clerk hovered behind him. He contemplated Nick. His brown hair had acquired more silver since Nick had seen him last.

"I came to see you, Master Benedict, about my allowance."

The man blinked. "Your allowance." He collected himself. "It has grown for some time."

Nick blinked himself. "My father hasn't canceled it?"

Master Benedict hesitated. Then he lowered his voice. "Master Mortimer has never spoken to me of it. Mistress Phillipa, may the Lord grant her peace, ordered that it be paid in the first place. And—I have not drawn it to your father's attention."

So, thought Nick, when my father notices me, he might well remember. Seize the money now. He wondered whether it would cover lodgings.

Master Benedict said, "It is good to see that you are well, that the sickness did not touch you."

Sickness? Feeling cold, he remembered the wizard and his students, talking about the winterheart—and the graves, and the gossip at the party. "I—haven't been in the city."

In the hallway, Mistress Janet arched one eyebrow. "I was surprised to see you here, Felicity. I was under the impression that you would wait until St. John's Day." Her eyes flickered over Fliss's short hair.

Fliss felt strange in a student's black robes, but unwilling to surrender them. "Once you recover, the white sickness leaves quickly."

Outside an open window, mating birds twittered and chirped. And I wanted to study, she thought fiercely. If Edgar's spell failed, others might not.

"Few of your—fellows have come. Marie...."

Fliss flushed. Break off with them, she told herself, and be *glad* you are not of their birth. "Many have little interest in magic. Only one ever cast a spell that surprised me."

Mistress Janet smiled and gestured at the walls. "Most spells they could cast are taught here at the university."

Perhaps she could—"Nicholas Briarwood knows a spell to create an invisible wall."

Mistress Janet frowned. One eyebrow went up.

"He called it a wall. I could not see it, but it was enough to stop a moving wall of snow."

Both Mistress Janet's eyebrows went up. "I fear I can not teach you it. Mortimer Briarwood's studies are notoriously broad. Indeed, I would be interested to hear more of it."

Ships sailed in and out of the harbor, their sails filled with enchanted winds—a craftsman's wizardry that any master wizard would scorn, but beyond his powers. Nick squared his shoulders and walked up the hill, toward the university, in search of a scholarship.

He had bought clothing second-hand with his old clothing and some coins—probably at unreasonable prices —and it felt strange. He had bought clothes there before, but that time, for a prank.

About him, armed young men swaggered down the street. People pulled out of their way. Looking for a fight, he thought. He shook his head and walked more quickly.

Strange voices echoed sonorously down the street. Frowning, he came around a corner. A procession filled the street, blocking the way: gray-clad penitents, their heads covered with hoods, their hands holding candles. The candle flames, faint in the sunlight, flickered with every step. The chant was long and lamenting. Nick glanced nervously away. It was Lent—but it was a market day, and the poor had to sell produce and buy food, even during Lent.

Finally, the procession passed. He crossed the street they had blocked.

Swifter than seemed possible, the university buildings appeared ahead. Nick found his pace slowing. A flowerbed of violets marked the beginning of the grounds. Some were white and some violet, but most of them were garnet red, from the Wizards' Wood. The university had wizards enough to transplant such flowers.

Even his slow pace bore him among the buildings. A student caught his eye: a graceful young woman in black robes, her black hair cropped exceedingly short. She stood on a flight of stairs, deep in conversation with a master wizard, red-haired, wearing a yellow robe. Nick frowned, wrestling with a teasing but uncatchable memory.

The master, a woman not much older than the student, looked at him and spoke to the student, who turned.

"Nick Briarwood!" Fliss called.

Nick stood as if frozen. No wonder that he had not recognized her, not with her banner of black hair gone.

Fliss frowned, anxiously. "Nick!"

You have to face someone who knows you sometime, Nick told himself. He walked over, the students eddying about him. The master looked inquisitive and faintly amused. Fliss looked shocked, but so clearly herself that he wondered how he had mistaken her. Still— "What happened, Fliss?"

Fliss blinked. After a moment, her hand went to her hair. "The white sickness." Then, in a rush, she said, "What happened to you?"

The master wizard glanced at him, her yellow robes almost reminded him of something, but he had to answer Fliss. "After I got home, I quarreled with my father. He turned me out."

Fliss's mouth pursed. Moments inched by. Nick felt an insane urge to blurt out anything, but he had nothing to say that would be better than silence—not before a master wizard, not when Mortimer's sly accusations still burned in his memory, not when he had fled the city like any criminal. Even Fliss—he had fled the city rather than seek her aid. How could *he* ask her to trust *him*?

Four students came out of the door behind her, and Fliss pulled to one side. "And since?"

Nick hooked his hands on his belt. "Oh, I've been around."

Fliss looked him up and down. The master looked over both of them in innocuous silence.

Fliss said, "Have you decided to come to the university?"

"Yes," Nick said. "I hoped a scholarship had fallen open." He faltered, remembering the graves and Master Benedict's surprise at his appearance. He had meant that usually some scholars did not, after all, attend, freeing their scholarships.

"I presume this is the Nicholas Briarwood with the spell you spoke so highly of, Felicity?"

Fliss bobbed her head and looked embarrassed. Nick's mouth twitched; she had never spoken highly of his spells to his face.

The master's face took on a gravity that did not match her age. "I am Janet Whitehall, Mistress of this college. Two scholarships *are* still open. And, the colleges may have a place." She nodded to Fliss and led Nick briskly off between buildings, without glancing back at him.

Nick followed.

She picked out a gate that Nick was quite certain that he should not open himself, even if he became a student. Behind it, a garden was filled with roses in full bloom. Some were even past their prime and shedding petals of scarlet and pink. Mistress Janet brushed by as if not noticing either the petals that cascaded from her passing, or that was still early spring, with a nip in the air.

Then, this was the university of magic.

A great rose bush before him was laden with royal purple flowers, from buds until past bloom. Nick closed his mouth and wondered whether the old gardener had seen such plants, when he grumbled about magic in the garden.

Trying to not stare about, he followed Mistress Janet in a back door.

Sunlight shone over the vast oaken desk. Master Otto looked up from the papers there. "Mistress Janet." His voice was not welcoming.

Nick wished he had arrived at the semester's beginning.

Mistress Janet said, cheerfully, "I brought an applicant for a scholarship. Nicholas Briarwood."

Master Otto's hand, half way through picking up a paper, stopped in mid-air. "Nicholas Briarwood?" he said, like a sailor's parrot.

"Yes, Master Otto," Nick said.

"Mortimer Briarwood's son?"

"Yes, Master Otto," said Nick. He suppressed the urge to lick his lips.

"A scholarship." Master Otto's mouth pursed. "I'm surprised your father. . . ."

"My father and I quarreled." He met Master Otto's gaze. The story became easier the more often he repeated it. Practicing deceit, he thought irritably.

Master Otto sat back. Moments passed, and Nick felt chilled. Deceit might not suffice.

"I should set a master wizard to examine him, I suppose," said Master Otto. "His tutor, *if* he succeeds." He looked at Mistress Janet. "I suppose you will say that you have enough students."

"Yes." Mistress Janet's tone was calm, but her mouth tightened.

"You found time to investigate those students last term."

"When a wizard fulfills other duties for the university," said Mistress Janet, "he need take no more than three students." Her smile reached no further than her mouth. "I would never suggest that *you* take him on."

Nick felt a cold weight in his stomach as he placed her, and those yellow robes: while still a student, she had found that one master wizard had committed arson in the Wizards' Wood, and that another—Master Oliver—had practiced diabolerie.

The demoniac thing weighed in his chest. Master Oliver had gotten his heart taken out of his body, to render himself immortal. Mistress Janet had destroyed the heart and killed the master. The demonic spell that protected his from her would not endear him to her.

Master Otto's face was sullen. "We must find someone, then. St. Catherine's has room, but first he must be examined. By some master capable of judging."

Footsteps sounded in the hallway. Mistress Janet looked over her shoulder. Her face lit up. Master Otto looked sour.

"Master Umberto," Mistress Janet said. "You said earlier that you could take another student."

A large man, whose master's robe was flame-red, filled the doorway. From his dark brown skin and broad face—a foreign master.

"I did," Master Umberto said, his voice a deep rumble. "Is this the student?"

"He still needs examination," Master Otto interposed, sharply.

Master Umberto glanced at him. His tone was light. "To have time to tutor a student, I must have time to examine one."

Fliss walked into Lady Alicia's library. She no longer needed to master Edgar's spell in order to find Nick. That was well. She had found the book Mistress Janet had recommended but could not study. She dropped on the couch. *Nick looked frightened to see me,* her thoughts wailed.

Her fingers twisted on the book. She had to do better than this. She needed to do well at the university—and she had not let the white sickness stop her.

She swallowed. A few months ago, she would have agreed that Nick was numbered among those friends she might do better without. A few hours ago, even, she might have agreed with it.

A door closed, below. Fliss laid the book aside.

As she came down the stairs, Lady Alicia handed her cape to a maid. Her white eyebrows went up. "Has something happened?"

Fliss nodded and studied the floorboards. She did not know where to begin. Lady Alicia kissed her cheek and walked to the drawing room. Her heart beating faster, Fliss followed and sat in an armchair. At lost for words, she stared at her hands.

"What happened?"

"I saw Nicholas Briarwood today. Alive. Well." More or less well. Even with his fright, and his evasiveness, she had seen how gaunt he was. "At the university."

"At the university? As a student?" Lady Alicia arched an eyebrow, but her tone was placid.

"Not yet—he's applying—but he looked worse than I do!"

Lady Alicia pursed her mouth. "We knew that something had happened to Nicholas. He could not have vanished into air."

Fliss made a dismissive gesture. "Nick said he quarreled with his father."—just as his father claimed.

"Who wouldn't?" said Lady Alicia, sotto voice.

"But that can't be why he looks like that! Pale as a ghost, and thin. He looks like he's *been* deathly ill—and his hair looks like he cut it himself, and he's wearing something that could have come from a used clothes dealer."

She dragged in a deep breath. And he had not preened like a peacock, when he heard of her praise. The thought of saying that aloud sickened her.

Crockery clattered in the hall. The maid came in with tea.

"Mortimer also said that Nick had quarreled with him," Lady Alicia said.

Fliss poured the tea. Unless Mortimer used some spell to cast Nick across the kingdom, the quarrel did not explain Nick's vanishing.

"Nick," she said, "was surprised to see my hair. He could not have heard that I was ill. He. . . I'm not sure that he even heard of the white sickness." She drew a deep breath. She must have not have been awake, not to notice. "Which would preclude his having had it."

Lady Alicia nodded.

Fliss added cream to the cup and handed Lady Alicia it.

Lady Alicia put it on a side table and laid her hand over Fliss's. Fliss did not move.

After a minute, Lady Alicia said, "There is no way for us to learn what Nicholas has done since he left his father's house, if Nicholas does not tell us."

Fliss remembered Nick's expression when she asked. Her mouth compressed.

Lady Alicia's dark eyes half-closed. "Does Mortimer know that Nicholas has returned?"

"I don't think so." Fliss poured herself some tea.

"All we can do, then, is wait and see."

Fliss felt her expression move.

Lady Alicia laughed under her breath. "I know. But I do not think you will have to wait forever."

Fliss looked down at the pale brown surface of her tea, at her tiny reflection.

"Invite him to dinner. The colleges do not set profuse boards." Lady Alicia smiled, wryly. "Tell him that it is but an ordinary meal, not a dinner party."

Fliss opened her mouth to say that she needed to cut off from that crowd, who would interfere with her studies. Then she shut it again. Would Nick be a hindrance?

She sipped the tea.

In the Bird's upper room, Edgar collected the cards. Randall appeared in the doorway.

Greetings came from around the table, from players who barely looked up.

"Next round?" said Edgar, shuffling.

Randall shook his head and took a mug of ale, only to stare into the cup. The cards moved around the table, until Edgar shuffled them again. He watched Randall with narrowed eyes. Randall had acted strangely ever since his cousin Luke had come.

Christopher had sat with his feet on the table, balancing the chair on two legs. He sat forward. The chair hit with a crack that jolted them all. Even Randall looked up.

"Randall, you're acting as if there was something wrong with the Bird's ale. If the news gets out, old Watkin'll turn us out on our ears."

"I had to be dreaming," said Randall.

"Dreaming?" said Christopher. "If you were asleep, you would have fallen and put your nose in your ale. Wasting good ale at that."

Randall's voice was low, as if he did not intend them to hear him. "I saw Nick Briarwood today."

"Nick?" Christopher's voice was sharp.

Edgar sat back. From the expressions around him, everyone was shocked. He clenched and unclenched his hands. Nick Briarwood. After Nick's mischief, after he had quarreled with even his indifferent father, Edgar wondered that he had nerve to show his face.

None of them noticed, their attention was so bent on Randall.

"I must have imagined it—"

"How could you?" said John.

Randall glanced at him. "He wore the clothing he wore the day of the party—I must have just—"

Christopher said, "Whatever happened to him?"

"I didn't speak to him," said Randall. "I must have imagined it—or—he was pale and gaunt and ghostly, maybe he was a ghost—but he was in the middle of the street at noon. I must have dreamed it."

Edgar snorted. "Nick Briarwood all over." He threw the cards into the air, and they fell to the table, shuffling themselves. "Day before the sleighing party, a student went flying through the air. Nick tried to convince me that I was seeing things."

No wonder he had no shame about ruining his snow spell. Nick had no shame about anything at all.

The smoke from the candle took shape: a long body, with a long tail, a head, four limbs. Nick glanced at Master Umberto and could not read his expression. He gave the dragon eyes, a mouth, and scales running down its back. Nick narrowed his eyes, reminded himself how much he needed this scholarship, and made finely grained scales.

Master Umberto made a note. Nick broke the spell. Smoke dissipated. Nick sat back in his chair and felt bruised. He had been proud of that spell.

"A light spell?" said Master Umberto.

Nick shook his head.

Master Umberto made another note. It was a basic spell, Nick knew, he had always known, but he never—

"Did your father tutor you in wizardry?"

Nick shook his head again. "A governess taught me to read." And his mother had hired the woman. "Then I raided his library." He could have applied himself more. Or—he could have asked his *mother* for a tutor.

Master Umberto laid down his pen. His voice was tranquil. "You show promise, and good eye for detail, and some remarkable gaps in your knowledge. Now, the theory of magic. . . ." He turned to a new page. "Why, if we do not deal with spirits who comprehend language, do we use language? Invocations? Commands?" He picked up his pen again.

Nick drew a deep breath and prayed that curiosity had led him to the right books. "Principle of similarity. We command because the response is similar to commanding the animate. It is not the same, because the energy must be derived from outside it, while an animate being could generate its own motion."

When Umberto did not speak, Nick added, "That is why a wizard grows weary—or, among the great, the air about him grows cold, or silent, or things rot."

His voice turned dry. "My father *did* tell me that tale of the wizard who cast a great spell and died in the collapse of the building."

Master Umberto made another note.

Sunlight slanted across the room. Dust motes floated through the beams, gilt like gold dust. Nick watched them in an attempt to not look at Master Umberto, who had said that he had no more questions, but studied his papers.

The bells rang. Nick started—and then, as they picked out the hour, he realized that it had not been that long.

Umberto rose and went to the door, where he called for a servant. They spoke in voices too low for Nick to hear.

He kept his attention on the sunbeams. He would not act like a small boy before Mortimer for some prank. Master Umberto was not determining whether to punish him.

Umberto returned. "Since you are a suitable student, and they intend me to oversee your studies, we must meet. I fear it will not be for several days. Only then will we have time enough to discuss lectures."

Nick nodded. He had known he would have to scramble to catch up. Umberto opened his mouth again, but a faint noise from the hallway made him turned away. "There." He gathered the black cloth the servant offered and held it before Nick. "Do you know why the students' robes are black?"

Nick could not look up from the cloth. "The color of truth. Because it takes in whatever is before it. Masters wear brighter color because they both learn and teach, but students must learn—"

Umberto held the scholar's robe out.

Nick took it: plain, black, long-familiar from passersby on the street. An hour ago, he would have said it was all he desired. An hour ago it meant only security to him. Now—the cloth weighed on his hands, ready to transform him, to require studiousness and obedience.

He pulled it over his clothing. His breath came light and rapid. Even knowing that his heart should beat faster could not calm him. He was a student at the university.

Light filtered down the hallway. A wizard looked up as Umberto approached the dining hall. "I heard a pretty story today—have you? About one Nicholas Briarwood."

"I have," said Umberto, "heard a great deal about Nicholas Briarwood today."

Another wizard laughed. "Didn't you hear? It was Master Umberto who examined him, and has him to tutor."

"You'll be pleased." The first wizard smiled warmly. "If the boy is like his father, you have a student of promise. Mortimer Briarwood was a wizard of skill."

"Was?" said a third—this one Umberto could name: Master Francis. "He still is, Master Vincent."

"How could you tell?" said Mistress Meghan. "He's a recluse. I'm surprised he emerged from his study long enough to quarrel with his son." She hesitated, glanced at Umberto. "If that tale is true."

"Over here, sir." The servant swept his hand toward an ivy-covered brick building. The sunset, deep red in the west, cast a sideways glow over it. Lamps flickered in the masses of windows. A statue stood to one side, and Nick glanced over: a woman with a wheel, of course, but he might not have recognized it had he not known that the college was St. Catherine's.

The servant ushered Nick up the stairs. Inside the door, a whitewashed corridor led into the building; beside it, a dark wooden stair led up. Firelight flickered in a side room; it shed orange light into the hall and cast shadows.

A voice floated out of the room, with rough peasant vowels. "New student?"

"Yes," said the servant. "I must see the house master." He vanished down the hallway.

"They're bent on filling up the college."

Nick could not pick out the speaker, who was not even silhouetted against the fire.

"It wasn't that empty," said another—the man who asked about a new student, Nick thought. "Didn't lose that many. And fewer got scared."

That room was a kitchen, he realized.

The speaker rose, a dark shape against the fire. Other students watched. He looked speculatively over Nick. "Jack Easton." The firelight fell on him. Tall, easily Nick's height, and more solidly built. His hair looked auburn, but the firelight made that hard to judge.

"Nicholas Briarwood."

Narrowed eyes looked up from the fire. Then, his accent was as clear as theirs.

"Where is this Nicholas Briarwood?" A pudgy man of middle years walked down the hallway, holding a candlestick; the candle's flame jerked about with his motion.

"Over here, Master Humphrey," Jack called, not looking from Nick.

The housemaster scowled. "Well, you're the last. We have only one room left, and it only sleeps one."

Nick swallowed. He had not thought that he might find himself sharing a room with a stranger, who might wonder about his scars. The housemaster climbed the stairs, and Nick scrambled to follow.

"Do you know, scholar, what manner of place you are at?"

Nick nodded, realized the housemaster had not glanced back, and said, "Yes, sir."

The man snorted. "The oldest college of the university. Benefactors established it centuries ago, to aid poor students. And not one scholar in ten knows that well enough to act with seemly gratitude—"

He reached the top of the flight and started down the corridor. Curious glances came from the rooms, but Nick had no time to even glance back. He followed with no more impression than of black robes and small, sparse, rooms, and they reached the next flight.

The housemaster talked on. "Dinner is at nine. Chapel at three, and breakfast after it if you were at chapel." He glanced back at Nick. "Feed yourself, if you like, but if you do not show up for dinner, there is only bread and honey. A *benefactor*"—his voice did not approve—"left the college a magical cabinet that will provide that."

Nick nodded again.

"And the morning chapel, you *must* attend."

Earlier than he was used to, but at that, he would need to rise early for lectures.

"Candles are six for a gild. Another *benefactor*."

Cheap, Nick thought, and then considered the coins. He had only the clothing on his back, and four years of study ahead. He might have to rise early for the sunlight, as well.

Master Humphrey turned. The candle shone sideways on his face, casting enormous shadows. Nick faltered.

"Remember, Nick Briarwood, that I am a master wizard. In other colleges, at other universities, servants can deal with scholars. Here, no less than a master wizard can subdue your mischief—and so I am here, to subdue it."

Umberto sat back. A spell cast a circle of light on his desk and the stacks of paper on it: one for each student, and his notes about the Wizards' Wood. His single visit had whetted his curiosity, but—Nicholas Briarwood first. Once Nicholas started his studies, he would have time for his own.

A minute longer, he contemplated the notes. The library held far more volumes than he had read already. He had seen no more of the wood than an hour's walk had shown. The violets he had fetched were grown by wizards, in the public view.

"I might as well have stayed at home, and studied there."

His voice echoed in the whitewashed room and left him in silence.

He snorted. First his students—but especially Nicholas and his ill-ordered studies. Whatever were his parents about, teaching such a student to read and nothing more?

In their black robes, the students gathered about the foot of the stairs. Nick came down. None of them carried weapons. Then, they were too poor, or they would not be here. His mouth twitched. Even if he had snatched the sword in Mortimer's chapel, he would have pawned it by now.

I hope, Nick thought, that this means they are not as touchy as the gentry are.

"Ah, Nicholas Briarwood," Jack drawled. The other students followed his gaze.

Nick walked slowly down. He had to live with these men, but if he were friendly, they might discover his secret. He reached the bottom stair.

"They wake you last night?" said a student.

"I slept like a log."

"You must have been dead to the world!" said a second one. "Bunch of drunken bastards came down the street, singing at the top of their lungs."

"Caterwauling," corrected the first one.

"Students," said a third one, morosely. "They aren't doing much studying."

Probably gentry. They could tarry at the university for as long as their studies took. Nick was glad that Edgar had never persuaded him to stay up all night in the tavern. "Do they do it often?"

"Often enough," said the third student.

Jack snapped his fingers. "I forgot—Giles isn't getting enough copies from his press, Matthew, and I heard you were looking for work."

Matthew looked distracted from the frequency of the singing, and Nick felt aware of his allowance. His old friends would scorn him as poor. He doubted that the other scholars would.

Other students clambered down the stairs, and Humphrey came to open the chapel doors. Even with the housemaster's sidelong glance, Nick felt relieved; he filed in with the rest, into the hardwood benches, and on the kneelers.

In the front, a priest opened a book. "Almighty God. . ."

Nick bowed his head over his folded hands. All about him, other students did the same, though some of them looked bored and some lost in thought.

And you, he told himself, are more interested in the students than the prayers. He looked back at the priest.

"Grant us keen understandings and retentive memories. . ."

A minute later, something glinted red to one side. Nick glanced to see a tiny imp, crawling over a student's fingers. His mouth went dry. The creature was the color of the demon that had torn his heart out, but—his fingers tightened—he could *not have*, not within the very chapel.

Someone else spat a dissolution spell, and the imp—the illusion—dissolved.

The priest looked at the smirking student. "Grant that we may act with prudence and not folly in all uses of our knowledge."

Marie pulled Edgar over to the garden's corner. By lamplight, the bushes cast monstrous shadows over them. "Is it true? What they say about Nick Briarwood?"

Nick, thought Edgar. If vanishing was so fascinating, he should try it himself. "What did you hear?"

"That he showed up at the university!" Her hand tightened on his arm. "Looking like death."

"I've seen him," Edgar said. "He looks under the weather." He shrugged. "Keeps to himself. Acts like nothing happened." I would bet you that he brought it on himself, he thought, the way he collapsed that snow wall on himself, and now he doesn't want to admit to his folly, but the consternation on Marie's face kept him silent. Even from silly Marie, defense of Nick's folly would smart.

"Randall was a damned fool. Said he'd seen Nick's ghost." Edgar smirked. Nick's clothes had not been what he wore the day of the party.

"He must be poor, if he's on bad terms with his father." Marie frowned in thought. "Knowing Nick, he will be intent on his studies and boring, don't you think?"

Edgar spread his hands, brushing against the hedge. Nick *could* be a pain that way.

"Nick could not entertain in the old manner. We would not want to embarrass him when he can not reciprocate, wouldn't you say?" Her gaze went past him, and Edgar realized that someone had come up behind.

"Embarrassing, too," said Marie's older sister Cecily, now respectably married, "with the young ladies." She gave Edgar a stern glance. "No hostess would want a young man with such poor prospects about her daughters, would she?"

Marie nodded.

Settled matters to her own satisfaction, Edgar thought. "I hope he did not get into real trouble." Marie's eyes grew wider. "Mortimer Briarwood was not. . . an attentive father. He seldom objected to Nick's deeds. What could Nick have done that would inspire Mortimer to turn him out of door?"

Marie shrugged. "Knowing Mortimer, anything annoying."

Edgar grimaced. So ready to believe Nick as pure as snow.

George said something, across the garden, inspiring laughter from those about. Marie flitted off, but after that trick with the blue fire, George would believe Nick had done something.

In the dark confessional, Nick shifted his weight. The kneeler was hard under his knees. "And—I am concealing a crime that someone else committed."

"My son, concealing another's wrongdoing is a virtue, not a vice. 'If he who is flesh cherishes wrath, who shall forgive his sins?'"

"It was a serious crime, and I fear he. . . ." Nick trailed off. He had no idea what his father might do.

"Have you good evidence against him?"

"No," said Nick. "Indeed, he—has evidence that makes me look the culprit."

The priest's indrawn breath was sharp. "Were you?"

"No," said Nick, flatly. In the silence that followed, he said nothing. He felt truculent, but had no desire to babble.

"My child, it is not well to brood on other people's sins." The priest prescribed his penance. Nick barely managed to heed him. The thought emerged again: what might his father do, now?

He knelt in the sanctuary to say the penitential prayers, but as he rose, it came back to another question: what should he do now?

The bells chimed. He left the church without answers. He looked up at the walls and windows of All Angels'. If he threw himself on Mistress Janet's mercy *now*. . . .

He heard a snort of laughter beside him. "Be careful what you do about here, or Mistress Janet Whitehall will think you're up to no good."

Nick glanced sideways at him. From St. Catherine's. David, he thought.

"If you can't control a spell, for a moment—she had a dozen of us sentenced to slave over the white sickness because *she said* we lost control of our spells." David nodded at a window. "Be careful where you practice."

Nick nodded slowly. The masters of the university might overcome the demon's spell—to execute him.

"Mistress Martha animated something," said David darkly. "Mistress Janet didn't make *her* track it down and destroy it."

Nick's mouth twisted. Hardly a friendly warning, but he did not think David meant him ill by it.

The sky was almost black.

It *was* cloudy, and now and again, rain splattered on the path, but, though Nick resentfully, it would have been brighter if it had been day. He glared at Humphrey ahead of them, and joined the other students in yawning.

The housemaster, as if oblivious, hurried them past flowerbeds where yellow of daffodils, and pink and orange of tulips, only underscored how dreary the rest of the scene was.

"The service is not for hours," muttered Jack. "What was the need to wake us?"

Humphrey chivvied them into the Cathedral of the Magi, and they resentfully took their places.

As the crowds of the devout, the excited, and the reprobates who had decided not to be utter infidels filled the cathedral, Nick was glad of it. More came. And yet more.

Some fashionable women, radiant in white and gold, peered over the crowd. Nick stiffened. Marie pointed at the students. Her voice carried: "Edgar saw him." Robina's giggle followed.

His face like stone, Nick turned his gaze on the altar and the lilies. His clothing felt stiff. Even peasants strove to wear new clothes for Easter, but he had not dared risk the expense.

If the black robe was drab, still it covered his attire.

His mouth set. And, he was poor. He should thank God on his knees for the coins he could still garner from Master Benedict, and his scholarship, and his place at the college.

The choir began the deep and measured music, from the entrance of the church. "The strife is o'er, the battle won."

Nick let his breath out. "Now let the Victor's song be sung: Alleluia!"

When the servants bore it in, the dish of lamb looked large to his eye, but as it came around, students eyeing it, Nick compared it to the table it served. He could not keep from glancing over when dishing himself some spring greens. He had not imagined that he might not eat meat on Easter.

He turned his attention to the greens.

"At least," said one student, "the bishop stopped those processions for Easter."

"Maybe," said another, "they'll forget their fright over the white sickness."

Nick grimaced, remembering how long that one had blocked the way, and doubted it.

"Hey, Hendrik," called an older student, "there's barely enough for all of us." The student with the lamb glared, but passed it on.

Nick looked away. The headmaster might insist that every scholar receive meat; he could not. The eggs, on the other hand, came in profusion and flamboyant colors, bearing every image imaginable. Nick picked up one with a peacock. It unfurled its glittering tail under his fingers.

Matthew took a flame-orange egg and started to crack it. Nick, remembering a few tales and that Matthew was not from the city, caught his sleeve. "Be careful," he said, his voice low.

Matthew gave him a strange look.

"The eggs are decorated by the upper students, and they can be mischievously done. . . ."

"Ho, Nicholas Briarwood," called a student, four seats down. "What story are you pouring into Matthew's ear?"

An upper student, Nick noted. "Why, I slandered every generous soul who decorated these eggs for us." He hoped no one wondered how he recognized the trick egg so quickly—but he slid the egg from Matthew's hand and held it over the table. "Crack the egg for him and show him what a slander it was."

The student looked at the egg as if it were a poisonous snake, Matthew reached for another, and laughter resounded.

Chapter 8—Beginnings

The sunlight passed through the vine leaves and shone green over Master Umberto's study. Behind his desk, Umberto considered. Nick forced himself not to sit forward. He had the scholarship; Umberto only considered how to direct his studies.

The thought did not calm him. If he proved a poor student, if he lost his scholarship, he did not know what would become of him. Already, weeks had passed in the term. He would have plentiful work ahead—even if he let the demon's work be.

His gaze flitted about the room. Violets, strangely colored, sat in pots before the window, but even they could not hold his attention long.

Master Umberto's dark brown hand moved the sheet of paper aside, the flame-red sleeve of his gown brushing the desk. It seemed to take a very long time. Nick forced his breath out.

"A spell works by means of speech and similarity, which the will uses to produce changes." He caught Nick's gaze. "Changes in existing matter?"

"Yes," Nick said, but his voice slowed. He had not made a fool of himself at the examination; he could manage this. "God alone can create," but he remembered traveling conjurors, with lights and handkerchiefs.

Umberto laid aside the sheet. "You seemed weak on that point when I examined you. God alone can create. When you have claims otherwise, the wizard is wicked."

"Diabolerie?" Nick could not keep a high-pitched note from his voice—but the conjurors were nothing like Mortimer.

Umberto did not release his gaze, but his voice was urbane. "Only in the sense that the devil is the father of lies."

Nick drew in a deep breath.

Master Umberto looked at his notes again. "Like many a self-taught student, your practice seems haphazard, and you are poor at compounding spells."

Nick felt the heat rising in his face. His fair skin would hide nothing. He had known that compounding spells was a skill he lacked, but being more difficult than any spell of simple intent, it had always seemed too much of a bother—and now he felt like a child.

"Also, you lack skill at breaking spells—perhaps your greatest weakness. Simple spells can achieve much, but a wizard needs to know how to break them." Master Umberto sat back. "A wizard loses control of a stone guardian, but it is trapped. How would you stop it?"

"The students at St. Catherine's talked about it," said Nick, warily.

"Having reviewed her work, I think it within your abilities; she did not attempt an elaborate thing. Still, it requires both compounding and dissolving spells." Umberto sat back. "Have you seen a stone guardian before?"

Nick remembered the creature guarding the tunnel. "I wouldn't know one if I did."

"Then you have much to learn." Master Umberto held out papers. "The spells Mistress Martha cast to trap it should last half a year. Week by week, you will tell me how your studies progress. I will direct you as you need."

Nick took the papers, remembering how dark the tunnel had been where Mortimer's creature had lurked. The papers crinkled. The cellars of All Angels' would be as dark. "First, I ought to master a light spell, to spot the creature."

"Lenore's work perhaps has the best one to learn. Study, also, how the spell works, without *creating* light."

Nick tucked the papers into his spell book.

"Then, there are lectures. A pity you did not arrive earlier."

Only a couple of weeks, Nick thought. "There have to be other students in St. Catherine's who take the same lectures. I might borrow notes—"

"It would be wise to do so in haste," said Umberto tranquilly. "I think Mistress Elise's sequence on transformations, and Mistress Janet's on the compounding of spells, would be most valuable for you."

Common among new students. "That would be tomorrow, in All Angels'," Nick said, "and on Friday, in the King's College."

"Even so. If you need assistance in mastering the earlier work, speak with me, and swiftly. Each lecture *builds*." He paused. "Is there any branch of magic in particular that you wish to study?"

Yes, thought Nick fiercely, but he could not tell Master Umberto that he wished to learn about diabolerie. He hoped his face was as unreadable as Master Umberto's. "Nothing I am certain of. There are things that fascinate me, but there have always been such things, and they often lose their luster after a little study."

"A prudent observation." Umberto laid his papers aside. "If you find that one branch or another does not lose its interest, tell me of it. No wizard can master every kind of magic; it is best to study those that please you. I will speak with you next week on your studies. God keep you until then, Nicholas."

Nick nodded and rose to his feet. His gaze went over to the violets. After a moment, he frowned and walked over.

Umberto, reaching for a book, stopped.

"You're over-watering them. Their roots will rot."

"You," said Umberto, "mentioned nothing of plant magic."

"I don't know it," said Nick. "Only plants. The gardener taught me." If he had suggested magic to him, he would have refused to let him even to *weed*—but he did not come here to tell tales of his childhood.

Umberto nodded. "I thank you for your advice."

Nick left for the walkways. The spring breeze tossed the maples' branches and the red veil of flowers they carried, and it tugged at his still ragged hair. He walked along the path. Birds flew away, squawking, at his passage and settled again as he walked past.

Lenore's work—he had no need to consider a plan before he took that from the library.

He came around a corner. The path went through the beds of tulips, scarlet and crimson. Here and there grew pink ones with red streaks. A handful of black-robed students walked on the paths, and one was Fliss. The short hair still startled, but she had no such shock in seeing him. She hurried toward him. Nick slowed.

She smiled. "I've seen you, but I haven't been able to speak with you."

Fliss was clever. With the way she heckled about mischief, she would be merciless about diabolerie, but putting her off would only rouse her suspicions.

"Lady Alicia wanted—wants to invite you to dinner." She frowned in thought. He felt guilty, to think with suspicion of such a friendly greeting. "In three days?"

Nick blinked. The dinners at St. Catherine's were wholesome but bland, and if Lady Alicia and Fliss were willing to have him—"Gladly."

"How are you finding the university?"

"I like it," Nick said. "Different from my father's library."

"And from Lady Alicia's lessons." Her voice lowered. "I tried to find that spell that you used against Edgar's snow. I have not had any luck."

The wall of will, he remembered—and what she had said of it, at the time. "I've only read it in one book. Was that the spell that impressed Mistress Janet?"

Fliss nodded.

"I remember—"

Fliss flushed. "Having it collide with Edgar's was foolish," she said, with dignity, "but it was still impressive."

Despite himself, her interest felt pleasant. "I can hardly send you to my father's library for the book. When can I show you?"

Before the lecture hall, a twelfth of the garden glowed orange with dawn's children in full bloom. Beside it, other flowers lay in bud, and night flowers were withering. A floral clock, but he was not here to become a gardener.

Nick walked into the hall, where students took their seats on the benches. Edgar sat three rows back, laughing with — Luke, Randall's cousin, from the party. Edgar glanced past him without—apparent—recognition. Nick chose a bench to one side and sat.

Matthew, from St. Catherine's—and Jack, as well, came in, looking about. The room had filled quickly, and Nick raised a hand to wave. They came over.

Mistress Elise, inelegant in her violet robes, emerged. The room settled. Nick opened his spell book. It had taken a startling amount of his allowance, and all of it was blank.

Mistress Elise stopped. Nick still scribbled. He had written everything, whether it made sense or not. He had neglected transformations before; Master Umberto could only have omitted it because his other skills were worse. His hand was stiff and his legs ached when he twitched.

Jack and Matthew already stood. Nick hesitated. But he could not ask Edgar, or the others he had known before, and he knew these two as well as anyone else in St. Catherine's.

"Since I wasn't here for the first lectures, I need the notes—" Jack eyed him. "Can I copy yours?" He glanced between them. "Either of—"

"Of course," said Matthew with a half-smile. Nick returned the smile. His father found advantages in being a recluse that he never would; he would never have the money to.

He glanced at his notes as they joined the students flowing from the hall—and glanced up by the door. Red and white flowers nodded. Some blossoms differed in color though they were on the same stalk: knights-and-damsels. "I thought the lecture was over at noon."

Matthew blinked. "Of course." He gestured at the clock.

"Knights-and-damsels don't bloom until the afternoon— nearer two than noon."

"Enchanted flowers," said Jack, dragging out the words. "Why wouldn't wizards enchant a clock?"

Nick felt his face set in mulish lines. The gardener's hatred of magic in the garden inspired him, perhaps, but this—"So it won't tell the *wrong* time. Who'd enchant a clock to chime two at noon?"

The clock tolled out the noon hour. St. Catherine's appeared ahead of them. Jack's mouth twisted.

"Besides, all these plants grow about here. Plants that aren't native would show off the enchantment better."

Jack laughed. "Talk like that too much, Nick, and they'll put you in charge of the clock."

"I can imagine worse fates."

Matthew lifted both eyebrows and glanced up at St. Catherine's, towering beside them. "Both of you—I have something—come with me."

Nick looked at Jack, who looked at him. Jack shrugged and followed Matthew, through a back door. After a moment, Nick followed.

Up two flights of stairs, Matthew pulled open the door to a side room. Despite the three beds arrayed in it, it was empty. He went over to one and scrambled for a box.

"My mother sent me—hardly enough for the college, but more than I could eat." He opened it, and Nick saw the Easter buns.

"Your mother lives nearby?" he said.

Matthew nodded and held out the box. Jack took one. "I'm—my father's a farmer, living upriver." He smiled. "I'm the seventh son, and I've three sisters as well. Father was glad when I decided to become a wizard instead of a farmer, and Mother sends me things."

He should have guessed that, from the accent, thought Nick. Though he could not place Jack's.

Jack was already eating, and Matthew eyed Nick. "Not that I would have appreciated them after that egg."

Nick's mouth twisted. That, he would not have. He took a bun, and Matthew took his own before sliding the box back under the bed. He sat on the bed to eat.

The cook had always made them, thought Nick. Feeling odd, he turned to Jack. "Do you come from nearby, too?"

Jack glanced sideways. "Nearer than some. I just came through the Wizards' Wood."

Nick opened his mouth and shut it again. Only those who lived in the hills just beyond found the road shorter—or safe enough, no matter how far they had to walk around. He took another bite of the bun.

"Then," said Jack, "that's not close next to you. They said your father lives just outside the city."

Nick nodded. "I lived with him until a few months ago."

"And now," said Matthew, "you're—no longer on good terms with him."

Nick snorted. "I was never on good terms with him. I don't think anyone ever was. Now, I am on *bad* terms with him."

In the library's back corner, Nick reread Umberto's notes. Even using all haste, copying Matthew's notes had taken time, and he had to say *something* to Umberto. The stone guardian was made of the same stone as All Angels', which made it harder to find by spells.

"The stone guardian was animated normally." His tongue touched his lips. The tomes might tell what was normal, and he had to keep his scholarship by his studies.

Besides, if he hoped to learn how to restore his heart, he had to learn the books.

He looked up. Row upon row of oaken shelves, beneath an arched roof. Balconies held further shelves, reachable by cast iron stairways. He had trouble finding spells in his father's library, and this one dwarfed that—not even considering the books tucked away in other rooms.

Those he did not need to fret about. He needed Master Umberto's sanction to reach them, which would be excuse enough to offer his tutor—he let out his breath. Good enough excuse for the stone guardian, which could be taken from his hands if he proved unable. Not good enough for his heart.

He was studying the stone guardian now. As long as he did not lose his scholarship, he could study to restore his heart. For years, if need be.

He walked among the shelves, past dozens of students and masters and hundreds of books. For all its order, the library's size, and the uniform shelves, made it a maze. He picked out a bird-like librarian in the library's indigo robes. She pointed him to the correct shelf.

In one of the darker corners, he found it, laden with dark bindings and black writing on them. He wished he had learned the light spell already, but he looked for a book on guardians.

On the Breaking of All Manner of Spells.

His hand hesitated on its spine. He could tell Master Umberto that the stone guardian was a spell, but it was a pitiful rationalization beside the burning desire to read. He flipped it open.

"Most particularly, all manner of spells are wrought by diabolists. All manner of lore is needed to break them again."

Nick set out in search of better light.

Charcoal gray clouds lowered overhead. The streets about Lady Alicia's house were already emptying as Nick walked down them. Even the cats seemed to have seen the storm clouds, but he reached the doorstep dry. He knocked and glanced at the sky. A drop splattered on the ground, and then another, but the door opened before a third one fell.

The maid ushered him into a drawing room, where a pair of lamps had already shone. Lady Alicia sat in a high-backed chair, like a queen at ease. Fliss perched on the edge of her chair and hopped to her feet to greet him. Lady Alicia did not move except to survey him. Clean, neat, his robes covering the condition of his clothing—but then, his clothing had never needed to be covered before.

Lady Alicia rose. "I am glad to see you. Come, let us go to dinner."

Nick bowed.

In the dining room, a pair of windows looked out a tiny garden, barely visible in the gloom. A few white flowers were blurs among the dark greenery. A small table, candle-lit, was set with white china and silver, and adorned with blue flowers.

What I was used to, just a few months ago, Nick thought. He handed Lady Alicia to her seat, he and Fliss sat, and the door opened. The maid brought in the soup.

"I hope it didn't rain on you," Fliss said.

"Some raindrops," Nick said, "but it has just threatened." The maid ladled the soup.

"Rather ominously," Lady Alicia said. "Then, spring storms often do."

The conversation rambled about the weather, over the soup, but as the maid cleared the soup plates away, he commented on the snow being heavier than usual.

Fliss said, "I had not noticed. The white sickness kept—we all kept inside."

"What else could we do?" said Lady Alicia. "Even those of us who did not contract it." Then she looked at Nick.

Nick looked at his own reflection in the plate. He had seen more of the snow than anyone in the city. The maid bustled about, laying out the meat and bread, and Nick picked up his fork. He had known this would come.

"I was surprised that you vanished." Lady Alicia held her fork, but did not put it near the plate. "It was distressing, once it was clear you had not contracted the white sickness."

Fliss fretted with her fork and did not look at him.

He should have dreamed up some explanation, before he had such urgent need of it.

Outside, suddenly, rain hammered on the street and drummed on the roof. Nick jumped. Rain covered the window so thickly that everything in the garden blurred. Both Fliss and Lady Alicia looked. After a moment, they turned back toward him. The rain settled down to a steady drumming, loud, but not too loud to drown him out.

"I quarreled with my father."

Lady Alicia inclined her head. "And did not come to a friend?"

Nick's tongue touched his lip. He had known that returning to the city was folly.

After a minute, Lady Alicia said, "Were you that afraid of him?"

Relief rushed through him. It was even the truth.

Do not sound too glib, a dark thought warned him. "Yes, I think so." He looked at her. "I was tired, and not thinking straight, and he threatened me. All I wanted was to get away."

"That sounds like Mortimer," said Lady Alicia.

Nick cut his meat. Fliss, with wary glances at him, ate hers.

"Felicity said you were studying with Master Umberto?" Lady Alicia said. She picked up her wine glass.

"I am," Nick said. "He has assigned me to destroy Mistress Martha's stone guardian."

"How is your research going?" Lady Alicia said. Candlelight glinted off the glass.

"I lost myself in works on how to break spells," he said. "I did not find how to destroy a stone guardian." Or, for all its talk on diabolerie, how to restore my heart.

"The university will teach you how to study." Lady Alicia smiled. "Being at the university will require more application than either of you are used to, as you will need to learn more."

Nick looked at his wine glass. More than you know, my lady.

The rain had sunk to a drizzle, but clouds still blacked out the stars entirely. Once she had quenched her candle, the room would be dark.

Fliss readied herself for bed with unsteady hands. She hoped that Nick had made it back to the college without being soaked to the skin. He could not fall ill and hope to keep up with his studies.

She knelt by the window and tried to pray, but her thoughts, untamable, kept returning to one point: *how* could Nick have fled the city in fear of his father? She pressed her hands together. How had Mortimer threatened him?

Luke snapped his fingers. Randall, his face set in discontented lines, looked from the candle-lit table, but he had been begrudging since Luke persuaded him—he would have tried to flee this evening if rain had not trapped him—and Luke ignored that. It would not be half as spectacular without Randall, and if he let Randall go, the coward would go drivel to the master wizards.

"I wonder," said Luke, "if Nick was a diabolist. It would explain much. His father was caught at it, and so scared that he married to become respectable. To find his son was not such a coward—he would be jealous."

"So why," said Randall, "did it take him forever to come back? If the power is so great?"

"You saw the wall of snow," said Luke. "If Nick was—careless with his father as well as with Edgar, he could need time to return."

Randall grunted and waved a paper at him. "Unless you pay more attention, you'll be as careless as Nick."

I doubt it, thought Luke.

"And Nick wouldn't have done any such thing," said Randall. "Perfect little prig."

Luke smiled. "He had to keep his secrets, too."

Between the day's uncommon warmth and the stove, the kitchen was hot. Nick perched on the rough bench. Sunlight came in the window. Perhaps he ought to put the practice off until nighttime, until his feeble light would be visible, even flashing in and out of existence.

But, simple as the spell was, he had to master it before he met with Umberto again. He had spent too long on that book.

He looked into the shadows and muttered the incantation. Light flashed, distinctly, and vanished. He scowled and concentrated again. Mistress Lenore's book was filled with light spells, but this was the simplest of them.

The door to the outside swung open. "Morning, Nick," Jack said. He walked over to the wooden cabinet, carved with bees and ears of wheat. "Studying here?"

"Darkest place in the college," Nick said. "And I need to learn a light spell."

Jack looked up from fetching out the honey and bread— looking, to Nick's annoyance but not surprise, astounded.

"My studies were—irregular, before I came to the university." He could change a fire's color, but he could not cast this simple Lenore's candle. He doubted anyone else in St. Catherine's could say that same.

"What was your teacher *thinking*?" said Jack, tearing off a chunk of bread.

"Teacher?" said Nick. "I told you I was not on good terms with my father. He never hired a tutor for me."

Someone shouted outside, loud enough to jar them both. Jack, bread and honey in hand, yanked the door open.

Something swooped in the air like a crow —no, someone, his black robes fluttering.

"What sort of fool is that?" said Nick. They went out to the gathering crowd. From the clamor, no one else knew, either.

Then, abruptly, the swooping stopped. The student landed on a wall. Exclamations arose, and he grinned.

"And just what did you think you were up to, *this time*, Gerard?" Mistress Janet stalked from the crowd and tilted her head upward to look at him.

Gerard's grin deepened. "Ensuring that my flying spell will not go amiss. You minded that I had no way to break my fall, before...."

Mistress Janet put her hands on her hips. "I suppose you tested the spell first?"

Nick glanced at Janet's face. This was what David had spoken of. He withdrew, into the shelter of the college.

"I wonder if she caught the white sickness," said Jack.

Nick glanced at him. "You can tell."

"Usually, but with her—fiery temperament, who could?"

Mortimer scowled at the book. The bookseller grew less useful by the day. The only new book he had bought here in over a year had been that piece of demon-summoning folly, so flawed that Nick had easily corrupted it.

He rifled through the pages. Despite that disservice, the mousy little creature acted more nervous about him, complaining and scuttling about with the books—as if the man had any purity to suffer corruption.

From the doorway, a gust shook the page. It swept out the shop's warmth and must for the smell of spring mud. Francis's voice boomed. "Ah, Mortimer Briarwood!"

Mortimer's mouth twisted.

"I heard your boy does well at the university."

Mortimer looked up. At the university? The boy had run off, but if he had not left the city, all his friends would not have pothered about him. He lowered the book. Then, perhaps he had regained his courage and returned.

"Promising boy. You must be proud of him."

Mortimer's mouth tightened. Proud of the brat's cunning, to twist his hard-won handiwork? He had been a fool not to keep a better eye on him, keep him in check.

Francis peered at him, as if disconcerted. "They say you quarreled with him."

If he knew that, he had only think to realize why Mortimer might not be pleased. Then, that required *thought*.

"They said the truth," Mortimer said. "He had best not return to my house." He laid down the book and walked out, before Francis asked what the quarrel had been about.

He drew a deep breath. It would be folly to risk revealing his secrets for the sake of destroying Nicholas. His eyes narrowed. The boy must have thought that, to flaunt himself in Mortimer's city.

"Under my very nose."

At the sharp word, a vendor stopped in the midst of her cry to peer at him rather than hawk her candied fruit. He scowled. She scurried off.

He forced his breath out. If he could find a better spell to preserve himself, he would have all the time in the world to deal with Nicholas.

Umberto waited for the dish to come around. It was amazing, how quickly they grew used to eating meat again.

"I saw Mortimer Briarwood, the other day," said Master Francis. "At the bookstore. Shocking. So fine a son, and he's not proud of him."

Master Bernard's voice was as querulous as ever. "Fine a son? Perhaps a fine scholar, but his father threw him from the house. An unfilial son."

"Do you think Nicholas picked the quarrel?" said Mistress Janet, sharply.

Perhaps less than helpfully, thought Umberto, as Bernard sneered.

"They all say they didn't pick the quarrel. They mean if their father indulged him, they would not quarrel." Bernard slapped his hand on the table. "Nicholas Briarwood is not fit for my lectures until he reconciles with his father."

Umberto considered how to learn what Master Bernard taught; his first duty would be to steer Nicholas from it.

Master Francis leaned forward. "I hope you are proud of your student. Someone should be."

Chapter 9—Studies

In a study room at St. Catherine's, Nick looked over his notes. Most wizards who studied stone guardians wanted to make them, not destroy them. He doubted the rest of the spells would be as easy as mastering the Lenore's candle.

He found tantalizing bits on breaking spells in general, but Lady Alicia had been right. Haring off on such topics earlier had left too little time for the stone guardian.

He sighed and rose to stretch his legs. His own studies had not merely been various, they had been lackadaisical; on any day, he had never spent so much time studying as he had to every day, here. He looked out the window. A student and a master stood by one garden, deep in talk over the sprouts. Nick looked at them until the student gestured. The flowers bloomed, pink engulfing green in the patch.

The gardener, thought Nick, would not have approved. The plants could not be as sturdy as those that grew and blossomed on their own. He looked at the pink flowers a minute longer. He could have sought a job as a gardener, he had learned a great deal of those skills as a child, but that would involve even more work, and they would expect a master gardener. . . .

Those reflections did not draw his gaze from flowers.

In the corridor, Jack said, "Over here." He stepped in the room and blinked.

"There's room," said Nick. He felt wary, but that was no excuse for discourtesy.

Matthew glanced in. Jack, after a moment, stepped forward to let him in.

"Working on the spell Mistress Janet talked of?" Matthew dropped his books on the table.

Nick shook his head. "Destroying the stone guardian that Mistress Martha created."

Jack whistled. "Master Umberto doesn't believe in starting out small?"

"No," said Matthew. "I'm another of his students."

Nick managed a smile.

Jack sat. "Hear about the fires?"

Fires? Rumors spread faster than flames—he shook his head and glanced out the window. He could see no untoward smoke.

"Not here. Down along the docks," said Matthew. "In empty warehouses."

"And," said Jack, "fires are all the colors of the rainbow."

"At once?" said Nick.

"No, each one—the last one, I heard, was green."

"Arson then," said Nick. And magic. "Mistress Janet must on it."

"Oh, she is, she is," said Jack. "She's on it like a terrier on a rat."

Matthew colored. "She was right," he said, though he sounded half-strangled.

Jack raised an eyebrow.

"Gerard could have killed himself," said Matthew, strength returning to his voice. "He didn't get my help the second time. And this wizard will be *lucky* if Mistress Janet catches him. The mobs'll tear him to pieces." He glanced at Nick. "After the white sickness—there was an old woman who would sell curses by the dock. They blamed her."

"It was centuries ago," said Nick. "And that wizard's *dead*. Took the white sickness."

"Anyway, a *real* wizard," said Jack, "has less to fear than that old fraud. A powerful one, coloring the flames. . . ."

"It's not a difficult spell," said Nick. "Coloring the fires."

"It isn't?" said Jack.

For a moment, Nick could not breathe. If they discovered, if they learned—they knew less of him than those friends he had not trusted with his secrets.

They are just being friendly, he thought. They weren't prying into when he vanished. He forced his breath out. They had already proven better sorts of friends than his old circle. "I'll show you in the kitchen sometime. I'll even show you one better, how to make it every color of the rainbow. After I finish this."

Jack and Matthew looked at his papers and grinned.

Matthew poked the logs. The low kitchen fire leapt up. Jack added a log, making the orange flames rise. "No point in not having sufficient flames for proof."

"Dinner's almost ready," said an older student, sticking his head through the doorway.

"Nick's showing us a spell," said Jack. "Won't take long."

Such confidence, thought Nick. He drew a deep breath and cast the spell. Violet light surged from the fireplace. For a long minute, the crackle of the blaze was the only sound. With a grin, Nick turned it green, then red, and then blue.

"I think you proved your point," said Matthew.

Nick sat there in the blue. He should have sought a scholarship long before, however rich his father was. To have friends that did not scorn his studies—

"Hey, what's that?" said a voice at the doorway. Other students pressed around—but none came into the colorful kitchen.

Though the blue light made him look sickly, Jack grinned. "Nick's showing us. The spell to color the arson flames isn't as hard as it looks."

After exclamations, Nick said, "I want to eat my dinner!"

"Are you the only one who does?" Master Humphrey pushed his way through the students—and his mouth fell open. Students chuckled. The housemaster scowled. "What is this meaning of this?"

"An experiment to show that the arsonist need not be so powerful a wizard," said Jack, tranquilly.

"Transformation," said Mistress Elise, "of a living thing to another form is therefore the most dangerous and difficult of transformations, because the thing must be alive at every moment. Once it is dead, it can not be transformed back to life, whatever is done to the corpse."

Fliss scribbled. This, at least, was intelligible, even if the theory before it was not.

Mistress Elise turned a scowl on the students. "Forget your fairy tales about werewolves—you will make no such transformations. If you did, you would have a wolf so drained of life that he would have to rest until the moon set—and still, most likely, be too weak to change back ."

Fliss stretched her legs. It woke her body. All her muscles complained of how long she had sat.

"Are all the stories false, then?" said a student, with a foreign accent.

Mistress Elise's mouth grew narrow and pinched. "No one can *prove* an absence." She dismissed the class.

In the commotion, Fliss surveyed her notes. Lady Alicia had been right; this was not her former studies.

She put them away. Nick was leaving the lecture hall. She had not seen him since a week ago.

"Nick!" she called. He stopped. Two others—one dark-haired and solidly built, one lean and red-haired—stopped with him. She faltered.

"Fliss," said Nick.

"The wall spell that you were going to teach me—."

"That would be—" Nick glanced at the other students. "I promised her before I—"

Both of them grinned, one wryly.

"Fliss, these are Jack Easton,"—he gestured at the red-head— "And Matthew Graybrook. This is Felicity Seaborn."

The last name raised Jack's eyebrows, but both greeted her pleasantly.

"We've met," said Matthew, after a moment. "At the orphanage. You came down with the white sickness—"

But others labored on. "The sisters were most grateful to you." She hesitated. She did want that spell.

"They won't let you into St. Catherine's," said Matthew.

"The weather's pleasant enough," said Nick. "We'll sit on the steps." He started to walk. "Did you understand Mistress Elise's lecture, Fliss?"

"Every third word or so," said Fliss. Nick snorted.

"Alive in every step," said Jack. "How could you tell?"

"It must be possible," said Fliss. "There are gryphons, manticores." She waved a hand in midair. "All manner of creatures half one beast and half another—or a quarter another, and a quarter a third. Traveling entertainers show them. They must be half-transformed creatures."

The young men looked thoughtful. Fliss glanced at Nick through her lashes and felt relieved. Nick's manner must have stemmed from his quarrel with his father; it had eased already.

"Unless you believe the tales about interbreeding," said Nick. "I think that possible—at the hands of a greater wizard than one who could transform it."

"How long do you think it would take to teach her?" said Jack. "That spell?" He looked at Fliss. "He's teaching us how to change the colors of fires."

"Like that—" Fliss shut her mouth abruptly. The picnic by the lake—but also the shore blazes. Her gaze flickered over Nick. He *had* cast the wall foolishly by the lake.

"I can't teach both in one evening," said Nick. "I have my own studies."

Rain pelted on the library windows, blurred the already dreary landscape outside, and turned the flowers, the only brightness, into blobs of color. Nick ran his finger down the books beneath the window. Between the rain and the evening, the dim light made reading the titles difficult, but bright enough that he could not decide to cast a Lenore's candle.

He should have put off Fliss and come earlier. He would have to put off Jack and Matthew. He had to ready these spells.

His finger caught on one jagged spine. *On the Dissolution of Spells.* He snatched the book before he had consciously read the title and dropped it on the bookcase to read by the gray daylight. The books on stone guardians did not deal with *destroying* them.

It opened with pother about the difficulty of dissolving spells, and the problem of discerning what the spell did.

"One must determine the right way to discover how the spell may be reversed."

Nick read on, but it offered little to accomplish that. Then he turned a page. The formula for a pentacle faced him. For a moment, he read it, long enough to be sure.

He slammed the book shut. For a minute, he stared out at the rain-distorted scene and wondered why his heart was not hammering.

He should have seen it earlier. Everything he had read in the tome hinted that right way to discover it was to summon a demon, which would know.

But while he had heard that the grimories would appear in the path of students vulnerable to them, he had never even known someone to whom it had happened, before.

He let his breath out. He could not leave it here. His fingers tightened on the book. The library must be the most likely place for any number of grimories to be hidden—he hoped. He could consign it to the hands of the librarians. He picked it up and walked toward the central desk. He felt himself moving slowly, as if very old.

The demons thought he would practice diabolerie to remove false evidence that he had practiced it. Despite himself, Nick laughed.

"Now," said Janet, "determining which spells are compounded and which simple is seldom as straightforward as it appears."

The students crowded on the benches. With the summer, she had abandoned lighting the room by spell. Gray morning light lay over the students perched on the benches like so many crows. This lecture meant the newest students, and it had not yet lasted many weeks; many young fools still had to learn that being a student was arduous. Some still clowned about in the upper benches—though some had found that the university was not as easy as it seemed. The benches were not as crowded as the first lectures.

"A spell that sets an effect in motion does not become a compounded spell because the wizard casts another upon the effect. If a wizard casts a light spell, and then makes it colored, he must compound the spell, because the light must be conjured still. It does not remain if the spell ceases. But if the wizard lights a fire by magic, he can then color the flames, for the fire will burn without further magic on his part."

Mutters ran about the lecture.

An unfortunate example, Janet thought, but I had not time to conjure up another for you.

Felicity Seaborn stared in front of herself, looking bemused, not writing.

The dark brown bookcase, carved with vines, stood against a back wall. The floor was well worn in front of it. Nick glanced over the titles, with lettering half rubbed off.

The Most Foul Arte of Diabolerie. The thing in his chest weighed heavily. He picked out *The Tome of the Stone Guardian.* The tantalizing bits, promising release, seemed to have doubled in number since he stuck to his lesson. He carried off the book to a table.

The clouding sky darkened the library. Nick laid his chosen book down and recited the light spell. A globe of silvery light sprung up over the desk—not created, he reminded himself, but brought from beyond the clouds. There he was ready for Master Umberto, at any rate.

He opened the *Tome of Stone Guardians.* An ink sketch looked back at him: the stone guardian crouched and snarling. Its mouth gaped with sharp fangs.

Nick kept his face steady, but his arm itched. The sketch bore more than a passing resemblance to Mortimer's creature. He sat back. He wanted to destroy it, but for that, he might have to reverse the spells. He started to read the lore about shaping the stone. He skimmed that, but when the text came to the automaton, he slowed.

"'. . .many wise men have said that no natural spell can give perfect liveliness and judgment to the stone, in the manner necessary for the perfection of its duties, that to have a true stone guardian, a wise guard for its master, diabolerie must be performed. Truly, the most perfect of such creatures have been found among the works of these men. . . .'"

Nick's fingers paused. He wondered whether Mistress Martha had used diabolerie, but the masters would have had to check. No one would have given a student such a task.

Then, if the master wizards looked for diabolerie around the university. . . . Nick shoved the thought aside and jotted notes about infusing motion, sense, and a kind of judgment in the guardian.

He read his notes again. The motion spells animated the creature continually; once broken, they would not start again. The hard part would be flushing the creature out. He scowled. For all the talk of its judgment, he could not judge how to outwit it.

"Nick? Are you busy?" said Fliss, behind him.

"Not really," Nick said.

"I—have a few questions about the wall spell," Fliss said. "It's harder than I thought."

A break, Nick thought with relief. "I will be glad to stretch my legs." He started for the shelf, book in hand, and Fliss came with him.

"Mistress Janet hasn't seen anything like it," said Fliss. "She hasn't mastered it herself."

He reached the bookcase. "Father must have gotten it from aboard."

Fliss's eyebrows pulled together, thoughtfully. Nick wondered how Mortimer had discovered it. A demon could fetch a spell-book from a foreign land as easily as from the

library, and Mortimer had admitted to selling his soul. He put
back the book. Mistress Janet might guess at how Mortimer
had done it.

They headed for the door.

"It's tricky," Fliss said, "and worse, it's almost impossible to
tell when you are successful. It's invisible!"

"I practiced windy days. You could feel it, then."

Fliss tilted her head to one side, listening.

"It took months before I could conjure a wall that would
protect me from the wind," Nick said. "I'm surprised I didn't
give it up."

Then the memory returned: Mortimer had found him
pouring over the book and declared the spell beyond his
powers.

Fliss licked her lips. "I was working at the orphanage the
other day. They—the white sickness is over, but there are
other things—"

Nick nodded. It did not surprise him, that even her studies
could not keep her away.

"If you have spells that you need to practice that could aid
the orphans, the sisters would be glad of your aid."

There was color in her cheeks, but she met his gaze, and her
blue eyes were clear.

I must put on a convincing show of innocence, Nick
thought, bitterly.

"The librarians mentioned that you gave them a book the other
day," said Umberto.

Nick froze. They couldn't have- - how could they have—he
had not given his name.

"They always mark such students, for the times we must
learn who has tried the spells and grown the wiser for it."

Nick tried to look up and failed.

"Considering how they tried to tempt you, are you finding the work too hard?"

"*No.*"

Umberto looked at him in silence.

"Not to resort to—" Nick fell silent himself.

"To tell your tutor, on the other hand?"

Nick still could not look at him. Umberto still sounded urbane, calm. "Not even to tell my tutor. I still think—" He let his breath out. "I can't believe anyone would be tempted by something so trivial."

"I envy you your innocence," said Umberto.

"Fliss!" Giggles flooded the street.

Fliss, her arms laden with books, stopped. She had not seen them in the crowd, but having stopped, she could not pretend that she had not heard. The women hurried toward her.

Marie pounced. "Fliss, you must come to our party tonight."

Catherine and Robina nodded agreement.

"We just found Edgar," Catherine said.

"It's been so long." Robina's lips formed a pretty rosebud pout. "We'll think you are evading us."

Fliss smiled thinly. "I have to study."

Marie threw her hands in the air. "But you must not exhaust yourself! When you were so much sicker than I was! Don't you *see?*"

Fliss's smile grew sour. She wondered whether Marie remembered how rumors spread.

"Edgar studies and comes to parties," Robina said.

"We don't wish to lose track of friends who go to the university." Catherine glanced at Fliss through her eyelashes. "You do not wish to sacrifice your friends to your studies."

Yes, thought Fliss with new resolve, if my friends are not friendly enough to let me study. The books shifted in the crook of her arm. Fliss adjusted them with her free hand, puzzled for a way to phrase that without scandalizing the gossips for a month, and said nothing. Considering how they spoke of her birth, they were reluctant to free her from their circle.

"We knew you would see it our way," said Robina. "All work and no play make Jill a dull girl, don't you see?"

"It's noon," said Marie. "You have been studying *all morning*, isn't that so?"

Inspiration struck. "Are you inviting Nick?" Fliss said, innocently as she could.

Silence fell. Catherine looked away.

After a minute, Robina said, "He's poor. We. . . don't want to embarrass him."

"He has to keep his scholarship," said Catherine. "He has not much free time."

"True," Fliss said. "Not to study hard would be base ingratitude to the benefactor who gave his scholarship." She raised the books. "I, too, must show my gratitude—especially as Lady Alicia will know it."

She hurried toward the library, disappearing into the crowd before they could recover from that sally. I have to cut myself off from them, she thought. They will strangle my studies if they can. It is only spite, that I have given them up, not they me, as they have with poor Nick.

She came around a corner. Throwing Edgar in my face. He can not be the student Nick is, not when Nick stopped his wall of snow so readily, before either of them ventured here.

"Felicity," said a voice from a side path. Fliss stopped. Mistress Janet emerged, her yellow robes brilliant in the shadows.

"How are your studies going?"

"I am still puzzling out Nick's spell."

Mistress Janet smiled, showing strain. "You will have more time to study it. I have to deal with the fires."

Fliss wondered that so blatant a display of magic had not left Mistress Janet enough clues to catch the wizard. Then she remembered, again, another fire that burned strange colors, the day before Nick vanished. She swallowed. Nick would not be involved with diabolerie. Then again. . . . her thoughts drifted on.

"That need not be diabolerie," she said, subdued.

"No, it need not," said Mistress Janet, "but I must ensure that. And what Mistress Anna did over the fire lily was not diabolerie. Just within an inch of murder."

A master wizard had lit a fire in the Wizards' Wood, to produce a flower that only grew after fires, and nearly burned someone alive. Fliss glanced at her face and said, thinly, "This looks less serious."

"Thus far."

Fliss swallowed again. Nick would not show anyone his color-changing spell if he were the arsonist. He would be too wary to *speak* of it. . . .

Her tongue felt heavy, but she spoke. "Nick—Nicholas Briarwood—knows a spell to do that—those colored fires. I've seen. . . ."

Mistress Janet glanced sideways at her. "I saw him in the library while one fire was burning."

Relief flooded Fliss.

"I saw him in the library," George said. The firelight played on his face. "Hunting through the books of diabolerie."

Edgar stared into the fire, low in the fireplace. It burned pale orange and left most of the room dark. Taking a private room in the inn so they could make their plans, that was one thing, but when George came up with such frail reeds to base their plans on, the expense was unwarranted.

The flames licked at the air.

"The little prig. Too pious to visit a whorehouse. Nick's not going to summon up a succubus."

"Who said he would? Everyone knows about his father."

Edgar looked dubious.

"Everyone who's gone by the house late at night sees strange lights," George said, his voice animated. "Mortimer Briarwood never shares any of his studies." He leaned forward. "Mortimer would not muck around with a succubus, but he would deal with devils for other things—if Nick takes after his father. . . ."

Edgar scowled, but after a minute, nodded. Nicholas Briarwood was Mortimer Briarwood's son.

Along the path, daffodils bloomed. Trees shaded it from the sun. Fliss walked briskly down it, and Nick followed. He had spent too long on the stone guardian, his thoughts were in a tangle, and leaving the university behind was the best thing he could do. His progress did not displease Master Umberto yet.

A small girl, her blond braids falling back from her rosy face, peered from behind the nearest tree. "Fliss?"

"Good morning, Charity," said Fliss.

"I *knew* you would come. Angelina was saying that you wouldn't, but I knew." She looked at Nick, as if just noticing him. "Who's he?"

"A friend of mine," said Fliss. "To help at the orphanage."

Charity came out to study him. "Tom fell down and broke his arm. The doctor fixed it but Mother Humiliata says he has to stay in bed *all the time*—for a week!"

Within the orphanage walls, there were no other men.

Fliss led the way through the neat, whitewashed halls, punctuated only by the almost black doors, until she greeted Sister Macrina. "We came to help, and Charity said something about Tom—"

"Tom's a good boy," said Sister Macrina, "but the doctor says that he has to rest." The young sister fretted with her wimple. Nick felt even more out of place. "The spell cured him, but he doesn't realize that he must still recover."

Fliss nodded.

Sister Macrina lowered her voice. "I think he's scared. Because of the white sickness."

Nick remembered his own impatience, in the woods. "Let us see if he can be entertained."

Sister Macrina looked grateful and led them off to a stairway. "I know that Mother Humiliata will want to speak with you, Fliss," she said, her voice echoing oddly in the stairwell. At the top of the stair, she opened the door. A room held half a dozen plain beds, and was lit by three windows where lead held diamond-shaped panes. A red-haired boy stared at the wall opposite. As they came in, his shoulders hunched.

"I've tried *everything*," said Sister Macrina.

"Let me check the spell," said Fliss.

Nick walked over to the fireplace. The smoke was sparse. The firewood had burnt down to a bed of coals, deep red only beneath a blanket of gray. Still, as the women whispered, he whispered the incantation even more softly. Smoke gathered, like a small ghost, summoning a flickering memory of the demon. Nick fought down the memory and drew the smoke into the room.

"What is that?" Like an owlet, Sister Macrina blinked at him.

"Smoke." He ushered it over to Tom's bed. Not even the scent of it escaped.

Tom's face set in sullen lines.

"Or, perhaps, a castle." Nick detailed towers, ramparts, flying banners. Tom sat up, gasped in pain, and leaned back, but his eyes never moved from the castle. After a moment passed, after he chose a tale, Nick sent birds flying about it.

"What castle is that?" said Tom.

Fliss gave him a grateful glance and slid from the room with Sister Macrina. Nick sat on the next bed. "It's a castle where, a long time ago, the lord heard that if a baby drank his first sip from the skull of raven, he would grow up knowing what birds said when they spoke."

He transformed the smoke into a bedchamber, a lady in the bed, and a baby in the cradle, with a man leaning over it. It took longer than he liked, but Tom watched in delight.

"So he ordered that a raven's skull be found before his son was born and with his own hands, gave the baby the sip."

"Did it work?"

Nick transformed the smoke again, into a little boy and birds flitting around him, and told Tom how the boy had climbed to the nooks of the castle, where the birds nested, and how he had cleared a maid servant of theft, by finding something stolen by a crow in its nest, until Tom chafed a little.

"And then, one day. . . ." Nick drew up a young man. Easier without the scenery about him. "He and his father were in the courtyard, and his father asked him what the ravens were saying." He summoned up the courtyard. It took longer, Tom wriggled in anticipation, but smoke ravens perched on the walls. "The boy said that it was nothing important."

Tom stared.

"His father ordered him. The boy said that what the ravens said was that one day, his father would go on one knee before him, and serve him."

Tom turned to stare at Nick, ignoring the smoke.

Nick drew a deep breath and kept his voice steady. "His father flew into a rage, beat him, and threw him out of the house. His son wandered out into the wide world, without friend or money." Tom looked at the smoke. At least, he was past the beating and did not have to show it. Concentrating fiercely, he transformed the scene into a forest, with the dejected young man. He drew a deep breath to steady himself before he went on.

"But he could talk to the birds," said Tom. "They could tell him where to find money, 'cause some of them *steal* it."

"He did not think of that," said Nick. Tom pouted, and Nick hurried on. "He walked in the woods until he came to a village where the well had run dry. He listened to the birds and heard that a snake had climbed into the well and drunk all the water. . . ."

Nick drew up the well in the smoke, Tom leaned forward, and Nick wound the story on, with all the adventures where his hero's ability to speak with birds let him work marvels—rather easily—but Tom was rapt.

But his voice started to go, and Nick said, "He came to the emperor's palace, which was plagued by birds day and night, calling and stealing food from all who lived inside it."

He let his voice rest as he drew up an enormous castle.

"The emperor promised lands and a noble title and the hand of his daughter in marriage to whoever could free them from the birds. So, the young man spoke to the birds. He told the emperor that his men were chopping down the trees in the forest, so that the birds lost their homes. The emperor gave the orders to no longer cut down the trees. The birds left the castle for the forest." The enormous flock, even in smoke, bloated out the light. Nick let it drop, leaving only the imperial castle behind. "So the emperor married him to his daughter."

Tom grinned.

"Then he and the princess went traveling on a ship." That one took some doing, with all the flags and pennants suitable for an imperial ship. "A storm blew them to his father's lands, and his father saw that a great nobleman and a princess had come to his castle. He went down to greet them, and knelt on the dock before so great a lord, held in such honor by the emperor.

"His son jumped to embrace him and begged him to realize that he had never meant him any ill will, and had not desired this to happen."

He drew up a smoky image of the father and son embracing. Even if he were not hoarse, he could have said nothing more.

"In here," a woman said in the corridor. "The doors are hard to tell apart."

Nick sighed in relief.

"Merciful heavens, what is that?" said the sister in the doorway. Fliss gawked behind her.

"An amusement for the ill," said Nick. He conjured the smoke back toward the fireplace before the room reeked of it, and swallowed, trying to ease his throat.

"I told you that Nicholas Briarwood came to help, Mother Humiliata," said Fliss, her voice meeker than Nick had ever heard it before. "He kept Tom quiet."

Mother Humiliata glanced at Tom. "So you did. But now we need you to inspect the work."

Fliss and Mother Humiliata talked behind him. Nick ushered his creation over to the chimney. For a minute, he held it over the flames and studied the father and son. Lucky son, lucky father, to live in a fairy tale, where such a meeting was possible. He dissolved it into a puff. The smoke drifted up the chimney.

Chapter 10—Rumors

Light barely reached through the clouds to the street. Mistress Janet looked at the low, dark building and its empty windows and felt hot-tempered enough to set it ablaze with a look. At the street corner, people pointed at her and muttered.

She watched a minute longer. Whoever had seen someone skulking might have been mistaken. There would be no telling whether someone had prowled there, or whether it was her arsonist—until the blaze started.

The windows remained dark. Janet strode up and tried the door. The knob rattled but did not give. She muttered the spell under her breath, and the knob turned.

The dust covered the floor like a gray blanket in its evenness, but a path went through it, where the smooth surface was disturbed—not by a horde, or often, but by a pair of feet, once.

Light filtered in the windows. Janet drew a deep breath and suppressed a cough. She intoned another spell. The light in the room shifted, turned more grayish, as she conjured up invisibility for herself. It would not hide the dust she stirred up, but it was better than nothing.

Janet followed the path through the rooms. The culprit had managed before only because no one had seen him. In the second room, she heard a noise. She could not place it, but she hardly dared to breathe. Even empty room after empty room did not ease her wariness.

Three rooms down, she heard a petulant voice. "No, I don't want the fire to be red this time. I want it to be green. Blue, if you *must*, but you've made it red three times."

A squeaky voice answered. Janet could not make out the words, but the high pitch made her scowl.

"I conjured you, you did not conjure me."

Janet felt like ice. She walked over to the next room. A youth, scarcely more than a boy, stood over a magical circle, crudely laid out in the dust. In the center stood a bright red imp, little taller than a cat, its long, barbed tail longer than it was. It scowled and squeaked, "But I like red."

Janet nearly felt her heart stop. How petty could diabolerie get? She had wasted her spell on these fools. They would not realize if she had galumphed up to them, unhidden. She let her spell drop.

The imp's mouth fell open. The diabolist stopped. He started to glance over his shoulder, looked at the imp, and then turned to face her.

"Oops," he said.

Beneath the trees, students walked by, and Robina's glance darted about. Catherine studied her.

"There he is," she said.

"Edgar?" said Marie.

Robina giggled. "No—Nick. Can't you see him?"

Nick walked under the trees. His hair was roughly cut, and his black robes did not quite cover his shabby clothing. Catherine slowed. Robina would not dream of inviting him.

"I've wondered," Robina said. "Where's he been?"

"He hasn't told anyone," said Marie. "I've asked all about."

"Have you asked him?" Robina said. Marie and she glanced at each other and hurried toward him. Catherine fell behind. Gossipmongers, she thought, but she walked quickly enough to hear Nick's response.

Robina pounced. "Nick! I wondered where you were, all those weeks when you vanished."

Nick faced her, looking surprised. His gaze shifted from Robina to Marie, and on, to Catherine, and back to Robina. Catherine cringed.

"About," he said, firmly.

Marie wheedled. "It's not as if quarreling with your father would keep you away from us for so long."

Nick's face set.

Robina pouted. "Come, Nick, you can tell us."

"I can't talk. I have to study." He walked past, and they saw only his back.

"How unfriendly," said Robina.

"Well, I like that," Marie said, putting her hands on her hips to stare after him. "How could quarreling with Mortimer make Nick vanish?"

Robina's plump face lit up. "Magic!"

Catherine gave her a sidelong glance.

Robina pouted. "Even the masters of the university are impressed by Mortimer Briarwood's wizardry." She waved her hands in the air. "He and Nick quarreled, and he used magic on Nick, sending him far away. It took him this long to get back, don't you see?"

"You don't *know* that," said Catherine, but her voice lacked conviction. It would explain everything.

The skies rumbled, and the day was dark. Wiser heads scrambled for shelter, even cats and birds were nowhere to be seen, but studies or none, he had to retrieve his allowance. The other scholars scrambled for every coin, and they would not welcome a rival—and he should not be a rival when he could get the coins. Bad enough he took up a scholarship when his father could have paid.

Nick came around a corner. Great, slate blue clouds billowed in the sky. Before him, a tree stood, still in sunlight, with every leaf brilliantly cut out against the storm.

He let his breath out. Besides, he thought, the time they spent earning those coins, he could spend learning to restore his heart; he did not think they had a need as urgent.

Smells wafted from a bakery, of fresh pastry and candied fruit. Nick swallowed and looked away. He had spent coins there since his mother had first entrusted him with them, but he could not afford it.

Lying in bed, Nick gave his notes one last glance over. They contained everything he had thought of. He put them away. He had a plan, but the details needed work. He rose. The only way to study in his room was in the bed, but besides the lighting, it left him stiff. He stretched and picked up the candlestick by the door. The flame flickered as he walked over to the door.

Someone muttered, outside. Someone else laughed, low. Nick opened the door. Out of the candlelight's reach, shadowy forms pulled down the last of the stairs, but lingered in the hallway there.

Nick's eyes narrowed. Perhaps they didn't realize how visible they were. He looked down the stairway. Something lurked on the step. The candlelight didn't reach that far, either, but he could make out the low, flat form.

Smoke rose from his candle. He lifted his free hand to conjure. The smoke took time to accumulate, but gathering it, he made the form of a hound—an enormous hound. The noises from the hallway had stopped, except for one movement, which might have been a start.

He sent his hound snuffling down the stairs.

A startled yelp made all three of them bolt until one tripped. The clatter inspired shouts of "What the devil's going on?" and footsteps from other doorways. Nick dissipated the spell, but the smoke still lingered. Candles, and light spells, lit up the corridor.

"WHAT IS GOING ON HERE!" Humphrey looked indignantly about. Scholars fell silent. Nick tried not to bother with how he looked; nothing would make him look more guilty than trying to look innocent—and everyone looked at him.

"I wondered that myself," said Nick. "There's something on the stairs, I tried to learn what—"

"It's his fault!" The student who fell—Vincent, Nick realized, a student of three years' standing—pointed up the stairs. "Because of him—"

"What were you doing up here?" said Nick. "I thought your rooms were on the first floor."

Students chuckled. Vincent gaped. One scholar laughed, and for all Master Humphrey's glares, laughter sprouted all about.

Humphrey drew himself up to his full height. "Have you all looked at the north wall? Outside?"

Nick tried to remember. Master Humphrey could have chosen a less obscure subject.

"Where the brick is purple?" said a student, lightly, from the shadows.

"And has been purple for many a year," said Humphrey. "A miscast spell discolored it scores of years ago—"

"What's so terrible about being purple?" said one student.

"Master Humphrey'll turn you purple, if you want to find out," said another. Laughter sprouted again.

Another third-year pushed through the crowd. "Should I get that down, Master Humphrey?" Looking at Nick, he smiled wryly.

The harpsichord played in the corner of the party.

"Has anyone seen Fliss lately?" said Christopher as he shuffled the cards. "She's at the university, she would have a chance to talk with Nick."

In spite of herself, Catherine drifted closer.

"*I'm* at the university," said Edgar. "*I* don't see Nick. He sticks with scholars like—you'd think all his old friends took the white sickness."

Robina sniffed. "Lady Alicia invited him to dinner, and he went." She leaned forward. "But I heard that Mortimer use magic on him—threw him out of the city, didn't you?"

Before Catherine could speak, Marie said, "Mortimer Briarwood might, but I doubt he would restrain himself so much." Robina turned on her, wide-eyed at this treachery, but Marie prattled on. "Mortimer would have turned him into a wild animal, or into stone, or a tree—"

"If he did that," said Catherine, "what is Nick doing at the university?" At least Robina's idea was *possible*. "They don't accept stones or trees—or even deer or foxes."

Marie's gaze was mild. "He was disenchanted. . . ." After a moment, she said, "Somehow."

Didn't they remember anything about Nick's father?

"Mortimer Briarwood," said Catherine, "would not have left Nick where he could be disenchanted."

"So a beast," said Stephan, "or a bird—able to wander."

The whole party seemed to listen.

"How was he disenchanted?" said Catherine. "No master wizard would have dared keep it quiet. And Mistress Janet—" She spread her hands.

"He could have had to travel," said Christopher. "Stephan's right—not a stone or tree then."

"Or," said Stephan, "he was *trapped* in a tree, and it got struck by lightning, or something."

They were impossible, thought Catherine. Robina's story was the most plausible, shockingly enough, but they seemed content to babble of impossibilities.

"Fliss," said Lady Alicia from the shadows of the room. Fliss, her arms laden with books, stopped in the doorway.

Giles sat with Lady Alicia. Fliss felt hot and sticky from the walk in the heat, but he already rose from his chair and conjured up blossoms.

She had to juggle the books to take the flowers, but she thanked him. He had mastered the spell. She smiled, wondering if she could flirt, and said, softly, "I had heard that another woman received such flowers at a party."

"From another man—John wished to woo, and I wished to help. I felt a certain sympathy." Giles smiled. "But I also heard at a party a—distressing tale that might concern you."

Fliss glanced at his grave face and shifted her books.

"They said that Mortimer Briarwood used evil magic against Nicholas, and *that* is why he was gone so long."

Fliss felt frozen into silence. Her fingers tightened on books and flowers.

"I know you see him—"

"I have not heard such a tale from him," said Fliss, but even she could hear how wooden her words were.

Both his eyebrows went up. "I hope such magic does not linger. It might be painful for those about him."

In St. Catherine's, a handful of students sat about the fireplace. David leaned toward Jack. "You know Nick."

Not that well, thought Jack.

"Would he spread tales about his own father? He didn't toss *Vincent* to the wolves."

Jack scowled.

"So how did the tales get started?" said Matthew. "When Nick wouldn't?"

"It slipped out." David sat back. "Someone asked him when he wasn't expecting it, and he told the truth."

If Nick was ever surprised *into* talking—"Why would he want to shield his father?" Jack said.

Next to the fire, Jan roused himself. "So where was he? I came from afar, and I was here long before he was. Do you think that Nick sat around and waited?"

A loud snort came from the door. Humphrey looked in. "So eager to defend a rich man's son! Do you not know how lazy they can be? They expect everything o fall into their laps."

He stalked off before they could argue. Matthew looked ready to burst with indignation. Jack stared at the fire. Nick had expected neither the notes for the earlier lecture nor understanding the lectures to fall into his lap.

"He's getting money from somewhere," grumbled Tom. When no one answered, he rose and left.

Jack contemplated the fire a minute longer. Jan rose; Jack nodded but did not look at him as he left. Nick did have money, without copying jobs, or any other task that poor students scrambled for, but he was not rich.

Footsteps sounded on the stairs and in the hallway. Jack looked up, and Nick met his gaze. His eyes were a hard-to-distinguish color by daylight; in firelight and shadow, Jack could not have laid a name to the color to save his life.

"How goes it?" said Jack.

"Finished my work," said Nick. "Until Master Umberto tells me where I went wrong."

Matthew's mouth twisted. "When do you meet him?"

"Day after tomorrow." He made no move to sit.

Jack leaned back on his chair to study him.

"With Vincent and the other two—" said Matthew, curiously.

Nick glanced at him, like a cat eyeing a dog.

Matthew leaned forward. "What did you do to their spell?"

"Nothing."

Jack blinked.

"I startled them, and they gave it away." He sat and, leaning forward, cast a spell Jack did not recognize. Smoke billowed into the room, where it took on the shape of a hound. "Quicker here—it took minutes to gather the candle smoke."

Jack's mouth twitched. They had assumed the smell sprung from the *pranksters'* spell. "The hallway smelled of candle smoke."

Nick smiled and twisted his hands. Smoke transformed into a tree.

"What else can you do?" said Matthew.

Nick drew it down, into an oval—and then a dragon burst from the shell. Jack grinned. Matthew laughed aloud.

Nick's smile faded. He gestured, ushering the smoke back up the chimney. "Anything I dream of, really, but I should have left some work until tomorrow. I am *exhausted.*"

Jack gave a long sigh before grinning. "You don't want to teach us the color spell tonight."

Nick looked ashamed of himself.

"Have you heard the rumors?" said Jack.

"Many," said Nick. "Which ones?"

"Those that say your father enchanted you."

For a long moment, the fire's crackling was the only sound.

"My father did nothing to me that resulted in my being unable to come here."

About him, the master wizards talked over their meals. Mistress Elise complained about the number of new students. Umberto ate soup and pondered. The road that went through the Wizards' Wood was as magical as the woods—nothing else could have lasted—and laid, not by misbehaving students as punishment, but so long ago that the records were lost. He ate some cheese. He ought to see for himself. If he confined himself to reading of the Wizards' Wood, he might as well have remained at home—but he had to be ready for Matthew, whose session was the next day.

"Damned, irresponsible IDIOTS!"

Mistress Janet slammed her books down on the table as if punctuate her statement. Her cheeks were flushed. All about the room, the other master wizards stared. She glowered until they looked away. Her gaze went around the room until settling on Umberto. He looked back steadily.

Janet's mouth twitched. After a moment, she picked up her books to walk over to him.

"I heard you found the starter of fires," he said.

"A young idiot." Her voice rang, but not as if she pitched it to carry, and she sat. "He didn't see a difference between casting the spell himself and summoning an imp to do it."

"No one," said Umberto, "warned me how lightly diabolerie was taken around here."

"It is a horrible crime." Janet's tongue was laced with acid. "So, of course, a young idiot can't commit it—he is clearly not a horrible criminal." She glanced sideways at Umberto. "Did you know that Mortimer Briarwood was caught at diabolerie when he was a student?"

Umberto rummaged through the tales of Mortimer he had heard. He shook his head.

"He was—not like Nicholas." Janet shook her head. "I wonder how that happened."

"Mortimer married Nicholas's mother," said Master Francis, "because he wanted to settle down, and have us *see* he had settled down. It was a wretched marriage."

"A flibbertigibbet like Phillipa Greenleaf and a scholar like Mortimer Briarwood?" said Master Bernard. "Of course it was wretched." He scowled at Janet. "Of course he is like Nicholas—fine young scholars, both of them. Nicholas should take his father's marriage to heart. A wizard ought to marry a woman who can take *some* things seriously. She wanted to drag him from his books."

"Were it not for her, he would have never left them," said Master Francis. "He's a hermit now."

"I dare say Nicholas saw little enough of his father, then," Umberto said, mildly.

"Still too much for his father's liking, apparently—or haven't you heard the tale?" Mistress Elise looked smug.

Who had not? thought Umberto, unless a new tale had sprouted.

She rapped her knuckles on the table. The soup tureen crawled down to her. "You know how Nicholas arrived at the university after the term started—when his father threw him out weeks before!"

Silence spread. Mistress Elise ladled herself some soup and glanced sideways at the masters. "It must have been magic.

Master Mortimer threw him not only out of the house, but half way across the realm. Nick needed the time to return."

Janet looked as if she had been stabbed. The other master wizards babbled. Some pointed out that that need not be true: Nicholas Briarwood had been enchanted into a beast or trapped in a tree. A man proclaimed that to offend his father, Nicholas must have done something dreadful, and a woman answered, bitterly, that all he need have done was inconvenience Mortimer.

Umberto laid a hand on Janet's arm. She let out a ragged breath. "He should have told me. That would be unlawful magic."

Umberto raised an eyebrow. That had not been what he first thought of. "How long ago did Nicholas arrive at the university?"

He drew many glances, if not that silence that Mistress Elise had inspired.

"Why, you met him that day—it was. . . ." Mistress Elise hesitated. "Five weeks ago—more than a month."

"Strange that this tale has just begun now. Nicholas is not spreading the tale, when he could have done so at once." He sat back. "My own reckoning would be that someone has invented a tale."

Mistress Elise looked as discontented as a child whose toy had been stolen, and the murmurs about the room were not entirely satisfied, but Janet looked relieved.

"It would explain the white sickness," said Master Francis.

Mistress Janet's eyes narrowed. "What do you mean by that?"

Several wizards flinched. Master Francis went on, "It's attracted to evil magic. For Mortimer to cast such a spell—and on his own son!"

"If the white sickness were attracted to evil magic," said Mistress Janet, "we would never be rid of it."

Master Francis's mouth twisted. "It is said that it is attracted to *evil magic*—not to folly."

Mistress Janet looked ready to denounce his folly, if not cast an evil spell of her own.

Umberto, his voice measured, said, "Nicholas did not vanish before the white sickness. It had come, it had killed, while his friends will testify to his presence here in the city."

After a pause, Mistress Elise said, sourly, "You weren't here."

"A pity. My aid was needed. But when helping those unfortunates who have lost their bread-winners, I have heard of when it first struck. While rumor varies in much else, it agrees on the night when Nicholas Briarwood was last seen."

Grumbles came, all round. Someone snapped her fingers to summon the bread tray.

Nicholas walked by All Angels', his arms filled with papers. He had not promised to present his plan this time, but his stomach roiled at the thought of waiting.

Mistress Janet Whitehall crossed the path, to plant herself in his way. His mouth went dry. What did she know? Or guess? The scholars talked of how she had found the students who flew their automata. And she did not look happy.

Her voice was flat. "I must speak with you, I will not keep Master Umberto waiting, but I heard a rumor. . . ."

Nicholas stopped, waiting for the blow.

"Any—and all—misuse of magic is my concern. It is the duty of all, but especially of wizards, from the masters to the newest students, to report such misuse to me." Her eyes narrowing, Mistress Janet went on: "Did your father cast you out of the city by magic? Or trap you, or transform you?"

Yes, thought Nick. He cast a dreadful spell. The mere fear of it drove me from the city in terror.

But that would reveal him as like Master Oliver, and Mistress Janet looked ready to burn him at the stake.

Nicholas drew a deep breath. "My father did not cast any spell on me to move me anywhere." After a moment, he added, truthfully enough, "Nor any other spell on me."

Janet nodded.

He hurried by to the door. He had committed himself to lies now. Mistress Janet would not forgive the deception, when he could have told her the truth at once.

He had to free himself from his heart.

Chapter 11—Discoveries

Master Umberto flattened the map on the table. Sunlight, coming through the ivy on the window, splattered over it. He moved the paper from the direct light and frowned.

Nick sat with his hands in his lap. His governess would have approved; he had finally learned to sit still. He fought the urge to blurt out something.

"To search the rooms one by one, and seal off the doorways with your wall spell." Umberto looked up. "You realize that the stone guardian will hide in the largest and most crowded room. It has wits enough for that."

"Giving the guardian free run of the rooms would be worse," said Nick, feeling glib. "We could scare it into the smaller ones, by starting with the larger." He leaned forward to trace the path with his finger.

"That would be better." Master Umberto sat back. "And then?"

"Break it down to sand," Nick said. "I know a mending spell that works on stone; I tested it. Then I reversed it."

"I know a similar spell, if not the identical one."

Nick licked his lips. So much for the simple issues, he thought. "All the books I read about the stone guardian—"

A breeze outside sent drops of sunlight dancing over his papers. He wondered if the question would be taken as accusation. He could not afford to be questioned about diabolerie.

He forced his breath out. He had taken a silly fright at Mistress Janet's questions about his father, and Master Umberto said nothing, waiting patiently for him.

"They agreed," Nick said. "The most dangerous—the best—stone guardians are made by diabolerie. How do we know that Mistress Martha did not use diabolerie to make her stone guardian?" He drew a deep breath and reminded himself that Master Umberto's expression was always unreadable. "Mistress Janet found a master practicing diabolerie, but no one had found out for years before."

"They searched her quarters," said Master Umberto. His gaze was steady on Nick's face, and Nick wondered what he read there. "If there had been any work on diabolerie, they would have found them. Since they are so easily found, a diabolist would have at least one."

Nick bobbed his head. Mortimer, even, had had his stack of papers. At least, said a fugitive thought, their searching for diabolerie can not find you.

"It was well-thought of. Such questions must be raised." Umberto laid his hand to the map. "Still, you would be ill-advised to speak freely of it. Malicious rumors spring from less." He folded the map back up. "We must bring your plan to fruition. Tomorrow, I think."

The sunlight in Mistress Janet's chambers was golden with afternoon, and dust motes drifted through the beams.

Fliss looked at her notes; these would keep her busy. She started to rise.

"A moment, Felicity." Mistress Janet sat back but looked more uneasy than Fliss had ever seen before—and younger. "Not about your studies."

Fliss met her gaze.

"You know Nicholas Briarwood?" At Fliss's nod, she said, "Has he told you anything about why he left during the white sickness, and did not return?"

"He did not take the sickness." Fliss groped for words. "He was astounded to see that my hair—" She gestured up. "But he told me only that he fled his father, and was too frightened to return."

Mistress Janet drew a deep breath, as if startled by something she had said.

"I do not believe the rumors," Fliss said, hastily.

"I asked him," said Mistress Janet. "He denied that his father had cast a spell on him, but he has more of his father about him than his eyes. He kept *some* secret."

"Perhaps he doesn't want to defame his father," said Fliss.

Mistress Janet scowled.

Fliss considered. She could not say whether Nick might keep his tongue about his father's faults—though he usually held his tongue about anything. She felt quite certain that he would not like their talking about him.

"I should have demanded why," said Mistress Janet. "I may yet, if I can surprise him. If he *feared* his father, perhaps the spell was not cast *on* him."

"Nick!" Matthew said. "I asked for the bread twice."

Nick blinked, and passed the bread.

"Still figuring out that stone guardian." Jack grinned.

"I showed Master Umberto my plan today," said Nick. "We will hunt the stone guardian tomorrow."

Comments and congratulations flew, with sardonic comments that it was odd that Master Umberto demanded no changes. "That would put me in a study for sure!" one called.

Nick ate his soup.

"Students," said Master Humphrey severely. The scholars settled.

Jack leaned over. "Be too busy tonight to show us that spell? The color one?"

Nick swallowed. "I would be glad of the distraction."

Jack looked pleased, and surprised.

"Does it work on light spells, too?" Matthew said.

Someone is learning from Mistress Janet's lectures, Nick thought. "I never tried it."

"We can try it tonight," Jack said, when Nick's mouth was full and he could not answer.

Matthew's eyebrows went up. "Learn the spell, and then to compound it? If it is as easy as Nick says, and you cast it with Leonore's candle—that would still be more than a work of an evening."

Jack started to object. Nick put down his spoon with a click. "Start with the spell. Then we can see how far we get."

When he reached the kitchen, Jack and Matthew already sat before the fire. Their tutors ought to give them more work, thought Nick. He dropped in a chair.

"What's the spell called?" said Matthew.

Nick blinked. He learned it so long ago, and no one asked—though he would hardly have expected his old friends to ask? He dredged up his memory. "Rainbow fires, I believe."

"Really?" said Jack.

"No," said Nick. "The most common name I heard was 'what Nick did with the fire'." From their wry smiles, he had managed to put the condescending inflection in his voice. "Or some such—but I didn't devise it."

Matthew laughed. Nick leaned forward and cast the spell. The fire turned rose red, from the tips of the flames, surging down to the logs.

Jack let out his breath, long and slow. "Show us that again."

Nick dismissed the spell and, by the orange light, went through it, gesture by gesture, word by word.

An hour later, the fire blazed; red, blue, green, violet. Jack, with a grin, turned it into a dark hue—indigo or green or blue—hard to tell, so dark the shade was.

Nick snorted. "Someone will break his neck on the stairs." With a gesture, he turned it white. For a moment, he wondered if the white fire was quite as bright as the natural hue. Then he yawned. He could ponder the matter tomorrow—or in a week or two. "Compound it without me, if you want to try. I have to sleep tonight."

"Luck," said Jack.

"God bless you," said Matthew.

Nick nodded to them both, but could not smile. Teaching the spell had distracted him from tomorrow, but no more.

In the dawn, gray sunlight slanted on the fresh leaves of the maples. Nick walked down the path to All Angels'. Half a dozen stone angels, by as many artists, looked upon the path and the handful of students and masters on it. The stony expressions ranged from benevolence to insipidity. Nick stopped under them. St. Michael, Archangel, defend us in battle, he prayed silently, be our protection. . . .

"Nicholas," said Master Umberto behind him. "Are you prepared to begin?"

"In a moment." Nick closed his eyes. Be our protection against the snares of the devil. May the Lord rebuke him, we humbly pray, and do you, O Prince of the Heavenly Host, thrust into hell Satan and all the evil spirits that wander the world seeking the ruin of souls.

He opened his eyes.

Master Umberto stood beside him. At his glance, he nodded and walked into the shadow of All Angels', where he opened the side door. Nick followed him down the stairs, to a room where sunlight cast a white square on the dusty floor. Shadows stood behind, their shapes indistinct.

Master Umberto cast the light spell. Silvery light flooded the boxes and cast black shadows with edges like knives'. Nick let the door shut.

"Cast your own light spell, Nicholas. Watch the shadows."

The shadows jumped and shifted under a second globe. Nick surveyed the room for motion, but the light settled, and the shadows fell in place. Nothing else moved: neither the crates nor the discarded enchantments.

"Seal the door," said Master Umberto, "and we will search."

Dust lay, not evenly but thickly, on every box and inch of bare floor. Their light spells followed them, staying only a small distance from their casters, but shadows started with every motion. Nick whipped his head around to stare several times, certain he had seen the stone guardian. Each time, a closer look showed the enchanted thing responsible.

Master Umberto identified some of the more curious contraptions: a magical clock; the bat-winged one, a machine for flight; a grumpy face in bronze, no bigger than Nick's hand, a doorknocker that would ask who the visitor was and admit only the desired ones.

"What's that one doing down here?" Nick said.

"It does not work properly," Master Umberto said. "The wizard never could give it enough intelligence, and it frightened off visitors at that."

"My father would have appreciated it."

Master Umberto glanced at him, but—his father's character was well-known. Nick searched on.

They reached the other door, and the conclusion that the stone guardian had not hidden in the room.

Nick looked back, over the vast store. "Do they stow every failure here?"

"Most, I think." Master Umberto opened the door, on a room with a handful of barrels and four doors.

Nick looked at the shifting shadows. "I hope there aren't rats down here." He sealed off the door they had come through: the stone guardian could slither through these shadows.

This search passed more quickly.

Nick stood in the empty room's center to pick a door. The rooms behind were, from the map, the same size.

"Seal them off while we search the next." His voice echoed strangely. "That way, the guardian can't sneak between them."

A minute later, Nick chose the rightmost room, and they entered it. From across the room, three windows filled it with vague gray light that shone over a few piles of boxes. Cobwebs hung from every rafter like veils, but the dust covering the floor had been stirred, and the worst about the boxes. Nick forced his breath in and out. He could not see any clear footprints.

Master Umberto gestured at Nick's light spell and quenched his own. Nick did the same. The light decreased only a little; they could hope that the stone guardian had not noticed them. He thought how his heart ought to pound.

They crept toward the stone guardian's lair, ducking under cobwebs and getting their noses tickled by the dust. Beneath one window, a ramshackle pile of metal stood. Nick frowned. It looked like none of the other contraptions—and there was no reason for it to be here.

A grumble came from behind the pile. A low, gray creature edged out. Its head bent at a right angle over its legs, and its long tail jutted out behind it, as it sniffed at the metal. One claw adjusted a piece. Nick fought to keep from gasping: the guardian had built the thing. His thoughts flew. None of the stories even of the diabolical ones had described any as *that* clever.

The guardian jerked its head around, as if it had heard or smelled something. Its mouth gaped, showing fangs, and it sprang across the room. Master Umberto started the breaking spell, but the guardian pounced, gashing his arm and breaking his spell. Blood splattered the dust.

It jolted Nick into action. Corner it with the wall spell, he thought in panic—and then, corner Master Umberto with it? I have to get it away.

The guardian, its mouth and claws red, gathered itself and turned to Master Umberto again. Nick gabbled the light spell and threw the Lenore's candle into the guardian's goggling eyes. It whipped around, growling and shaking its head, trying to throw off the light. Master Umberto hurried back, his hand going to his injured arm.

The guardian leapt from the light and snarled. Nick threw up the wall of will with only a moment to spare. The guardian flattened itself against the invisible wall, and he grunted from the force of the blow. It gathered for another attack. Nick bit his lip; throwing the spell from wall to wall had blocked off the guardian, but trapped him in the room.

The guardian threw itself against the wall. He felt as if a boulder had struck him. Breathing hard, Nick braced himself. Master Umberto had to be doing something.

The guardian glared at him. Glad of the respite, knowing it would not last long, Nick fought to regain his breath. The guardian stalked along the wall, testing it here and there. He had not planned for this, Nick thought forlornly. He could not break the guardian and subdue it at once.

Master Umberto's voice rumbled in his ear. "Stand still, Nicholas." An arm passed around his waist and yanked him back. He did not feel the wall; his vision went black, his breath caught in his throat, and a moment later, in the next room, he staggered from the wall by the light of Master Umberto's spell.

Master Umberto's mouth set in an inflexible line, and he gave Nick only a moment to regain his balance. "You must trap the creature in that room. Then, you must hold it in while I get help. Mistress Martha lied. This guardian is not within a student's powers to destroy."

Frightened, Nick nodded. If the creature escaped—if it mauled him and he lived—

Master Umberto laid a hand to his shoulder. "It will be difficult. I would not put even holding it back to a student, but I had not the sense to master the wall spell as well."

"There's only two doors," Nick said, hoarsely, tentatively. The first door stood ahead of him, and quickly, he cast the wall spell.

Master Umberto said, "Are you sure you can hold these walls?"

"They are only difficult if something pushes against it." Nick hurried to the other door, where he could see out, and see both doors. "It can only try to break through one at a time."

A gray head looked at him from the other doorway. So quickly he almost jumbled the spell, Nick walled the stone guardian within. Its maw gaped, and it threw itself with bruising force against the spell. Even after a frenzied minute, when it retreated from its attack, his ribs ached as if it had struck him indeed.

Master Umberto looked at him. Nick could almost feel how pale his face was, but the guardian was inside. "I'm fine. I can hold it—if you hurry."

Master Umberto said, "Nicholas, the quickest way from here lies through one of your spells."

The guardian snarled and lunged. Nick held up a hand. Master Umberto fell silent. The guardian fought, and fought, against the wall. Then it stopped to glare at Nick. He spared the attention to drop the other spells and gestured to Master Umberto. He heard the wizard's leaving as the swish of his robe, and footsteps on stone. He had no time to watch; the guardian hurled itself against the wall again.

Minutes later, the guardian ran its claws over the wall. Sweating, Nick wondered how much time Master Umberto needed. This early in the morning, the master wizards would be scattered about the university. Some would not even have arrived. And Master Umberto would have to convince them of the need, that he was not started by a shadow.

The guardian shoved again. Nick drew a deep breath and felt strangely aware that his heart was not beating like a drum.

"Nick!" Fliss's voice echoed from the open door behind him. He blinked. The guardian leapt to the attack again, and he turned his attention to keeping it in. Fliss's footsteps hesitated, then rushed. She glanced in the room and threw up a second wall, over his. He felt the relief in an instant. It was not gone, but Fliss took half the burden.

He drew a deep breath. "What are you doing here, Fliss?"

"Master Umberto found me. Mistress Janet had told him of the wall of will." The guardian whirled indignantly, its tail thwacking the walls with jolting strength. "He warned me about attacking it before. . . . where's it going?"

"There's another door. I put up a wall there, too." Nick walked closer. The stone guardian stalked off, raising a cloud of dust, but it was not going to the other door. His breath hissed between his teeth. "The contraption. The stone guardian built—something of its own."

Fliss gave a startled cry. "How did it manage that?" He looked at her. What a question to ask *now*. She looked away and drew a deep breath. "Very well—it managed it. What can it—the contraption—do?"

"We don't know. The guardian was still working."

"Can you wall off the contraption from here?"

He had not realized he was that tired, not to be thinking straight. Nick peered through the dusty air and cast the spell. It felt as if it took, and then the guardian pounded on it. He gasped, but a moment later, with a scream of rage, the stone guardian charged back. It hurled itself against the walls. Fliss nearly wilted. It had not felt this strong the last time. He said so, between strained teeth.

"Then," said Fliss, cutting out each word, "we must be threatening it." Her bone-white face set in determined lines.

Minutes later, a querulous voice spoke behind them. "Don't hurry me, Francis. These old bones can not move that fast." Fliss started, her wall eased, and Nick gasped with the sudden weight of the stone guardian. She threw her strength back into it. They did not turn as the master wizards entered the room.

"What the devil. . . ." gasped Francis. "Bernard, did Umberto tell you of such a thing?"

Nick wished the master wizard would wonder later, but he had no breath to say it.

Bernard stomped his staff on the ground and, with a firm though thin voice, began a spell of dissolution. Chips flaked off the guardian's nose. Warily, it pulled back, eyeing the master. Nick braced himself for the moment when it realized, but after a moment, Francis joined in, and its legs collapsed. Footsteps resounded, and the guardian crumbled. Minutes later, half dozen master wizards stood near a pile of gray dust.

"Well," said Mistress Elise, "Umberto overreacted. He and Nick could have handled the guardian."

A clamor arose. Nick let the wall drop and looked at the dust. He could not have contained it alone. And Master Umberto was only one man.

The dust moved. Nick's breath caught. A draft might have caused it, but he had felt nothing. The dust shifted again, sharply. A draft could not have caused that. He raised his voice, "It's not dead."

Fliss looked at him with a puzzled expression. Some wizards gave him angry glances. Most did not even look over. Nick drew a deep breath and shouted, "IT'S NOT DEAD!"

Silence fell. Nick drew a dozen baneful glances.

"It was never alive," said Master Francis.

Mistress Elise, her expression furious, looked. Then she screamed, her voice resounding. "Look, look."

The guardian's head rose from the dust. The master wizards stood, or inched away, or turned pale.

Nick felt queasy but threw up three walls to surround it. I will be tired to the bone tonight, he thought.

"That's not possible," gabbled Mistress Elise. "The stone guardian—the spell moves it, it does not restore it."

"Of course not." Master Umberto's voice resounded in the cellar. He and another man moved swiftly through the wizards; he had brought not another master wizard, but a priest. The master wizards fell back from them, muttering. Some looked terrified. The priest began the exorcism, sonorous words ringing over stone. The stone guardian collapsed back into dust.

For a minute, silence reigned in the cellar.

Master Umberto said, "This will be unpleasant. Who declared that Mistress Martha used no diabolerie?"

"Why, Master Umberto," said Master Francis, "you can't mean. . . ."

Babble broke out.

"I doubt it was Mistress Janet," Master Umberto said, his voice too low for anyone but Nick to hear. He turned to Fliss and Nick. "You twain will be needed, to testify."

The priest sniffed. "They will. Unpleasant, indeed—when did you learn such mealy-mouthedness about diabolerie?"

"How dare you accuse Mistress Martha?" said Mistress Elise. "She would never have committed such evil."

Chapter 12—Speech

On the paths about All Angels', students and townsfolk gathered—far more than were usually about at this hour. They stared and whispered. Where they could not be easily overheard, they talked. Several pointed at the priest, but they hung back from the company.

Mistress Janet walked from a doorway toward them; her coppery hair streamed behind her, like a banner. She looked at the wizards with narrowed eyes. "I received the news." She glanced at Mistress Elise, who would not meet her gaze, and to another—Master Lawrence, who also looked away.

In surprised, Nick remembered that Mistress Janet was not that much older than he and Fliss.

"The matter must be brought before the chancellor," said Master Umberto. "Mistress Martha's case must be reconsidered."

Mistress Janet walked alongside Master Umberto. In a low voice, she said, "They said it was diabolerie."

Master Umberto nodded, and her mouth tightened.

The crowd followed the wizards—at a distance, but they whispered, and accumulated. Perhaps he imagined that they looked more at him and Fliss, or perhaps it was only that their black robes stood out among the colorful master wizards; they glanced at the priest, too. Then, the priest was proof that this had dealt with demons. He felt sick.

He thought that he saw Edgar in the crowd, looking sharply at him, but he could not be sure, and the chancellor's office loomed ahead. Moments later, they walked into the hall. The polished floor spread before them and up a flight of stairs to either side. The last master wizard closed the doors behind them, blocking off the crowd.

"There won't be room in his office," Mistress Elise said. "I'll bring him down." She climbed the stairs. The master wizards stood about.

Master Umberto's gaze lingered on Nick and Fliss, before he said, "How long will it be?"

Mistress Janet's nose wrinkled. "Long. Hours."

"We need the students' testimony, but at once?"

"Hardly." Master Bernard sniffed. The other masters looked contemptuous at the thought. Mistress Janet looked thoughtfully at the two of them.

"I apologize," said Master Umberto. "I should have let you twain go at All Angels'. Since you held off the stone guardian for so long, you must be in need of rest."

Master Bernard blinked.

"A well-deserved rest," said Mistress Janet. "The university is in your debt. So are the master wizards."

Fliss turned scarlet. Her head dropped to hide her cheeks, but her black hair no longer swung freely enough to veil her face. Nick felt his own face heat.

Master Francis folded his arms and looked them over. "Servants could show you a back entrance—to avoid the crowd."

Nick and Fliss murmured their thanks and hurried down the hall. Nick felt like a small boy again, running off to the garden, evading his governess. Then, Master Otto's querulous voice sounded on the stairs. Nick ducked into a back hall, holding the door for Fliss, before Master Otto could insist they remain.

"Sir?" said a servant, disapprovingly.

"The master wizards—Master Francis—said you could show us a way out." Fliss glanced over her shoulder. "Avoiding the crowd."

The servant hesitated, bowed, and showed them a door into a walled garden. They went out, and the servant shut the door after them, closing them into the silence. The air had grown warmer since he had awaited Master Umberto outside All Angels'. The garden bloomed with white and purple violets, and lilies of the valley, and they walked slowly among the flowerbeds. He was glad; he did not think he could have endured the crowd, as weary as he was.

Fliss breathed a sigh of relief. "I wonder how long the crowd will linger."

Nick dragged in a deep breath. If Master Umberto had included lessons on how to keep off the curious—"I didn't realize how it would draw one."

Fliss laughed. "No, I believe you didn't." Even with her hair short, she looked lovely; the smile lit up her face. "You thought more of the stone guardian than of the fame of having destroyed it."

Nick felt himself flushing again. He remembered Fliss's disdainful glance at the party, and his face grew even hotter. A thought whispered to him: if the master wizards accepted him, he could live at the university, even become a master himself, without a way to undo the demon's spell.

That thought chilled him. He had been lucky in the basement. Master Umberto might have noticed when dragging him out of the guardian's reach. His heart should have raced.

What would Fliss think, thought Nick, if she knew what the demon did to me? His chest felt as if it held a leaden weight. The master wizards would not take the matter lightly; they had not taken Master Oliver lightly, and did not take Mistress Martha lightly now. And he had already lied to Master Janet.

He pled exhaustion. Fliss was quick with sympathy. "How long were you down there alone?"

His mouth twitched. "Too long," he said—which was true enough, however much he meant to deceive her.

Feeling guilty, he headed through the streets. Once or twice, he heard sharp comments about himself, but he did not care.

At St. Catherine's, half a dozen students talked in the kitchen. When he opened the door, they fell silent. Matthew rose. "Nick? What happened? There are rumors. . . ."

Nick raised a hand. "About what?"

"They're accusing Mistress Martha of diabolerie," said Matthew.

"That's true."

"The stone guardian?" said Jan.

Nick nodded. "I had to stand off the guardian, while Master Umberto got the masters and a priest." Several students looked commiserating. Others flinched. "I'm going to bed."

Master Humphrey's voice echoed down the hallway: "At this hour?"

Nick called back, "I must obey Master Umberto," and took to the stairs.

The three flights had never seemed longer. It was an effort, even, to open and shut the door. He lay down and felt the demon thing still heavy in his chest. His plea had been true, but in bed, he stared at the ceiling. If the stone guardian had savaged him, the master wizards would have treated his injuries and noticed his lack of a heart.

He rolled on his side, laying his cheek to the pillow, and sighed. His eyes closed.

In the tavern's shadow, George looked uneasily about. "You saw it."

In exasperation, Edgar scowled at him. Without a doubt, George had looked for an excuse as soon as he wearied from the task. "You can't believe that."

"The master wizards! If they listen to him, they won't listen to *us*."

"They could have been listening to Fliss—"

"They'll listen to her again, when she talks about Nick. She was always sweet on him. *She* won't believe it."

Edgar reminded himself of the collapse of his snow wall. If Nick had wanted to, he could have shoved the wall to one side. Nick must have meant to humiliate him. And Fliss had not been so sweet on him then!

George seemed not to remember the brazier, but he could be brought into line. "All we need," said Edgar, "is more care. There will be *something* we can use."

"The master wizards don't like tale-bearing," said George, and his voice turned triumphant. "If you lie about a crime— they could throw us out of the university!"

"You wail as if you needed your degree to support yourself," said Edgar. "I thought Fliss was the foundling."

George's lips pulled back from his teeth—as if it had been Edgar and not Nick who had humiliated him before them all. "You're the one who's so *fond* of these studies. *I* am keeping my father from sending me off on a ship to trade."

"I don't need the university to study—"

"You sound like Ni—" George stopped abruptly, his mouth hanging open as he stared at Edgar's face.

Edgar was vaguely aware that his hands had clenched into fists, but he did not care. Nothing, certainly not this fool, would stop him. "If you speak of anything, to anyone, you will regret the day you were born."

He forced his breath out. George was useless. Let him go. He could deal with Nick himself. He could have dealt with him by now if he had not let George distract him.

"Ho! What are you two doing down there?" Stephan waved.

Edgar waved back. One advantage, he would not be caught sneaking about, trying to meet with George.

Master Umberto's room was empty. Nick glanced at the clock and sat, glad of the respite. The other students at St. Catherine's had exclaimed over the stone guardian until they turned him scarlet, but their friendliness would make keeping secrets difficult. Searching for a way to undo the demon's spell might prove harder than the spell itself. He scowled. He had to deceive Jack and Matthew anyway—who were already better friends than any young man he had known before.

"Ah, Nicholas."

Nick started, bumping against the chair arms. His gaze skittered over the clock, and he scrambled to his feet.

Master Umberto came into his study. "I must beg your pardon. I did not realize how long the meeting had taken." He sat. "The matter of Mistress Martha will take up time. People might have died if that creature had escaped." His arm shifted.

"The creature attacked you—" Nick remembered the flow of blood, but not how much had flowed.

Master Umberto inclined his head. "And I left you to hold it within the room while I healed myself. I would have been of no aid to you had I lost consciousness." He shifted back his sleeve. The scars were stark on his skin. "It persuaded the most obstinate masters."

Nick glanced away. Master Umberto pulled down his sleeve.

"There must be a trial, and I must help. On the other hand, you have shown yourself to be an excellent student even with little guidance. Even without full knowledge, your plan worked almost as you intended. I blame myself only for not mastering the wall of will; then I could have sent you for aid."

Nick imagined trying to persuade the masters that they were needed; his imagination failed.

Umberto put the tips of his fingers together. "There is the guardian's contraption. We have investigated it and know that there is no trap. You could dismantle it, to see if you can identify what it is intended to do."

Nick nodded. Another field of study, but this one had nothing that could help him with his heart. He could not tell Umberto that.

"You have no need for haste. Your studies have been excellent—and holding off the stone guardian was taxing enough for you."

Nick nodded again.

Master Umberto hesitated. "Also, when our investigations are complete, I would like to learn this wall of will. On other occasions, it might prove useful, if learned before the need."

"Of course," said Nick. He remembered the golden spell the demon had entrapped his heart with. His heart ought to be beating faster. "I found the spell you used to get me out of the room fascinating."

"It is not easy, but if your studies progress well, I may instruct you in it—next year. Or even by wintertime."

Nick smiled. One needed spell was at least in sight.

"You need more work on compounding spells," Master Umberto said. "I will assign you some work there—a theoretical problem, I think."

Sunlight shone over the street and vendors, but Lucia, seeing Fliss, had to stop and gossip.

"I can not believe it!" She laid her hand over her heart. "Our Nick? A pleasant fellow, a good hand with tricks, he showed up George properly—but Nick stood off a monster that the master wizards fear?"

Fliss smiled thinly. She had to study, and neither the weather nor the prospect of illness would distract Lucia now. Lucia's maid shifted her basket, and Fliss wondered how much Lucia had already bought.

"I knew that he wanted to be a monster-slayer, when he was young, but. . . ." Lucia shook her head. "So many children believe in fairy tales, don't they?"

"You needn't wonder, you know," said Fliss. "Lady Alicia invited him to dinner tomorrow night. You can come, too."

Lucia's tongue touched her lips. "He would be uncomfortable, wouldn't he? After all, he is used to being one of us, which can hardly be when he's so poor. . . cut off by his father without a coin! Lady Alicia is different, she is often generous with the poor—he's living in a college, don't you know?"

The sky to the west had grown yellowish, but the day was still bright. Nick walked along the street, where householders and their servants still bustled. Even out of his scholar's robe, he looked like neither.

A little maidservant, rushing with her basket, nearly collided with him, gave him an odd glance, and hurried off even faster. Nick smiled wryly and turned a corner.

Mortimer stood on the opposite side, ready to cross. Their gazes met. Nick's mouth tightened, but he held his father's gaze steadily.

Mortimer's mouth twisted as he turned away. Briefly, Nick's eyes closed. He did not care. He did not care what he had done, and he lived on in prosperity and not in fear of discovery.

Nick drew a deep breath. When he opened his eyes, Mortimer was gone. He walked down the street more quickly.

Mortimer walked into his study, gestured to light the lamp, and poured himself a glass of wine. He glared at the books. Nothing, not in all these months, to replace the work that Nicholas had so blithely ruined.

And now he had to endure torrents of praise for Nicholas's cleverness. He could escape if it were only Francis, but every wizard chattered of his *promising* son.

Mortimer drank. He had been right, the night Nicholas foiled his spell. The boy was too clever by a half. The ruin Nicholas had made of his spell could not have been chance.

He looked into the cup, saw his own face looking redly back. Now Nicholas won himself praise and acclaim, and a place in the bosom of the university, and no one guessed what he carried in place of his heart. He drank again. This was what came of giving the brat the run of his library.

He lowered the cup. His eyes narrowed. Nicholas was clever to have found a way to subvert his spell in the library. He put down his wine. Nicholas could not have found it elsewhere; the library at the university had no such lore, and neither did the booksellers. It had to be here, in this room, among the fruit of thirty years' collecting.

"What he can find, I can find. He is not *that* clever."

Mortimer slowly recalled a spell and raised his hand to cast it. All about the room, the books that Nick had touched glowed pale violet. Mortimer got to his feet to haul them down. There were hundreds, but one held the knowledge he looked for.

He flipped through the first. The pages glowed, here and there. His eyes narrowed. He pulled down another. This one gleamed only on the outside; the pages remained dark.

Better yet, thought Mortimer. He went to select the tomes.

Light, in little round drops, skittered over the pages as the breeze stirred the leaves, outside.

Umberto looked up from his notes and out the window. The only trees visible grew in the square—perfectly ordinary trees. The university buildings blocked out any further view. Perhaps he should not have applied for a place in the university. He had come to learn of the Wizards' Wood. He had barely touched the literature they had on it, and not enough that he would venture into the deep woods.

I ought to assign my students work on it, and then I would have an excuse. The thought lightened his mood. Students—particularly Nick—were the better part of the university duties, and they would profit from the study. He inspected his notes. Cecelia and Matthew, perhaps, could look at the woods, but Nick had to learn how to compound spells.

A shout made him stop and turn. Jack and Matthew hurried up, and Nick waited, uncomfortably. To be in this street, they had to have been delivering their copy work for the coins it would bring them. He, also, had been here for money. Master Benedict had handed it over.

Both Jack and Matthew smiled. "It's quicker this way," said Jack, gesturing at an alley.

Nick followed them, saying, "I thought. . . ." The stone wall he had remembered was there, cutting through the hillside.

Lightly, Jack gestured; then he climbed, on nothing, to the top. Nick watched. Matthew scrambled up. His hands and feet caught—something. Shaking his head, Nick strode forward and tested it. The stone was far rougher than it should have been; tiny cracks served as hand and foot holds. It felt uncanny, but he reached the alley on the other side.

"This'll take us past St. Ursula's," said Jack, leading on. "Did you get Mistress Elise's lecture?"

"In parts," said Nick.

Jack lowered his voice. "All the older students say she must be *furious* about something. The way she's lecturing, so fast."

"We have only to survive," said Nick. "We can puzzle out what she means from the notes."

"It could be worse," said Matthew, but chanting from ahead made him scowl. Nick followed his gaze. Gray-clad penitents, with candles and psalms. This might prove the longer way.

"It's not Lent," said Nick.

"It's not Eastertide, either," said Matthew. "The bishop forbade such displays during Eastertide."

Nick closed his eyes and shook his head. "But Pentecost was yesterday."

"You're lucky," said Jack. "You don't know what you missed. During Lent, they went all over the city. Some even came down the university paths, not just the outer buildings. Some mornings, getting to lecture—" He shook his head.

"White sickness," said Matthew. He pointed out a side street where they could escape the procession. "Rumors that it's caused by fell magic."

Nick snorted. "Everyone knows that a diabolist created it. A man who is *long dead*."

"Drawn by fell magic," said Matthew.

"There were all the stray automata," said Jack. "Not counting Mistress Martha's. And—other—rumors—"

Both Matthew and Jack looked at him. Both looked embarrassed enough to not ask the question.

"My father cast no spell on me at all, that night," said Nick.

Jack lifted an eyebrow, but neither of them said anything, making Nick fell all the guiltier. It was true, but still, he meant to deceive them.

They walked along. The street was empty, but the penitents paralleled them; their chant reached over the walls, lamenting the sins of the city.

The sunlight shone in the window, over the musty chamber.

"He's a clever fellow," Luke said, perched on the desk. He eyed Randall carefully. More would be better than fewer, *if* they could be trusted.

"I told you what he was like," Randall said.

Luke shrugged. "I hadn't seen it. That blue fire—that was clever."

"He's a prig," said Randall, mulishly.

"A prig wouldn't have burned George," said Luke. "Or shown up Edgar."

Randall leaned back in the stuffed chair. "And you think he would help?"

Luke's mouth twitched. Why do you think I mentioned him, if I do not think he would?

"He hunted down a stone guardian," said Randall. "They say he kept it prisoner. And he'll testify against Mistress Martha."

"Not like he *chose* it," said Luke. "Master Umberto palmed the job off on Nick. If he has any spirit at all, he must mind being pushed about like that."

Randall looked at the floor. "I haven't spoken to him—not since he came back."

"He must be embarrassed by his poverty," said Luke. "Maybe he'll get over it. We should approach him."

Mistress Janet looked over the lecture hall. Nick wondered if he imagined her picking him out with particular intensity. He glanced at his notes.

"The story is true, but Lord Harold, being blind, did not need to see," Mistress Janet said. "Therefore he cast a simple spell of invisibility on himself.

"Most cases involve those who are not accustomed to blindness. One can cast invisibility as a simple spell, but it renders one's victim blind—and blinding spells are easier. In actual use, invisibility spells are compounded." She glanced at the questioner. "Class dismissed."

Coughs and the rustle of paper rippled across the room. Nick looked at his notes again, considering the problem Umberto had set him.

"Nicholas," Mistress Janet said, appearing beside him. "Did Master Umberto tell you the details about Mistress Martha?"

Nick rose and shook his head.

"You were in more danger from it than anyone else. You are entitled to know." Her mouth set in wry lines as they walked to the door. "They had seized her papers and declared they weren't diabolerie."

"She had hidden the real papers?"

"The papers spoke of 'spirits', and neither Martha nor the wizards who looked at them had the wit to realize what manner." Mistress Janet rolled her eyes toward the ceiling. "I even believe Martha when she says that."

Nick winced. "The devil is a liar."

"And the father of lies," said Janet. They stepped into the sunlight by the door. "At least the students have stopped with automata that they can not master." She stopped. "Umberto said you dealt with the guardian's contraption. He has told us little else."

"He checked that it was not dangerous. I dismantled it." His mouth twisted. "It held a warning spell. If the guardian had completed the thing, it would have warned of our arrival, and let the guardian flee."

Her eyebrows went up. "I am glad you took no longer than you did. Master Umberto's scars are nasty enough, when you surprised it."

Nick nodded. For a moment, he wondered how to say he had to go to the library. A laughing clamor down the street caught his gaze.

"So they did succeed," said Mistress Janet.

Down the street, two—no, three—scholars led a deer not much larger than a dog, its hide leaden gray with silvery spots. They grinned like idiots. The deer mildly paced along, eyeing the buildings.

"A shadow deer," said Mistress Janet. The threesome laughed and answered comments, but never left the deer for a moment. Except one glanced away, and the deer took a hesitant step, into a tree's shade, and then Nick could not see it at all. Exclamations echoed. One scholar frowned and gestured as if beckoning. The shadow deer rose into the sunlight.

"They have a place ready for it—a small garden, heavily enchanted, holding grass and bushes. They'll find it can vanish there, too." Mistress Janet smiled. "Such are the studies that the university offers. You will not even have to reach mastery to engage in such things."

Nick walked toward the library, pondering.

"Hey, Nick," said a voice beside him. Nick turned. Randall grinned at him. Nick smiled, without enthusiasm, but Randall's grin did not falter.

"Luke, this is Nick Briarwood. I told you about him—you met him at the party by the lake."

Luke smiled. "Randall told me about your exploits together."

"How do you do?" said Nick, recalling times he would have preferred to forget.

Randall's grin widened. "I told him about the crows."

Nick winced. He had been uneasy about that one at the time.

"We're going to pull one on the university," whispered Randall. "Wake these sleepy old masters up."

"Give them all a surprise in the square," Luke said.

"How are you going to do that?" Nick heard the harsh note in his voice when it was too late to take it out. He glanced between them and was not certain that he would have wished to speak more gently.

"Oh, magic," said Randall. "We could use a third to help us get them all." He clapped his hand to Nick's shoulder. "We'll tell you all about it when you join us."

"Why do you want me?" said Nick.

"I told him how faithful you were, when we were children," said Randall.

"We heard about the fuss with Mistress Martha," said Luke. "It impressed us."

Nick glanced between them again. "You think you will need help in stopping whatever you're going to do?"

"When did we ever have to *stop* these things?" Randall grinned. "You can join us—"

Nick pulled away from Randall's hand. Randall blinked.

"I don't think I will."

"Well." Randall pulled back. "Well, if you're such a coward."

Luke's smile was sardonic.

"I have to study," said Nick.

The smile only grew the more sardonic. Nick fled.

Chapter 13—Practice

In the kitchen, firelight laid orange light and black shadow over the young men's faces.

"I figured it out," said Jack. "If spells *can* be compounded, one of us can cast the first spell, and another can cast the second. Then we will know that the spells *can* go together."

"It's not compounding them," Matthew said.

Nick sat with one leg pulled up in the chair, one arm slung over the back of it, and listened.

"It shows that they can be," said Jack. "That's not always possible." He looked over his shoulder. "Right, Nick?"

"Right," said Nick. "We would never try to compound my color spell with a healing spell."

In the silence, the fire crackled.

"If you wanted to turn somebody purple?" said Matthew.

Jack laughed.

"*Why* would anyone want to turn anyone *purple*?" said Nick, loftily. "You would do it to turn someone *orange*."

Jack's laughter echoed back from the stairway. He cast the spell, and a Lenore's candle hung in the air before him.

Nick drew a deep breath and cast his spell. The light shifted to purple, and mingling strangely with the firelight.

"All right," said Jack. He filled the room with Lenore's candles. As quickly as he could, Nick colored them until the room glowed like a rainbow.

Matthew, his face discolored, smiled. "Try this—three spells." He lifted a hand and muttered. Lights flitted about like fireflies.

A furious voice broke in from the doorway. "And what are you fools up to?"

Master Humphrey glared at them all. Matthew dropped his spell, and the lights hung in midair.

Jack hooked his thumbs into his belt. "Studying, Master Humphrey." When that drew no reaction but a flare of nostrils, he added, "Ensuring that we do not waste our benefactor's generosity by putting our scholarships and our places in the college to good use."

With a snort, the housemaster left. Nick could not match Matthew and Jack's grins.

Early morning light lay gray about the library's shelves. Nick suppressed a yawn. Students who supplied the taverns with custom had sung half the night in the university paths, and he still had to study. He ran a finger down a shelf, over the titles, and spotted one: *Concerning Demons.*

For a long minute, he looked at the book.

That Sunday's sermon had dwelled on the evil of summoning succubae. Even with the example of Mistress Martha, the priest had not thought of there being worse in the city.

He pulled the book out and studied the cover without opening it.

"Nicholas! What studies brought you to these books?"

Nick recognized the voice: Mistress Janet. He felt like ice. She would see the book in a moment. If he were to hide it, she would see that. He turned to face her, trying to think. He could only conclude that his heart ought to be pounding.

In the silence, Mistress Janet's eyebrows went up. "*I* was looking for that book."

He handed it over with a half bow. Her hands closed on it, but she did not look away.

"After the stone guardian proved to be diabolic, I was curious." Nick spread his hand before he could claim more—as if he had not already deceived her.

Without lying. He wondered if he should lie before he fooled himself into thinking that omitting the truth was right in itself.

Mistress Janet glanced at the book and back at him. "If you still wish to appease your curiosity, I will give you it when I am done. It *is* about how to break demoniac spells, and your curiosity has yet to interfere with your studies."

The demon thing felt bitter in his chest. If Mistress Janet's interest in his studies was more than the polite comments other masters had made, he could hardly repulse her; that would attract her attention .

Few masters had arrived; luncheon was just beginning. Umberto peeled an orange—from the orangery, not imported. He thought the color somewhat off, but the spells might be interesting.

"You would think," said Janet, "that when the spells are commonly known, the students would have the wit to learn them." She leaned back against her chair. "Why deal with a devil—even an imp—to lock your box when you could lock it? Then you could unlock it yourself. I spent two days unraveling it."

Umberto smiled. Clear enough how Janet had found this one. "I dare say that one had not sold his soul. The demon gave him a poor spell for that reason—to induce him to."

"Well," said Master Otto, "if it was not to gain some dreadful wicked power, I do not see why you harp on it. Do you, Master Umberto? Hasty, perhaps, but wicked. . . ."

"Wicked?" Mistress Janet spat out the word. "Does it matter why? The devil hands out the powers with a generous hand. Considering their ultimate source, they are poison."

Umberto's eyebrows went up. "Their ultimate source? Mistress Janet, their ultimate source, like a miracle's, like those we derive from our natural philosophy, is God."

She looked at him with bitter eyes.

"The devil is also a creature. His powers are not his, but derivative. Though they are tainted by passing through his hands, it is certainly false to think that anything's ultimate source is the devil."

For a moment, Janet looked ready to claw his eyes out. Then she, reluctantly, sat back.

Master Otto preened. "I did not realize what a master philosopher you were, Master Umberto." He leaned over and whispered loudly. "She is often so. . . ."

"Young?" said Umberto. "Prudence is the province of the old, those whose judgment, 'by reason of use, has learned to tell good from evil.'" He shrugged. "*She* is learning by using her judgment."

Master Otto's mouth tightened.

The river lapped against the bank, and wavelets threw rippling lights against the trees, on their shadowed trucks and the undersides of leaves. Fliss tilted her head to one side, thinking. She did not want to look like a fool before Nick.

"Actually," she said, "these spells compound more easily than you might think. The principles are not that antithetical. The healing spell works by drawing like things together." She pointed her index fingers into the air and drew her hands together, so they lay side by side. "The cleansing spell works by removing unlike things." She popped her fingers apart. "The basic principle is to restore the soundness to what—and only what—the body naturally is."

Nick nodded but scowled.

"It does not only apply to cuts and bruises," said Fliss. "We can endear ourselves to the sisters by cleaning and mending the children's clothing. Not worn clothing, any more than healing spells restore youth—"

"They'll let you?"

"That's where I practiced," Fliss said. "Doing it by hand is easier, but this way, they do not have to do it."

They came out into the broader sunlight of a street, and Fliss glanced sideways at Nick. A handsome devil, she thought, but his face was still solemn. She looked away. She had not thought him so fond of his father, to be distressed this long.

In the trees ahead of them, the orphanage appeared. Fliss led the way around, to the back entrance. At any rate, his studiousness was charming. They reached the sewing room, by the back door.

"Felicity," said the sister there.

"Sister Audrey. Nicholas Briarwood and I have come to impose on your kindness; we would like to use the children's torn and dirty clothing to practice our spells on."

Sister Audrey's eyebrows went up. "It must be both?"

"Ah, yes."

"How you impose on our kindness, Felicity!" She gestured them to a basket.

Fliss set to with a will, tossing aside the merely dirty beneath Sister Aubrey's curious eye. She pulled out a shirt with a tear the length of it, and mud all over, raised an eyebrow, and tossed it to the other pile. Nick might not master the spell that well today, but she would learn how quickly he learned today.

Sister Aubrey returned to her sewing. Nick shifted his weight. A minute later, having sorted out half a dozen things, Fliss fetched them to the door and sat on the flagstones. They were dusty from many feet, but she and Nick needed the sunlight. She began to demonstrate the spell.

Nick sat, listened, and tried. His first two ventures either repaired or cleaned, with only the faintest traces of the other. He reached for another cloth. Fliss put her hands about her bent knee and watched. Less flamboyant than the spells cast every day at the university but far more practical.

He dropped yet another piece. The dust marked it at once. A yellow butterfly alighted on it for a moment, and fluttered off. Nick grimaced and reached for the next.

"You are quite certain you are doing it right?"

Nick blinked. "I—I am too used to working from a book, with no one to ask."

Fliss lifted both eyebrows. To be sure, she would not ask Mortimer Briarwood for help, but—"I shouldn't've teased you. You are doing well."

Nick cast the spell on the last cloth but one, and it lay clean and whole beneath his hand.

"Ah, you've got it," Fliss said. "See. . . ." She laid a hand to his arm.

Nick flinched.

Fliss stared, lowering her hand. His shoulders hunched, Nick looked at the shirt. Her breath came out slowly. From the rigidity with which he sat, he would say nothing.

She could not keep her voice from sounding high and breathless. "You see, the threads are both clean and intact. This does not work for worn threads." Her voice prattled on while formless thoughts of what Mortimer could do shifted through her mind, refusing to take shape enough to accuse Mortimer of anything.

"I think you mastered it well enough to use on wounds." She laid a hand, flat, on the last piece. "Notice that it works because the cloth is flat, and the dirt came up out." She pulled her hand away. "Never try it on dirt when the wound has scabbed over. It will be –- messy."

Nick nodded. Fliss's gaze fell to his arm. What had happened that night, to make him flinch at a touch? He had never been a chatterbox, but he would not meet her gaze.

Nick looked over his notes on coloring the Lenore's candle again. He had mastered Fliss's spell. There was no reason for this to evade him.

He drummed on the table with his fingers. No reason at all.

The sky was flamboyant in the west, and just growing darker in the east. Jack and Matthew had gone to deliver enchantments to a shopkeeper, but they ought to be returning by now.

He pushed back his chair. The other students in the room barely twitched. Moments later, Nick stood outside St. Catherine's, in the cooling air. Across the way, on the steps of St. Agnes, students talked and worked spells. An ivy vine grew up, supported on a trellis of thin air, and sported colorful if tiny birds, trilling away—for a minute.

Nick walked by. Down one street, he saw light cast by a spell.

"You're trying to make trouble," said a voice. Nick stopped in his tracks. That voice he recognized. He walked more quickly.

"I beg your pardon," said Jack, but Edgar would never take such an apology. Nick turned the corner. Edgar, his face flushed, faced Jack and Matthew. Edgar stepped closer to Jack, looming in his face. His hands clenched into fists as Jack pulled back.

Drunk, thought Nick. Again. He stepped into the street and threw an arm about Edgar's shoulders. "Fancy meeting you here!"

Edgar paused for a long moment. If he remembers the flying student, thought Nick, I have done Matthew and Jack no favor. Edgar turned to face him.

Nick smiled. "I thought you were studying."

"Going to the Blue Fish. . . ."

"Why, then—" Nick stepped back. "We won't keep you. Much too dreary here."

Edgar pondered a moment, and Nick held his breath. Then he wandered off.

"Hope he doesn't end up in the harbor," Nick said.

"You know him?" Jack said.

"Used to." After a silent moment, he said, "He does not wish to embarrass me with reminders of my current poverty."

Jack snorted.

Matthew said, "There are dozens of students in the taverns, but some of the drunks are looking for trouble."

Nick tried to remember the excuse. "Some feast day the students claim to celebrate—at least the richer sort."

Both men snorted. "So that's the Feast of St. Folly," said Jack.

Nick hooked his hands on his belt. "I came to find if you had any more luck with the compounding than I have had."

"For that," said Matthew, "we need to know how much have you had."

"Little," Nick said. Walking back, they talked of spells. Jack suggested that Nick should teach them the spell Fliss had taught him when the sound of drunken singing came down the street.

Nick said, "That comes from the colleges,"

They walked in wary silence, but they could hardly avoid the revelers. Students could not enter St. Catherine's through a back door.

They turned the corner and could see St. Agnes's and St. Catherine's. Women from St. Agnes stood on its steps. A couple dozen students stood about them—all men. Three carried jugs. One pressed the drink on the nearest woman, and his haranguing voice crossed the path.

"Know any of them?" Jack said, with a touch of disdain.

"I do not think so," said Nick coldly.

Matthew glanced about. "They are probably, some of them, not first-year students—we should get a master wizard—"

"How?" said Nick.

Matthew grimaced.

"Though—we might get Master Humphrey—or better, St. Agnes's housemistress," Nick said. "If we drop the Lenore's candle before it draws attention. . . ."

It vanished on the word, but a voice came across the paths: "Hey, you!"

Nick almost hoped that the drunk had not meant him, even when he waved the jug of ale, but then the man, and three others, headed toward them.

"I think," muttered Nick, but he had no time. He cast the wall of will.

The nearest student hit it and bounced back. He rubbed his nose in puzzlement.

"Hey, what you up to?" said another, glowering. "That's no way to treat friendly folks." He gestured, unsteadily, at the jug. "Offering you our—hospit-ality."

His friends muttered agreement and shoved against the wall. It was not enough to stagger Nick, but he felt it.

"Worked on the guardian, works on them," said Jack.

Matthew looked worried. "Can you move it?"

Nick shook his head. "I doubt I can cast it many more times. It was a rough day." He drew a deep breath and lowered his voice. "They'll get around it in no time. It doesn't spread very far." And if they thought of *spells*, he thought—

"Distract them somehow, then," said Matthew, gloomily.

Nick turned to Jack, with a glance at the men. Too drunk to get around the wall, but he could not hold it forever. His voice low, he said, "Cast Lenore's candles. I will color them, and Matthew will move them about, and we will see how drunk they are. They puzzled Master Humphrey, sober."

A grin spread across Jack's face, and lights sprung up about him. Nick dropped his wall. The foursome pressed on, rich with promises about requiting unfriendliness. Nick cast garish shades of red and orange, blue and green; the lights discolored their own faces and all the things about them.

"This will never work," said Matthew, but he sent the lights streaming toward the drunken students.

The first drunkard gaped. His companions hesitated behind him. He bolted, nearly colliding with his fellows. A second later, as lights flowed toward them, the other three turned so quickly as to stumble, and chased after him.

"That shows them," said Jack.

"There's still the rest," said Matthew.

Ahead, a man grabbed a woman by the wrist. She yanked her arm away, but an ugly mutter ran through the drunken students.

Matthew's eyes narrowed. Lights poured across the grass. Jack conjured new lights, and Nick colored them to add to the stream.

"Diabolerie!" wailed a drunk. Panic sent them staggering down the path. Even the women looked taken aback. Two darted for the door of St. Agnes's, but only one went in; the other one glanced back.

"Humph!" Matthew let the spell drop, and the lights stopped.

The nearest woman took a step forward. The lights colored her face. "What was that spell?" she said eagerly.

"Three spells," Nick said. "We haven't mastered the compounding...."

The housemistress, severe in black, appeared in the doorway of St. Agnes's. "You can't let those young men *into* the college."

"Who said we would, Mistress Thomasina?" called one woman. The others giggled.

Scores of Lenore's candles gleamed whitely over the lawn, and dozens of scholars were intent. One after another blossomed into color. Mostly, Nick noted, at the hands of students who had studied at the university for several years.

Still, he cast a Lenore's candle and, concentrating fiercely, turned it blue. If he had not seen them learn it more quickly than he, he would never have mastered it by now. He shook his head.

"Nick," said Fliss, by his elbow. He blinked, and she said, "I was in the library."

"I hope the drunks did not—"

She snorted. "Masters are in the library. They weren't *that* drunk." Her gaze followed the candles. He explained.

"It would," said Fliss gravely, "be unwise of me to return alone, to Lady Alicia's, at this hour and with them about." He looked sideways at her. "And unkind of me to ask you to leave your studies, so necessary for your scholarship. But I could safely stay here to be taught." She smiled.

He drew her into the company. A few eyebrows went up at her accent, a few more at her name, but soon she practiced as intently as any. When she, smiling, set one candle in the midst of another, washing out the green that Nick had lent it, Jack laughed.

"Serious at her studies," he said to Nick, in a low voice.

"She was a foundling," said Nick. "Her guardian provides for her schooling, but she has as much need for her studies as anyone in the colleges."

Jack watched her for a moment. Fliss turned a candle gold, and he said, "I see."

Nick felt a burst of jealousy that astounded him.

She found them on the steps of the colleges. Students from St. Catherine's and St. Agnes's, and from farther colleges, cast spells all about. Nick Briarwood saw her first, and froze. Students fell silent. Candles stopped careening about. Others lost their color, or even winked out.

Mistress Janet spoke dryly. "I heard tales."

"They were drunk," said one woman quickly.

"The diabolists?"

"No!" and the confused stories broke out. Mistress Janet sighed. Nick sat on the steps of St. Agnes. This would take some time to untangle, she supposed.

"We were practicing the compounding of spells," said another student—Jack, she realized. He wore an expression of studied innocence. About all, students chorused agreements and declarations of guiltlessness.

Nick Briarwood rose to his feet. "We can show you." He smiled. "And then we can plague you for what we are doing wrong, since you are the lecturer on compounding spells." Quickly, he expounded.

"This color spell—"

Nick hesitated. Matthew cast it on a Lenore's candle.

"Jewel-light," said Mistress Janet. "I am surprised that the upper students have learned it, let alone started to teach the first years it."

Nick flushed. The colored lights altered but could not hide the color. "I learned it in my father's library."

Half an hour later, beneath colored Lenore's candles, Mistress Janet strode off. Jewel-like colors stained faces they shone on, but other students smiled at Nick as if they shared a secret, and not one cast a wary glance. Not even at Fliss—Nick smiled himself. Rosy-cheeked and light-headed from the success, the students chattered, but still slowly moved toward their colleges.

Fliss glanced about. "I must get home. Lady Alicia will wonder. . . ." Her black hair had grown long enough to frame her face, but she looked more young than stately.

Nick rose to his feet. "You were right. You shouldn't go alone. The drunks might be trouble, even now." He looked at Jack and Matthew. "Her guardian will not—"

"Guardian?" said Matthew.

"She's a foundling." Nick lowered his voice. "And she is not entitled to an inheritance. She can not offend her guardian and must do well at the university."

"Foundling?" said Matthew.

Jack laughed. "What did you think 'Seaborn' meant?"

"I wondered," said Matthew, "if she were akin to some families back home—at Kingsport."

"No," said Fliss softly. "At least, I would not know, if I were."

A cat skittered across the street. Fliss looked ahead, to the house.

Their Leonore's candles shed nearly the only light in the street, but she could see the lamp, and knew which room it was lit in.

On the doorstep, she hesitated. They had come to escort her, not to visit, but—"Lady Alicia is still up."

Nick glanced at the sky. His mouth twisted. "We have to get to lecture in the morning, so we will see you to the door."

Both Jack and Matthew seemed to have flinched Lady Alicia's title. Fliss nodded, slid up the stairs, and let herself in. The young men set out without a word; they too had stayed up late. She climbed the stairs.

"Dear me," said Lady Alicia. "I did not expect this hour."

Fliss felt the heat rise in her face. "Neither did I. But the— there were students roistering. And Nick was studying. They escorted me here when they were done."

Lady Alicia laid her book aside.

"We lost track of time."

Lady Alicia glanced at the window. "I heard your voices. They left at once?"

"For bed. There are lectures tomorrow."

After a moment, Lady Alicia smiled. "I did not realize the hour myself. I stayed awake to warn you that my nephew Lord Baldwin will visit. He will come with us from the St. John's day festivities."

Fliss flinched away, her arms tightening about her books.

"Just a visit, Felicity. I will at most give a party, and your studies will not be interrupted." Her voice hardened. "If he tries—"

"Disgraceful," said Master Bernard with unusual firmness. "Utterly disgraceful."

Janet snagged some bread and snapped her fingers over the honey. Golden drops rose with wings and six legs and, buzzing faintly, flew to spread itself on the bread. She wondered what master wizard had *bothered* to make that spell last.

She bit into the slice. She did not want to hear more about the lights, least of all more accusations of foul magic. She had spent more time than she had realized with the students, even if it had given her a useful example for her lectures.

"Banning them from each other's colleges *ought* to suffice," said Master Bernard. "So they flirt on the grass. In the public view."

Janet sat back. "They were practicing spells."

"They were *flirting*," said Master Bernard.

Smiles appeared up and down the table, some half-hidden as masters turned their faces away.

Master Bernard glared at them all. "They are *scholars* and should *study*. Look at what happened to Mortimer Briarwood when he married Phillipa Greenleaf."

"He didn't let it interfere with his studies long," said Master Francis. "And Mistress Phillipa managed his money well."

"She meddled long enough," said Master Bernard. "If Nicholas Briarwood wants to avoid his father's folly, he should take care, and so should every scholar."

"Nicholas Briarwood," said Mistress Sybil, "quarreled with his father. Now there is a serious student. Quarreling with a master who can teach him so much."

Master Ivo looked up from his soup. "What would he be willing to teach?"

Well, thought Janet, she knew the truth there. "He learned the jewel-light spell in his father's library."

"Jewel light?" said Ivo. "He knew that?"

"He didn't know Leonore's candle," said Master Bernard. "Or so Master Umberto said."

"He knows it now," said Janet.

From her chamber door, Master Otto said jovially, "So, you have learned that boys will be boys."

Janet looked from her papers. "I what?"

"Why, those students last night, who plagued the university with spells. Sending them after the other students!" Master Otto grinned. "I heard it was diabolerie."

"Taking the word of drunks is foolish," said Janet. "I saw the spells. Two are taught in lecture, and one is not because the students come, knowing it. The fool arsonist could have learned one and spared himself his bargain with an imp."

"Three?"

Janet permitted herself a smile. "They were too drunk to realize the scholars compounded three spells?"

Master Otto gaped like a landed fish.

"It was not even a proper compounding. Three students had each of them cast one spell. They were still testing whether the spells could be compounded, but they learned quickly afterward. They show promise."

Master Otto scuttled away.

Ferns nodded. They turned the forest floor as green as its canopy. Umberto sighed. Into the Wizards' Wood, the place he had ventured so far to see. And now, it impressed him mostly at the place to hide from the university's intrigues, when the St. John's Day festivities already gave him some freedom.

A red bird fluttered by, startlingly bright. He did not know whether he had seen a bird of that breed before. Umberto walked on, the ground sloped upward, and he came to a hilltop. Trees continued for only another stride. A barren valley lay before him, with every tree in it blasted. Only the sturdiest boughs still held to trunks. The ground bore a scraggly scattering of ferns and wildflowers, but the brush was as dead as the trees.

The sun beat down on it, heating the air.

The trees showed no sign of charring. Not a fire, Umberto concluded. He walked into the valley. The dead leaves underfoot were still thick. The lopsided flowers were none of the radiant and enchanted blooms that the books in the library babbled of. He laid a hand on the nearest dead tree. The destruction lay in a circle, a circle too perfect for nature, as if a spell had done it.

"Of course," he whispered. "Master Oliver."

The pale yellow flowers of the nearest plant waved a little in the breeze. It was a feeble and stunted plant, but even all the master wizards would be hard put to undo Master Oliver's destruction. He appraised the distance. The heart had been in the center, and yet Mistress Janet had managed to destroy it, while yet a student. His mouth twitched. She had proved she could do a master's work.

A bird trilled in the trees. Master Umberto shook his head and walked through the valley. The marvelous Wizards' Wood, and the first marvel he found in it was the hand of man.

Trees closed around him again, and the rise of a hill cut off the desolate valley. The air cooled, in the shade. Again ferns flourished underfoot, and a squirrel—an ordinary one, he thought—bolted across the forest floor and up the nearest tree in front of him.

A flash of color drew his gaze. He looked through the ferns. A small red flower grew there. It took him a moment to be sure of it, but it was a violet. A garnet red violet, in the middle of summer, but it could be nothing else.

He remembered half a piece of lore and looked about. Other garnet violets lay here and there, almost in a line. Where the blood of a certain, enchanted deer was shed, he remembered. Once they planted, they would bloom in the proper season, like those he had taken that spring, but here, some rash poacher had tried to claim the wrong deer.

Sunlight pounded on the stone of buildings and walkways.

It was too hot to walk about the university, thought Janet crossly. She stopped under the nearest tree, but even the shadow, splattered with light through the leaves, did not cool the air. The master wizards had taken advantage of the feast; half were in the Wizards' Wood, gathering herbs. Master Umberto had talked of what he hoped to find. Others, she had seen leaving that morning.

"I hope none of them get up to mischief this time," Janet muttered in her general annoyance. But, worse, the other half could not be found either.

She considered her students. If she could find them, neither Yves nor Gilbert had the spellcraft to deal with this. Lady Alicia had taken Felicity with her to a party in the country, and the spell she had mastered with her.

Janet let out a long and exasperated sigh. The perfect spell, which she could have mastered in the time she spent dealing with that arsonist.

She looked about. Nick Briarwood emerged from the library. Her mouth twitched. She knew where Felicity had learned it. Her task was not facing a diabolist with all his powers, but breaking a fool's spells. It would be less dangerous than the stone guardian.

Nick walked on. He would pass her in a moment.

Besides, Janet thought, there was no one else.

"Nicholas."

His gaze flickered over to the shadows. "Mistress Janet." He turned to face her but did not approach.

"You were interested in learning about dispelling diabolerie."

Nick nodded, looking at her with wary eyes.

"I have a case of misused magic now. I need assistance." She spread her hands. "The master wizards are not available, and you showed considerable talent with the stone guardian—it will teach you more about breaking spells."

Nick swallowed.

"Have you read *Concerning Demons*?"

"Parts."

That, Janet thought, would make him a better choice than many master wizards. "It should not be dangerous. The practitioner was not much, and all that remains is breaking the spells." She smiled. "It might not even be diabolerie, but merely throwing around spells with abandon."

Nick glanced at his books.

"Master Umberto will find this an addition to your studies, not a distraction from them. Mastering how to dissolve spells is always tricky."

Umberto dug. Silver flowers chimed, sweetly, and it was still morning. The flowers came free, their pale roots shedding bits of earth. He stored the plant away. He could venture much further. This was the Wizards' Wood, and if the wonders were well-spread out, yet they were there. He wandered on.

A clearing, filled with sunlight, exploded with a rainbow of butterflies. He smiled as they fluttered off.

Then he heard voices. No words were clear, but the note of panic was.

He strode off—not too swiftly. It might be a lure. Worse, he might fall to the danger and be of no aid to anyone.

Firs rose up, about a pond; their needles were dark and blue. Some were low bushes, near the ground, and their needled boughs stuck out jagged points. And across the pool, seven bushes snarled and pranced. From moment to moment, their forms shifted: now more like bushes, now more like wolves.

Like wolves, they surrounded three students. No, four, Umberto realized as the wolves snapped and snarled. One lay on the ground, his hands about his calf but blood trickled about his fingers. One branch—or maw—was marked with red. Umberto looked again. The bushes actually changed shape; it was not just their movements that made their forms appear to shift.

The spell leapt to his mouth. The lead wolf lunged into the wall of will. It yapped in surprise. The students looked about as the wolves leapt again and again, their barks growing less baffled and more angry. The force of their assaults gave Umberto new respect for Nicholas and Felicity.

"Stay there," Umberto called.

"We can get him out of here," one student called back, bending to his wounded companion.

Another put out his hand, and hit the wall. "We can't."

The wolves circled the students. The first student eyed Umberto uneasily.

He walked as quickly as he could. The rocky ground was uneven, in places slippery with needles, and he did not think that he wished to fall into the pool, no matter how shallow it was. The stream held uneven stepping stones; though he had to pick his way with care, he reached the other side.

Snarling, the pack leapt toward him. He threw up another wall, only inches away from himself. It barely landed before the first wolf's nose, but the wolf hurtled into it and howled.

The students stared in silence. Umberto drew a deep breath and considered how to construct a corridor to them.

Minutes later, they edged from the grove. Two students carried the wounded one. The wolfish bushes prowled along and sometimes tested Umberto's wall of will. The wizards stepped from the grove, and silence fell. Seven bushes stood where none had stood before.

A student breathed out a long sigh. "We had best get back to the university."

"So we had best." Umberto looked at the wound. "And instruct ourselves on these wolves and how dangerous their bites can be." Not exactly the lore he was looking for, but on St. John's Day, he could hardly direct them to find their tutors.

Nick looked up the flight of stairs. Like Lady Alicia's, the house stood inside the city walls, but even finer. The owners were noble, and not minor nobility.

Mistress Janet walked up as if she had never heard of a back door. Nick followed her with less confidence. He had never been as glad of how the plain black robes covered the clothing beneath.

A maid bobbed a curtsey and ushered them inside, giving Nick a nervous glance. He followed Mistress Janet into a hall far greater than any he had seen before.

A gray-haired woman walked into the hall and looked at Janet. Her voice quavered. "He meant no harm."

"Your Tristram meant no good, Dame Petronella!" Janet looked over her shoulder at Nick. "Tristram wished to hide something. He cast protective spells on his room. He did not know there were protective spells on the house."

Nick looked over the great hall again. An old and grand house, within the city walls, would have spells enough to ward off danger from any feud, and more than a little war. And the spells that could ensue from either. Everyone knew that. Nick followed her up the inside stair.

"First, of course, we have to find out what manner of spells he laid. A spell of discernment—I could have used one on the stone guardian, if I had realized in time."

Stand behind her when she discerns, Nick told himself, or she will learn something about you.

Mistress Janet reached the top of the stairs and stood aside to give him room. Nick looked down the corridor, at the spread of mist—not evenly but in cords.

"Walking down there will sicken you." Mistress Janet put her hands on her hips. "That spell you taught Felicity is needed here. There's no telling what Tristram laid on this room."

"From his spellbook?"

Mistress Janet jerked her thumb at the mist. "Cast the wall between me and the door, and I will start the spell-breaking. Stay behind me."

Nick bobbed his head. The safest location for him in more than one sense. The demon thing in his chest felt like a burning weight. Despite it, he cast the spell.

Mistress Janet intoned a spell. Silver strands spread through the corridor, making the cords of mist look like a spider's web, but they did not reach back toward Nick.

"A spider-spell. What a thing to throw about!" Mistress Janet stretched out a hand for a second spell. The first strands curled back and disentangled with a faint scent of must, and lightning. The unraveling spread, faster, until Nick almost expected dust to fly. Sunlight reached a plain corridor, paneled with dark wood.

"If *that* kept Tristram out of his room, we have little to fear," she said.

Nick dissolved the wall spell. Mistress Janet walked to the first door and yanked it open. Silver spangled the room: thick as snow on certain books and the desk, a mist over the walls, and in between, like dew, on the bed and floor. Its glow filled the room, greater than the sunlight from the three windows.

"Still, better to be safe." She glanced back.

Nick cast the wall spell.

Mistress Janet cast hers. By the door, for the span of about an inch, silver trembled and dissolved, but no further. She grimaced. "He did not lay a single spell. No, that would be too easy. He cast a score, and we must dissolve them one by one." She swept back the hair from the nape of her neck and held it up. "One by one by one. . . God help us, it's too hot for this work." But she went on casting—and did not tell him to give up the wall.

She worked across the floor toward the desk. Every now and again, she told him to shift the wall until, at the desk, she inspected the glow, narrowly.

Nick dropped in a disenchanted chair. "It doesn't look like the rest."

"That's because he laid the spell so thickly. It's just many, many, many strand, even though this spell does not work the better with more." The glow cast odd shadows on her face, making her concentration look unearthly. "Tristram did not get much instruction with his spells—a fool, to sell himself so cheaply."

Or perhaps only a fool would have been caught, thought Nick. His father's plan had failed, but he had not revealed himself, not even to Mistress Janet. He fought to keep his mouth from twisting. If she had caught Mortimer, he would have had nothing to fear.

Mistress Janet looked at him and arched an eyebrow. Nick, flushing, laid the wall between her and the desk. She intoned the familiar spell. The desk subsided into plain brown. The silvery light dimmed to so little that the afternoon daylight, tinged with gold, filled the room.

"At least *that* was only one spell." Mistress Janet considered the bed and walls. "I think you should try them."

Nick sat up, so abruptly that he banged his arm on the chair's.

"The spell is simple." She cocked an eyebrow. "You could learn it now, if—"

"It's a variation on a spell I learned very young."

Mistress Janet smiled. "You will learn, here, as well as help. Master Umberto will be pleased—if you were not, to be lectured on a holiday."

Nick stood. He could not refuse such friendly interest, he thought gloomily.

Was this fair to Nick?

His expression deathly serious, the young man worked his way across the bed. Silvery threads shriveled and vanished—less quickly than beneath her hand, but quickly for a student, let alone a first-year student weak in dispelling magic. If he had quarreled that badly with his father, Mortimer would disinherit him. He would need his degree, and he show enough promise to win it, if politics did not interfere.

Nick scowled and looked under the bed. He moved closer and went on casting the spell.

She might not manage to exert the influence on his behalf that she had exerted on her own.

Her mouth tightened as Nick reached the bed's foot, and the last thread vanished. He turned to bed stand, unwrapping it, visibly faster. He opened its drawers, lifted his eyebrows, cast the spell again, and pulled out a book. "I think this is his grimorie."

Janet hopped up. She should have seen that, but Nick had done well enough that she had not seen him falter. "Tristram was clever enough to hide it, then." And Nick to find it, she thought. I will speak with Umberto about his studies, and ensure I am at the university when they are done.

Mistress Janet looked about. The sunlight had grown orange with afternoon, and the room steamed. "I think we have them all, but I will check." Nick hurried out the door and hoped she thought he was getting out of the way. She cast the spell. He could see no silver in the sunlight, but she circled about, eyeing every corner, and finally approached him.

"I should warn you that not all such breaking is easy. We did not need your spell this time, but many a wizard has been killed or crippled breaking spells."

Nick could not feel his heart baeat. He was in no danger of thinking spell-breaking easy. He glanced sideways at her. Perhaps she would believe him. He wavered. He had lied to her before, and telling the truth would be confessing to that lie.

Perhaps she would believe that he came to trust her because of this.

"Tristram will be condemned," Mistress Janet said with satisfaction. "It amazes me, the stories they can come up with. Long, convoluted stories about how they did not do what they obviously did, or did not know what they obviously knew. And they think I—or anyone—would believe them." She grabbed a handful of hair and threw it over her shoulder. "Even the fools who harm someone bleat about how they didn't mean any harm, and therefore it doesn't count."

Nick smiled back. He hoped it fooled her, but he could not meet her gaze. No one was perishing from his silence.

"Go and enjoy the bonfires tonight," Mistress Janet said. "You have earned a respite."

Nick remembered the silver. "Tomorrow—I would like to learn that spell of discernment."

The sky was still red and orange, and the air still heated by the day, but down in the city, the first bonfires were being lit. Then, thought Umberto, standing in the university square, by the heaped firewood, the summer nights came later here; it would have been full dark by now in Metharia. He glanced over the hillside. Torches streamed up the streets toward the university.

A preaching friar appeared by the piles of wood, ranting on the wickedness of such celebrations when the white sickness had revealed their sins. Laughing students hustled him away. His voice rose and was suddenly cut off. Umberto glanced over. The friar's mouth still worked, but nothing came out. He tore himself from his captors' hands, and laughter chased after him.

"Master Umberto." Young Matthew looked cheerfully at him. "I thought you were going to the Wizards' Wood."

"So I did," said Umberto and realized how few masters there were about. Perhaps he could have ensconced the wounded student in the infirmary and left again, but they might have needed his spells more than he needed anything from the Wizards' Woods.

Either fewer students had gone, or they returned more quickly. Beyond Matthew were Nicholas and other students, young men and young women, looking eagerly at the wood.

"I had to return early," said Umberto. He nodded to Nicholas. "I heard—I hope that Mistress Janet's labors did not exhaust you."

Nicholas smiled, though it looked strained. "I rested this afternoon. I would not have missed this; I've only seen it from afar, before."

Umberto had seen the gathered wood, outside the city. Even now the fires were springing up. Mortimer Briarwood's house stood close to where one blaze burned, and he doubted that Mortimer could have kept his son that subdued.

A student—a third-year student, in a scholar's robes—cast a spell. The wood smoldered and started to burn. Flames leapt up—and up. An enormous firebird burst from the blaze, flapping its wings as it soared. Cheers went up, scattered about the crowd, but so did rival creatures: more birds, one an entire flock of creatures no bigger than Umberto's hand, butterflies, dragons. . . more and more as more bonfires were lit about the university.

An ill-formed bird blazed from the fire before him. A student poked Nicholas. Moments later, the bird burned blue. Nicholas set it rippling through the colors.

"That's Nicholas Briarwood," said a wizard beside him. Umberto turned to Master Ivo. "You must be proud of him."

"He mastered that spell before he came under my tutelage."

Master Ivo snorted. "Someone should be proud of him. Lord knows that his father isn't."

It was a day and a night like other days and night—suitable for studying. With the problem Nick had given, he had no time for frivolity.

Mortimer scowled. The laughter and shouting would make study difficult for anyone. Orange light danced on his study walls. Despite himself, he looked up.

An enormous bird burst from the bonfires at the university, gold and red. And then colors shimmered across it. Purple firebirds, he thought disdainfully. He looked back at his notes. He had learned the folly of showing his skill during his first year at the university. The slightest error drew raucous laughter from fools who would never venture the spell. Even showing only spells he had mastered drew no respect, only deprecation and futile attempts to outdo him—by envious fools who did not care if they were mocked.

He looked up again. Birds in blue and green. He wondered if Nicholas had a hand in that. *He* had times for such frolics. Mortimer's fingers tightened on the books. Once he hunted through the books that Nicholas had touched—he looked back down.

Sitting on his bed, Nick looked at the parchment that Mistress Janet had given him. For all his interest, he had been too weary when she had first given it. At night, even with the bonfires lit, the light might have been seen—and he had, he admitted, feared what it would reveal to himself as well as to anyone else. Jack had talked him into spell-casting at the bonfire, but he had no excuse except cowardice. He had slept late, and the spell was simple.

He cast the spell and looked into the battered mirror. Even in its distorting reflection, by broad daylight, he saw the silvery glow. He saw its shape as well.

Quickly, he broke the spell. The light took a long time to fade. Cold and sweating, he leaned against the wall. It was just as well that he had left it until daylight. That spell glowed like no other spell. Someone would have gossiped.

Chapter 14—Association

Beneath the dreary sky, the air was hot and wet. The trees were darker than usual against the charcoal clouds. Across the grass, the young women of St. Agnes had half a dozen Leonore's Candles glowing in the familiar white-blue light.

"Hey, Nick," called one. "Come tell us what we're doing wrong with the spell!"

"You cast it so easily on the bonfire—there has to be a trick," said another.

Nick grinned but shook his head. "Business."

The second woman snorted. "Come when you're done. I swear, this spell of yours makes compounding look simple."

"I wish," said Nick. "But some of you *did* learn it that night, and you could ask them." He walked down the paths. Cheerfully doubting statements followed him. The light did not, not for long. The day was so dreary that marigolds, in yellow and orange, flared and made the grass seem all the drabber by contrast.

"Nicholas Briarwood?" came a voice from the nearest building. Nick saw a master's green robes. He stopped.

Master Ivo emerged. "You dealt with those knaves, were you not? Scared them off before St. John's Day?"

Nick nodded, trying to remember Master Ivo's reaction to learning Mistress Martha had practiced diabolerie. "They were drunk."

Master Ivo smiled. "Excellent. Those roisterers could only be improved by being shown up. A most promising student to do that—both of you show promise."

"Three," Nick said. "Three of us were needed."

"Were there?" Master Ivo peered at him, shrugged, and went on. Nick headed down the paths again. A breeze shook the trees' leaves. He walked out of the university and down the almost empty street toward Benedict's. A few vendors, hopeful or unafraid of rain, still hawked their wares, but could not disturb his thoughts. Someone emerged from a corner and stepped before him.

"No wonder," said Randall, "that you have no time for your old friends. Tossing nasty spells at students who are just having some fun."

Some fun, thought Nick sourly.

Randall's face contorted. "Little prig. I bet you impressed the master wizards all right."

"What are you up to now, Randall?"

Randall's shoulders hunched.

"Do you think the master wizards—Mistress Janet, if no other—will let you play pranks forever? You're not a child anymore, Randall."

"You'll see soon enough—and then you'll be impressed." He darted off.

Nick sighed. An idle threat. Mistress Janet had not caught his father, and he doubted Randall was half the danger that Mortimer Briarwood was.

"Did you hear the latest about Nick?" said Robina.

Marie bent over her teacup. She supposed that the university had not actually eaten Nick up, but Robina's interest was imprudent. "No, what is it?"

For all that Robina sat sedately, her eyes danced with mischief. "Some gently-born students got drunk and wandered around the university—last week it was."

"That doesn't sound like Nick, does it?" said Marie.

"If," said Robina's Aunt Dora, "one can call Nicholas Briarwood gentry, nowadays. Quarreling with his father, being thrown from the house, and getting cut out of the will—"

"Nick wasn't one of them, don't you see?" Robina said. "What happened was, Nick cast a spell on them."

Marie put down her teacup with a click. "Really?"

Robina nodded. "Scared them off."

"He's only been at the university a few months." Marie stared out at nothing. She had never known Nick to cast frightening spells.

"Perhaps he knew it before." Agnes looked at her tea cup. "He might even have had to use it to get back, after the spell. Practice makes perfect."

"He would have shown us before," said Marie. "But this, and that business with the stone guardian—Nick will end up a master of the university."

"So he will," Robina said, warmly.

Marie hesitated. An impoverished student was one thing. A master of the university would be respectable and not poor. "I wonder if I should invite him to a party."

Aunt Dora shot her a glance like lightning.

"Should. . . ." Robina gaped. "He *is* poor, that might be awkward for him."

"Oh yes," said Marie, but if Nick gained a position at the university—Agnes looked disapproving, but *her* banns of marriage were already being read. She did not have to consider that a master of the university might be better than to be an old maid. "We don't want to lose track of him."

"You would be wise not to encourage him before he gets his place," Aunt Dora said.

Marie widened her eyes and looked at her. "But if he remembers how we treated him before?"

"The next thing I know," said Aunt Dora, "you will declare that *Isobel* should still be a welcome guest here." She sat back.

"Nicholas Briarwood quarreled with his father in a *most* unfilial manner. Do not encourage such a rascal."

Ah, thought Marie, Aunt Dora does not think Nick will be well-to-do enough.

"Besides," said Agnes, "it would be unkind. He will need his degree. He needs no distraction."

Lady Alicia presented Giles to Lord Baldwin. Giles stood in the middle of the room and looked flustered. As if, thought Fliss, he had forgotten that Lady Alicia was a noble.

He turned to Fliss and presented her with flowers again, but his chatter was nervous, and his visit, short.

As he vanished down the street, Lord Baldwin stood by the window and said, "A young man of the gentry, I take it."

"Yes," said Lady Alicia.

"He seems taken with your ward."

Fliss did not dare to twitch, or raise her head from the flowers.

"Young men's fancies—you know how fickle they are," said Lady Alicia.

"Ehem. But both are of age to marry. And it ill befits our house for a ward of it to have no place—"

"Your father would tell you that Felicity is *my* ward."

Lord Baldwin glanced at Fliss. "Come, young Felicity, do you wish to be a poor scholar at the university?"

Fliss remembered. She had only had glimpses of the scholars scrambling for anything that brought coin, but enough to remind her of what Lady Alicia gave her. On the other hand, they survived. Even Nick Briarwood. "It would only be until I received my degree."

Lord Baldwin snorted. "Not every student receives a degree. Not every master receives a post. Even if you did—you would end up like Mistress Janet Whitehall, scrambling like a clerk, though she's of higher birth than I."

"She's my tutor," said Fliss, and wondered why. That would only confirm Lord Baldwin's distaste.

"A duke's granddaughter can marry as she wishes, and leave her position. *You* would be well advised to assume your chances at matrimony will be few. Even as Lady Alicia's ward, to wed among the gentry would not be easy."

"It would be rash," said Fliss.

"If you want to continue your studies. . . ."

"Nephew," said Lady Alicia, "marrying this man would bring her prosperity and the chance to continue, if all goes well. But it is folly to marry for money." Her voice turned dry again. "If only because money can prove fleeting."

Lord Baldwin grunted. "It is folly to reject a wooer because he has money." He gestured at the flowers. "Besides, I would think this man a wooer after young Felicity's own heart."

Felicity flushed and bent over her head over the flowers. Only the delicate scent hinted that the flowers were magical.

"A prosperous young man, a student of magic—a father for her own children. When she gads about the orphanage. What more could a prudent woman ask of marriage?"

Fliss swallowed at the mention of children, envisioning little children with dark hair and pale faces. What did Giles lack that she wished for in a husband?

Robina called down the street, "Oh, Nick."

Nick stopped in the hot sun and let out a long breath. Marie was with her; both of them looked cheerful. He hoped they did not want to talk for long.

Marie looked at his books and tossed her head. Her curls
went flying. "All work and no play makes Jack a dull boy. I am
having a party tonight. You must come."

"I can't."

Marie's mouth narrowed. "Oh, come on, Nick. You didn't
use to be such a stick-in-the-mud."

"I didn't use to be a scholar," Nick said.

"You were bad enough. With all we hear of your
spellcraft—you must have *long* neglected us to hide among
your books."

They had complained of that often enough when he came,
thought Nick.

Marie put a hand on one hip. "St. John's Day was Sunday,
it's at the beginning of the new term, you can't be that far
behind—and I've heard the students in the taverns."

"Not for long, if they were scholars," Nick said.

"You don't want to cut off your old friends, do you?"
Robina said.

Yes, he thought, but hesitated to say so, after all the old
accusations of being like Mortimer.

Then, the scholars at St. Catherine's or St. Agnes's would be
surprised to hear he was a hermit. "I have to study."

He smiled. "But you were going to attend the university,
before the white sickness. Now that you've recovered—if not
this term, the next. You will have to study then and still see
more of me."

Marie narrowed her eyes and stalked off with Robina. Her
voice carried back. "Well, I never—he's turning into the image
of his father."

"It's ridiculous," said Marie. Despite the evening's heat, she was
never still. "To act as if *we* offended *him*."

"Of course it is," said Catherine, "but he was always fond of his studies."

Robina snorted. "Too fond."

Entirely too fond, thought Edgar. Young women were silly geese, but losing their heads over Nicholas Briarwood was uncommon folly. "Perhaps you shouldn't have been so cool after he reappeared."

Robina bit her lip.

"You've seen his spells," said Edgar. "He could always support a wife as an entertainer. In some tavern."

From the twists of mouth about, he need not fear meeting Nick at another party.

"*And*," said Robina, "he must be corrupting Fliss. I haven't seen her *at all*, at any party."

"She was one of the mischief-making students with the light spells," said Edgar. "Associating with the scholars."

Into the stillness, someone muttered, "Considering her birth. . . ."

Tactless to mention that, thought Edgar, but probably for the best. He lifted his cup. Giles, white-faced, stared at him. A good warning to him, as well.

"How are your studies coming?" Fliss asked.

At a library table, Nick looked up. Clouds had gathered; light from windows had grown far dimmer. He must have studied longer than he had thought, unless the clouds had come in *very* quickly. "Well enough. I am starting to understand compound spells. In fact, I have just about mastered my latest lesson." His legs felt stiff; he shifted them.

Fliss cocked an eyebrow. "Have you?" The tip of her tongue touched her upper lip. "If you have some free time, you could come with me to help at the orphanage." She glanced down and up again. "Of course, if you have something else to do—for your studies—I know you need your scholarship."

Nick thought of *Concerning Demons*, but he was tired of desperate and secret studying. Especially as the tome went on and on about the various ways that demons could work, and how difficult it was to work out which one. The only thing he knew was that if Master Umberto asked him now if he had interests in magic, he could answer, *not* in breaking spells. Except that he had to—

Not, he resolved, now. "If you think I would be any use, I'll come."

Fliss smiled. "The sisters and I are checking the children for sickness. You can entertain them. Keep them still. They know you're good at that."

In the kitchen, smoke wafted from the low fire. Nick watched it closely. The smoke hesitated, stopped, and took form. He needed a tale—a new tale, because Tom sat there, and his eyes were brighter than any other child's. After a moment, he formed a knight on a steed—not a fairy tale, but a tale of chivalry.

"A knight in shining armor," said a boy.

Nick smiled. As if he could make smoke shine. "Even so. This knight rode through a forest." He gestured. More smoke floated out. It flew, more easily now, into the trunks and boughs and leaves. Wide-eyed, the orphans stared.

"He was an exile from his father's house because his stepmother had poisoned his father's mind against him, because she wished for her children to inherit his father's lands, and he was his father's only son." Don't I wish for so simple a reason, he thought, but kept his voice grave. "He ventured into the wilderness, where there were monsters, so as to get to another land."

A sister came out to usher a girl away, and the girl, with some pouting, went.

Nick conjured a dragon up, and a lady of noble blood that the knight had to rescue from it. His voice grew hoarse. He swallowed and went on, recounting how the knight's father had been invited to the wedding, the step-mother having conveniently died in the meantime, and was reconciled with his son.

". . .and they all lived happily ever after." Nick dissipated the smoke. The children's cheers did not lift his spirits.

"I'm going to be a knight when I grow up," one boy said.

Nick's smile was bittersweet. He looked over the children's heads. Fliss, smiling, and the sisters watched him.

Mother Humiliata raised her voice. "We're done, children, come back inside."

As the children groaned, complained, and inched toward the door, Fliss picked her way among them to him. "You wanted to be a knight yourself, at that age."

"So I did," Nick said. He could declaim on what a fool he had been and leave Fliss wondering what caused it. He could not tell her that his one encounter with an evil wizard had not ended as a tale of chivalry would have. His chest ached. Amazing what one learned as one grew up.

"Let's go back," he said, "if the sisters don't need us." He looked at the sky. The air crackled with anticipation, and thunderheads threatened.

"They're grateful for what we've given," said Fliss.

His mouth twitched. "Better than Edgar's wall of snow, and my wall of will?"

Fliss looked down. He let his breath out. He would have sworn that nothing could abash her.

Her voice was low. "The problem was Edgar's wall of snow. Perhaps nothing could have prevented some kind of misfortune." She looked up, trying to smile. "The collapse could have been bad regardless, and I—we might owe you nothing but gratitude, for your wall of will."

Lilies lined the way: yellow, orange, red, pink. Fliss was distant in thought, and Nick wondered whether to rouse her.

"Nick!"

Coming down a side path, Jack waved a hand. "What brings you down this path?"

"Going back to St. Catherine's," said Nick dryly.

Jack glanced at the way. After a moment, he said, "From?"

"Practicing spells at the orphanage," said Fliss. "Though— Nick seems to have his down."

Jack fell in alongside. "Jewel lights?"

"No, he formed smoke," said Fliss, and told what he had done.

Jack had a strange look on his face. He said nothing, until Fliss flitted down a different path, toward Lady Alicia's. Then he stopped. "I came to the city just before the white sickness. Before I came to study."

Nick stopped, and his gaze went to the path.

"Not alone—with some others, through the Wizards' Wood. We went back that way to avoid the sickness." He turned his face toward Nick. "Do you know anything of a wyvern?"

"That I didn't do it," said Nick. "It came out of the wood."

Jack studied him for a minute.

"Do you know any spells to tell what manner of monster lurks in the firewood from Wizards' Wood?"

Jack snorted. "Know a trick or two that help. Sometimes."

"You should learn the wall of will," said Nick. "For protection."

The thunderstorm had led into solid rain the next day. After charging for the library, Nick was just as glad to read in its shelter, even if the grayish light needed supplementing from time to time. Finished with one book, he went back for another.

Matthew came around a corner as if looking for someone. He was pale and held a book like a poisonous snake.

"What is it?" Nick said, with some exasperation.

Matthew silently opened the book. Nick's mouth tightened. An impish thought compared it to his own experience. Matthew had found a grimorie, a summoning for a succubus.

Matthew grew paler. "Demons think they can tempt me by putting this in my path."

"You don't know that," said Nick. "It could be the target restored it to the shelves and fled. He might have hid it there and you are rescuing him from himself."

A shadow of a grin appeared on Matthew's face.

"Hand it over the librarians and never mind it again."

"I suppose you would have done that," said Matthew.

Nick drew a deep breath. He would never have told anyone in his old circles this—except, perhaps, Fliss. "Yes, that was what I did."

Matthew's eyebrows went up. Nick smiled, but it felt uncomfortable. Matthew's grimorie, the demons could have put in the path of any young pup, but his they had aimed at him.

Chapter 15—Revealing Secrets

More compounded spells, thought Nick as he left Master Umberto's office. He could devise the spell to restore his heart as part of his studies—if he could explain it to Master Umberto. He doubted Master Umberto would consider it studied unless he could see him perform it.

He walked down the stairs and outside. The storm had washed the air, but the heat was growing again. That was—he could, if only he could find the spells to compound.

His mouth tightened, but he walked toward the library.

From the corner of his eye, he saw furtive movement in an alley. He looked over, for a glimpse of pale faces in the shadows, but when he walked over, he saw an empty alley.

Standing in the shade, Nick looked about. It had only been a glimpse; he could have been mistaken. He laid a hand on the wall. On the other hand, an invisibility spell would hide anyone. They wouldn't even have to compound it, if they could just wait for him to leave.

"And it's just the sort of thing that Randall would love," he muttered. He had thought—but nothing moved in the alley, and he knew no spells to detect the invisible.

He walked out, more slowly, to the bustling square, where he hesitated in a tree's shade. The square held nothing odd, nothing that would inspire anyone to look.

"Watch what you're doing. . . ."

Nick stepped aside. A student, laden with books, hurried past, and other walkers eddied about him. He walked over to the nearest building, and its shade. A dozen statues stood about: two lions guarding the entrance, a great merman blowing his horn, with mermaids about in the fountains, and men and women. People hurried through, but in the growing heat, some gathered by the fountains.

One child splashed about the mermaids. Nick smiled fondly at the sight of her—and suddenly, she squeaked with frightened surprise. A stony mermaid lowered her arm and stretched, the motion stiff. The child inched back. The mermaid turned her head, looked at the child with marble eyes, and slid from her place with a flip of her stony tail. Water sprung up. She rose in the waves and thrashed ahead. Nick's stomach felt cold. Behind her, other mermaids stirred. The merman, his expression cruel, lowered his horn.

Someone screamed.

He could not see it all; no one could look in all the directions at once. Men and women descended clumsily from their pedestals. A lion shrugged, its stony muscles rippling, and leapt down to the pavement, with a resounding thump. Everywhere people screamed and panicked.

His mouth set in grim lines, Nick forced his way to the fountains, though people pushed by him. Mermaids writhed, splashing the water over the square, and people thronged about, stared, and did nothing.

The child scrambled back to the fountain's edge, wailing with panic, but could not climb out. Flailing arms and tails brushed against her, with bruising force. Then a mermaid spotted the child and reached for her with stony hands. The child screamed. Nick snagged her by the waist and dragged her out. She screamed on, blood on her arms and legs. Nick stepped back, as the mermaid's arms reached for the girl. She stretched until half her body was over the edge. Nick retreated. The mermaid might not be able to move on the ground, but falling on him would do all the harm that she would need.

The mermaid did not follow. She pulled back and looked from the child to meet Nick's gaze with her solid gray eyes. Her expression was vague, imploring.

"Angela!" A woman reached for the girl. The still screaming child held out her arms. Nick handed her over without a glance at either. A student groaned on the pavement, blood oozing from a crushed leg onto his black robes; a dozen people sat, or lay, bleeding. Statues blundered about, but their motions grew smoother and more confident.

The lion growled, its eyes intent on a cluster of students, and gathered itself to spring. It was far larger than the stone guardian; the claws and teeth were perhaps the same size, but it would bite and claw with more force. Nick threw the wall of will between the lion and its prey.

The lion hurled itself into the spell with bone-shaking force. Nick gasped. How strong a spell had Luke and Randall used? He would be as exhausted after another attack as after all the guardian's efforts.

The lion's head whipped around to look at Nick, its eyes dark and fervent—no longer stone. Its tail twitched. It lunged again, as quick as a thought.

Nick tried to cast another wall, but the lion pounced more quickly and knocked him, sprawling, on the stones. He fought for breath, unable to scream. Its stony claws raked his arm and ribs, tearing cloth and flesh, staining themselves red. Hot blood flowed down Nick's side. The lion pulled back. Nick gasped with pain, his vision darkening. The lion looked at him and pounced. Fighting the pain, Nick cast the wall again. He threw the lion back, but it crouched, watching him. Nick pushed himself up against the stone, reaching only half-sitting before he reeled back toward the ground. For a second, he thought that its eyes held intelligence.

Not important, he told himself sternly. Lying flat without stirring, Nick wove the spell of breaking. Jabs of pain made him hesitant, and slowed his spell—for a moment, he doubted the spell could affect it, standing so solid there—but the lion was not the stone guardian Mistress Martha had conjured. When the spell left his lips, its stone flaked and broke down into dust, easily blown away.

Nick dropped the wall and slumped, feeling as broken as the statue. His blood soaked his clothing. All about the square, around the bleeding bodies, the statues broke beneath the spells of wizards, masters or students. Nick bit his lip. He had to heal his injuries. Sweat beaded on his face, but he could not hesitate. Someone would help him and learn that he had no heart in his body.

Shouts resounded, and footsteps echoed. Someone ran through the courtyard, and Nick knew it was toward him.

"Nick!" Fliss dropped to her knees beside him. Her already pale face went white as she looked at the blood. She dragged in a deep breath, and her hand took his wrist. His mouth could not move; his hand could not pull away; he could only watch her hand descending on his wrist with the slowness of a feather falling. His breathing was harsh in his ears.

Her fingers probed. Bewilderment flooded her face. She glanced at his chest, rising and falling with his breathing, and her fingers probed hard. Nick wondered how guilty his face looked. A second later, her mouth set like iron.

Nick swallowed. "Fliss, please," he said, hoarsely.

She did not move.

"I swear to you, I did not do anything wrong." After another moment, he said, "Fliss, I am bleeding, let me cast the spell. . . ."

Fliss's mouth tightened, and she cast the spell herself. Blood oozed back, from ground and clothing—her clothing as well as his, she had knelt in his blood—into the wound. His light-headedness eased. His knowledge that he was trapped grew firmer. Flesh and skin knit where the lion had rent them. Nick closed his eyes, feeling weak as a kitten. At least, Fliss had hidden the evidence. He would only have to explain to her and not the entire university—until she denounced him.

His words tripped over each other, getting out. "It is not like Master Oliver's. It is not blighting anything—and I didn't do it. . . ."

Fliss leaned over him. Nick fell silent. How could he persuade Fliss that he had no heart in his body for innocent reasons?

"You will tell me what happened. And soon." Her voice was low but grim.

It was not a request, but he nodded.

Fliss rose and offered him a hand. He took it and stood with more steadiness than he thought possible. About them, master wizards stood over destroyed statues or bent over the wounded. Someone screamed in agony, and Nick winced.

A master wizard eyed them. "Nicholas Briarwood? The student who dealt with the stone guardian?"

Nick nodded.

The wizard glanced at what had been the lion. "Were you here when the. . . ." He gestured at the scattered stone and was silent a moment. "Trouble," he finally selected, "began?"

Nick bobbed his head.

"Then we wish to speak with you."

"The lion clawed him," said Fliss. "Badly. I mended the injury, but he's not well yet."

He glanced at her. "Who are you, and were you here?"

"Felicity Seaborn. I wasn't." Her voice was sharp. The master wizard had, after all, forgotten her part in destroying the guardian—or perhaps she hoped to drag him off at once for her answers.

The wizard raised his eyebrows. He looked at Nick. "Are you well enough to talk?"

Nick considered for a moment. He would have to do it some time, and best while the memory was fresh. "I think so."

"If you ruin my spell work, Nicholas Briarwood—" The threat in her voice made the master wizard start.

"I'll plead off before I am too tired," said Nick. She eyes him as if she wished she could threaten him, to make him stop before he was too tired to speak with *her*, but she did not betray him.

His arms laden with books, Edgar walked toward the square. It was just as well that Marie had taken the white sickness. She would never have survived these studies. George would fall out soon. Even Nick would last only as long as his studies did not meddle with his mischief.

Luke and Randall came out of an alley and brushed by him as if he were not there—as brusquely as they did Nick. Edgar looked after them. His eyes narrowed. If he had just met Luke, he had known Randall long—

Screams cut off his thoughts.

People fled the square, shouting in panic. Others flooded toward it and filled the air with questions. Edgar hurried. It took him a minute to reach the scene: shattered statues, bleeding bodies with wizards going from one to the next, wails of agony and panic rising. His hands tightened on his books. The screams were clear enough: the statues had come to life. Had been brought to life.

Randall and Luke had fled from the alley, minutes before, when Randall had always been a troublemaker as a boy. And he could see Nick Briarwood, down in the square.

Edgar ignored the chatter about him. Fliss helped Nick to his feet. His eyes narrowed. What was Nick doing in the thick of this?

George had told him that Randall and Nick had met recently. Edgar looked about, at the blood. Some of the victims were children. It would be wrong to keep such a thing to himself, with these goings on. He shook his head sadly. Far worse than boyish pranks.

A master wizard Nick and led Nick away. Fliss left, as well, but his gaze followed Nick. With his silver tongue, Nick would spin them some tale. But he did not know what Edgar knew, about Randall and Luke.

His thought flicked over Fliss and dismissed her. Nothing that three could offer—not even a good marriage—would seduce Fliss's icy self-righteousness.

But Nick . . . Nick he knew.

Fliss watched Nick go. For all the mugginess, and the glare from the sun, she felt like ice. Her hands trembled, she noted distantly. She hoped that he had not agreed with the master in order to avoid her.

No one watched her. No one needed her; every injury had a master wizard bent over it. She hurried up the stairs out of the square and scrambled down the path.

All about her, stories flew. Fliss heard scraps and walked on. Anyone who saw her must have attributed her pallor to the scene. At least, no one asked her if she were well. Or perhaps she met no one she knew as she scurried toward home.

Then, she saw the Cathedral of the Magi. She drew a deep breath and turned aside. Up the stairs, and she stumbled into the darkness inside.

The sanctuary light glowed like a red star in the chapel's depths. Fliss drew a deep breath, genuflected, and looked about. Half a dozen candles glowed in a side chapel. Fliss walked over. Behind them stood a crucifix cast in bronze, gleaming in the light. Fliss walked up to the railing before it, pulled a coin out, and placed it in the box. It rattled against the opening. She pressed her hands together for a minute and then, with great care, lit a candle. The flame quavered, but took.

She sank to her knees. His heart was outside his body. The only thing she could think of was Master Oliver. Master Oliver's spell would have cured those injuries before she saw that Nick had fallen, but that thought could not calm her. She would not have believed it of Nick. Of half a dozen other young men and even some young women, but not Nick, even before he vanished and reappeared so deathly serious.

She flinched. So deathly serious—she raised her eyes to the crucifix. She would not believe it of Nick. Even Nick's folly was not petty, she tried to explain to God, but she could not keep her thoughts coherent. She buried her face in her hands. Other young men might, perhaps, be willing to cast the spell, but only Nick had the studiousness to actually master it.

The master wizard drew himself up to his full height. "Young man, do you think we have time to hear you tell tales out of school? This was no schoolboy prank."

Beneath the master's stern gaze, Edgar flinched and regrouped his thoughts. "I beg your pardon, sir. I phrased it badly." Telling them about George would be an unnecessary complication. "I saw Nick Briarwood associating with another friend, named Randall, also fond of pranks—and this friend fled the scene, when the statues first came alive."

The wizard said nothing.

Edgar arranged his thoughts. "Not from the scene itself. From an alley near it. They could barely have seen the statues, let alone the damage they did, but they ran like the devil was on their heels. They had to know what had happened already."

One bushy eyebrow shot up. "They?"

Edgar nearly kicked himself. *Nick* had not fled; he must not have felt the horror that the others did. "Randall was the one who met Nick. There was also Luke, a cousin of Randall's." His heart hammered. Nick's accomplices were as guilty as he. He should have denounced them all together. For Nick to escape justice because of his sloppiness, that would be wrong indeed.

"If Nicholas Briarwood knew about the statues," the master wizard said, "he would have been a fool to stay there. He was gravely injured, you know."

They were determined not to see it, thought Edgar. "I have seen with my own eyes Nick being injured by his own spells, because his judgment was poor."

Even in Lady Alicia's library, Fliss hid herself in a corner. She sat with a book in her hands, holding it tightly, but did not read.

Lady Alicia walked into the room. "A shocking affair. Have you heard about the statues in the square, Fliss?"

Fliss plopped down the book. "I was there. Not when it happened, but not a minute after."

"No wonder you look so pale."

Fliss gulped. "Nick was there. When it happened. A statue mauled him when he was destroying it."

Lady Alicia murmured her shock.

"I patched him up, but I was going to go see him, to make sure he is all right." She sat back. "In a bit. The master wizards wanted to speak with him, and they'll ensure he doesn't collapse while they question him."

Lady Alicia nodded. "A worthy mission." After a moment, she shook her head. "It is surprising that Mortimer has never spoken with Nicholas. The boy has given him reason to be proud."

Fliss blinked at this unexpected offshoot. If Mortimer Briarwood knew—Lady Alicia kissed her and left, wishing her well on her trip.

My trip, Fliss thought. She would ensure that Nick was well before she got the story. She looked back at the book. "Love is not love, that alters when it alteration finds."

Fliss's mouth drew into a thin line. That was only if she loved him.

She blinked. And then had to blink again.

Chapter 16—Consequences

On the wall opposite, sunlight shone orange. Nick's head ached. He had been rash to promise Fliss.

"The mermaids only thrashed about. One eyed the child at first, but ignored her after. They did not try to do anything, except reach for the child—only one of them did that."

As if this were not the twentieth time he had said that, the wizard wrote something.

"Now, about the lion."

Nick slumped. Every inch of him ached. He should have heeded Fliss. Even if Fliss might have insisted—

"All these things may be important, Nicholas Briarwood." He sat back. "What else do you have to add?"

"Nothing." Nick's head bowed. "I told you everything." He thought of adding, "More than once," but the effort was too much.

"How is the matter going?" said Master Otto from the doorway, not quite managing an authoritative tone.

"He says he has told us everything."

"Send him away, then." Someone moved in the corridor behind him. Master Otto looked over his shoulder. "Yes, what is it?"

The person spoke in a low voice. Master Otto grunted. "Come with me, Nicholas."

Nick suppressed a groan as pointless. He rose and followed Master Otto down the hallway, into his office. Master Otto gestured him to a chair. Nick sat.

"You responded with admirable speed in this matter." From a flamboyant sky, sunlight shone through the windows, over the table and Master Otto's papers.

Nick's eyelids dropped. "You are welcome."

Otto's mouth tightened. "You responded so quickly that I wonder how you managed it."

Silence reigned a moment. Nick stared at the chancellor. His tongue felt heavy in his mouth.

"Without knowing what the scoundrels who summoned up the imps intended."

Nick felt like ice. His heart ought to hammer. He might have guessed that Randall would ramble into diabolerie, but he had not known. And how on earth could Master Otto have come to think that he *might*?

Master Otto said, "Two students said that it had gotten out of hand when they fled. We will catch them, sooner or later."

His side ached. Fliss's spells, however skillfully cast, could not heal all the damage. "I do not doubt it."

"I've half a mind," said Master Otto, "to have Umberto set you catching them as a lesson."

"Without a doubt, Nicholas would do it masterfully." Master Umberto's deep voice echoed through the room. "Given enough time." He walked in and met Master Otto's gaze. "Do you wish to set it? A promising student—but not that promising. I would think that you would wish the culprits caught quickly."

Master Otto's mouth tightened.

"I fear I must steal my student back."

Nick let out a long breath. Master Otto hemmed and hawed, but Master Umberto watched him with the air of a lion, awaiting the moment to pounce.

With relief, Nick rose to his feet. Master Umberto bowed, and Nick trailed after. No sooner were they in the dim, red-carpeted hall than Umberto slowed enough for Nick to come up beside him.

"Master Otto has a point," he said, his voice low. "It would be wise of the culprits to throw themselves upon the mercy of the master wizards while they might still have some."

Nick remembered the blood in the courtyard and wondered how the master wizards could have any now. "I do not know who they are."

Master Umberto said nothing.

"Some friends of mine told me they were planning a prank, but I do not know what."

"A prank," Master Umberto muttered. "May God grant that this, they consider more than a prank."

Nick spread a hand and winced.

"Are you well?" said Master Umberto. "I knew you would be tired."

"I was injured. Fliss—Felicity Seaborn restored me."

They walked out into the sunlight. Birds twittered in the nearby trees.

"You are weary to the bone from your healing and spells—and that interrogation. Go home now, Nicholas."

Nick nodded but looked past Umberto. A crowd came down the paths, toward the building. The sounds were vague but ugly.

"What's that?"

Master Umberto turned. The center of the crowd came into view. A master wizard stalked along the path. Behind him floated two golden globes, each one holding a black-robed figure. One captive started to speak, his words unintelligible with distance. Something hurtled through the air to bounce off the globe. The master wizard stopped to reason with them. Nick made out Randall and Luke.

How could even Randall not see that this would be disaster? Nick looked away. Master Umberto watched him.

"Did Master Ivo catch the culprits?" Umberto said.
Nick nodded.

Nick walked toward St. Catherine's, through the tree-lined
streets. Roses clambering over walls had started to blossom.
Most flowers were still red or deep pink buds, tightly furled,
but the scent of full-blown ones filled the air.

Summer was in full season, Nick thought. He looked at the
roses. Escaping from Master Otto meant facing Fliss all the
sooner, and Fliss would tell Mistress Janet. His shoulders
hunched. He should have told her when she was full of praise
for what he had done to Mistress Martha's creature, or when
the Leonore's Candle had amused her. Perhaps not on the
stairs of St. Agnes—but he could have told her that he had to
speak with her. Or even when they had dealt with Tristram's
spells.

His mouth twisted. Oh, let him admit his own folly. He
should have sought aid at the university the night that
Mortimer had tried to kill him. At the latest, when he
returned to the city.

He walked on. His pace was slow when St. Catherine's
came into sight. Be with me Lord, for I am in trouble and
need.

Fliss hovered on the steps of St. Catherine's. Several students,
passing by, gave her perplexed glances. Across the way, the
students of St. Agnes talked, looking too anxious to practice
anything. Her heart began to beat no faster than before, but
much harder.

"Felicity," said a rough voice behind her.

Fliss looked quickly. "Jack."

Jack leaned against the doorway. "Nick's not here. He was in the square, and the masters still have him."

"I know, I was there. I healed him—the lion mauled him. I suppose the rumors did not spread *that*."

"No," said Jack. "At least, not yet."

"I healed him, but I worried about the spells—" She choked off the words, before Jack could think her more frantic than her reason would justify. If Nick collapsed before the masters, they would tend him.

"He'll be back," Jack said. "The housemaster would not object if you sat by the doorway." His mouth twisted. "Well—not too much."

Janet looked at the papers on the desk. Master Ivo had found the papers with the twosome. She picked a yellowing one up. The paper was brittle and dry beneath her touch. She wondered how long this one had lurked, to look so ancient. One culprit—Luke—claimed to have found it in his family's library.

Perhaps a demon had planted it there and yellowed it to confound him. Her mouth twitched. Not that confusing him seemed difficult. He still looked bewildered that the statues had acted as they did.

"Impudent little wretches!" Master Otto fumed. "They could have killed someone!"

"So they could have," said Janet. "Of course, so could Mistress Martha have. Master Umberto's injury could have been much worse. The good Lord alone knows what would have happened to Nicholas Briarwood if Master Umberto had been unable to pull him through the wall." She turned. "Let us thank a merciful Providence that in neither case was the full harm fulfilled."

"That's different."

Of course it is, thought Janet.

Nick climbed the stairs to St. Catherine's and pulled open the door.

Just inside the door, Fliss perched in the chair, one leg folded up so she could watch the door. She looked at him.

Nick felt as if struck by an ax. God in heaven help me. "We can't talk here."

Fliss glanced back at the hallway. "They won't let you have a woman in your room, I dare say."

Nick only nodded.

"There is the library," she said. "There are places where we could see anyone coming."

Dozens of students and masters filled the paths and the library's doorway, many of them talking of the horrors in the square. Nick pulled aside, into the stacks, as quickly as he could, and walked toward the back windows. There, benches sat in the sunset light, and few people were about.

Fewer than usual, which was to the good. He glanced at Fliss. She was rigidly controlled, but still pale.

He bowed Fliss to the bench. She sat and folded her hands in her lap. Silence reigned for a moment.

"Why do you have no heartbeat?" Fliss said, her voice clear.

Nick's gaze fell. He had promised the truth, and he was too tired to lie. He sat at the bench's other end. "Because I have no heart in my body."

Fliss's hand tightened on her robe, wrinkling the cloth.

"That night, I did not quarrel with my father. When I came home, he called me into his study and gave me something to drink. It was bespelled."

Fliss shifted. He stared at the wall behind her. "When I regained my wits, he had me chained in a secret lair—with a pentacle in the floor."

The memories of the icy stone and chains stopped up his mouth. Nick swallowed. Glancing at Fliss, he could not read her face.

"He intended to sacrifice me to a demon to gain immortality—since I would not be missed, anyone would believe we had quarreled." Words had to be forced through his lips. "He summoned the demon, and he forced it to grant immortality, but the spell did not work as intended. The demon...."

His chest throbbed with remembered pain. Fliss sat still. Her knuckles were white, where they gripped her robes, and he could not look at her face. Outside a bird fluttered and chirped around the window, oblivious to what passed within.

"The demon took my heart from my chest and put— something else in its place. My father had not compelled it to make *him* immortal." He glanced at her face. Her expression had not changed. "And it wrapped up my heart in a spell so that my father could not harm it—or anyone else."

The bird chirped and flew off. Fliss did not move.

Nick's shoulders hunched. "Father drove me out—into the arms of what had to be a stone guardian. I escaped it, with some injuries, and fled to the woods to recover. Which was how I know it wasn't Master Oliver's, to drain life out of things. I ailed there a long time. In the hermitage."

Fliss's indrawn breath was sharp. "He practiced diabolerie," she said, cutting out each word as if with a knife, "and you just *fled?*"

"What could I do? Accuse him of diabolerie?" Nick rose to his feet in a surge.

Fliss looked at his face and flinched.

His voice was still low, but he could not take the intensity from it. "I have no heart in my body. I have a diabolic thing instead, and it is making me immortal."

Fliss's white face did not move.

"Would you think that a demon would give such a thing to a man who did not bargain—and pay—for it? It was proof enough of diabolerie when Master Oliver died."

Fliss's voice sounded half-strangled. "I don't." Her hand went out to his arm.

Nick pulled his arm away, feeling ill. "You don't. Who else wouldn't?" His breath came harshly; he fought to steady it. Fliss did not twitch. "Perhaps if I had come at once and thrown myself on their mercy. But I was—afraid. And there have been other times, when I thought to confess, but each time I didn't, I had more to explain the next."

After a moment, Fliss spoke, her voice very soft. "At the orphanage—that was why you flinched, when I touched you. You were afraid I might find out."

"It was not likely," said Nick, "but I did not think of that."

"Perhaps something can be proven," Fliss said. "It was *not* the only evidence against Master Oliver. In his chambers, they found tomes on diabolerie."

"They'll be in *his* home, which was also *my* home."

Her voice grew softer still. "Don't you want your own heart back?"

"That was why I came," said Nick. "The university has the most knowledge, and I want to learn—"

Fliss bit her lip.

"I've looked. In the library, when I should have been studying. But I haven't had much time for it."

Fliss rose to her feet. "Nicholas," she said formally, "I wish to speak to Mistress Janet, and Master Umberto."

Nick closed his eyes. His chest ached.

Fliss twitched, her robe rustling. "Perhaps not today. Not with the statues. But tomorrow, or the day after."

"Yes," he said, without opening his eyes.

Chapter 17—Decisions

Nick's head hung, and his hair fell over his face. Fliss bit her lip. The lion had mauled him, the spells had drained him, and he had not received the same gift as Master Oliver: if his heart drained life from others, he would show some liveliness. "You need some rest."

Nick nodded, but did not even look up. Fliss put a hand on his arm.

"The housemaster will not let you into St. Catherine's."

"Then, I will get another student to help you to your room." She hesitated. "No, wait a moment."

He raised an eyebrow. She muttered the healing spell under her breath. Little responded, to draw back together what had been broken, but she had done as she had said she would, and check his injuries.

She led the way back to St. Catherine's and pulled open the door. Jack came out of the kitchen, and she breathed a sigh of relief.

"How did your spells work?" Jack said.

"Well. But he should have told the masters that he was too exhausted for questions." She pushed Nick on the shoulder. "Go to bed, Nick. I would hate to have wasted my spells."

Jack laughed.

A voice rose from the kitchen. "We should make sure that he doesn't—test some spells to keep him in place."

Nick smiled a little. "To test the spells, you would need to know that I would *get up* if you did not cast them. Now is no test." After the shout of laughter, he climbed the stairs. Fliss walked him go up, and when he was lost in shadow, she saw Jack looking at her.

"Really think he might not make it?" said Jack.

Fliss nodded.

"I'll make sure he does." Jack started after.

Fliss sighed. She was weary herself, the way healing spells drained, and so she left.

She walked into the fierce afternoon air and, despite the heat, drew a deep breath. She kept barely aware enough of the people around her enough to avoid walking into them and nearly blundered into a bed of blood-red roses. The evidence against Nick was very black. But she thought he would never. . . .

She put a hand to her hair. The diabolist who had created the white sickness, and died of it, had meant no harm to the innocent—at least, to most of the innocent. If Nick's tale was true in every particular, there was a diabolist about. Nick's own words showed how a demon could warp tales.

She changed her path.

She tried not to hope that Mistress Janet would not be there as she reached the office and knocked.

"Yes?" The word crackled with impatience.

Fliss opened the door.

Mistress Janet looked up from her desk, scowling. Fliss's tongue froze.

Mistress Janet said, "No one will die—I think—but at least two will be lame for life. I can't talk."

"I have to—"

Janet looked back down. "They've caught the fools."

"It's not that," said Fliss. "We do not have to talk today, but you will not want to put it off until after the day after tomorrow." She spread her hand. "Tomorrow would be better."

Mistress Janet stared at her. Fliss looked away. In the silence, she heard leaves rustle, and her heartbeat thunder.

"I have to speak with Master Otto, and Master Ivo, and the culprits." Every word Mistress Janet spoke was clipped. "I will be busy on the morrow, from the hour that the university rouses until it sleeps again."

"Then we must speak at dawn," said Fliss, "before it does."

Mistress Janet scowled but nodded. "You should rest," she said, as if the words were strange in her mouth. "You look weary to the bone."

In the charcoal gray coolness, voices intoned psalms.

Fliss bit her lip. The penitents thought they had just reason to fear. God help them all, they might be right—but she had to get to Mistress Janet.

She skittered down alleyway and burst across streets, into the university before the procession reached it. Thank God that Mistress Janet was in charge of such investigations.

She skittered like a mouse through the silent buildings. Even the scholars were just stirring, but it was warmer than it had been when she left Lady Alicia's. Mistress Janet did not rouse that much before the rest.

She came around St. Catherine's. Nick stepped in front of her.

Her breath came in sharply and went out with the words, "You shouldn't be up."

He shrugged. She admitted, though not to him, that he looked strong enough to stand—for a time.

"I've suffered worse," he said, and she felt cold, but he went on, "Have you spoken to Mistress Janet yet?"

Fliss shook her head. "She was busy yesterday. I am here to catch her early."

"And I," said Mistress Janet, "came early to be caught." She came up to them. "Does Nicholas Briarwood know of what you speak? Because you are right, he should be abed."

Nick's smile was not natural. "Better than she does, but I will go rest. She can tell you of it."

Mistress Janet's eyebrows went up.

"Let me show you your student's skill." Nick held out his wrist. "Check my pulse."

Fliss bit her lip, but neither one glanced at her. Mistress Janet looked at Nick a moment before reaching. It took her a minute before color leached from her face.

"I dare say there was another of whom the same could be said, once, at the university," said Nick, lightly, though he looked as if the lion had just mauled him. "But our stories are not the same. I told Fliss the main of it. I will tell you the rest when you deem me well enough."

Mistress Janet looked after him until the door closed behind him. Her voice sounded creaky and unused. "Master Francis was astounded that you managed to save Nicholas's life. I think you didn't." Her face set, she turned on Fliss. "You said it was not urgent."

"It did not happen yesterday," said Fliss. "It was before he came to the university."

Janet's gaze was murderous.

"I did have to heal him, so it was not Master O—"

"Inside," said Mistress Janet.

Janet rapped on Master Umberto's door and entered almost before he answered.

Umberto rose. "An unanticipated pleasure. I thought the statues pressed you too hard for any other duties."

"The fools have been dealt with. I have another matter."
She forced herself to sit back and not perch on the chair's edge.

He sat again. "I presume that you came to me because I
might aid you?"

"Your student, Nicholas Briarwood, was at the squares
when the statues came alive. One mauled him."

"And your student, Felicity Seaborn, healed him. With
skill. He was well enough after the masters questioned him—
though I had to rescue him before exhaustion overwhelmed
him."

He was fond of Nicholas. She drew a deep breath. That did
not affect her duty—or his. "Felicity learned something while
she did it. Nicholas has no heart in his body."

A breeze fluttered the leaves in the tree outside. Janet met
his gaze without flinching.

"That," said Umberto, "is a matter that admits of few
explanations."

Janet's mouth felt dry. "Diabolerie. Nicholas admitted as
much to Felicity. But not his own. His father's, or so Nicholas
told Felicity."

Umberto shook his head. "I do not think it was his own—
though I confess to partiality."

Janet turned in her chair. "Neither do I," she said
scornfully. "Then I am as foolishly fond of him as any master
was of Mistress Anna, or Master Oliver. . . ."

He glanced at her. "I have heard of his father."

"Nicholas said it happened the night that his father claimed
to have quarreled with him. So he hid it for months on end.
He told Felicity he has tried to break the spell, but how could a
student expect to do that on his own?"

Umberto raised a hand. "Unless he tries to flee, this can
wait until he recovers."

Janet grimaced.

"It may not be proof," said Umberto, "but if he does not flee, it is some evidence of innocence." His chair creaked as he leaned back. "And you know that it is not Master Oliver's, when he is so weak."

There was that, thought Janet, drearily. The first thing that Felicity had leapt to say. Her eyes narrowed. Students were not the only ones who could make automata, and unlike Mistress Martha, she would make no error about the source—especially as she wanted no wits at all, only eyes.

She wanted the tale from his mouth quickly enough.

Sweat trickled down Nick's neck. He walked in the building's shade, as slowly as everyone else in the heat, until he reached the doorway and climbed the stairs. Inside, it was cooler, but he walked no faster.

Master Umberto sat behind his desk. Mistress Janet sat in a chair next to it. Fliss perched in the window seat, her hands clutching each other. The light that outlined her shone into the room, but left much dim.

A chair awaited him, before them. After all, they expected him. He sat.

Mistress Janet inclined her head. "Your story. In detail, Nicholas."

Nick drew a deep breath. Without looking directly at any of them, he told how he had come to his father's study. The only sound in the room besides his hoarse voice was the occasional voices floating cheerfully in the window. He described the room he had woken in. Mistress Janet shifted her weight. He looked at her, but she said nothing.

"My father arrived a few minutes later." His gaze went to the wall behind Mistress Janet. "He summoned a demon."

Mistress Janet looked at him. Nick described what he remembered of the ritual. She did not interrupt with questions, and Nick told how his father had offered him, as his own flesh and blood, the child of his body.

"Child of his body," muttered Mistress Janet. "Would that more spells had prices like that." Her mouth twitched. "Or perhaps not."

He found himself slowing as he described the demon's final trick and almost whispering as he recounted what the demon had done to his heart. Fliss blanched, Mistress Janet twitched, and he thought perhaps even Master Umberto looked perturbed.

"The demon vanished once it was done with my heart—and with bragging to my father."

A breeze picked up. It pulled at the curtains and carried the scent of flowers in the sun-warmed air. Nick shivered.

"My father—threatened me then. He said I had made the demon do it. He said that if I denounced him, he would denounce me." His chest ached. "And that all the evidence was against me and not him. I was the one with no heart in my body. And—then he threw me out."

He recounted his tale up to the creature at the entrance.

"A stone guardian?" said Master Umberto.

"It looked—when I saw the books, I knew it looked like one." He drew a deep breath. "I escaped, but it injured me. I fled to the woods."

Mistress Janet's eyes narrowed in thought. "Did you," she said.

Though it was not a question, Nick nodded. "I was tired when I left the party. The bespelled sleep did not rest me. And the injuries were worse than I had suffered at the lion's paws, and I had to enchant them myself. I was too tired to think straight."

Mistress Janet's expression had not changed in the least.

He bolted through the rest of his tale, until his arrival at the university.

Silence prevailed for a minute. On the walkway below, someone laughed, the noise carrying.

"So you returned here," said Mistress Janet. "Where your heart was most likely to be revealed." Her lip curled. "Did you think that you could safely hide it, since it was not Master Oliver's spell?"

"Where else could I study?" His voice sounded flat in his own ears. "Learn to reverse it?"

"There are other schools that teach wizardry in the world," said Umberto, as if they spoke of the weather.

Nick turned his face toward him. "Not like this one."

"And yet," said Mistress Janet, her voice as light as a delicate steel dagger, "you discarded it best provision for such a reversal: its wizards." She leaned forward. "Indeed, after I had cleared your name—and the names of your friends—in the matter of the light spell, you asked me what books might be useful."

Nick did not look up. "So I did. I found nothing of use."

"I could have told you that," said Mistress Janet.

For once, no sound came from the outside, as moments inched into minutes.

"If," Master Umberto said, "the demon's spell is new, we will need to construct a new spell to deal with it." His voice was grave. Nick was not entirely certain that Umberto believed him, only that Umberto did not utterly disbelieve. "Sooner would be better. I have heard many tales of the heart outside the body, but every one ended badly for the wizard."

He gestured at Mistress Janet. "The case of Master Oliver did not, alas, diverge from legend."

Mistress Janet's expression turned meditative. "We will have to break into your father's house to get you your heart back." She clasped her hands about one knee. "And then I will denounce your father for his diabolerie."

Nick's shoulders slumped. Whatever the evidence was, she would, he knew.

"About the pentacle—you said it was inlayed gold?"

Nick nodded.

"Perhaps we could find where Mortimer got the gold, to lay it to his name."

Nick swallowed. Did she believe him, and think that would prove it, or doubt him and think that would settle the matter? He glanced at Fliss. With the light behind her, he could not read her face.

The morning mist was burning off. The sticky air grew hotter, and the sunlight struck with force. The students murmured hopes that it would be done soon, but like a flock of crows, they stood in the square. Anyone who wanted to evade it had already done so.

Nick stood with the other students from St. Catherine's. Master Humphrey would notice if they evaded this. Logs for the fire lay on the stones—Nick's mouth twitched—where one statue had stood. Luke and Randall were chained near it. They did not look grateful—though if someone had died, they would not only go to the royal court, but from there to the fires.

"Students of the university!"

Master Otto's haranguing voice almost managed to sound impressive as he began with succubae, to proceed to the more dangerous arts that Luke and Randall had used. "We burn now the works in which they dabbled. It is, for them, a blessing, to be caught now, before they commit crimes that would cause us to consign them to the flames."

Luke and Randall wore identical expressions: hunted, like wild animals, but not remorseful.

Master Otto marched to the wood to cast the fire spell. Flames leapt up, swiftly growing vigorous; with a minute, all the logs blazed, bright even in the morning light. Hot as well, no doubt.

Jack said, his voice low, "Bet you that's magic. The wood, not just the way he lit it."

"Won't bet against it," said Nick.

"Got it from the Wizards' Wood," said Matthew. "I'd bet."

Jack looked as skeptical as Nick felt.

From a box on the steps, Master Otto pulled out a parchment. Solemnly, he displayed it to the crowd and cast it into the blaze. It fluttered, as if trying to escape, but its path led down. The flames licked it up, turning its edges black the instant it touched them, and consuming the rest before Master Otto threw in the next.

The box held only half a dozen. The firelight cast shadows across Randall and Luke's faces, almost making them look ashamed.

He had forgotten that this shortcut through the university would lead him here.

Mortimer looked at the ashes, cool in the sunset. Young fools, and no rivals to him in the art. To throw your learning away for a prank was folly.

At least, Nicholas had not, associating with them, corrupted them into his ways: to steal another's learning for one's own profit—and burning the books. His eyes narrowed. The most diligent study of the books that Nicholas had touched had not revealed the brat's secrets. He must have burned his own books, not wishing to be stolen from.

The wind stirred the ashes.

Mortimer walked on. From the praise the master wizards heaped on him, Nicholas was deep in his studies. It seemed he could not leave the house without an ambush claiming he should be proud of the little wretch.

He toyed with the notion that Nicholas, having all the time in the world to study, would bend himself to becoming a master at the university, but after a moment, he scorned himself. Nicholas had meddled once; he would not stop. Unlike some masters of diabolerie, there could be no bargains between them. Bargains required honesty. Nicholas found stealing knowledge easier than finding it.

He walked past the Cathedral of the Magi, and his lip curled.

The demon had encased Nicholas's heart in golden magic. He had thought he had time to deal with that, once he had claimed his own immortality, but Nicholas might decide to end their rivalry himself.

Mortimer drew a deep breath. He had not even found Master Oliver's spell, and he had no adequate protection against Nicholas. Even denouncing him to the masters would bring a counter accusation. He had to protect himself.

"He must study, Marie!" said Stephan, his voice carrying.

Edgar looked up from his ale to give Stephan a baneful glance, but across the room, Stephan was not looking in his direction, or even at Agnes, hanging on his arm and looking distressed. "Did you think Nick could impress the master wizards without studying? He's not *that* clever."

Clever enough to weasel out of blame, Edgar brooded. It had all been Randall and Luke. No one even mentioned Nick. He took another swig of the ale.

George came into the room. Edgar glowered at him. The other man glared back—startling enough— and stalked toward him. He spoke in a low voice. "You told the wizards that you had seen Nick talking with Randall."

Edgar raised an eyebrow.

"*I* saw Nick talking with Randall."

"So long as the wizards knew. . . ." Edgar spread a hand.

George's eyes narrowed. "You just hate Nick. Do your own dirty work."

He turned his back on Edgar. Edgar drank more ale. He would never have guessed that George would revolt over such a point, but he should have; everything worked out for Nick.

"Your young Nicholas Briarwood," said Master Otto. "How are his studies coming?"

Umberto stopped in the porch's shadow. The day's heat still penetrated there. "Well. Nicholas is a promising student."

"Is he now." Master Otto's mouth was thin. "He decided on studies abruptly after his quarrel with his father—and he was a friend of Randall's. By some accounts, of the other *prankster* as well."

Master Otto, Umberto thought, would take Nicholas's situation exactly as Mortimer had threatened. "Had Randall no other friends?"

"Has Nicholas Briarwood shown no strange interests?"

Umberto looked at Master Otto's face and the cunning he thought he was showing. "Between Mistress Martha, and Mistress Janet's using his help at Lady Petronella's, Nicholas has been fascinated with diabolerie. He shows promise at dispelling it."

Master Otto stalked off.

Nick walked from the library. To either side, lilies bloomed in violet and blue. He hesitated, trying to work out how they had been enchanted, and noted they should be thinned.

Edgar emerged from the evening shadows beside him. "So you got away with it."

Nick stared.

"You talked with Randall. George saw you." Edgar's eyes burned. "You were at the square, you were the first to move— you must have known—"

"They were in the alley?" Nick stepped forward. "How did you know that? Were they talking with you?"

Edgar blanched and retreated. Nick's fingers tightened on his book. It was a good thing that Edgar had not looked at the book, about the practice of diabolerie.

His heart ought to be pounding.

Chapter 18—Plans

"Before the end, he had a dragon, conjured out of thin air, to devour his foe. Alas, the foe had died for the want of air, first. So did the dragon, which would have prevented its eating him, but he himself also died." Mistress Elise looked about the hall. "The substance is the same, whether dragon or wind, but a dragon is far more compact."

Jack sat back. "If transformation on that scale is that arduous, how was it possible?"

Mistress Elise looked banefully at him—undercutting her warning to the students.

Nick looked at his notes. Last night, at the kitchen hearth, Jack had asked the question. Nick had pointed out they were not masters, to know *everything*. He had not expected Jack to take up the notion. Not when Mistress Elise gave the lecture.

But—she might answer. He listened.

"There are," said Mistress Elise, "sources of power other than one's self."

"But," said Matthew. Nick did not look up but felt keenly aware that he sat between the two of them. "If he drew power from the house, it would have collapsed. Even stone would have collapsed before he transformed all the air into the monster."

"Actually," said Mistress Elise, "stone is less useful for power than wood is." The lecture went on.

At the end, as students gathered up their notes, Matthew said, his voice low, "She didn't say how."

"If," said Nick, "he worried about power—that would have distracted him from the air—"

Jack's eyes narrowed. Matthew looked intrigued.

"But I can't talk about it now." Master Umberto wanted to inspect his—the demon's thing with spells. Umberto had said he would wait until after the lecture; he could hardly make the master wait for more than that.

Jack snorted. "Master Umberto's been running you off your feet lately."

Nick opened his mouth and shut it again. Matthew, who had glanced idly at him, scowled.

Then, Matthew had him as a master, too. "Yes. And I'm keeping what is it secret. Master Umberto wishes that."

Jack looked considering. Even with that much of the truth, Nick felt guilty, but if he said that Mistress Janet had ordered it, Jack and Matthew would only wonder why she was in the position to decree. And Master Umberto *did* wish it.

"If this is anything like the stone guardian," said Matthew, "you have quite high enough a reputation as a promising young wizard. Leave some for the rest of us."

"I hope I can tell you within a month," said Nick, and knew himself for a liar. He would tell them if he could, but he did not hope for it.

Mortimer walked across the room slowly. Like an old man, he thought; then, he felt old. He restored the last book to its place. He had been a fool to try twice. He had inspected every tome, however petty, that Nicholas had ever touched. He had demanded every book that could be found in the city from the bookseller, who denied that Nicholas had ever bought anything from him, and would not dare lie.

At his desk, he poured himself a cup of wine. He glared at it. Some foolish diabolists sold their souls for intoxicating, diabolic brews beyond any human vintner's skill. He could wish for such a wine now. A promising student indeed. Mortimer raised his glass. The sunlight glinted from the wine, making it shine like a ruby.

Mortimer drained it. Nicholas had done it. Briefly, he wondered if the boy could be forced to tell him. It would serve him right.

It would draw attention.

He twisted the empty cup. It glinted in the firelight. Nicholas's friends in the university were not his friends before he went. Perhaps he had learned the folly of associating with fools. But he ate dinner with Lady Alicia and her Felicity. Worse, Nicholas aided Mistress Janet. He could not rely on the white sickness to again confound those interested.

Mortimer poured himself another glass. Had it been wise to let Nicholas escape? Heart or heartless, immortal or perishable, if he had held the brat prisoner, he could have learned more.

He contemplated the cup without drinking. He could not let pride go before his fall. Nicholas had found the lore in the city, but he could not. However humiliating he found it, he should search elsewhere.

Besides, he had not gone aboard for many a year. Who knew what he might find? He looked out the window. The sea glinted, near the horizon. Whatever a thief like Nicholas could find, a skilled scholar could find.

With annoying and unmusical persistence, birds cheeped in the trees. Outside the window, the clouds were charcoal gray. Nick groggily thought about going back to sleep.

A knock sounded at the window, but when he looked, nothing was there. Nick smiled sourly. Randall's spell—originally. But Randall had then taught half their circle the spell. Even those who knew no other spell could wake him that way, if they admitted to knowing him.

The knock came again. Nick rolled out of bed to grab his clothing. The shock of the cold air woke him completely as he scrambled to dress to decency.

He looked out. From the empty paths, Fliss waved at him. She seldom looked so bright-eyed.

He scrambled to pull on his robes and headed down the stairs. No sounds even of movement came from behind the doors, but he opened the door to the college, and Fliss, her cheeks rosy, stood on the threshold.

"I thought of a way."

Nick's eyebrows went up.

"Oh, the library," Fliss said, and headed off.

He was not a stride behind her, but said, "I have to make it back by chapel."

"It won't take long," Fliss said.

That simple a spell. After *weeks* of two masters straining for such a spell. . . .

A librarian cast them a side-long glance, but once they reached a bench inside, Fliss did not sit. Nick hesitated. She whirled to face him.

"I thought about the heart, and the thing in your chest, and—what difference is there between putting back your blood, and putting back your heart?" Her eyes shone. "You can hardly find two things more like."

Nick's breath caught. He felt how his blood was not pounding in his ears. Fliss smiled.

His voice sounded distantly. "There is the thing the demon put in instead."

Fliss waved a hand. "I taught you how to take dirt from a wound."

"You warned me against using it in a wound that had closed," said Nick. "My chest would be worse."

"The demon. . . ." She stared at the floor. Color rose in her face.

Oblivious, birds cheeped outside the window.

It was the right sort of idea, Nick argued with himself. Fliss's spells worked as he needed, if only they could reach through—through flesh and bone. His thoughts flinched away. It would be like passing through—a wall.

Nick drew a sharp breath. "Umberto's spell."

Fliss glanced up.

"When we fought the stone guardian, Master Umberto drew me through solid stone. If we compounded that with your spells, the spell could work." Nick thought for a moment. "Or you and he could cast your spells to work together, as Jack, Matthew, and I did, with the lights—that would be simpler." He grinned. "Better, since the first casting will be on me. It would work on the spell the demon encased my heart with, too."

Fliss began to smile.

On a half-conscious impulse, he leaned toward her, his lips an inch from her cheek.

Fliss turned scarlet and pulled back. "Come. We have to talk with Mistress Janet, and Master Umberto."

The air grew cool with evening. Nick sat on the steps of St. Catherine's, and a rose-red light glowed between his hands. He slowly moved it up, shining over the group. Nothing to do with his father, or his heart—but it whiled away the hours before they discovered a way into his father's house. One, as Master Umberto had said with uncommon severity, that assured they would not be interrupted in their spellcraft.

And with the prospect before him, Master Umberto wanted to distract him with roses.

He lifted the light. With the spells proposed, Mistress Janet praised his cleverness and consigned all the work to those who would cast the spells. *He* would not.

One woman put a hand on her hip. "You make it look easy," she said, her tone quarrelsome.

"It is easy, Hilda!" called another woman—Marjory. Two blue and violet lights flew about his, with more speed than he could have lent his own.

"Hey, Nick," Jack called. "We've got this spell down—how about the transformation spell we argued about?"

"Oh, that one's simple," said Marjory.

Jack rolled his eyes. "We mere mortals have to wrestle with it."

Some students laughed at him, and some at Marjory. Nick managed to emerge from the crowd.

"Master Umberto working you to death?" said Jack.

Nick shook his head. "Some transformations—he said I needed more practice on spell breaking, but he thought he would give me some other work for a moment." His mouth twitched. "I asked if transformations bred true. Master Umberto set me to studying why blue roses sometimes do not last even on the same stalk, and sometimes can be grafted for generations."

Jack snorted. "Wish Master Francis felt the same way."

You'd think, thought Nick, that we imperiled the city with our lights.

Lamplight gleamed in Umberto's room, more against the clouds than the approaching evening. Fliss sat on the edge of her chair. Master Umberto discussed the matter as if with a fellow master, and not with a student new to the university.

"The spell," he said, "must work right the first time."

Fliss's imagination attempted to imagine the spell misfiring and, after a vague, gristly image, failed. She wondered if Nick had considered the chance of failure. He had looked so radiantly happy when he realized that her spell could be used.

She bobbed her head, seriously.

"How do you know that the thing the demon created will come out, like dirt from a wound?"

Fliss opened her mouth, shut it again, and then said, "The spell identifies that which is native to the body." The very words from the book, she thought.

"The demon can not abrogate this spell? To conceal its handiwork?"

"I—can devise a spell to test," Fliss said, weakly. "Based on the cleansing spell. It ought to be simpler, even."

"Probably will be," Master Umberto said. "Nonetheless, Mistress Janet will inspect it, before she commits herself to its use."

Someone walked down the corridor. The moment of silence, inside the room, extended. I feel like a burglar, Fliss thought, afraid that someone will hear us plotting our crime.

Mistress Janet bent over a crystal, which glinted by lamplight. The window mirrored the scene, but where the room was dark, he could see the scraps of moonlight that came through the clouds.

Nick stepped inside her office. She gestured him to a chair. "Anyone about?"

Nick shook his head, watching the crystal. That morning, he had snapped up the spell that Master Umberto had thrown to him like a starving dog snatching a bone, but he had mastered it before an hour was out. Shoots from the roses were set in a greenhouse, awaiting blossoming, but if he used spells to force them, he would not know whether he affected more than their growth.

His gaze went to the crystal. He wondered for how long this would occupy them. He doubted Mistress Janet lacked things to do.

"One can see through the crystal, and so it is useful for far-seeing." Mistress Janet straightened. "Moonlight will get us into the tunnel, but I will need a light spell once inside. Still, light goes both ways—that will be simple enough."

"What if my father is doing something?"

"We will retreat. At least he will not interrupt the spell to restore your heart."

"He'll see us," said Nick.

"And we'll see him," said Mistress Janet. "If he is up to no good, he must be stopped *at once*. I have seldom been so glad as when you mentioned 'child of my body.' It gave me hope that he had trapped himself with too narrow a spell. But since he found one spell, he could find others." Her hand spread over the stone. "You were not here for the white sickness, but you have seen the graves. There are many spells he could use."

Nick looked away.

Mistress Janet fixed her gaze on the crystal. Words slipped from her mouth. After a minute, she straightened. "See, Nicholas."

Nick walked over. As tiny as a miniature on ivory, and far more delicate, the crystal showed the moonlit and puddle-covered road that he had stumbled on, last winter. The grass grew thickly by the ditch, enwreathed with flowers colorless by moonlight, but on the hill, trees stood.

"Up there," Nick said, "by the stream."

The crystal's image slid up the hill. The brook babbled in unnatural silence. Nick touched his lip with his tongue and considered the trees. The wet grass and brush grew thickly, hiding more than the snow had. Rabbits, now and again, darted through them. He had not looked back at the tunnel once he left it—and Mistress Janet already looked impatient.

"There," he said. "By the Queen Anne's lace."

Mistress Janet plunged the scene through the flowers. The stairs gaped, with dimness below.

She stopped the crystal. After a moment, the stone guardian ambled from the shadows. "I hope," Mistress Janet said, "that that is not a demonic being. There are many good priests about, but I don't know one I trust to bring into this." She glanced at Nick. "The light spell, Nicholas."

Nick cast it. The guardian snarled in silence and leapt, its fangs trying to close on the bare air. Nick's side ached in memory. Mistress Janet pulled back, reflexively, and the stone guardian landed in a heap. For a moment, it looked as if it were wincing from a pain in its jaw, but it turned to attack again.

"What a pleasant greeting," Mistress Janet said, and moved down the tunnel. The guardian followed, jumping on the light more than once. Even tiny, in the crystal, its claws and fangs were sharp.

"If it claws at the door," said Nick, "my father will notice."

Mistress Janet lifted her eyebrows, but retreated to the stairs, and up. The stone guardian followed only to the stairs.

She sat back. "We have to get by it. This time. I can not send us inside without knowing what we will find there."

Her gaze settled on him and did not move. Nick swallowed. He was—he did know of stone guardians. And he was the only one to know this one. His gaze flickered back. Even if they could destroy it through the stone, that would warn Mortimer.

"It did not attack me before I reached the stairs, that night." His arm itched. "If we got by it before I cast the light spell. . . ."

She nodded. He dissolved the spell. Mistress Janet sent the crystal scene back down, into the tunnel. She frowned. "You went down *this* tunnel—in the dark?"

Nick flushed a little. "I was desperate." He cast his spell. The stone guardian shuffled in the shadows, but did not leap out. Mistress Janet swept the vision down the tunnel and through the door. The spell burst out into the room, gloomy and vacant. Books and things sprawled over his father's table with a sloppiness Nick did not remember, but the pentacle, the altar, and the walls had not changed.

Over the pentacle, gold glowed. Through its translucent shell, he saw a dark shape, about the size of his fist. His breath became shallow and fast.

"Mortimer can not have put his safety in the hands of that stone guardian alone," said Mistress Janet, her voice unusually deep. She looked at the room with narrowed eyes.

"No one suspected him," Nick said. "Wards would draw attention to the tunnel. That would bring more danger than anything they could protect against."

"The houses about here," said Janet, "have so many wards that it would be hard to pick out any of them as more than the others."

"Less out there," Nick said. "The houses in the city were built when feuding was a real danger, or at least a real memory. But this was built merely by my great-grandfather."

Mistress Janet looked back at the crystal. "The door has something odd. We shall have to check it when we venture there."

"The spell of discernment? Can't it be cast through—"

"It does not dissolve quickly, and we can not break the original spell." She glanced at him. "What did you use it on?"

"Myself," said Nick. And then he had moped, long enough for it vanish.

She gestured, dismissing the spell, and stared at the wall. "Simpler than many a diabolist's lair. We can even reverse the spell there, which would be simplest and safest. And then—"

Nick looked down at the crystal. Then she would accuse
Mortimer Briarwood.

Her accusing his father was his father's accusing him.

Chapter 19—Commitment

China clinked in Lady Alicia's parlor.

"Shocking," said Lady Sylvie. "Mortimer's ignoring his son like that. I knew he was rather—but *what* could Nicholas Briarwood have done to inspire that?"

Gossip, thought Fliss, wearily. She sat back, letting her hair fall free. In the muggy weather, it clung to the back of her neck, and it was too short to tie back.

The hideous weather did not help. Though it had been only two weeks since Mistress Janet had resolved to put Nick's heart back, and four days since she and Master Umberto had made their plans, her nerves were overwrought with waiting.

Listening to nonsensical gossip did not ease them.

"There has to be something about the stories about Nicholas Briarwood," said Marie's mother, Isabelle. "Mortimer Briarwood has his faults, but he and Phillipa Greenleaf were such a bad match because of her folly and his studiousness. He can not complain of that in Nicholas."

Marie nodded as if she had not declared those studies made Nick dull. Fliss sipped her tea. Then, Marie thought Giles's flowers charming, and Fliss did not want to think on that.

"For Mortimer not even to acknowledge his son, when Nicholas shows such promise." Isabelle's hands fluttered like small birds. "There has to be some reason."

"Mortimer Briarwood," said Lady Alicia, as if commenting on the weather, "is so secretive that it is hard to know what will offend him. Having dined with Nicholas Briarwood several times since the quarrel—he did not seem dreadful to me."

"Well, of course, Nicholas finds Fliss charming," said Isabelle.

"Secretive, to be sure," said Lady Sylvie. She looked as if she had picked up a stick and found it a poisonous snake. "Why, Mortimer is off on a journey—leaving the country—and I just heard about it this morning, did you know that?"

Words leapt to Fliss's mouth. She bit down on them. She had to sound as if it were idle gossip to her. Mortimer was not a hermit. He had heard how promising Nick was. He might hear that Fliss Seaborn was fascinated by his departure.

She surprised herself with the coolness of her voice. "When is he leaving?"

"Next week," said Lady Sylvie, "can you believe it?"

The other women exclaimed. Fliss wondered how she would endure. It was a fight to keep her voice steady.

"How long is he going for?"

"At least a month." Lady Sylvie shook her head. "You would not think that even Mortimer could keep his preparations for that amount of time secret, wouldn't you?"

"He could hardly go for less," said Isabelle. "What would be the point, to go and come back?"

The heat had just started to slacken outside, and the room was still muggy. Ruddy sunlight shone on Janet's desk. She glared at the paper before her. She had denounced diabolerie before. She pulled back her hair from her neck to let the faint breeze under it.

"If I do it wrong, Master Otto will hold that I have slandered a master of whom no evil has been said since he was a student—and I have not accused Nick because he is a pet of mine." She rapped her pen against the desk.

Her thoughts flitted, to Symond's advice. If she had taken it, she would have left by now. She might even be married.

She remembered Nick Briarwood's white face. She wondered if Felicity would have denounced him to anyone else. She shifted her weight. She had conscientiously spied on him and found nothing, but she was still spying. Nick might end up glad of evidence toward his innocence, she told herself.

Footsteps echoed in the corridor, and Felicity hurried into the study. Her face was sweaty, but she smiled.

"I've learned when."

Sitting back, Janet raised an eyebrow.

"At tea at Lady Alicia's. Half a dozen of the society ladies, talking about how shocking Mortimer Briarwood's behavior is. One said that Mortimer would leave the city for a month—leaving next week."

Janet's hand froze with the pen in midair. After a long minute, she grinned. "That will be it, then."

On the steps, Fliss smoothed her skirts. She should have long ago devised a tale to explain herself. With the prospect before her, she could not collect herself.

But she could spend the night in the street, either. She opened the door.

"Fliss?" said Lady Alicia.

Fliss drew in a deep breath. It did not steady her much, especially when the noise revealed that Lady Alicia was not alone.

She walked forward. By the time she reached the door, Giles had already conjured up flowers for her.

"I thank you—but I fear I can not—my studies—" Her words tripped over each other.

"You've been busy lately," said Lady Alicia.

Her tongue felt leaden. She managed to move it. "Mistress Janet." Her fingers tightened on the flowers. "She does not want me to talk of it."

Giles sighed deeply. "I hope your studies will not occupy you always."

She bent over the flowers. He had mastered the spell; he never had any difficulty conjuring this bouquet up.

The sea breeze pulled at Mortimer's clothing. He stalked along the dock. A ship's officer bowed to him, but he barely heard the man's greeting, knowing that his wealth, not his scholarship, bought the respect.

On the deck, two wind wizards inspected their tools, the only thing about them that marked them as not sailors. At his glance, they pulled off their caps. Slowly, Mortimer walked up the gangplank. Petty wizardlings, mere technicians—but no worse than any "master" at the university. Better, in that these fellows would keep to their place.

The steward offered to show him his cabin, and Mortimer followed the man. The thing could be done; what Master Oliver could do, could be done again. And he would exercise more prudence than Master Oliver, so that Mistress Janet could not whimsically murder him.

The steward bowed him into the richly arrayed cabin. As he left, Mortimer settled into the chair; its carvings of vines and beasts on the legs, arms, and back were over-intricate, but the expense showed they did not take him lightly.

His gaze went to the porthole. He could only glimpse the university. With Nicholas looking as ill as he did, it was clear that the spell he had found was not Oliver's. Mortimer smiled. Let Nicholas fret over his health over an endlessly prolonged life. *He* would get both life and health.

Outside, a sailor shouted. Footsteps drummed on the deck, and the ship lumbered from the docks.

Umberto lingered among the trees. Sunlight dappled the dead leaves of the forest floor, and a golden squirrel ran through them, making them rustle.

He had no real reason, now. All his students were hard at work; even Nicholas transformed roses and made cuttings— after refusing to force the blooms, for fear that would affect the transformation. He chuckled. Promising bright-eyed students. He had time enough now to look at the Wizards' Wood, as he had come here to do.

The leaves rustled, and the spangles of light shifted about him. The woods held greater marvels than that squirrel.

But if he discovered a marvel he would—if it were fascinating enough—be lured away from attention to Nicholas Briarwood.

Umberto stopped and tilted his head back, to look at the maples, towering pillars in a green-roofed cathedral. Great shafts of sunlight pierced those leaves. No, he would not risk the distraction, of even a study to be laid aside.

He let his breath out.

To his right, sunlight moved oddly. He glanced over. Among the dust motes, a yellow wing fluttered, and then another. A flock of sunshine birds, trilling, flew from the sunbeam. Bird after bird took form from the light, and glowed beneath the boughs. Trees echoed with their song, until their flight bore them back into sunlight, and with sweet notes, they dissolved back into light.

Umberto did not move, not for a time after the last had vanished again.

A few strides way, giggles sprang up from a gaggle of students; half a dozen young women turned from a student from St. Catherine's, and protested that he was impossible.

Nick grimaced. He had thought that practice might distract him. With Lenore's candles floating colorfully about him, he envied Fliss, who had only to put off Lady Alicia.

Green exploded in his face, and he sputtered. A handful of students laughed—several of them older ones. One had been in the threesome, whose little prank had been foiled by his smoke dog. He drew a deep breath. At least he did not look malicious about it.

Around the door to St. Agnes's, laughter burst. A woman walked up to it. It opened of its own. When she entered, it snicked shut again—and then opened to let her out again. Nick wandered closer.

One woman looked him. "What do you think?" She spread her hand, as the door slid open for others.

He raised an eyebrow and walked over. The door opened. "The housemistress would—not approve."

The student leapt forward, and others hurried to help her break it. Nick pulled back. It distracted, but he had to rise early in the morning.

Before the sky was quite dark, he was abed, but not asleep. Then lights flood his room: rose, blue, green, yellow. He peered at the window, at the Lenore's candles clustering there. More appeared, in violet, orange, and pink, even as he watched.

Speaking of spell-breaking—but even if he had mastered the spells, he was outnumbered. He could not break faster than they could conjure. He pulled a blanket over his head. They were, he reminded himself, friends of his; they meant no harm; it was not their fault he could not tell them the truth.

He would sleep badly whatever happened.

Nick stepped inside the chapel. He shivered from the chill before dawn, even here where the air was still. Starlight did not reach through the few windows. The half dozen candles were the only light. Nick genuflected toward the sanctuary and, rising, picked out the statue of St. Jude from the side altars. He found a coin, slid it into the box, and dropped to his knees. "Lord, have mercy. Christ, have mercy. Lord, have mercy." He shivered. "St. Jude, pray for me."

He had confessed the night before and only lingered with the other scholars after—he was not an utter fool—but he still felt cold with dread. "Lord prosper our work and defend us from our enemies," he whispered.

Moments slid by. For all that Mistress Janet wanted to venture before chapel, he was too early to leave. He should not have gotten up—except, why should he lie abed, staring at the wall or ceiling, thinking these same thoughts? Here at last, he could collect himself enough to pray.

"Keep me safe, O God, I take refuge in You. I say to the Lord: 'You are my God. My happiness lies in you alone.'"

The candle barely flickered. The smoke arose like a little ghost.

"I will bless the Lord who gives me counsel, Who even at night directs my heart."

He managed to keep his voice steady, but he stopped after that verse.

He watched the candle flame a long minute.

"I keep the Lord ever in my sight: with Him at my right hand, I will stand firm. And so my heart rejoices and my soul is glad, even my body shall rest in safety. For You will not leave my soul among the dead, nor let your faithful servant know decay."

The candle flame stood steady and straight ahead of him. His mouth was dry as he finished: "You will show me the path of life, the fullness of joy in your presence. At your right hand happiness forever more."

On the roadside, the air was still cool, but it grew warmer, and the sky had turned from black to charcoal gray. Birds chattered from every tree. Nick dragged in a deep breath. The waist-high grass—thick with blue chicory, white Queen Anne's lace, and yellow hop clover—lashed at his legs and splattered him with dew. A faint light, bobbing over the grasses, showed where Umberto stood, but the other two were only visible from where the grasses shifted.

None of them spoke. Then, neither did he. He walked up the hill, into the birch grove. Footsteps swished through the grass. The tunnel gaped before them, dark among the silvered grass; he wondered that no one had fallen into it.

You faced a stone guardian once before, Nick reminded himself. "Master Umberto, shine the light in here." Without thought, he pointed; a moment later, he dropped his hand.

Even without it, the silver light flew over the grass, making the blades cast knife-sharp shadows, and settled over the tunnel. It cut out the steps in light and black shadow.

For a moment, Nick imagined bloodstains on the stone.

Something moved inside, too vague to show anything more than the motion. Then, with a sound of rock grinding against rock, the stone guardian crept into the light. Its eyes fixed on the opening.

Clever enough to know that we are here, Nick thought. He cast his spell quickly. It turned its head to stare at the noise, but when it moved forward, it crashed against the wall. Nick braced himself. Its expression turned baneful, and his side twinged. Mistress Janet's voice rose quickly beside him. Chips of stone fell from its limbs, and it raised its head. Then its nose flaked off. Mistress Janet intoned on. It crumpled into dust.

A long minute later, Nick dropped the wall. The dust stirred in the breeze, but showed no signs of reforming.

"So, Nicholas," said Master Umberto. "Your plan for a stone guardian not made by diabolerie must be deemed a success."

Nick almost smiled at that, but his nerves were too overwrought. He climbed down, into the tunnel's chilly, damp air. He had imagined the stains. All traces of his blood had washed away.

The tunnel stretched into the gloom. It was warmer than in the winter, but he shivered.

"I think," said Mistress Janet, "that you can drop the spell now, Felicity."

Silently, the others appeared. For a moment, they all stood still.

Her coppery hair swirling behind her, Mistress Janet walked down the tunnel as if she had no fear. Nick stepped aside, and they followed her. The air smelled of wet earth and rock, and not at all of greenery. Soon summer warmth was excluded from the air. Their footsteps resounded.

Nick glanced down. There was no dust—and no trace of his flight. Had it taken this long at midwinter?

The solid oaken door appeared in front of them. Mistress Janet stopped, putting her hands on her hips, and looked over every inch.

She did not glance back. "Did your father do anything with the door?"

"He opened it to throw me out, and closed it after me, both with a spell."

She cast the spell of discernment. The door lit up. Fliss shifted her weight. "Nick—you're...."

Mistress Janet glanced back at Nick and again eyed the door. "No traps. On the spell, at least." Umberto's weight shifted, but Janet went on. "Do you remember the gesture to open the door?"

Nick closed his eyes, summoned up his memories, and slowly moved his hands. He had looked more at his father's face than his hands, but it had gone like. . .this.

With a faint snick, the door slid open. It showed a sliver of the dark room behind. Nick breathed a sigh of relief. Mistress Janet gestured for silence.

"Do not touch it," said Master Umberto. "I have seen such a spell. . . ." His words trailed off as if he forgot their presence. Mistress Janet rolled her eyes toward the ceiling, but gestured for Nick and Fliss to stay back. Master Umberto's hands rose to push the tunnel's still air; a breeze blew the door the rest of the way open.

"Do not touch the door, passing by it." Umberto pulled his robes aside to walk in. Nick followed.

Except for what lay on the table—and the jumble there had only shifted from when they saw it in the crystal—the room had not changed since he had fled it. The chains sprawled as they had fallen from him. The gold enchantment encased his heart like amber, and gleamed.

Nick drew a deep breath. His heart beat the harder. He felt the void in his own chest.

"Let us do what we came for," said Mistress Janet.

Nick's breath caught. This place held only one place where he could lie down, since the floor would make the task harder for Fliss and Master Umberto. He still felt bitterly cold.

He forced himself to walk over, shedding his robes and pulling loose his shirt. The glow from the discernment spell had yet to fade. The others waited in silence. He yanked the shirt off and sat on the altar. Fliss looked pale and uncertain; Master Umberto, grave and unreachable.

Mistress Janet tried a heartening smile.

Nick lay down and stared at the ceiling. No longer needing to meet or avoid his gaze, the others moved in rustles of clothing. Master Umberto spoke in low voice.

I waited in the hermitage while I recovered, Nick told himself, for longer than this. His hands tightened into fists.

Beside him, Mistress Janet began an incantation. Master Umberto and Fliss fell silent. Mistress Janet's fingers traced against his shoulder. Numbness spread through his chest. Nick drew a deep breath. Lord, have mercy on me. Christ, have mercy on me. Lord, have mercy on me. Blessed Mary, pray for me. St. Jude, pray for me. St. Catherine, pray for me.

Master Umberto pronounced the wall-passing spell. His resonant voice sounded even more authoritative than Mortimer's had, the night he had lost his heart. He swallowed. St. Michael, Archangel, pray for me. St. Raphael, pray for me.

Fliss's light voice rose. Their words collided in a jumble. Nick's fingernails dug into his palms. He would not look. He would not watch his own heart float across the room.

The thing in his chest weighed in spite of the numbness.

God help me, he prayed; God have mercy on me. Mistress Janet's hand touched his arm, and he flinched.

Fliss and Master Umberto walked across the room, their footsteps racking Nick's nerves. He closed his eyes. Master Umberto's deep voice rumbled beside him. Even with his eyes closed, Nick could feel Fliss lean over him, her words reaching his ears as a barely distinguishable murmur.

Something wrenched his chest, not painfully, but so violently that it shook his body to his fingers and toes. His eyes popped open. For a light-headed second, he saw Fliss leaning over him, her spell pushing his heart back. The demon's thing hovered in air. Nick looked away. Fliss's spells changed, to healing. Master Umberto joined her, his deep voice and her light tones harmonizing in one spell. Nick felt his blood pounding in his ears.

A long minute later, Fliss and Master Umberto fell silent. Looking more strained than ever, Mistress Janet pronounced two sharp words. Sensation flooded back. His chest ached, but the bone-draining fatigue was worse—and his heart beat.

The other three stood silently about him.

Nick started to sit.

Master Umberto put a hand on his shoulder. "Rest, Nicholas." He looked over at Mortimer's table. "While we deal with Master Mortimer's work."

Mistress Janet walked across the room with determination in her eyes. Nick leaned back. No, Mistress Janet would not leave his father's house for a long time.

He snagged his shirt. With the numbness fading, it was cold.

Janet pronounced a short, crisp spell and looked at the papers. Nick frowned. He could not see a thing. Then she pronounced it again, with only the faintest of variations, and the papers glowed—but it was not the spell of discernment.

Still, she looked pleased. Waving one paper in the air, she said, "Do not even come close to them, Nicholas."

Chapter 20—Tales

The sun had risen over the trees. Even in Master Umberto's study, the air was already warmer. Nick sat in the corner. His head bent. As they had come into the building, students had whispered among themselves. Rumors were flying.

Mistress Janet stood before Master Umberto's safe and stolidly loaded it with the books and papers. Fliss added her armload to the stack. Nick and Master Umberto watched. As intently as thieves hiding their loot, thought Nick.

From the doorway, Master Otto said, "Mistress Janet, wherever did you get those—books?"

They all started.

He slid into the room. "Despite the care you lavish on them, they are not written on sheet of gold."

"From Master Mortimer Briarwood's secret lair." Mistress Janet's voice was sweet. "He's practiced diabolerie."

Color drained from Master Otto's face.

She stepped away. Master Umberto locked the safe without glancing at Master Otto, and Janet's voice grew sweeter. "At his house, I laid a spell to keep him out, but he might break my spell. It's hard to judge his abilities when he has hidden them for so long."

Master Otto's face took on a lupine delight. "Nicholas Briarwood, do you support this slander? Of your own father?"

"I told her of it."

Master Otto blinked. Then he sniffed. "No wonder he threw you out—making such claims. How did you know it was diabolerie?"

He *was* the chancellor. Nick rose politely. "Because I saw the demon. Heard what he bargained for. Knew what he offered the demon: myself."

Master Otto's face worked as if he fought even that.

Nick steadied himself on the chair. "He failed—the demon outwitted him. He threw me out of the house because he blamed me for the failure."

"Meddling in his diabolerie?" Master Otto's lip curled. "The apple never falls too far from the tree."

"He lied." But it sounded unconvincing even to him. "He could not conceive of the demon's outwitting him on its own, finding a loophole in his demands—though he had me bewitched and chained up before I laid eyes on it."

Master Otto's scornful face mocked him.

"Mistress Janet aided me in reversing the demon's works on me—"

Master Otto suddenly had a cunning look. He turned to Mistress Janet. "How long have you known this?"

Her eyes narrowed.

"Since Nicholas Briarwood first discovered it? And yet you let it slide." He shook his head. "We should never have given you sole charge of investigating diabolerie."

Mistress Janet raised an eyebrow. "The king's justice might listen to your request, but. . . . " She spread her hands. "They will ask why, and learn that the magic imperiled Nicholas Briarwood. I will charge Mortimer Briarwood with diabolerie and attempted murder—now, when his son is free from peril." She lowered her hands. "Judge whether they will listen to me or to you."

Nick envied her her cool voice. He thought he would feel sick if he were not so tired.

Master Otto's voice carried to the next room—and probably to the ears outside the building. "We can summon him to face charges."

Nick slumped on a bench. He had underestimated what terror had done for him, the night he had lost his heart. Now, he could barely keep his eyes open. He could never have made it to the woods today.

Fliss perched on the bench, with her hands folded in her lap, and gave him anxious glances.

"Nonsense," Mistress Janet said. "If Mortimer Briarwood does not come willingly, we must force him. So we must have the force at hand."

Fliss whispered, "You need to rest, Nick."

Nick sighed and slumped further. "Tell Master Otto that."

Fliss leaned forward. "If you collapsed—"

Nick pondered it. It seemed too much of an effort.

The door opened. Nick wearily wondered whom the servants had been unable to put off.

Fliss hopped to her feet. "Lady Alicia!"

Lady Alicia nodded to her. Nick collected himself and started to rise.

"Sit, Nicholas," said Lady Alicia. "It is clear—" She looked him up and down and shook her head.

"What. . . . what brought you here?" Fliss said.

Lady Alicia smiled. "Why, what deals with my ward concerns me." Her smile fading, she went within.

After a minute, her voice rose. "To see to my ward, and learn the truth, when the rumors are so many. Some said she was hurt. Though anyone can see that it is Nicholas Briarwood who has suffered."

Mistress Janet's voice was quiet enough that Nick could not make out words. He wished he could sleep on the bench.

The door flew open again. Master Humphrey eyed Nick, aghast, and walked by Fliss.

"Good God, what are you doing here?" Master Otto said.

"What did you mean, putting that pup in the college? If half the tales are true, you could have brought down the oldest college in the university with your folly!"

"You can tell us these tales—in a civil tone!" said Mistress Janet, "and we will tell you how many lies you are lending credence to."

From the way he flinched, Humphrey had not realized that she was there. Nick's mouth twitched.

Fliss whispered, "Your friends will know the truth."

Well, it would prove who his friends were. His old circle had not proven faithful. He remembered practicing spells on the lawn with scholars. But he had known them—and they, him—some months. . . .

Lady Alicia's crisp voice rose. "In this, his complaint is just. Saint Catherine's has nothing like enough protection against a diabolist as powerful as Mistress Janet describes. Nicholas would be in danger, and so would all the students."

"Mortimer has not been convicted yet," Master Otto said.

The crisp voice turned dry. "If Mortimer murders Nicholas, that will be proof enough—but little consolation to Nicholas."

"Considering that you came here for news of your ward, Lady Alicia—" said Master Otto.

"Considering that I also am a master of this university," Lady Alicia said, "that is a rash assertion. But—in view of any trouble I have given you, I will aid you. Nicholas Briarwood shall remain at my house. Centuries of feuding have given it wards enough to deal with Mortimer at least as well as anywhere else you could conceal him."

"An excellent proposal," said Mistress Janet. "Nicholas will be safe at the university when he is awake and well, and can defend himself, but asleep or recovering—best if you took him now, while I show Otto the evidence. Felicity can help me."

Nick sat up, met Master Otto's poisonous gaze, and wished Mistress Janet were not so bold. He still had to avoid being convicted of diabolerie on Mortimer's evidence.

And nothing would acquit him, in Master Otto's eyes.

At midday, Fliss walked toward St. Catherine's. Even picking her way for shade, she escaped the sun little, and the stares not at all. Lucky Nick, to be so ill he could not stay.

Master Otto will doubtlessly require him later, said one virtuous thought.

Fliss grimaced. From the steps of St. Catherine's, a couple of students looked at her and whispered—but it was so hot. She wished she had not offered to fetch Nick some clothes. Even on an errand of mercy, the housemaster would hardly allow her into the college. She should have said that Master Humphrey should send the clothing on.

"And gone home myself." She plodded toward the stairs. She had not realized the extent of the spell she had cast.

"Fliss!" Jack came up beside her. "We heard—"

"What are the rumors saying?"

"That Mistress Janet and Master Umberto and you and Nick were up to your tails in something—maybe diabolerie." His mouth twisted in derision. "And that some of you were hurt."

"Only one of us was hurt. Nick."

Jack flinched.

"It was *because of* diabolerie. Lady Alicia—my guardian—is giving him shelter to recover without—"

She hesitated. The news seemed to have sunk in: Jack turned gray. "Without what?" he said, slowly.

Fliss dragged in a deep breath. Master Otto would babble to anyone who would listen, but she was not him. "I do not know how much of this Mistress Janet wants talked about. But to protect him from the diabolist." Jack did not speak, but her words had carried far enough; other students stared at her. "I spoke with your housemaster about getting his clothing from the college."

"Fliss!" A woman hurried toward St. Catherine's, her black robes flapping; Marjory, Fliss thought, remembering the Lenore's candles. "Thank God you are all right."

Fliss smiled, weakly. Other students came out of St. Catherine's, glancing toward Marjory, and her. She nearly groaned. "Please, I came...."

"I'll find Master Humphrey," Jack said. He took the stairs two at a time. The students crowded around Fliss,.

"Already?" Master Humphrey's voice carried, silencing the students. He peered out at Fliss. "At least you haven't—"

"You were there when Lady Alicia agreed to shelter him," said Fliss. "Because you insisted he wouldn't be safe here."

Protests rose from the scholars. "He wouldn't even need the masters," said one man. "*We* could do it."

"Lady Alicia," said Fliss, "has centuries of wards woven about her house. They wouldn't *dare* put that many on the college. *Your* spells would mix up with them and then—well, that's what we *don't* want to find out."

Scholars laughed. Master Humphrey slowly turned red.

"But is it dangerous?" said Matthew. His voice carried and silenced.

"We can hope not," said Fliss, and the silence lasted long—until broken by raucous laughter from the next street. Several students grimaced.

"We will remember him," said Marjory, "in our prayers. At chapel."

"This—ridiculous horror—" said Master Francis, in the corridor of All Angels'. While Janet's glance stopped up his words, he showed no signs of repentance.

"I did not—" Janet reached out to grip his arm. "I did not show any of you."

Master Francis looked too startled to free himself, and she did not give him a chance, drawing him into her rooms.

"Stay there."

"Really, Mistress Janet," said a voice from the doorway, but she already turned and hauled open a box.

It lay there.

It was no larger than Nick's heart, the size perhaps of his fist, but it lay, dark and contorted. On its surface, shapes hovered on the edges of appearing as—something—but never took enough appearance to tell what evil form they had.

Neither Master Francis nor the wizards at the door spoke. She pushed it under their noses. They jerked back.

"Look," she said. She did not know how long this work, but still—"None of you dare leave without looking."

Fliss stepped through the back door. The cooler hallway was lit only by one window at its end, and she let her eyes adjust. The case Jack had brought for her felt far too heavy for the few pieces of clothing it contained. She eased it to the ground and used her free hand to pull the hair from the nape of her neck.

Lady Alicia's voice carried from the sitting room. "Certainly, I let Nicholas Briarwood stay here. Do you want Mortimer to—dispose of the evidence?"

Fliss closed her eyes. She had come in this way to avoid notice, but there was no way up but past the sitting room. Suppressing a sigh—the noise could carry—she sneaked.

Lady Alicia's voice rose again. Perhaps she had guessed.

At the stair top, Fliss hesitated. Weary, but if she saw for herself how Nick was, it would not take long. She had to leave the clothing anyway.

A conscientious wizard would ensure she had healed him correctly and completely.

Fliss glided down the hallway. Behind a guestroom door that lay half open, there was movement. She crept over. The housekeeper sat and knit. Keeping an eye on Nick, Fliss thought. She pushed the door open with care, so that it did not creak.

The window of the north-facing room left it nearly as dim as the hallway. Nick lay abed, his eyes closed though he still wore everything but his boots. Fliss put the case inside the door and slid closer. He sighed, stirred, and settled again without opening his eyes. The housekeeper's mouth twitched, but her knitting did not hesitate.

His chest rose and fell. She walked toward the bed. Weary though she was, the spell had been simpler than she dreamed possible. Perhaps he—her hand went out, to lie against Nick's chest.

Beneath her fingers, his heart beat. Fliss let out a long breath. Thanks be to God. Behind her, the needles no longer clinked, but she did nothing more than notice. Not when she had dreamed of Nick's having no pulse.

Nick grunted. His dark eyes, opening, met her gaze. Still unreadable, those eyes, but Fliss jumped back, feeling heat rise to her face. "I was. . .I was just. . . ."

Nick smiled and caught her still extended hand. "I can hardly believe it myself." He tugged her down to sit on the bed. "Ensure that your handiwork holds. If I sicken while this tired. . . and the good housekeeper will ensure no wrongdoing."

The housekeeper snorted but said nothing. After a moment, the click of knitting began again. Fliss laid her hand on his chest again. The steady beat reassured her.

His eyes were half-closed. "Are they—the master wizards—done?"

Fliss nodded. "The warrant is out, and the evidence is stored." She suppressed a yawn and leaned against the bed post, to steady herself.

Nick's eyes closed again.

She thought she heard the housekeeper moving, behind her, but she had already had a weary day.

A cool breeze, damp with dew, spread from the window with the hazy morning light. Fliss, her hair tied back with a ribbon, walked into the breakfast room.

At the table, Lady Alicia smiled. "So this is what you have been about, all these odd hours."

Fliss nodded, not meeting her gaze, and took a muffin.

Lady Alicia picked up a cup. "From time to time, I have talked with Mistress Janet concerning your future."

Fliss nodded again.

"I extorted a promise from my brother—many, many years ago, when you were small—that if need be, you would be raised and sent to the university by him."

Fliss swallowed her mouthful quickly. She wondered if Lord Baldwin, with his offer, knew that.

"But Mistress Janet assures me that you will not need to rely on his goodwill. At need, you could become a scholar. Like Nicholas Briarwood."

"I would do my best." The softness of her voice surprised Fliss.

Lady Alicia nodded. "Now, I have something to ask of you. I wish you to finish your studies at the university and take your degree." She put down her cup. "Before you marry. For that matter, before you betroth yourself."

Fliss felt cold. What had the housekeeper said?

Then, she had fallen asleep on Nick's bed. Her fingers tightened on the muffin, and crumbs fell.

"I will." She drew a deep breath and remembered the day when Nick had almost kissed her. "You have my word."

Lady Alicia's voice was as calm as if speaking of the weather. "I will tell Nicholas of your pledge."

"Have you heard about Nick Briarwood?" Catherine looked about the parlor. Someone had to have heard more than she had; they could hardly have heard less.

Robina's Aunt Dora put down her teacup with a click. "Which? The rumors swarm like flies. Even Mortimer Briarwood would not throw his own flesh and blood out for no reason."

Catherine wished she had picked her audience with more care—but how could she wait, not knowing? "Lady Alicia was always a model of rectitude, and she's sheltering him." She picked up her teacup. "Nick, that is, not Mortimer."

"I don't believe it," said Robina. "Mortimer was a horrible man, and he did something horrible to Nick—that's why Nick has to recover, don't you see?"

Catherine looked at her tea. She could call on Lady Alicia and Fliss. Interest in their responsibility would be merely polite, and she doubted there was a better place to discover the truth.

But Nick was still disinherited—and worse off now, if he accused his father of crimes. It would still embarrass him. Catherine drained her teacup. He had troubles enough.

"This," said Mother Humiliata, "is ridiculous." She glared at the children whispering in the garden. Despite the heat, she found herself furious that they did not run about and play. "Are we to be a hotbed of gossip? Like flibbergibbets with nothing better to do?"

"But," said Sister Audrey, "the children are concerned, with all these tales of diabolerie."

"What good would their tale bearing do?" She scowled at the sister. "Consider what harm it might bring. Tales borne by rumor do not remain the truth. And consider what harm they are doing themselves. Gossiping is not an easily lost vice. And what man wants a hireling who can not keep his tongue?"

Sister Audrey sighed. "I do not think they will calm unless they see Nicholas Briarwood for themselves."

Mother Humiliata scowled. Two girls retreated behind a tree and whispered. "For the nonce, if they are that anxious, they should go into the chapel and pray."

A little boy ran up to her. "They said that the white sickness—" he said, shrilly.

The street overflowed with black-clad and gray-clad figures, many in rags. Though the university's buildings stood about, students and masters alike crowded by the side, unable to break through.

Janet scowled. Wails weighed down on the air. Friars intoned penitential psalms, now and again rising over the ruckus. Those rags were assumed, not normal attire.

"Rend your hearts and not your garments," she muttered. "I've never seen such a—"

"I saw the penitential processions earlier," said Master Umberto. "After the white sickness."

Janet did not turn to face. "Not this size. Not here."

"Then, now they know of the evil magic that might have caused it."

"White sickness," said Janet, "was created by diabolerie centuries ago. It has needed no aid since. This is superstition, not piety."

Umberto spread a hand. "But the sickness moves strangely. Perhaps it has an—affinity for evil magic."

"If so," said Janet, "it would never leave. Master Oliver nearly murdered someone with his spell." She gestured at the procession. "Are they all repenting of diabolerie?"

"Perhaps not," said Umberto, "but do you not think it good for anyone to repent of wickedness, for any reason?"

The rear windows stood open. Outside, red and golden blossoms flooded the narrow garden. The morning air, already growing warmer, carried in the flowers' almost spicy smell. Nick sat on the couch and looked at a history volume. He would never have thought that he would long for the days when he had to gather firewood in the Wizards' Wood, but if he got up, one servant or another would harry him back to the couch.

A voice carried in from the street. "Is that the house?"

Jack? His heart seemed to beat faster—still a surprise.

Matthew's answer came. "Think so." Nick started to rise.

"We were here once before, it ought to be plain."

"Once," said Matthew. "And at night."

Nick pulled back the curtain. On the street, Jack and Matthew garnered strange looks from passing servants. He opened the window. "Are you looking for Lady Alicia's?"

Jack and Matthew both gaped. Nick wondered if he really looked that bad.

"I don't even have to present you to Lady Alicia; she's out."

Minutes later, the maid wore a disapproving expression as she ushered them into the library.

Jack sat. "Is what they're saying true?"

"I don't know what they're saying," Nick said. "Lady Alicia would tear Fliss's head off if she disturbed me."

Jack's mouth twisted. "The worst one is that you've been accused of diabolerie."

"Not that I know of," said Nick, but—his father was not even needed, then. "Mistress Janet would insist on my declaring my innocence."

Matthew sat back. "Fliss said that you accused your father of practicing diabolerie—and trying to kill you.

"That's true."

Both Jack and Matthew sat in silence.

"Mortimer—my father—hasn't been captured. That's why Mistress Janet is having me stay here. It's safer."

"Did you surprise him at his work?" Jack said, as if dragging the words out. "Is that why he tried to kill you?"

Nick shook his head.

"Don't wear yourself out." Matthew leaned forward. His attempt at a smile did not keep him from looking grave. "Your Lady Alicia will throw us out on our *ears*—if Fliss let us live that long."

Nick smiled, but— "I'm well enough to talk." He drew a deep breath. "He bargained with a demon for immortality. The demon tricked him and gave me the immortality. It ripped the heart out of my body and gave me something else."

Jack whistled. "Like Master Oliver."

"Similar," said Nick, "but not the same." His hand went, without his thinking, to his chest.

"You got the heart and Mistress Janet believed you?" said Matthew.

"Good God, Matthew," said Jack, "don't you?"

"Do *you* think that sounds like Mistress Janet?"

Nick said, sharply, "She was angry that I didn't tell her when I first came to the university, but she believed me."

Matthew nodded, slowly. "Half the masters are up in arms. They say that Mort. . . your father —a respectable wizard, not involved in such matters. . . ."

After a minute, he added, "We're watering your roses now and again."

Nick blinked. He smiled, feeling the movement before he realized that he would do it.

"Like father, like son," said Master Francis. His voice carried down the hall from the dining room. "I was impressed by his skills, I grant you. I wondered that Mortimer wasn't proud of him—but who's to say that the son didn't ape his father? That would explain Mortimer's anger as well as Nicholas's far-fetched tale."

And who defended Nicholas, to inspire this assault? thought Janet. She closed the distance to the master's hall.

"Mortimer Briarwood," said Master Benedict, "was a diabolist when he was a student."

The murmurs sounded like a mob. Janet pushed the door open, and silence fell. Many faces were sullen, resentful.

"If you wondered, perhaps you should have asked." She met Master Francis's gaze for the moment it took him to glance away. "There is a spell I recently found in the library. It shows whose hand had touched a work. Mortimer had laid a hand on these tomes on diabolerie, and when he was caught,—" she nodded to Master Benedict, "—the works he had then were burned. These were new. But whether new or old, Nicholas Briarwood has not touched them."

One master laughed, but she could not pick out who.

"No doubt," said Mistress Elise, "you would have thrown him to the wolves, if this spell had shown otherwise."

"No doubt," said Janet, sedately enough. If that were true, he would have betrayed her, but even that could not make her eager for the act. She would not admit that here. And she would have done the deed.

"The spell," said Master Francis, suddenly. "It was Mortimer Briarwood's. That of touching the manuscripts—that was his masterwork."

Janet said, elongating each word, "How fitting."

Master Francis looked away.

"Has this—" said Master Benedict. "Has this affected your severity on cases of diabolerie? After all, that was the evidence against Master Oliver."

Outside the window, leaves rustled, and laughter resounded. She heard it clearly because the masters sat in silence, watching her with avid eyes.

"Of course it has," said Janet. "I can show you the thing the demon conjured into Nicholas Briarwood's chest—if Master Francis's tale of it does not affect *your* judgment of diabolerie."

"Master Oliver had the heart," said Mistress Elise.

"And if Nicholas's heart had murdered another, I would have stopped it even at cost of his life—" With a queasy twist, she remembered how bone-chilling it had been to find that she had killed Master Oliver, and that when she had not doubted his guilt.

"After all, someone else found Master Oliver's works of diabolerie. It was not my imagining."

Chapter 21—Transitions

"Mistress Janet!" A servant ran toward her.

With an exasperated sigh, she turned from her chambers. The sky was already purple with evening, and held stars, but the heat had barely slackened.

"Mistress Janet, a bookseller in the city vanished— yesterday." He dragged down a breath. Younger than even most students, he looked almost green. "They looked through his papers. There were—diabolic pieces."

"Had he heard of Mortimer Briarwood, and how the university wants him?"

The servant blinked.

"I will ask," said Janet. "Show me the way to his store."

Candlelight shone, none too brightly. Few though they were, they added heat to the party.

"I thought you were fond of Fliss," said Lucia.

The cards leapt up to shuffle themselves. Shuffled, they jumped toward the dealer's hands but not into them—the dealer, intent on Giles, had not raised his hands.

Giles looked at the table.

"She's sleeping under the same roof as Nick Briarwood," Lucia said.

"Lady Alicia," said Stephen, "would ensure that nothing scandalous happened."

And she could not place a mutter behind her, "As if a prig like Nick—"

"Scandal?" said Lucia. "Whatever pittance Lady Alicia leaves Fliss, I am sure it will seem rich to Nick, and he could woo her at any hour, in a manner respectable enough to appease Lady Alicia."

In Lady Alicia's library, the lamp flickered. Fliss glanced up. Nick's head was still bent over the notes. She wondered whether it would weary him more to attend lectures, but she had her own studies. She looked back when she heard the door below, and the housekeeper declaring that Felicity was in the library.

Footsteps sounded on the stairs, and Nick glanced between her and the door. She scrambled to her feet. "Odd, if there's a visitor for the invalid—"

Giles reached the doorway. His gaze flickered over Nick, and his mouth tightened. He bowed and produced a bouquet of flowers.

"So you mastered that one?" said Nick, genially.

Giles gave him a bitter glance and did not stay long. When she turned to Nick, Fliss did not remember anything Giles had said.

"He taught Jack it," she said slowly.

"More generous than I. I only pointed him to the book." Nick's hand flashed through the air. The same pale blooms flooded his hands. He glanced at her, smiled slyly, and let them dissolve into sweetness. His hands moved again, until they were laden with red and golden roses. He held them out.

"But your hands are full."

Smiling, Fliss laid aside Giles's flowers, but when she had the roses, he conjured a bouquet of blue and violet flowers and expanded it to fill the room with blooms. She laughed and looked back at him.

Nick was no longer smiling.

"They match your eyes," he said.

She glanced down. A long minute passed.

"My," said Lady Alicia. "I did not know you knew such a spell, Felicity."

"It's mine," said Nick. He dissolved the blooms. "I—I wanted to see you. I want to return to lecture."

"I think you have proved your case," said Lady Alicia.

He smiled again. "I was just playing games." He gave Fliss a sideways glance. "And Fliss knew it."

She smiled back.

Musty, with racks of parchments and shelves of books, the tiny shop proved little shelter from heat and dry dust. The merchant rifled through parchments. "My lord will wish to purchase this. . . .."

Mortimer scowled. The parchment the merchant pressed in his hand was old and mentioned demons. He was three kinds of fool to let that seduce him into study, to be sure that it was an elementary work. He dropped it without further comment. The merchant shrugged, deducing—finally—that the foreign wizard was no fool.

Mortimer headed out into the noonday dust. Before he had sold his soul, the works had fallen into his hands like leaves from an autumn tree!

The sun beat down on the square. The few shoppers outside the shops haggled in the booths' shade, and their shrill voices did not intrude far into the hot silence. Even beggars lolled in the alleyways. In the shade, Mortimer glared. It had to be possible. Master Oliver had done it.

Scowling, he walked toward the inn, through the glare. A buzzard or some such bird floated on the air, circling in the heat. Even the gulls rested. Nothing could be done here at midday, at any rate.

He wondered what Nick was doing. *He* would have no worries about time.

Nick stopped on the riverbank. In the swampy curves of the river, trees showed scarlet—early, as the trees near the river always did. Students eddied about him. He might never have to face his father. Mortimer had eluded capture for a week already. The rumors had started to sink, as students grew agog over a third-year who found a spell-book with pages of gold, and other, lesser marvels.

On the other hand, he had felt like this during the months at the hermitage. It would almost be worth it, to face the charges and be done.

"Nicholas!" Mistress Janet came through the crowd. The wind tugged on her red hair, and she grabbed the strands to hold them down. "I can't wait until your father is captured. I need to ensure he has no more works—to find out if he has been up to other foul things. Maybe even learn what he is about, on this trip, and find him."

Nick swallowed, guessing what she would say next. He could not avoid his father's house forever, he supposed.

"I will need your help."

Old Warin would have grumped.

The flower beds had not been set out, the brush had not been pruned—Nick had known that his father had carelessly hired a new gardener after Warin had died, but he had not realized how much that man had heeded *him*.

The garden would never be his to fret over again, and
Mistress Janet had already reached the door. Nick tried to
quell thoughts of who might own the house next, and what
care he would give to the garden.

She cast the discernment spell as soon as she entered.
Rooms gleamed, but after a glance, Janet walked on. The
protective wards, Nick realized. He wondered how she could
recognize them that swiftly.

Her footsteps rang, and servants came out to gawk. A maid
looked ready to speak, but an older servant caught her arm and
shushed her. Then one noticed Nick, by the door.

The cook wrung her hands, as Mistress Janet went up the
stairs. "Ransacking your father's house—like a thieves' lair—
have they no respect for position?" With the aid of the son of
the house, her tragic eyes seemed to say.

"Mistress Janet is a Whitehall," Nick told her.

The cook's eyes bulged. Nick hurried up the stairs. Mistress
Janet had cast the spell, he had heard her, but nothing
glittered. He followed as she strode down the hall, opening
each door in turn. The windows gleamed, but nothing else.
She ended at his chamber. He swallowed, hesitated, and
walked up quickly. Since last he had been there, nothing in it
had changed. He dragged in a deep breath, trying to steady
himself. His father had not cared—

"Any other doors?"

"Secret ones? I looked many a time when small. None."

She turned. "Do you know anything about the lights in the
windows?"

"I've heard the talk before, but I never saw anything."

She glanced back at the room. "It couldn't have been you?"

Nick remembered the metal flitting through the air,
glinting. "Err—once or twice. No more. I mastered a spell the
night before... but I'm not sure it could have been. *Lights* I did
not master until the university."

Mistress Janet nodded. "Then—the library. The most likely place to find receipts is in the desk."

Nick blinked.

"For gold. He needed it for that pentacle."

Nick opened his mouth and shut it again, feeling foolish. "He could not have conjured up the gold, not without the pentacle."

Mistress Janet smiled.

They went down the stairs. The servants had dispersed. Inside the library, she pulled open the desk drawers, one by one. "I don't see any. . . ."

The thing, dark and winged, leapt up so quickly that Nick acted without thought; he threw up the wall before seeing the thing on the other side. Mistress Janet put her hands to the wall and stared at the bat-like creature. As dark as a scrap of night, it flitted out the window.

"I should have caught it," Mistress Janet said. "I shall have to read carefully, to learn how he avoided the spell—"

"A warning perhaps?" said Nick.

"Warning *him* that someone was meddling with his desk, most likely. Tell Lady Alicia. Mortimer knows now."

The bird flew from the sunset. Mortimer gave it a baneful glare. It flew closer, like a seagull no longer afraid of man. Mortimer started to turn when he realized that the blackness did not stem from flying against the sunset. The bird was black and, in fact, no bird—but it was familiar to him.

He stepped into the shadowed alleyway, which held neither beggars nor thieves for him to frighten, and awaited it. His heart hammered as if he had not known that he was in danger, and danger enough for him to have cast that spell in the first place.

He forced his breath out. He had no reason to play the fool because the bird's arrival demonstrated his prudence.

His creature alighted. The brief view of the intruders seared itself on his eyes: Nicholas, and a young master of the university with vivid red hair and yellow robes, both of them making free of his study.

The creature crumpled into dust, and Mortimer's hands clenched into fists. He dared. He dared. Not content with having stolen his immortality, the boy *meddled*.

"My immortality would not steal yours, Nick. For this, I *will* break through to your heart. *You* will be as mortal as you wished to keep *me*."

The words echoed, and he was glad that he had looked before the news tempted him into that folly.

He forced himself to plan. To the inn, to buy passage back, to learn what could be done.

As he walked through the evening dust, he placed the master wizard: Mistress Janet Whitehall, the woman who threw her noble blood about to win her mastership, a mastership which the masters had not seen fit to bestow. Mortimer snorted. He had needed no such favoritism, even when having to hide his finest work. If she had laid hands on his work, it would not be that hard to retrieve it.

Umberto looked at the papers. He could finish that night, if he worked at it. He stretched his arms. If he had known how long this would take, would he have undertaken it?

But Mistress Janet could not, not while hunting for Mortimer, and if it were not done properly, Mortimer might escape. Then, his hatred for Nicholas would drive him—and his hatred for Mistress Janet, and Felicity Seaborn, and (he had to concede) one Master Umberto.

Umberto picked his pen up. If he finished it tonight, tomorrow he could teach his students, and learn of the Wizards' Wood.

He remembered the birds of sunlight.

If he had wanted to investigate the woods, he could have avoided the university and not let himself be distracted by Mistress Janet and Master Otto, and by Nicholas Briarwood.

Then again—he looked at the papers—what would have happened to Nicholas, if he had? Nicholas's face had been as white as snow when he told his story.

He went back to work.

As the evening air grew cooler, Nick hurried. The sky had darkened to violet. Students and masters were all in their studies, some perhaps in their beds, and he could not help thinking how easily Mortimer could arrive. He should have insisted—as if he could have gotten Mistress Meghan to examine him the quicker, or to tell him earlier that Master Umberto wanted to see him.

Lamplight still gleamed in Master Umberto's window. Nick climbed the stairs and let himself in. Safer than wandering.

A single lamp cast a golden circle of light on Master Umberto's desk. From both the windows came a cooling breeze.

Master Umberto glanced at the window. "It had not occurred to me that Mistress Meghan would detain you this long."

"I came directly," said Nick.

"If you had lingered—it is not safe, this late." He laid aside his pen. "What was her pronouncement?"

"I have recovered," Nick said, with a ghost of a smile.

"You may recommence your studies, then." He glanced sideways at Nick. "I may question you about what you saw this winter in the Wizards' Wood."

Nick smiled fondly. To learn what those things were. . . .

Umberto laid a hand on the papers. "I fear you will lack my undivided attention for a time. In one thing you misled us." He sounded almost idle. "You spoke of the blood relationship. Although that is favored, it is not necessary. Your father could cast the spell again."

Nick winced.

"A mighty diabolist." He still sounded idle. "These magical circles that force the demon to give what the magician bargains for—" He gestured at a chair and twitched the papers. "One circle can force a demon to tell the truth, and get nothing in return but dismissal. Mortimer noted that it enraged the demon."

"My father had little use for truth. If he knew the truth, he could not blame me." Nick did not realize how poisonous his tone was until the words were out.

Master Umberto studied his face. Nick squirmed and felt young.

"Did anyone tell you that a master saw him near the city— less than a week ago?"

Nick shook his head.

"How are you returning to Lady Alicia's?"

"Walking."

"At this hour? Then, it is well that you came, though we can not discuss your studies. You will stay until I complete this; it will be but a few minutes. Then I will escort you to Lady Alicia's." He waved at the bookshelves. "Apply yourself to whatever suits your fancy."

Nick rose to look at the books, but his thoughts would not attend to the gilt titles on the spines. Mortimer had been seen. And Mistress Janet would not rest until she had him. And once Mortimer had accused him—the rumors already spread, but with his father's word, the story would never die.

Outside, the spell spheres glowed lily-white, casting circles in the gloom. Figures walked along the way, not glancing from their paths—even if he were visible against the window. No sound came from Master Umberto, neither the movement of paper nor the scratch of a pen, but Master Umberto took his duties gravely. He would read thoroughly, and not stare at his student.

Nick forced himself to look at the books. A simple and easy spell, a basic spell that his uneven education had not taught him. His hand hovered over the spines of a learned treatise on fire, an old tome discussing the intricacies of a spell that Nick did not recognize, a book mentioning transparency.

After a moment, he reached for the last. Flipping through its pages confirmed that the invisibility spell was the transparency it mentioned.

His mouth twitched. At times, he had wished he could vanish. If he had used it when Mortimer had him chained to the altar. . . . and Mistress Janet had told them that it was a compounded spell.

Nick took a chair, cast Lenore's Candle, and plunged into a lengthy discourse: on light, and seeing, and how the hard part of invisibility was not hiding, but allow the wizard to see once hidden. He had listened in lecture; he flipped through the pages in search of the spell.

The night grew cooler. Nick shifted in his chair to get away from the draft. He found the actual incantation and read it, and then again. Compounded or not, it was the easy spell he had looked for. He recited it, concentrating. For a moment, the air seemed to shimmer. Then, everything looked the same. Perhaps a trifle darker, as if he saw not the room but its reflection in a mirror.

Master Umberto shuffled his papers. Nick laid aside the book and smiled; Master Umberto should have asked what he studied, so as not to be surprised.

The air ahead of him shimmered. Umberto looked up. "Nicholas?"

Surprise was out, Nick thought, disgruntled. Except that Master Umberto did not look toward him. His breath caught. The shimmer thickened and took on the shape of a man.

Nick's lips formed "Father," but the word did not escape him. His heart raced.

Master Umberto's gaze went about the room. Nick bit his lip. He could not let Mortimer know he was there. His pulse hammered until he wondered that Mortimer could not hear it.

Mortimer smiled. "I waited until my fool son left before I came."

Nick forced himself to keep his breath even. An indrawn breath would warn Mortimer, but whatever he had used to watch, he had not seen *his* spell.

Master Umberto looked about again, as if wondering how—and why—Nick had left with such stealth. Memories of the secret chamber flooding back, Nick fought to keep his breathing quiet. Master Umberto looked straight at where he stood, and he turned his face away.

Mortimer's mouth twisted, as if tasting something bitter. "The little prig." His hand flew as he cast the wall to part him from Umberto, with the safe on his side. "Did you think, Master Umberto, I would let you meddle? I will deal with you as with my treacherous son."

Nick drew a deep breath and cast the wall himself. Mortimer grunted with surprise, turning toward the noise, and stepped toward Nick. He hit the spell. Mortimer raised his hand and mapped out its shape. With narrowed eyes, he looked at the safe.

"An excellent choice, Nicholas," Master Umberto said. Nick started, and wondered why he had betrayed him. "Useful."

Mortimer's gaze searched the shadows. "How dare you? You insufferable little prig, ruining my work again!" He threw himself against the wall. It was easier to hold him back than the stone guardian, but Nick found the invisibility spell melting away. Mortimer's face contorted.

"For years, I toiled on that spell! And you steal it!"

"Don't be a fool," Nick said, forcing his voice to iron.

"*You* were fool enough to throw it away, frightened once you had it, but not want it?" His voice turned sly. "But fortunate for me, your cowardice. I had looked for a spell to break through to your heart."

"What good would that do, if you want to be immortal?"

"It would have showed *you*! And it would have ensured that you never meddled again!" Mortimer raised a fist and, with a grunt of surprise, fell forward against the wall.

Nick gasped.

Master Umberto appeared again, standing over Mortimer. He nodded at the wall—the actual wall—behind him.

Nick nodded, swallowed, and released his wall. Mortimer sprawled. Nick realized, almost indifferently, that his hands shook like aspen leaves.

"I think," said Umberto, "that now it is safe for you to wander the night—and I can neither leave him here, nor hale him to prison by myself."

In the cold night air, Nick stopped under the trees. Light glowed down one alleyway and approached in gemlike colors.

"Nick! Is that you?" Jack had a green Lenore's candle over his head. "What are you doing here?"

A handful of students came behind him. "Looking for Mistress Janet. My... father's been captured."

"Why," said Cecelia, "that's wonderful."

In the babble, Nick raised his voice. "I have to get to Mistress Janet."

"She's around here," said a student in the shadows, and students swarmed about the buildings.

"Why the long face?" said Matthew in a low voice.

I will not confess to being afraid, thought Nick. "It's been a long day."

"You can return to the college now," said Jack.

Nick paused. "Not tonight. Lady Alicia would worry. And when she worries—" He spread his hands.

Chapter 22—Trials

Nick walked down the path to St. Catherine's. Half a dozen older students eyed the college and talked about protective spells. One waved to him. "We're looking at its protections. They're not strong enough."

Nick wondered what they feared. "Didn't you hear of my adventures on St. John's Day? I would not like to protect a college where students cast spells day and night—and dawn and twilight."

"And many of them badly," said another. "I told you there was a reason why no one builds with many spells nowadays."

"Mistress Janet might advise you," said Nick. "After the trial." As the dumbfounded faces turned toward him, he added, "If you ask her nicely."

From their expressions, they were not that eager to protect St. Catherine's.

"May God bless and preserve you," droned the priest.

Nick bent his head over his hands. Did the priest have to start the services late the one day he had to leave?

He stayed on his knees. He would need the college more than ever, after this.

"I will praise you, Lord, you have rescued me
And have not let my enemies rejoice over me."

Nick closed his eyes. Do not let my enemy rejoice over me.

"What gain is there from my lifeblood, from my going down into the grave? Does dust give you thanks or proclaim your faithfulness? Hear, O Lord, and have mercy on me; Lord, be my helper."

Moments later, Nick's thoughts returned to the trial as the priest meandered to the final blessings.

"Amen." Nick surged to his feet. He had to eat breakfast; he could not sit through this trial with an empty stomach.

"Today, isn't it?" whispered Jack as the porridge came down the table.

As if the sidelong glances did not advertise that everyone knew it. Nick scooped the porridge into his bowl, bolted a mouthful of it, and nodded. He was glad that a full mouth precluded his saying anything.

Sunlight glittered through the window. It turned the Magi in their robes of blue, green, and flame red to gleaming jewels and shed colors over the cathedral and congregation.

Umberto knelt. About him, the master wizards, as colorful but less brilliant than the windows, shifted on their knees. The priest intoned, as if oblivious, "Lord with your justice endow the king, and your judgment the king's son." But his back was too rigid to be as unconcerned as he appeared.

Nearby, a wizard whispered to another and pointed back. Despite himself, Umberto looked. Mistress Janet sat far in the back; she must have arrived late. Red and gold light fell from the window of St. Michael the Archangel on her. Gleaming, she looked ahead with such steadiness that Umberto turned back to emulate her.

Nick hurried down the corridor. Weeks to prepare for the trial—and he was nearly late. Mistress Janet's tart voice rose ahead of him.

"Even Master Otto can not convince the master wizards to acquit in the face of overwhelming evidence. I can go over their heads. Unflattering though it is to convict a master, it would be less flattering to lose that—prerogative."

He could not hear the answer, but he reached the room's door in time to see Mistress Janet's sour expression.

"They could ignore diabolerie when I did not bring it to their attention. They rather resent my finding it. It is so wicked—and they are not wicked, or so they would tell you."

"Good morning, Nick," Fliss said.

Mistress Janet nodded. Her yellow robes looked rumpled. Nick remembered that she was only a little older than Fliss and he were.

She looked out the window. The other master wizards filed into the building, formal in their robes. In every corner, students and other bystanders whispered.

"Not long now," Mistress Janet muttered. She turned, her robes swishing. "And just as well. We will be lucky to finish before evening. Mortimer being a master wizard, they will raise every pedantic point. They think it reflects poorly on them."

"Does it not?" said Master Umberto.

Mortimer, pale as bone in his dark prison garb, walked between guards toward the building. His arms were laden with chains. Nick could see no sigils, but the metal was pale—to reflect magic as well as light. Students pulled away, and Mortimer ignored them with imperial detachment. As if he felt Nick's glance, he looked at the window. Their gazes met.

Nick flinched.

In the paneled room, the evening light shone dully red through the windows. Here and there, Lenore's candles hung over masters' seats, never large. Where neither sunlight nor the candles reached, shadows gathered—most of the chamber. Masters looked solemn as Mistress Janet elaborated how she had tested the works they had found in Mortimer's room, and only Mortimer had laid hand on them.

In the back, where the newest masters sat, Nick sat beside Master Umberto, who sat in perfect serenity through all Nick's twitches and shifts. At least none of the masters were asleep.

Master Otto gave Mortimer leave to defend himself. With unnatural calm, Mistress Janet sat. Once she had folded them in her lap, her hands did not even twitch.

Mortimer rose, so lightly the chains did not rattle. His dark hair and clothing blurred with shadows, which only made his worn face the more vivid against them. His voice held a sneering edge. "Victim." His lip curled.

Mistress Janet glanced at Master Otto, but the chancellor raised no objection. Mortimer had a right to defend himself, but Nick's hand clenched into a fist. Master Umberto laid a hand on top of it, but he could not loosen it.

"Whoever heard of a victim who obtained the prize that the criminal had sought?" Mortimer's voice lowered. He stared at Nick as if they were the only two in the room. The murmurs of the wizards around them, Mortimer did not even seem to hear.

Mortimer's low voice held a knife's edge. "*He* got what *I* had slaved for. Only much knowledge of diabolerie would allow anyone to thus foul my spell."

Nick met his father's gaze but could do nothing more. He saw conviction in Mortimer's eyes.

"Have you heard of such a thing?" Mortimer looked about, and tried to catch the gazes of his fellow master wizards.

Sometimes, he succeeded Nick noticed.

"The devil," said Mistress Janet, "is a liar, and the father of lies. Those who deal with him are like him."

Mortimer scowled. Her face as expressionless as her voice, Mistress Janet looked back. Master Otto shifted his weight, as if about to declare she had not been given leave to speak.

Her clear voice rang. "If you have nothing to say in your defense, Master Mortimer Briarwood, be still." She rose to her feet. The last sunlight made her robes and hair glow against the shadows. "The claim about your son leaves only the question of why, having, with such difficulty, wrested immortality from your hands, Nicholas threw it away so eagerly."

Mortimer spread his hands, the chains barely rattling. "'Unstable as water, thou shalt not excel.'"

He still looked certain. He believes it, thought Nick. God help me.

"It could have *killed* him!" said Janet.

"Mistress Janet—you are here to argue the case, not quibble with the prisoner." Master Otto turned on Mortimer. "We are not here to judge your son. We are here to judge you."

A murmur of agreement ran through the wizards, nearly overwhelming Nick with relief. He leaned forward. His heart beat harder and harder as the masters registered their votes of condemnation. Even when more than half of them had voted, even when the last one voted, even when Master Otto solemnly pronounced, "The judgment is guilty," his heart raced.

Master Otto paused a second. "The sentence is death."

Nick's heartbeat slowed abruptly. He drew a deep breath. Mortimer's case would be appealed to the king, of course—the king had decreed that for all diabolerie, after cases where the condemned witch was nothing more than ill-tempered—but Mistress Janet, explaining, had said the appeal held no doubt.

Mortimer rose, with dignity, to his feet. The jailers led him off. He did not even glance about.

Low conversations broke out, punctuated with the rustle of robes. Nick rose. A master wizard glanced at him, and then, quickly, away. Nick felt color drain from his face. Wizard after wizard gave him a sidelong glance of distrust.

Mortimer was judged here, not I, Nick realized. He was condemned; I was not acquitted. He felt a mad twinge of doubt about his own memory.

He looked at Umberto and said, "Fickle? If I were to learn such magic as he claims, I would have had to study steadfastly and without—"

Umberto's hand touched his. "Every master knows how hard you study."

"Do they?"

Janet stood before the door to the chancellor's chambers. "That was improper, Master Otto."

Master Otto tried to sidle by.

Not bold enough to acquit Mortimer, but bold enough for spite. She could not complain to the king of that. "I have to speak to you concerning all accusations of diabolerie. You laid down the rule yourself. And one was made."

Master Otto did not meet her gaze. "In the chambers."

"How long do you think I will need?" Janet leaned forward. "You should have silenced Mortimer the moment he accused Nicholas. He was only entitled to defend himself. You did not even let me point out that he was spiteful about the demon's trickery—"

"*I* will not gossip concerning Mortimer's charges. Speak with those who do."

He stalked by her, and Janet fumed. He would never hold his tongue, but that was far from the worst. Why was he so lazy he could not bother with the least duty of his post? How dare he hate her for doing his job? Her hand clenched into fists, until the pain of the nails digging into her palms jarred her out of her thoughts.

Janet opened her hands and looked at the red marks. I am sorry, Nicholas, that I doubted your fear of your father. She let a long breath. She could not charge the gossips with diabolerie.

"Lord, have mercy," she whispered on a breath. "Christ have mercy. Lord have mercy." She ransacked her memory. "St. Margaret, pray for us, and all those falsely accused."

"Did you hear about Nicholas Briarwood?" said Robina.

Catherine stirred her teacup. "*Everyone*'s heard about his father's trial, haven't they?"

"But did you hear what Mortimer Briarwood said at the trial?" At Catherine's glance, Robina grinned. She lowered her voice. "Mortimer Briarwood said that his diabolerie didn't just go astray—Nick pushed it astray. He wanted to get the immortality for himself, don't you see?"

"Dear me," said Catherine's mother. She spread butter on a piece of bread. "There *was* something strange about the affair, wouldn't you say? Nick vanishing for months on end, and turning up so strangely."

Aunt Dora shook her head. "It would explain altogether too much for my comfort—but I would not like to spread gossip." She folded her hands in her lap. "Too much harm is done by idle tongues."

It doesn't sound like Nick, thought Catherine. "If he *wanted* it, why did he have Mistress Janet reverse it? He did, didn't you know?"

Robina looked as if Catherine had struck her.

"He had his heart put back. That was what he was recovering from, at Lady Alicia's."

Robina shrugged. "Mistress Janet caught him. She wouldn't have believed him unless he said he wanted her to." She considered a moment. "Or maybe he really did. Remember the picnic? He did that wall to block Edgar's spell, but he tried to weasel out of it with Fliss."

"Besides, Catherine," said her mother, "you shouldn't gossip."

Master Umberto laid down a book on the table. "I was thinking on a change in your studies."

Nick inclined his head. He could study. He could do nothing about petty gossip. There were murmurs even in the college, though he had solid friends there, far more than he had before his father's attack.

"Despite your stay there, you do not know much concerning the Wizards' Wood. Since the university was built here because of the woods, I do not think we should neglect it."

Nick remembered the flitting bird that had glowed under the trees, the smoke creature, the eye in the water. He let his breath out. "I would be glad to. Especially the plants."

Master Umberto nodded.

"I would like to learn anything magical about plants," said Nick. "Anything at all."

"Have you mastered any such spells?"

"Except for making the rosebushes blue—no. My father's library held none." Nick smiled. "But I know a great deal of plants before they are enchanted."

Master Umberto sat back. "How are the roses coming?"

In the shadow of All Angels', Edgar looked at the crowds of students. George looked at him dubiously, and Edgar fumed. Nick had been accused, the master wizards ignored it, and no one cared. Couldn't they see what a sneak Nick was? Even George still acted offended—at *him*.

"Mortimer Briarwood accused Nicholas in front of all the master wizards, and Mistress Janet dismissed it out of hand. She's supposed to investigate all charges."

The other students eyed him.

"*She*'s playing favorites. Those infernal lights the scholarship students were making—he was behind him, and they were plaguing their betters with them. She dismissed them too. When everyone knows that late at night, you could see lights dancing in the Briarwood home."

Students nodded—he had taken care that none of the college paupers were in earshot—and a couple muttered under their breath, but one said, "What about the rest of the masters? Mistress Janet is not a favorite with the university."

"They were embarrassed. They had to admit that Mortimer was a diabolist and a master of the university—for years. They couldn't bring themselves to say that Nick was, too. You've heard how they praised of him."

"I've heard of them," said a student, and a murmur of agreement ran about. In a moment, they dispersed into the morning heat. Some were already scowling, as if to compare the praise heard for Nick to that heard of other students—but the other students had not been accused of diabolerie.

"Gossiping to get at Nick?" said George. "That's petty."

"I wouldn't stoop to it if I had any choice," Edgar said. "But the master wizards are forcing me to."

George's lip curled. Edgar's most baneful glance did not strike the contempt from his face.

"That's not how the compounding works," said Jack, on St. Catherine's steps.

Nick, pouring over Matthew's notes, looked up.

"It *can* show more light after the transformation," said Jack. "It depends on the color. The white—"

"It can not," said Matthew. "It can look that way sometimes, in the dark, but the colored light. . . ."

Nick tried to decipher the notes. Something about drawing other stuff into the compounding—that the first spell effect might need more or less. And how this applied to the brightness of the Lenore's candle, after they had cast his spell on it, he could not work out, whatever they said. "The spell— the spell I taught you—takes away light. . . ."

"Marjory was sure of that," said Jack.

"Perhaps the candle is affected by the color," said Nick. "It might draw in more light of the proper color."

"Only if the light remains the same," Matthew said. "Even diabolists can't transform without all the matter."

"Ah, don't tell him that," said a sniping voice from the path—a student Nick did not know at all. "He's the expert on diabolerie. Let him tell you."

Bastard, thought Nick. To either side of him, Matthew surged to his feet, and Jack's hands clenched into fists. Nick rose to join them.

The student looked startled and scurried away. Nick felt sick to his stomach.

"Damn idiots," said Jack, sitting down.

The weather had cooled some since Mortimer's trial, but this evening was muggy. A student, his black robe fluttering, hurried by and glanced uneasily at Nick. Nick walked on, toward the library.

Fliss emerged from the street ahead, her cheeks flagged with red. Nick hurried to catch up with her. She glanced back and slowed, but her expression did not change. Her arms held the books as if to wall out the world.

"The damned fools," Fliss said. "It isn't the master wizards who are the worst—though they're old enough to know better. But I took tea this afternoon. You would think that no one ever *knew* you. As if you were a stranger that they could believe *anything* of."

Nick's gaze fell. The week had drained the spirit from him. He did not think that anyone in St. Catherine's, or even Saint Agnes's, believed the accusation, but he did not know how many believed them false. He held the door open and followed Fliss within. "My father believed—believes the accusation himself, I think."

By the door to a reading room, Fliss stopped. Her hand rested on the polished wood. "Then even a truth spell could do you no good, if you could find one of those legends."

Nick's mouth worked.

"And only you and Mortimer know the truth," Fliss said. "Only you were there."

Nick remembered Master Umberto's description of his father's work. It nagged at him: only he and his father had been there.

"Nick?" said Fliss.

His scowl deepened. He did not want his thoughts broken into. Then, as Fliss's hand touched his sleeve, it struck him.

He let out a long breath. The circle that made a demon tell the truth, that was what he remembered from Master Umberto. And he and his father had not been alone.

He smiled at Fliss. "Only my father and I, and the demon."

Fliss frowned.

"If my father were certain that I had stolen his work, he would demand that they let him summon up the demon again

to prove it. He could make it tell the truth, with his magic
circle—Master Umberto found it in his notes."

Fliss's mouth formed an O.

"At that—Master Otto would never let him to cast the
spell, and he knows it. He did not think of it because he knew
it would prove him a liar." Nick's smile deepened. "I will say
that the next time I hear someone repeat the rumor. You
should tell that to those friends of yours at tea."

"This insane story of Nicholas Briarwood's." Master Bernard
shook his head over the chessboard.

Master Umberto remembered Nick the day before: flushed,
guilty, and triumphant. Perhaps it was foolish for the boy to
spread tales like that, but how else could he defend his good
name?

"What in particular is impossible about it?" he said.

"A demon?" said Master Francis, from where he watched.
"Forced to tell the truth?"

"It was among Master Mortimer's spells. I myself told
Nicholas Briarwood of it."

Both master wizards stared at him.

Alas, I have joined the gossips. Umberto sat back.

Mistress Janet emerged from around a bookcase and said,
without preamble, "Nicholas, what do you think you are
doing?" She put one hand against the case, blocking his way.
"It's been three days since you started this rumor."

"It's convinced *some* people," he said.

Mistress Janet considered for a minute. Her eyes narrowed.
He stood still and hoped he did not look defiant.

She looked away, sighing, and her words were not so much spoke as breathed out, "It's better than anything I have to offer. May God prosper it."

Trees in the Wizards' Wood were turning red and gold and orange. Nick, his arm laden with wood, went about a grove and found a stand where leaves nodded blue and purple.

Though he was here to fill the hermitage's woodpile—he had benefited enough from it—he considered those trees. He had no need for the discernment spell here, useful as it was proving this day. He only wished he had seen the trees in the summer, to know if they were visibly enchanted then; now, he would have to wait.

Then, he remembered Mistress Janet at his father's home, dismissing spells at a glance. To recognize the patterns, he had to practice. He intoned. Light flew over the trees, shooting up trunks and along boughs, into branches, down to the twigs and leaves—like sap.

It might not even been dangerous to burn, the wood from there.

Still, the stray traveler would not be him, this winter; he would not generously fill the wood shed without seeing whether the fire would be more dangerous than the cold. "I do not think I will gather it any wood from there."

"Wise," said Master Umberto, as he emerged from the brush. He glanced at Nick's armload.

"The shed is not quite full." Nick looked at the grove. "I wonder if it's the trees. They look like oaks, except for the leaves. It could be the earth they grow in." His arms ached a little, and he shifted the burden in his arms, reluctant to leave. "Some nuts, and some dirt, could show—"

"Have you time for it?" said Umberto.

"Oh, yes," said Nick. "I'm no longer studying spell-breaking on the sly."

Though watching saplings sprout, like watching rose shoots, would not keep him too busy to listen to rumors, no matter how much he tried not to eavesdrop—

"Speeding the growth of the saplings might alter their nature," said Nick. "So—this time next year."

"True enough," said Umberto. "There's a flower here, called the hermit's hope. As soon as you put the wood away, and take what you need from the grove, come see it."

"Took you long enough to get here," said Master Otto. Sunshine slanted over the office.

Nick closed the door. "I only received the word less than an hour."

"I sent to St. Catherine's hours ago."

"I was in the woods, with Master Umberto, and I came back covered with dirt." He glanced about for a chair, and there were two, but Master Otto did not indicate one.

Master Otto's glance was poisonous. "What the devil did you think you were up to? Spreading rumors?"

His heart beat harder. "Rumors spread on their own around this university." If you had cut off Mortimer's rumor mongering at his trial, I would never have started.

"Bringing disgrace and discredit on the university," said Master Otto. "Sit."

Nick obeyed, but the lecture did not start. After a minute, his heart calming, he wondered what the chancellor awaited.

The door opened, and chains rattled. Nick did not move, but his breath came light and swift. Master Otto dismissed the guards to the corridor.

Nick looked sideways. At Master Otto's gesture, his father sat. His heart hammered again.

"What is this nonsense you have prattled?" Master Otto said to Nick, as if Mortimer were not there. "Half the students are gossiping about it."

While the other half gossiped about Mortimer's accusations. Nick's mouth nearly twitched, but he fought it and surprised himself with the evenness of his voice. "Master Umberto told me of my father's works. One was a magical circle that could compel a demon to tell the truth. He put that in the account he gave."

Master Otto's nostrils flared.

"I told Fliss—Felicity Seaborn—that if my father believed, in truth, that I had stolen his work, he would offer to summon the demon and make it tell the truth about me. He was angry enough to want to bring me down—if he believed as he claimed to believe. Only a guilty conscience would have silenced him."

Master Otto looked green. He sank back in his chair as if he had not expected the rumor to be true.

"I told others, as well. If they spoke of it—it was no secret. Master Umberto would not have told a mere student, in his first year, if it had been."

Mortimer lifted his head to look at Nick. Nick met his gaze. For the first time, he saw a flicker of doubt in them—not disbelief, but doubt. He kept his voice uninterested. "Master Umberto would know more than I. But even I could see that a man who threw away a chance to defend himself in order to attack me—he would not throw away a chance to bolster his case. He would only avoid anything to prove it false."

Master Otto looked as if he were choking.

Mortimer grew red, and spoke through clenched teeth. "Prove my case, you vile thieving little prig. . . ."

His heart hammered, but Nick raised his eyebrows. "Or, of course, disprove it."

Master Otto sputtered with rage, but he could barely be heard.

Mortimer sank back, the chains clanking. "No, no, you will foil me. Trick the demon into disobeying me. Again."

Nick marshaled his words. "If you have studied this since before my birth, you would be fool indeed to let me foil it when you expected it."

Mortimer's shoulders hunched.

"If your circle has the virtues you claim for it, I could not make the demon lie. Or are you perhaps not the diabolists of the skill you claim?"

Mortimer half-rose from his seat.

"This can not be," said Master Otto. "This can not be! We can not have a demon-summoning at the university."

"There!" said Nick. "You knew Master Otto even better than I. You must have known that a coward who let you slander me in court would not permit you to summon it. You could have bragged of how you could have confirmed it, had Master Otto not been such a coward."

Mortimer's face was shadowed with doubt. He sat again, his chains rattling.

"And so you were doubly safe. Whatever fresh lies you told, it would have been but another nail in my coffin—if your guilty conscience did not make you fear he would permit it. 'The guilty flee when no man pursues, but the righteous are as bold as a lion.'"

Mortimer breathed in and out. "No," he said, feebly. "No." Then his voice regained strength. "No, because everyone else would know that Master Otto and, worse, that Mistress Janet, would never permit it. They would know it for idle bragging, which would distract them." He straightened. "I could have cast it again. There is nothing wrong with my skills. That was how I knew that you meddled; I had done nothing wrong with the spell."

"Then why did you not?" said Nick.

"Cast that truth circle?" Mortimer raised an eyebrow. "I *had* the truth."

Nick swept a hand through the air. "The other one. The immortality one."

"That one failed. I needed a better one."

"Because I meddled?" Nick raised an eyebrow. "How could you need a better spell when the only reason for failure was my meddling?"

Mortimer's mouth opened and shut.

"I was misled by your comments about my being blood of your blood and flesh of your flesh, but Master Umberto read the work. You needed anyone at all to offer. The lack of a blood relation would be offset by the lack of knowledge to meddle—if I had meddled."

Mortimer looked at Master Otto as if expecting him to silence Nick.

As he did not silence *you*? thought Nick. "You did not cast it again. You knew that you could not force the demon to give immortality to *you* with it. That was the flaw."

Mortimer's arm jerked. The chains chimed like bells.

Master Otto sputtered. "But why—why would he lie?"

"The devil is a liar, and the father of lies," said Nick. The doubts he had squelched—vanished. His father had lied for so long, to everyone. Why would he not lie to himself?

"So, Father, do you wish to proclaim to all that you *could* prove my guilt?"

There was doubt in Mortimer's eyes.

"I will not permit it!" said Master Otto.

"And in perfect safety," said Nick.

Mortimer looked away. After a minute, he rose to his feet, but now the chains clanged.

Nick let his breath out, very slowly.

Chapter 23—Challenges

"Not even with Master Otto huffing that he would not permit it," said George. They walked by All Angels'. "Mortimer Briarwood was afraid to cast the spell. *He* knew the truth."

Edgar grimaced.

Nick walked around the building. Edgar moved to intercept him. Nick still looked worn. His studies must have drained him. From the corner of his eye, he saw George retreating, as if speaking with Nick endangered him.

"So you have been acquitted," Edgar said.

"I was not charged." Nick smiled.

Edgar turned away. George was long gone, but there was no use talking to him, or to anyone. He bade Nick a curt farewell and strode off the university grounds to be alone with his rage.

At least Nick would not plague him at the parties. The mothers and aunts had babbled about what a pity it was that Mortimer would disinherit him. For his sins, Nick would scramble for his living. He might end up entertaining others with those spells he found so amusing himself.

Nick walked beneath the trees, which held red leaves among the green. The orphanage emerged from the trees ahead of him. He should have come earlier. Catching up on his studies had not been *that* difficult.

Charity ran around the building. She turned, her braids flying with her speed, to shout, "It's Nicholas!"

A flock of children ran after her, and after them a sister, clucking like a mother hen. Tom, at the head of them, reached him and flung his arms around Nick's waist with such vigor that he nearly went over backwards.

"You're all right now, aren't you?" said Charity. "We've been praying for you—but you're all right *now*."

"Quite." He rumpled hair as the children swarmed around.

The sister snorted. "Quite well enough to be of aid, rather than make more work for the poor sisters."

"Come along," Nick said, "or the sister will lose her temper. It is wrong to expose her to temptation like that."

With a few wails, the children headed back to the orphanage. Another sister emerged to shepherd them. Nick glanced over. He supposed he had not seen all the sisters at the orphanage before.

"Ah, we have a new sister here, the mother house sent her. Sister Apollonia."

She bobbed her head. Nick nodded and froze in the middle of the motion. "Isobel?" formed on his lips.

"Apollonia," she said, serenely. Then, sisters took on new names.

One girl's shrill voice rose, "He's gone, now, isn't he? Like the witch who would've killed Snow White? They made her dance in red-hot shoes until she *died*. They made him—" When he looked at her, she whispered, as if she feared being overheard, "The evil wizard who did bad things to you."

His father. He did not think the children understood that. Nick pitched his voice to soothe. "They're going to." Mistress Janet left in another week, but his father was already in the hands of the royal officials. The children's questions chorused about him.

"Children, come inside," called Sister Humiliata from the doorway.

As the children moved toward the door, Sister Apollonia angled over beside him. "I asked Fliss not to tell. . . ."

Nick thought about the others who had known her, before. "Of course not."

She nodded and hurried inside. She stopped in the doorway, as Sister Humiliata spoke with her. She looked content.

Maybe once it was over, he would feel the same, but it would be a week before Mortimer was executed.

Nick leaned over his papers, so intent he did not notice the door opening. Jack held the door for Matthew, and Nick stirred, but to gather up his papers.

"I thought you met with Master Umberto tomorrow," said Matthew.

Nick blinked. "I do—" He looked at their books. "But I have to do something this afternoon."

Jack snorted. Nick threw himself into his studies as if Master Umberto had complained of his slackness. "Even you can not be about the greenhouse at all hours."

"It's not that," said Nick. "I have to visit my father's man of business. That's where I've gotten my money. My mother arranged it for me, and my father—never did pay much heed to money."

Jack blinked. Lucky Nick.

"His estate is not bound to pay it."

"There are jobs," said Jack. "Copying and the like."

"I know," said Nick.

He needed the money.

Soon enough, he would join the other students in scrounging for anything that paid coin, and he had seen how scarce that employment was.

In the dimness of Benedict's office, he pulled the door shut behind him.

"Ah, Nicholas Briarwood," said the young clerk. He pulled out the books and start counting out the allowance.

Nick waited and wondered who his father's heir was.

"Sir," said Benedict, from the back room.

The clerk hesitated. Nick looked over. Even when Benedict had explained his mother's rules to him, he had never heard such a tone in the man's voice.

Benedict nodded to the clerk. "Count out the money. I must speak with Master Nicholas."

The clerk opened his mouth, shut it again, and went back to the coins. Nick drew a deep breath and went to the back office. Benedict shut the door as when he had explained how his mother had set up his allowance.

"You know, no doubt, that Master Mortimer Briarwood never spoke with me concerning your allowance, either when your lady mother arranged it, or when he—when you left his house."

Nick nodded.

"You may not know that he never spoke to me of his will. Indeed, he never made up a will. And you are his natural heir."

Nick stared at him.

"He always was—unconcerned by money."

Unable to clear his thoughts, Nick shook his head.

"Nor," said Benedict, "are the crimes of which he was convicted of the sort to invoke forfeiture."

"My—my father's not dead yet." He heard how thick his voice was.

Benedict glanced at his desk. "Even up to the hour of execution, Master Mortimer might endeavor to alter his will, but you may appeal to the king. He has, under the law, no grounds to disinherit you."

Nick's mouth twitched.

Benedict put his fingertips together. "Until official word is received of your father's death, you do not inherit."

"Mistress Janet Whitehall," said Nick, "will bring back news of his death."

Benedict smiled. "Your inheritance is sound but not so much as permit great extravagance."

When, minutes later, he returned to the street, a golden-leafed tree stood ahead of him. A flock of birds flew toward it, and alighted one by one, until the tree resounded with their chatter. They rose and settled again on other branches in tiny flocks, never venturing far from each other.

Nick stood for a long minute, watching them—and let his breath out. He had to finish his work for Master Umberto, who could not wait forever for him to return to normal.

He walked back, slowly. The air was cooler than it had been, and he reached the university, however slowly he walked. Asters flowered purple beside the paths, and leaves sprawled over them, brown and scarlet.

"Ho, Nick!"

Jack and Matthew came up beside him. Jack grinned. "Settled matters with your father's man of business? Come down to the level of us mere mortals?"

Nick drew a deep breath. His gaze flickered between them. His old friends had abandoned him when they thought him disinherited, but his stomach had not crawled, facing them, as it did now. Jack's grin faded. Matthew frowned.

"I had thought that my father would disinherit me."

Jack's mouth opened and closed again, like a fish's. After a minute, he said, "You mean he didn't?"

Nick shook his head. A gust of wind blew by, carrying a ribbon of yellow leaves over their heads. Nick said, slowly, "I know he never concerned himself much with the money. He would have cut off my allowance if he had realized." He looked between them, and hope flickered. His old friends would have—leaves, red and brown, blew by their ankles and knees. "He can't, now. He was convicted on my evidence. The royal courts would overturn the will."

Jack whistled.

Matthew said, "They gave you a place in the college. Inheritance is not a reason to throw a student out."

His heart seemed to beat not faster but harder. "I do not want to leave, but—do you want to face Master Humphrey about my remaining when I have money?"

For a long minute, the only sound he heard as the pounding of his heart.

Matthew started to laugh. After a moment, Jack joined in. Nick opened his mouth, and laughter started, until students passing by stared at them. Nick fought for breath.

"No," Jack said, wiping his eyes, "we can hardly condemn you to facing him down."

"So you will live outside the city," said Matthew. "Not handy for the lectures, or the library."

"Not too far," said Nick.

Matthew smiled benignly. "Mistress Janet mentioned that your father had books in his library that the university does not have."

The chant intoned: "He will bid His angels watch over you, to guard you in all of your ways."

Feast of the Guardian Angels, thought Nick, on his knees. How fitting. He bent his head over his hands as the priest went on with the Mass at the cathedral.

". . .and especially those for whom we now pray."

Silence fell. Nick's fingers tightened about each other until his knuckles were white. Mortimer's execution would be within days.

He could not bring himself to pray.

He attended very badly to the rest of the Mass, and lingered after. He stopped before the icon of St. Dismas and surveyed the three crosses at Golgotha. A bank of candles stood before it, but the only one lit was the central one. He swallowed.

"My son, can I help you?"

Nick turned to face the priest, who inclined his head. "Nicholas Briarwood." His voice was cool but gentle.

"My father will be executed next week." His voice came out as little more than a croak.

"A just sentence."

"I tried to pray for him. I couldn't."

"'For such a man, you need not pray.'"

Nick bowed his head but could say nothing.

"I will pray for you," said the priest, and left, fumbling with his rosary. Nick turned back to the small altar. His hand shaking, he slid a coin into the box and lit a candle, holding the taper with care to the candle flame and then to the wick. It took the new flame several moments to leap up. Even then, it quavered. "O Lord our God. . . ." he began, but was unable to go on.

The cell was easily measured; five strides wide, three strides long. Mortimer strode it again. It was barren of anything but the cot, and a barred window looking on the courtyard.

He glanced out the window. The priest hurried across the flagstones again. His mouth twitched. Infernally persistent—he had no doubt he could demand for a priest after midnight, and the priest would scurry.

Fools, he thought. The circle of truth would prove nothing. The boy had tampered with the spell once. He could do so twice. Even if Master Otto had permitted it—and the coward would not have—it would not have proven Nicholas's innocence.

It had to have been Nicholas's tampering.

His fingernails bit into his palms.

It had to have been.

Chapter 24—Conclusions

"This is good work on the hermit's hope." Master Umberto laid Nick's paper down.

Nick looked down at his clasped hands and wondered why that did not sound like praise. "What do you want me to do next?"

Umberto watched him for a moment. "I did not intend you to do so much work so quickly. Perhaps you should attend to the lectures. . . ."

Nick thought of the blank times, even when working on the flower, and shuddered. "No," he said, "no, I came to the university to study. I have attended the lectures. I work with the other students at the colleges on—" Not for long, he thought. He could not remain in the college after his father died, after he inherited.

Umberto gave him a sidelong glance. "And your acorns."

"Planted and ready to sprout in the spring." Three kinds: some with both the nuts and dirt from the woods, and some with only one. It had taken him a time to find acorns outside the woods—but not that long.

Umberto inclined his head. "I said, when you came here, that you had some startling gaps in your knowledge. I commend your diligence in stopping them up—even when not part of your studies."

Nick swallowed. "Are there others I should look at?"

"None that would surprise me in a first-year student." He sat still a moment. "Have you done nothing but study?"

"I've helped at the orphanage. Matthew and Jack even came with me a few times."

Umberto assigned some other autumnal flowers of the Wizards' Wood for him to study. "And these ones I expect you to take more than a week to complete. If you can finish such a paper in a week, I wish you to study them more thoroughly."

Nick nodded.

"Are you going to the bonfire tomorrow?"

Nick looked up. "Of my father's papers? I will need to study."

Master Umberto inclined his head.

"I was thinking that the color spell might be compounded with the smoke spell. The light is the same, even if it does not come from within the smoke."

Nick ate his breakfast slowly. He had no need to rush, not when he still had to mull over the tomes he had read last night. Perhaps he could venture to the woods. Vesper blooms were an autumn flower, and actually casting the spells could only aid his studies.

"None of you are to go anywhere else this evening," rapped Master Humphrey.

Nick blinked. That would prevent his going—more than autumn, they were evening flowers. He looked up and realized the housemaster had spoken for some time, and the word still rolled on, speaking of horror of diabolerie, and the need for them to see.

Nick met his gaze. For a long moment, Master Humphrey was silent with his mouth agape. Only when Nick looked away did he go on, "You must learn of the evil."

Outside the window, the orange light flickered. He should have gone to the woods—but it was folly to go alone, more so this late. St. Catherine's was dark and still. Though Master Humphrey had only looked at him a moment while hurrying his charges out, all the other students had gone to the bonfire. He sat alone in the study room, his spell was the only light in the building, and the bonfire's glow carried far.

He looked at his notes. After a long minute in which he could not read them, he rose.

At the window, he could barely make out the square where the fire burned. The crowd blocked out the flames, and the figures throwing the books on the blaze were hard to distinguish. His fingers tightened on the window frame. His memory drew up each book lying beside the magic circle as Mortimer summoned up the demon.

Nick yanked himself away, his heart hammering and his breathing hoarse. He stalked over to sit down again and stare at his notes rather than the bonfire.

They would burn his father in a blaze much like that.

By the window, Janet contemplated the stars and felt numb. The first capital case she had carried to the end. A draft chilled her seat, and she shifted her weight. The moon, which had waned almost to the last quarter, was half up the sky: long after midnight, then, but she could not sleep. She knew her duty and had done her duty.

But why had Symond's yammering, and that of other relatives', not even perturbed her? They had told her that being a hangman did not befit her birth. Even now, the thought did not vex her.

Someone moved across the courtyard, from the tower where Mortimer was held. Janet scowled and hoped that Mortimer did not force them to capture him again, but the guard was not coming toward her tower, where the wizards lived. He vanished into the shadows beneath a different tower. She tried to calculate which of the royal servants he went after. She had not worked it out before the guard reemerged, with a priest.

Janet blinked. A priest had appealed to Mortimer that evening, as he had every evening. She did not doubt that he, or another, would appeal to Mortimer in the morning. But now? She leaned forward. And a guard had gone—

The guard had gone for the priest. Her fingers bit each other. The only reason for that would be if Mortimer had sent for a priest.

The muddy garden was laden with leaves. Wise not to go out, thought Catherine. She pulled back from the window. And when they did—she remembered Edgar's exploits in that place.

"That story about Nick Briarwood," said Lucia. "I would *like* to believe it, but even Mortimer wouldn't tell such lies about his own son."

"Of course it's lies," said Robina. "Why would Mortimer make such an accusation?"

Catherine drew a deep breath. "Did you hear?"

Agnes had been playing at the harpsichord, not a stride away, but stopped. Catherine swallowed. She was not sure she believed it herself. But Robina had turned a sneer on her.

"You know how Mortimer cut Nick off—disinherited him?"

Nods came all around. So did baffled glances.

"He wrote him back. Nick is his heir." The gasps about the room restored Catherine's confidence. "His father's man of business was talking about what they needed for him to inherit."

Edgar looked as if she had struck him.

"So," said Christopher. "Mortimer must have written Nick back in, in contrition for his lies."

Murmurs of agreement sounded.

"It's just a story," said Edgar. "How could anyone know? Mortimer might have summoned a lawyer for something else."

"If Nick is living in the house again," said Christopher, "we'll know."

"A most eligible young man," said a woman, her voice too low to be identified.

Jack and Matthew argued about the lecture. Nick hoped his note were good enough. Golden leaves skittered by.

"Nick!" called Robina. Behind her, Catherine looked shocked, but Robina walked toward him, oblivious. "You have to come to my party—you can't claim to *need* to study now—"

She gave Jack and Matthew a glance so dismissive that Nick thought they might go. He said, quickly, "Have you met my friends?"

She gaped.

"I presented them to Lady Alicia—"

Robina skittered off.

Nick glanced at them. Jack raised an eyebrow.

"I don't think much more of that will be needed," Nick said. "But I am deeply grateful for that part."

Matthew laughed. And then he said, "What's that?"

They listened. The chanting came clear. Jack said, "Yet another penitential procession," but Matthew was frowning.

"It doesn't sound right," said Nick, and walked toward the sound. Matthew and Jack followed, until they stood in an alleyway and saw the procession going by. The psalms were wrong for a penitential procession.

"Thanksgiving?" said Jack, as they pulled back to St. Catherine's.

"The diabolist has been caught," called David. "They figure that the white sickness wouldn't be back."

"The white sickness," said Nick, "lasted long after the diabolist who conjured it up was gone. What makes them think that this one's evil will end with him?"

A handful of scholars looked at him, in silence.

"Don't tell the penitents that," said Matthew. "Or we will never get to lectures."

A skein of geese flew through a sky with only a feathering of clouds. Their honking was faint but clear.

Father's probably dead by now, Nick thought. It would be evening soon, but he wandered along the riverbank. These last days, Master Umberto had no complaints of his frantic studying. Indeed, he hardly studied at all. He had not even asked Jack to come with him to the Wizards' Wood, though Jack would know better than most how to keep safe in it.

The sky showed shades of yellow, and the clouds were touched with pink. The air was still warm, though trees rained scarlet and yellow leaves with every breeze. Nick did not even bother to brush them out of his hair as he walked along the path. They scuttled along the way with him, with others that had long turned brown.

He headed over the bridge. The university had been unendurable. No one had spoken of the execution to him, but they had glanced, and whispered, and cut conversations short. He did not know which was worse, the curiosity or the pity. He struck out at random, away from the city.

A long minute later, Nick realized that the path led by the orphanage. He slowed—he should have known that his feet were likely to go where they had gone before—but he did not stop.

Half a dozen orphans played under the trees. One pushed up the heap of leaves that the others were half buried in, and their laughter echoed throughout the grove. Nick lingered as the last orphan burrowed within. The boy looked over his shoulder to try to pull up some leaves. After a moment and a step forward, Nick gathered up a handful and showered it over the boy.

"Nicholas!" squealed a girl. The nearest child threw his arms around Nick's leg, and all the children piled on to pull him into the heart of heap, sending the leaves flying.

Another shower of leaves came down. Fliss stood over them, rosy-checked and laughing. "When the sisters sent me out to fetch you children, I didn't expect to find Nicholas holding you here."

"He didn't," said a boy, earnestly. "He just got here. And we were holding him."

Nick sat up. "No matter. Time to go back." Children climbed out of the leaves. They shook to shed them, and picked the stubborn ones off one by one.

Fliss looked over to Nick. "I didn't expect you to be here," she said in a low voice.

"I was passing by," Nick said, his voice equally low. "I could not sit and study as if I were not awaiting the news."

Fliss's eyes fell. "Come along, children," she said sweetly. She touched his arm and spoke in a low voice. "I heard from Mistress Janet. I ought to tell you that the execution was not deferred."

Nick closed his eyes. Fliss's hand brushed his, no more, and was away again before he reopened his eyes.

A girl skipped around Fliss, and Fliss managed to rumple her hair before sending her with the others. "And," she added, her voice even lower, "the priests had given up hope on him, here and on the journey, but—" She looked up. "—he sent for a priest last night."

Nick glanced sharply at her. Did he? Mortimer? He had not thought even impending death would affect Mortimer. He remembered Mortimer's imperious stance at the trial.

Nick drew a deep breath. Had Mortimer repented of what he had done? Had he admitted to himself that he had wronged his son?

He twitched. What would be the point of the summons unless he had? The priest could not absolve him of sins that he did not repent of. And even summoning him, his father would regard as a weakness. Mortimer despised folly—"Did he?"

Fliss met his gaze. "He did. Mistress Janet said that he seemed subdued—for him."

Nick swallowed.

"That," he said, "is good news." He let out a long breath into the golden evening. He thought he had not felt this calm, since before his father tried to murder him.

"I suppose I ought to see the priest."

Fliss tilted her head to one side. "To have Masses said for his soul?"

"There you are," a sister called. Nick joined Fliss in herding the children into the orphanage. God willing, he would have long to talk with her.

A pile of leaves burned in the courtyard. Tom spotted Nick and called, "Show them what you can conjure from a fire!"

A sister reproved, and Tom said, "It will show us why we should study hard, if we want to be wizards!"

Nick laughed. Before any sister could speak, he conjured a great bird from the smoke—gray but enormous, and every feather detailed. As the children and sisters gaped, he glanced at them and colored it: crimson, violet, green, scarlet. The children gasped.

"Not only if you wish to be a wizard," said Nick. "If you wish to know what manner of bird—" He gestured, and it sprang up into the air, flying away. "You will discover it in the books."

He flew it far away before he let the bird dissipate. The children whispered guesses to each other. Fliss whispered to him, "The phoenix. Rising from the ashes."

He smiled back at her.